The Kill Switch

ALSO BY JAMES ROLLINS

The Eye of God
Bloodline
The Devil Colony
Altar of Eden
The Doomsday Key
The Last Oracle
The Judas Strain
Black Order
Map of Bones
Sandstorm
Ice Hunt
Amazonia
Deep Fathom
Excavation
Subterranean

ALSO BY GRANT BLACKWOOD

The End of Enemies
The Wall of Night
An Echo of War

The Kill Switch

James Rollins
and Grant Blackwood

HARPER LUXE
An Imprint of HarperCollins*Publishers*

HarperCollins books may be purchased for educational, business, or sales promotional use. For information, please e-mail the Special Markets Department at SPsales@harpercollins.com.

FIRST HARPERLUXE EDITION

HarperLuxe™ is a trademark of HarperCollins Publishers

Library of Congress Cataloging-in-Publication Data is available upon request.

ISBN: 978-0-06-230022-5

14 ID/RRD 10 9 8 7 6 5 4 3 2 1

To all the four-legged warriors out there . . .
And those who serve alongside them.

The Russian Federation

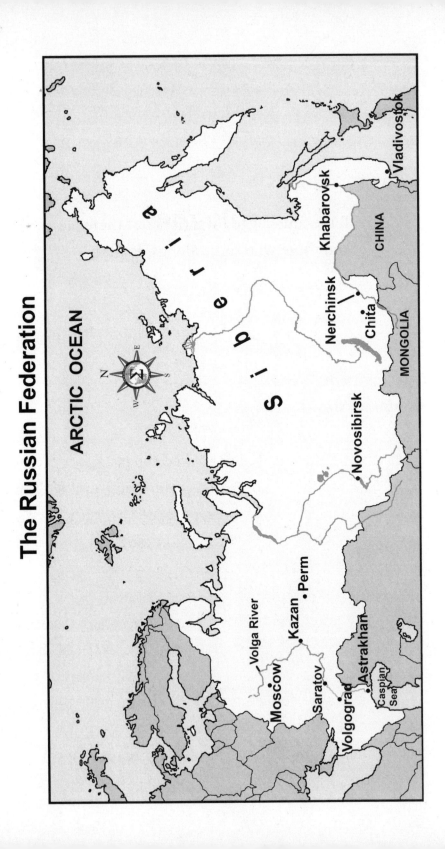

Prologue

Doctor Paulos de Klerk packed the last of the medical supplies into the wooden trunk and locked the three brass clasps, mumbling under his breath with each snap. "*Amat . . . victoria . . . curam.*"

Victory favors the prepared.

Or so he prayed.

"So, my good doctor, how goes the effort?" General Manie Roosa's voice boomed from the fort's watchtower above.

De Klerk shielded his eyes from the blazing sun and stared up at the bearded figure leaning over the railing, grinning down. Though not physically imposing,

Roosa had a commanding presence that made him look seven feet tall; it was in the man's eyes. The general always looked eager for a fight.

And he was about to get one if word from up north held true.

"Are we ready?" Roosa pressed.

De Klerk returned his attention to the other trunks, cases, and burlap sacks. Though the general's words had indeed ended with a question mark, he knew Roosa was not making an inquiry. At various times through-out the day their leader had posed the same "question" to almost every Boer soldier under his command, all of whom bustled around the plateau on which the fort sat, cleaning weapons, counting ammunition, and generally preparing for the upcoming march.

With an exaggerated sigh, De Klerk replied, "As always, I will be ready to leave five minutes before you are, my general."

Roosa let out a booming laugh and slapped the log railing. "You amuse me, Doctor. If you were not so good at your profession, I might be tempted to leave you behind, out of harm's way."

De Klerk stared around the bustling fort. He hated to leave its security, but he knew where he was best needed. As primitive as the fort was, with its palisade walls and crude buildings, this place had withstood countless British attacks, making it a bastion for Boer troops. Leaving the confines of its protective walls likely meant he and his medical aides would be seeing a brisk business in the coming days.

Not that he wasn't accustomed to the horrors of battle.

Though only thirty-two years old, this was De Klerk's fifth year of war in the past decade. The first *Vryheidsoorloë*, or *freedom war*, was fought back in 1880 and had mercifully lasted but a year, ending well for the *Boers*—the Dutch/Afrikaans word for *farmers*— as they won their sovereignty from British rule in the Transvaal. Eight years later, the second *Vryheidsoorloë* started, involving not only the Transvaal but also the neighboring Orange Free State.

Same issues, more soldiers, he thought sourly.

The British wanted the Boers under their colonial thumb, and the Boers were not keen on the idea. De Klerk's ancestors had come to the savannahs and mountains of Africa to be free, and now the *Engelse* wanted to take that away. Unlike the first *Vryheidsoorloë*, this war was protracted, with the British implementing a scorched-earth policy. Though neither De Klerk nor any of his comrades verbalized it, they knew their own defeat was inevitable. The one person who seemed oblivious to this was General

Roosa; the man was an irrepressible optimist when it came to matters of war.

Roosa pushed himself away from the railing and climbed down the rough-hewn ladder to the ground and walked over to where De Klerk was working. The general straightened his khaki uniform with a few well-experienced tugs. He was the same height as the doctor, but burlier of physique and bushier of beard. For the sake of hygiene, De Klerk kept himself clean-shaven and insisted his aides did the same.

"So I see many bandages are being packed," Roosa said. "Do you think so little of my leadership, Doctor? Or is it you think too highly of the *Engelse* soldiers?"

"Certainly not the latter, my general. I simply know that before long I will be treating throngs of enemy prisoners wounded by our bullets."

Roosa frowned and rubbed his beard. "Yes, about that, Doctor . . . about supplying succor to the enemy . . ."

It was a sore point between them, but De Klerk refused to relent. "We are Christian, are we not? It is our duty to provide such help. But I also understand that our men must come first. I will only provide enough aid so that a British soldier might survive long enough to be reached by his own doctors. If we do not do that, we are no better than them."

Roosa clapped him on the shoulder—not necessarily agreeing, but acknowledging the sentiment.

For reasons he had never fully understood, Roosa had come to think of him as a sounding board. The commander frequently shared information with De Klerk that had nothing to do with his medical duties—as if the general also saw him as his own conscience.

Still, he knew there was another reason Roosa took such an interest in his preparations. The men under the general's command had become his family, a surrogate to his own wife, three daughters, and two sons, all who'd been taken by smallpox two years earlier. The loss had nearly destroyed Roosa and left lasting scars. When it came to bullet and bayonet wounds, the general was phlegmatic and optimistic; when it came to disease, he was frighteningly anxious.

Changing the touchy subject, Roosa pointed to the leather-bound diary that was never beyond De Klerk's reach. "Cataloging more flowers, I see."

He touched the worn cover both affectionately and protectively. "Providence willing, yes. If we are going where I think we are going, there will be many species I have never encountered."

"We are indeed heading north, into the mountains of the Groot. My scouts tell me a brigade of *Engelse* soldiers are headed west from Kimberley, led by a new commander—a colonel fresh from London."

"And in a hurry to prove himself no doubt."

"Aren't they all? If we leave in the morning, their lead elements will spot us by early evening."

And then the chase will be on. Though not a military strategist by any means, De Klerk had been with Roosa long enough to recognize the general's favorite tactic: let the British scouts spot them, then draw the enemy north into the mountainous Groot, where the harsh terrain could be used to set up an ambush.

The British preferred to fight on the savannah, where their tidy formations and overwhelming firepower always won the day. The enemy commanders hated hills and mountains and ravines, hated that Roosa and his band of backward farmers refused to fight on their terms. And it was exactly such a strategy that Roosa had used many times to lure the British into murderous engagements. And still the enemy did not learn.

But how long would such arrogance last?

A chill iced through De Klerk as he gathered his research journal and pocketed it away.

The troops were up and on the move well before dawn, traveling northward without incident as the sun climbed higher. Then at noon, one of the Boer scouts overtook the formation from the south, pounding up to them on a sweating, heaving horse. He joined Roosa at the head of their formation.

De Klerk didn't need to hear the conversation to know its content.

The enemy had found them.

As the scout wheeled away on his horse, the general rode back to the medical wagon. "The British will soon be giving chase, Doctor. Your comfortable cart may see some jostling."

"I am less concerned with the wagon than I am my delicate internal organs. However, as always, I will survive."

"Fine mettle, Doctor."

Minutes slid into hours as the general led their unit north, steadily closing the gap between them and the Groot, whose foothills smudged the horizon, the details blurred by waves of heat rising from the savannah.

Two hours before dusk, another scout appeared. The expression on his face and the posture of his body as he rode past the medical wagon told De Klerk something had gone wrong. After a brief consultation, the scout rode off.

Roosa turned on his horse and shouted back to his leaders, "Prepare the wagons for fast travel! Five minutes!" He then rode back to De Klerk. "This new

Engelse colonel is trying to be clever. He has disguised the size of his brigade and split them into two forces—one the hammer, the other the anvil."

"With us the pig iron in the middle."

"Or so they hope," Roosa replied with a broad smile. "But hope fades with the light, Doctor. Especially once we lure them into the Groot."

With a jaunty wave, Roosa wheeled his horse and rode off.

A few minutes later the general's booming voice echoed throughout the Boer formation. "Fast travel . . . go!"

De Klerk's wagon handler snapped the reins and barked a "Hah . . . hah!"

The horses bucked slightly, then broke into a gallop. De Klerk grasped the sideboard and held on, his eyes fixed on the distant Groot Karas Mountains.

Too far, he thought grimly. *Too far and not enough time.*

And an hour later, his fear proved true.

A trail of dust marked the return of a pair of riders sent north by Roosa to scout the way ahead, but as the dust settled, it became clear only *one* rider had come back. He leaned askew in his saddle and fell from his horse as he reached the unit, wounded twice in the back by rifle fire.

Roosa ordered a halt, then signaled for De Klerk to come forward. Armed with his medical bag, he rushed to the fallen man and knelt down. Both bullets had torn through vital organs before punching through the front of the young man's torso.

"Collapsed lung," he told Roosa, who cradled the man's head.

The scout, a boy of eighteen, was named Meer. He clutched at Roosa's sleeve, tried to speak, but coughed up frothy blood before he could find any words.

"My general," the boy croaked out, "an *Engelse* battalion . . . north of us. Heavy cavalry . . . with cannons on fast caissons."

"How far away, son?"

"Eight miles."

Meer coughed harshly. A fresh gout of blood sprayed from his mouth. His body arched, fighting the inevitable, then went limp.

De Klerk checked him and shook his head.

Roosa closed the boy's eyes and gave his hair a few strokes before standing up. A pair of soldiers carried Meer's body away.

De Klerk joined the commander.

Roosa murmured, "All my talk of *Engelse* arrogance . . . it is I who was the arrogant one. This new British colonel is trying to stop us from reaching the Groot. If they can catch us out here in the open . . . well, then, my good doctor, you are going to have more work than you can handle in a lifetime."

He didn't respond, but Roosa must have noted his paling face.

The general gripped De Klerk's shoulder hard. "This *Engelse* colonel is clever, but the tongs of his pincer are still wide enough for us to escape through. And soon the night will swallow us."

An hour later, from the back of the bucking wagon, De Klerk watched the sun's upper edge dip below the horizon. Night was nearly upon them, but to the east, a plume of dust—red and gold in the setting sun—covered a quarter of the sky. He estimated the number of cavalry horses it would take to create such a cloud.

Two hundred riders at least.

And behind them, wagons upon wagons of troops and cannon-bearing caissons.

God help us . . .

But at least they had safely reached the foothills of the Groot, escaping through the enemy's pincers. With a final buck, the wagon rattled into a shadowy ravine, and the view of the British forces vanished.

He swung around and studied the broken landscape ahead, a veritable maze of hills, dry washes, and caves. Roosa had extolled many times about the "pocket fortresses" hidden in the mountains, Boer strongholds from which they could wait out any British siege.

Or so they all hoped.

Time ground slowly under the wheels of the wagon and the hooves of their horses. Finally, one of the scouting parties Roosa had dispatched to the south returned. After a brief consultation, the rider took off again, and Roosa ordered the formation to slow.

The general rode back to De Klerk's wagon.

"We have bought some time, Doctor. But this *Engelse* colonel is not only wily, but also stubborn. His troops still remain on our trail."

"What does that mean for us?"

Roosa sighed. He took a rag from his tunic pocket and wiped the dust from his face. "To quote Shakespeare's Falstaff, *discretion is in fact the better part of valor.* It is time we hole up. One of our pocket fortresses is nearby. Hidden, but easy to defend. We will tuck ourselves away, wait for the *Engelse* to tire of the Groot, then attack them from the rear when they leave. You are not, uh . . . what is the word? Afraid of tight places?"

"Claustrophobic? No, I am not."

"Good to hear, Doctor. I hope the others share the same fortitude."

For another half hour, Roosa led them deeper into the mountains, eventually turning into a narrow ravine before stopping at a large cave entrance. The men began transferring supplies into the cave.

He joined Roosa at the mouth of the tunnel and asked, "What of the horses and wagons?"

"All will go inside, Doctor. We shall have to partially disassemble the wagons, but there is room enough inside for a small paddock."

"And supplies?"

Again Roosa offered a confident smile. "I have been stocking this cave for some time, Doctor, and I have a few tricks up my sleeve as well. Unless this *Engelse* colonel is willing to loiter in these mountains for months, we have nothing to fear. Now, Doctor, if you will, take two men and begin transporting your supplies inside. I want to be safely settled within the hour."

As usual, Roosa got his way. As the last of the supplies were carried inside under the flickering glow of lanterns, the general oversaw the placement of black powder charges at the mouth of the cave. Having already set up a surgery of sorts in a side cave, De Klerk wandered back to the entrance to watch.

"Good, good!" Roosa called to one of the sappers. "Move that charge on the left a few feet higher. Yes, there!" The general turned as he approached. "Ah, Doctor, are you settled in?"

"Yes, General. But may I ask . . . is that wise? Sealing us in here?"

"It would be distinctly *unwise*, Doctor, if this were the only entrance. But this cave system is vast, with many smaller, well-concealed exits. I have given this tactic much thought."

"I can see."

From outside the entrance came the pounding of hooves. One by one, the marksmen who had been dispatched earlier to harass the British forces entered the cavern, each man leading a lathered, panting steed. The last rider to enter stopped beside Roosa.

"We slowed them considerably, my general, but their scouts are less than an hour behind us. I estimate three hundred cavalry, two hundred foot soldiers, and forty 12-pound cannons."

Roosa took this in, then rubbed his chin. "An impressive force. It seems the British have put a large bounty on our heads. Well, even if they manage to find us, the fight will be on our terms. And then, comrades, we will see how good the *Engelse* are at digging graves."

After blowing and collapsing the cavern entrance, the night passed without event—as did the next day and the six days after that. Most of the Boer troops settled into their new stronghold and went about the business of making the cave system not only comfortable, but as defensible as possible, too.

Meanwhile, Roosa's scouts used secret exits to slip from the caverns under the cover of darkness and returned with the same report: the British battalions remained in the mountains and appeared to be searching intently, but so far, they had failed to find the hidden fortress.

After a week, a lone scout returned at dawn and found the general sitting in the officers' mess hall, a small cavern in which one of the disassembled wagons had been turned into a trestle table with benches. Roosa and De Klerk sat at one end, going over the day's sick report under the glow of a hanging lantern.

Exhausted and disheveled, the scout stopped beside Roosa. The general stood up, called for a water skin, then forced the scout to sit down and waited as the man quenched his thirst.

"Dogs," the scout said simply. "Bloodhounds. Coming this way."

"Are you sure?" Roosa asked, his eyes narrowing.

"Yes, my general. I could hear them baying, not two miles away. I believe they are coming toward this position."

"Could they be jackals instead?" De Klerk offered. "Or wild African dogs?"

"No, Doctor. My father had bloodhounds when I was a child. I know well their sound. I do not know how they would—"

"They captured three of our men," Roosa explained, as if expecting this news. "Their scent is our scent. And concentrated as we are in this damned cave . . ." The general's words trailed off. He looked down the length of the table at the faces of his concerned unit commanders. "Gentlemen, let us man the ramparts, such as they are. It appears the *Engelse* will be here for tea."

The first hidden entrance the British found was on the cave system's southern side, a hole disguised by a jumble of boulders.

And so it started.

De Klerk found Roosa kneeling before a sandbag barrier with one of his unit commanders, a man named Vos. Beyond the sandbags the cavern's ceiling descended to shoulder height; at the far end, some fifty feet away, was the horizontal shaft that led to the secret exit. A dozen soldiers were stationed across the cavern floor, each one kneeling with his rifle behind a stalagmite.

As they waited, De Klerk glanced up. Finger-width fissures split the cavern's ceiling, casting slivers of bright sunlight across the stone floor.

Roosa turned, placed an index finger to his lips, then pointed to his ear.

De Klerk nodded and said nothing. In the silence of the cavern, he strained his ears. In the distance, he could make out the faint baying of the British bloodhounds. After several minutes, the bawling fell silent.

Everyone held his breath. A soldier behind one of the forwardmost stalagmites signaled back to the barrier.

Roosa nodded. "He hears voices. Multiple men coming through the shaft. Vos, you know what to do."

"Yes, my general."

Vos scratched his bayonet along the rock floor, and the men stationed behind the stalagmites turned toward him. Using only hand signals, Vos gave them their orders. Though De Klerk knew what was coming, he dreaded it.

Led by the faint glow of a lantern, the first British soldier appeared in the shaft. He crawled out of the entrance, then turned left and stopped, making room for the man behind him. One by one, the British scouts crawled out of the tunnel until there were six crouched at the far end of the cavern. Silently, the enemy played their lanterns across walls and ceiling and the stalagmites across the floor.

De Klerk watched, continuing to hold his breath.

Seeming to find only an empty cavern, the trespassers clipped the lanterns to their belts, then started moving forward, their rifles at the ready.

Vos let them get within twenty feet—then, with a double tap of his bayonet on the rock floor, his men sprang the ambush and opened fire. The fusillade lasted but seconds, killing all but one of the British scouts instantly. Moaning, the surviving soldier began crawling back toward the shaft, trailing a slick of blood behind him.

De Klerk grabbed his medical bag and stood up. Roosa grasped his forearm and shook his head.

"But, General, he is—"

"I said *no*, Doctor. The more terrifying we make this for the *Engelse*, the sooner they will leave. Vos, see to it."

At Roosa's nod, Vos hopped over the sandbag wall, drew a knife, then walked across the cavern to the crawling soldier. He knelt down and slit the man's throat.

Roosa turned to him. "I am sorry, Doctor. I do not enjoy ordering such a thing, but if we are to survive this, we must be brutal."

Such butchery settled like a cold stone in De Klerk's chest. He turned away, despairing, knowing one certainty.

Nothing goes unpunished under the eyes of the Lord.

Days passed, and still the British came. Soon the enemy had found all but one of Roosa's secret entrances.

Small but fierce battles raged at the *ramparts*, as Roosa had taken to calling them. It became clear the British colonel was not only willing to send his troops into Roosa's meat grinder, but he was also willing to make terrible sacrifices—five, six, seven of his troops for one Boer wounded or killed.

De Klerk did what he could to help the injured or dying, but as the days turned into weeks, the Boer death count continued to rise—at first from British bullets, then from illness. The first ailing soldier appeared in his surgery complaining of intense stomach cramps. The medical staff treated him with herbs, but within hours the man became feverish and writhed in agony. The next day, two more men appeared with the same symptoms; then four more the day after that.

His surgery became a madhouse of incoherent screams and squirming patients. Roosa walked into the surgery on the twenty-fourth day to check on the wounded, like he did every morning. De Klerk gave the general a grim status report.

Roosa frowned as he finished. "Show me."

Carrying a lantern, he led Roosa to a corner of the cavern where the sick men were quarantined. Together, they knelt beside the first patient who'd appeared with symptoms, a blond-haired boy named Linden.

The boy flailed on the makeshift cot. His face was deathly pale. His arms had been secured to the sides of the cot with leather straps.

"Are those necessary?" Roosa asked.

"A new symptom," De Klerk explained and reached down to show the general.

He lifted the thin cotton tunic away from the man's torso. The patient's belly was covered in wartlike nodules, but instead of dotting the exterior skin of his stomach, the protrusions appeared to be coming from beneath the flesh.

"My God. What is that?"

He shook his head. "I don't know, General. Without these restraints, he would be clawing open his belly. Look here."

Together, they leaned over the boy's body. Using the tip of a scalpel, he pointed to one of the larger nodules, about the size of a pea. "Do you see the milky green color, just beneath the skin?"

"I see it. It's as if something is growing inside him."

"Not *as if*, General. Something *is* growing inside him. All of them. And whatever it is, it is doing its best to break *out*. They are all showing signs of it. Look here!"

Roosa brought a lantern closer. The pea-sized nodule seemed to be writing, wormlike, beneath the skin. As they watched, a red blister grew at the edge of the nodule and quickly expanded to the size of ripe plum.

"What in the world . . . ?" Roosa whispered.

"Stand back."

The doctor grabbed a nearby rag and draped it over the nodule. The scrap of cloth bulged for a few seconds—then came a hollow *pop*. A yellow-tinged crimson stain spread across the rag. The patient began to buck wildly, banging the cot's legs on the rock floor.

One of the medical aides ran over to help them hold Linden down. Still, the boy's back arched high under them, his head pressed against his pillow. Suddenly dozens of nodules appeared beneath the skin of Linden's throat and belly, the blisters growing before their eyes.

"Get back, get back!" De Klerk shouted, and the three of them backpedaled.

They watched, horrified, as the blisters began bursting, one after another. In the flickering lantern light, a yellowish mist hung in the air before slowly settling back over the boy's body.

With a final convulsion, Linden arched off the bed until only his heels and the crown of his head were touching the bedroll. The boy's eyes fluttered open, staring sightlessly, then his body collapsed and went still.

De Klerk did not need to check, and Roosa did not need to ask. Linden was dead. The medical aide draped a blanket over his ravaged corpse.

"How many are afflicted so far?" Roosa asked, his voice cracking.

"Seven."

"And the prognosis for them?"

"Unless I can discover the source and counteract it, I fear they will all die. Like this boy. But that's not the worst news."

Roosa finally tore his eyes away from the boy's draped body.

"This is only the beginning. More will surely get sick."

"You suspect a contagion."

"I must. You saw the airborne discharge from the blisters. We have to assume it is a mechanism of some sort—the disease's way of spreading itself at the end."

"How many do you think are already infected?" Roosa asked.

"You must understand. I have never seen or read of anything like this. And the incubation is short. The boy here was the picture of health three days ago. Now he is dead."

"How many?" Roosa pressed. "How many will become sick?"

De Klerk kept his gaze fixed to the commander, so he could see his certainty. "Everyone. Everyone in this cave." He reached and gripped Roosa's wrist. "Whatever is killing these men, it is virulent. And it is in here with us."

PART I

A Simple Proposition

1

March 4, 7:42 A.M.
Vladivostok, Russia

His job was to protect the bad from the worst.

Not exactly the noblest of ventures, but it paid the bills.

Crouched at the edge of the Russian docks, Tucker Wayne let the weight of his duty fall over him. The icy wind and pelting sleet slowly faded from his attention, leaving him focused on a dark, quiet winterscape of cranes, haphazardly stacked shipping containers, and the hazy bulk of boats lining the pier. In the distance, a foghorn echoed once. Mooring lines creaked and groaned.

Tucker's training as a U.S. Army Ranger was always at the ready, but it was particularly necessary this morning. It allowed him to home in on two very important issues.

First: The port city of Vladivostok, which was a vast improvement over the deserts of war-torn Afghanistan—though he'd never add this frigid place to his list of retirement locations.

Second: The assessment of the threat risk—such as, who might try to assassinate his employer today, where would they be hiding, and how would they do it?

Prior to his taking this job three weeks earlier, two attempts had already been made against the Russian industrialist's life, and his gut told Tucker the third would happen very soon.

He had to be ready—they *both* did.

His hand reached down to offer a reassuring touch to his companion and partner. Through the snow-covered fur, he felt the tense muscles of the small Belgian shepherd. Kane was a military working dog, a Belgian Malinois, paired years ago with Tucker back in Afghanistan. After Tucker left the service, he took Kane with him. They were bound together tighter than any leash, each capable of reading the other, a communication that went beyond any spoken word or hand signal.

Kane sat comfortably beside him, his ears erect and his dark eyes watchful, seemingly oblivious to the snow blanketing the exposed portions of his

black-and-tan fur. Covering the remainder of his compact body and camouflaged to match his coat, he wore
a K9 Storm tactical vest, waterproofed and Kevlar reinforced. Hidden in the webbing of Kane's collar were a
thumbnail-sized wireless transmitter and a night-vision
camera, allowing the two to be in constant visual and
audio contact with each other.

Tucker returned his full attention to his surroundings.

It was early in Vladivostok, not yet dawn, so the
docks were quiet, with only the occasional laborer shuffling through the gloom. Still, he did his best to keep
a low profile, trying to blend into the background: just
another dockworker.

At least, I hope I look the part.

He was in his late twenties, taller than average,
with slightly shaggy blond hair. He further masked his
muscular physique under a thick woolen coat and hid
the hardness of his eyes beneath the furred brim of a
Russian *ushanka,* or trapper's hat.

He gave Kane a thumb stroke on the top of the head
and got a single wag of his tail in response.

A far cry from home, eh, Kane?

Then again, if you took away the ocean, Vladivostok
wasn't much different from where he'd spent the
first seventeen years of his life: the small town of
Rolla, North Dakota, near the border with Canada.

If anyplace in the United States could give Siberia a run
for its money, it was there.

As a kid, he had spent his summers canoeing Willow
Lake and hiking the North Woods. In winter, it was
cross-country skiing, snowshoeing, and ice fishing.
But life wasn't as perfect as that postcard image made
it seem. His parents—two schoolteachers—had been
killed by a drunk driver when he was three, leaving
him in the care of his paternal grandfather, who had
a heart attack while shoveling snow one hard winter.
Afterward, with no other immediate surviving rela-
tives, he'd been dumped into foster care at thirteen,
where he stayed until he petitioned for early emancipa-
tion and joined the armed services at seventeen.

He pushed those darker years away, down deep.

No wonder I like dogs better than people.

He brought his focus back to the business at hand.

In this case: assassination.

He studied the docks.

*From where would the threat come? And in what
form?*

Against his advice, his principal—the Russian billionaire and industrialist Bogdan Fedoseev—had scheduled
this early-morning visit to the port. For weeks there had
been rumors of the dockworkers attempting to union-
ize, and Fedoseev had agreed to meet with the leaders,

hoping to quash his employees into submission. If that tension wasn't enough of a threat, Tucker suspected a fair number of the workers were also Vladikavkaz Separatists, political terrorists whose main victims were the prominent capitalists in the Russian Far East, making Bogdan Fedoseev a high-value target.

Tucker cared little about politics, but he knew understanding the social landscape came with the job—as was knowing the *physical* landscape.

He checked his watch. Fedoseev was due to arrive in three hours. By then, Tucker needed to know every nook and cranny of this place.

He looked down at Kane. "What do you say, pal? Ready to work?"

In answer, Kane stood and did a full-body shake. Snow billowed off his fur, and the wind whipped it away.

Tucker started walking, with Kane trotting alongside him.

9:54 A.M.

By midmorning, Tucker had located six of the eight workers he suspected of being Vladikavkazists. The remaining two had called in sick that morning, something neither had done before.

Standing in a warehouse doorway, he studied the docks. The port was fully alive now, with forklifts moving here and there, cranes swinging containers onto outbound ships, all accompanied by a cacophony of hammering, grinding, and shouted orders.

Tucker pulled out his phone and scrolled through his list of PDF dossiers and found the two men who had called in sick. Both were former soldiers, petty officers in the Russian Naval Infantry. Worse still, they were both trained snipers.

Two and two equals a credible threat.

He set the men's faces in his memory.

His first instinct was to call Yuri, the head of Fedoseev's protective detail, but it would do no good. *I do not run,* Fedoseev had proclaimed loudly and frequently. But most damning of all, Tucker was an interloper, the American none of the other security detail wanted here.

Tucker's mind shifted again, visualizing Fedoseev's route through the docks. He judged the exposure windows, the angles of fire. He surveyed for any likely sniper perches. There were a half-dozen spots that would work.

He glanced at the sky. The sun was up now, a dull white disk above the horizon. The wind had also died, and the sleet had turned to big fat snowflakes.

Not good. Much easier to make a long-range shot now.

Tucker looked down at Kane, knowing they couldn't sit back and wait.

"Let's go find some bad guys."

10:07 A.M.

The six potential sniper nests were spread across the dockyard, some twenty acres of warehouses, catwalks, narrow alleys, and crane towers. Tucker and Kane covered the ground as quickly as possible without appearing hurried, using shortcuts wherever possible, never staring too long at any one spot.

As the pair passed a warehouse front, Kane let out a low growl. Tucker turned in a half crouch, going tense. Kane had stopped in his tracks and was staring down an alleyway between a pair of stacked containers.

Tucker caught the barest glimpse of a figure slipping out of view. Such a sighting would be easy to dismiss, but he knew his dog. Something in the stranger's body language or scent must have piqued Kane's interest: *tension, posture, furtive movements.* Kane's instincts were razor honed after several dangerous years in Afghanistan.

Tucker recalled his mental map of the dockyard, thought for a moment, then flipped Kane's collar cam into its upright position.

"GO SCOUT," he ordered tersely.

Kane had a vocabulary of a thousand words and understanding of a hundred hand gestures, making him an extension of Tucker's own body.

He pointed forward and motioned for Kane to circle around the bulk of containers to the far side.

Without hesitation, his partner trotted off.

Tucker watched him disappear into the gloom, then turned and jogged directly into the nest of giant container boxes where his target had vanished.

Reaching the first intersection, he stopped short and glanced around the corner of the container.

Another alley.

Empty.

He sprinted along it and arrived at the next intersection, this one branching left and right. It was a damned maze back here among the giant containers.

Easy to get lost, he thought, *and even easier to lose my target.*

He pictured Kane somewhere on the far side, hunkered down, watching this pile of containers. He needed his partner's eyes out there, while he hunted within this maze.

Tucker punched up Kane's video feed on his modified satellite phone. A flickering, digital image appeared on the tiny screen, live from Kane's camera.

A figure suddenly sprinted out of the line of containers, heading east.

Good enough.

Tucker ran in that direction. He caught a glimpse on the screen of Kane doing the same, tracking the man, still scouting as ordered.

Both were on the hunt now—which is what army rangers did. Aside from rare exceptions, rangers didn't patrol or provide humanitarian relief. They were single-minded in purpose: *find and destroy the enemy.*

Tucker had enjoyed the simplicity of that.

Brutal, true enough, but pure in a strange way.

He emerged from the container maze in time to draw even with Kane. He motioned the shepherd to him. Kane came trotting up and sat down beside him, awaiting his next command, his tongue lolling, his eyes bright.

They were now near the eastern edge of the dockyard. Directly ahead, across a gravel lot, lay a set of train tracks, lined with abandoned and rusted freight cars. Their quarry had vanished among them.

Beyond the train yard, a perimeter barbed-wire fence rose high—and beyond that, a dense pine forest.

Aside from the muffled dock sounds in the distance, all was quiet.

Suddenly Kane's head snapped to the left. A section of the barbed-wire fence shook violently for a few moments, then went still. In his mind's eye, Tucker envisioned a second target wriggling through a gap in the fencing to enter the dockyards from that direction, using the cover of the forest.

Why?

Searching farther to their left, he spotted a tall crane tower, once used to load the freight cars. The tower was one of the six potential sniper perches he had marked in his head.

Tucker checked his watch. Fedoseev would arrive in six minutes. Hurrying, he pulled out a pair of small binoculars from his jacket's pocket and focused on the top of the crane. At first he saw nothing but indistinct scaffolding in the swirling snow. Then a shadowy figure appeared, slowly scaling the ladder toward the high platform.

That's who came through the fence just now—but where's the guy I was following?

He considered calling Yuri with the abort code, but even if his message got past that gatekeeper, his boss's careless bravado would win out. Fedoseev would not back down from a threat. Bullets would have to be flying before the industrialist would consider a retreat.

It was the Russian way.

Tucker dropped to his belly and scanned beneath the freight cars. He spotted a pair of legs moving to the right, disappearing and reappearing as the figure passed the steel wheels. Whether this was in fact his guy, he didn't know, but it seemed likely.

He reached back and drew the Makarov PMM pistol from the paddle holster attached to his waistband. A decent weapon, but not his preference.

But when in Rome . . .

He looked over to Kane, who was crouched on his belly beside him. His partner's eyes had already locked on to the target jogging down the rail line, heading away from the man climbing the crane.

Tucker gave a one-word command, knowing it would be enough. He pointed to the target moving on the ground.

"TRACK."

Kane took off, silently sprinting after the man on foot.

Tucker angled toward the left, toward the crane tower.

Hunched over, he swept across the gravel lot, reached the train yard, and belly-crawled beneath a freight car and down the sloped ballast into a drainage ditch beyond. From the meager cover, he spotted the gap in the perimeter fencing; the cut was clean, recent.

To his left, a hundred yards away, rose the crane tower. Rolling to his side, he zoomed his binoculars and panned upward until he spotted his target. The assassin was perched on a ladder a few feet below the crane's glassed-in control cab. A gloved hand reached for the entry hatch.

Tucker quickly considered taking a shot at him but immediately decided against it. With a rifle, perhaps, but not with the Makarov. The distance and the scaffolding made a successful hit improbable. Plus the snow fell heavier now, slowly obscuring the view.

He checked his watch. *Three minutes before Fedoseev's limousine entered the main gate.* Fleetingly, he wondered about Kane, then brought his mind back to the task at hand.

One thing at a time, Ranger. Work the problem.

Let Kane be Kane.

Kane runs low to the ground, his ears high, picking out the crunch of boot through ice-crusted snow. The command given to him is etched behind his eyes.

TRACK.

He sticks to the shadows of the rusted cars, following the dark shape through the whiteness, which grows thicker. But his world is not one of sight alone. That is the dullest of what he perceives, a shadow of a larger truth.

He stops long enough to bring his nose to a treaded print, scenting rubber, dirt, and leather. He rises higher to catch the wafting trail of wet wool, cigarette smoke, and sweat. *He smells the fear in the salt off his prey's skin; distantly his ears pick out the rasp of a hurried breath.*

He moves on, keeping pace with his quarry, his paws padding silently.

As he follows, he draws the rest of his surroundings inside him, reading the past and present in the flow of old and fresh trails. His ears note every distant shout, every grind of motor, every wash of wave from the neighboring sea. On the back of his tongue, he tastes frost and winter.

Through it all, one path shines brightest, leading to his prey.

He flows along it, a ghost on that trail.

10:18 A.M.

From his vantage in the drainage ditch, Tucker watched *his* target slip through the hatch at the top of the crane and close it with a muffled *snick*.

With the man out of direct sight, Tucker stood up and sprinted toward the tower, holstering the Makarov as he went. Discarding stealth, he jumped onto the ladder's third rung and started climbing. The rungs were slick with snow and ice. His boots slipped with every step, but he kept going. Two rungs beneath the hatch, he stopped. The hatch's padlock was missing.

Holding his breath, he drew the Makarov and then gently, slowly, pressed the barrel against the hatch. It gave way ever so slightly.

Tucker didn't allow himself a chance to think, to judge the stupidity of his next action. Hesitation could get you killed as easily as bravado.

And if I have to die, let it be while I'm still moving.

In the past, he had pushed blindly through hundreds of doors in countless Afghan villages and bunkers. On the other side, something was always waiting to kill you.

This was no different.

He shoved the hatch open, his gun tracking left and right. The assassin knelt two feet away, crouched over an open clamshell rifle case. Behind him, one of the cab's sliding windows stood open, allowing snow to whip inside.

The assassin spun toward Tucker. The look of surprise on his face lasted only a microsecond—then he lunged.

Tucker fired a single shot. The Makarov's 9 mm hollow-point round entered an inch above the bridge of the man's nose, killing him instantly. The target toppled sideways and went still.

One down . . .

Tucker didn't regret what he'd just done, but the contradiction flashed through his mind. Though not a religious man, Tucker found himself attracted to the Buddhist philosophy of live and let live. In this case, however, letting this man *live* wasn't an option. Odd that he found the necessity of taking a human life defensible, while killing an animal was an entirely different story. The conundrum was intriguing, but pondering all that would have to wait.

He holstered the Makarov, climbed into the cab, and closed the hatch behind him. He quickly searched the assassin, looking for a cell phone or radio; he found neither. If he had a partner, they were operating autonomously—probably a fire-at-will arrangement.

Time check: *sixty seconds.*

Fedoseev would be prompt. He always was.

First order of business from here: keep the Russian out of the kill zone.

He turned his attention to the assassin's rifle, a Russian-made SV-98. He removed it from the case, examined it, and found it ready to fire.

Thanks, comrade, he thought as he stepped over the body and reached the open window.

He extended the rifle's bipod legs, propped them on the sill, and aimed the barrel over the sea of shipping containers and warehouse rooftops toward the main gate. With the cold stock against his cheek, he brought his eye to the scope's eyepiece and peered through the swirling snow.

"Where are you, Fedoseev?" Tucker muttered. "Come on—"

Then he spotted the black shadow sailing through the white snow. The limousine was thirty feet from the main gate and slowing for the cursory check-in with the guard. Tucker focused on the limousine's windshield, his finger tightening on the trigger. He felt a moment of reluctance, then recalled the SV-98's specifications. The weapon didn't have enough juice to penetrate the limousine's ballistic glass—or so he hoped.

He fired once, the blast deafening in the tight cab of the crane. The 7.62 mm round struck the limo's windshield directly before the driver's seat. As an extra measure, Tucker adjusted his aim and fired again, this time shattering the side mirror. To his credit, the driver reacted immediately and correctly, slamming the limousine into reverse, then accelerating hard for fifty feet before slewing into a Y-turn.

Within seconds, the vehicle was a hundred yards away and disappearing into the snow.

Satisfied, Tucker lowered the rifle. Fedoseev was safe for the moment, but someone had tried to kill Tucker's principal. He'd be damned if he was going to let the second assassin escape and try again later.

Tucker ejected the rifle's box magazine and pocketed it before pulling out his satellite phone. He checked the video feed from Kane's camera. Between the wet lens and thickening snowfall, all he got for his effort was a blurry, indecipherable image.

Sighing, he opened another application on the phone. A map of the dockyard appeared on the screen. West of Tucker's location, approximately four hundred yards away, was a pulsing green blip. It was Kane's GPS signal, generated from a microchip embedded in the skin between his shoulder blades.

The dot was stationary, indicating Kane was doing as instructed. The shepherd had followed his quarry and was now lying in wait, watching.

Suddenly the blip moved, a slight jiggle that told him Kane had adjusted position, likely both to remain hidden and keep his quarry in sight. The blip moved again, this time heading steadily eastward and picking up speed.

It could only mean one thing.

The second assassin was sprinting in Tucker's direction.

Hurrying, he scaled down the ladder, sliding most of the way. Once his boots hit the ground, he trudged through the thickening snow, his Makarov held at ready, following the rail line. He hadn't covered thirty feet before he spotted a hazy figure ahead, crouched beside the cut in the fencing. His quarry leaped through the gap and sprinted into the trees.

Damn it.

Kane appeared two seconds later, ready to give chase. But once the shepherd spotted Tucker, he stopped in his tracks, ears high, waiting for further orders.

Tucker gave it.

"TAKE BRAVO!"

Playtime was over.

Kane lunged through the fence and took off in pursuit, with Tucker at his heels.

Though now in takedown mode, Kane didn't get too far ahead of him. The shepherd wove between trees and leaped over fallen trunks with ease, while simultaneously keeping his quarry and Tucker in view.

Engulfed by the forest, the sounds of the shipyard had completely faded. The snow hissed softly through the boughs around him. Somewhere ahead, a branch snapped. He stopped moving, crouched down. To his right, forty feet ahead, Kane was also frozen, crouched atop a fallen trunk, his eyes fixed.

Their quarry must have stopped.

Tucker pulled out his phone, checked the map screen.

Two hundred yards away, a narrow canal cut through the forest, a part of the dockyard's old layout when it had belonged to the Russian Navy. His quarry was former naval infantry, smart enough to have planned for an escape route like this, one by water.

But was that the plan?

According to the map, there was also a major road on the far side of the canal.

What if the man had a vehicle waiting?

Decide, Tucker.

Would his quarry flee by land or sea?

He let out a soft *tsst,* and Kane turned to look at him. Tucker held up a closed fist, then forked fingers: *Track.*

Kane took off straight south.

Tucker headed southeast, hedging his bet, ready to cut the man off if necessary.

As he ran, he kept half an eye on Kane's position using the GPS feed. His partner reached the canal and stopped. The blip held steady for a few seconds—then began moving again, paralleling the canal and rapidly picking up speed.

It could only mean one thing.

Their quarry had boarded a boat.

Tucker took off in a sprint, darting and ducking through the last of the trees. He burst out of the forest and into an open field. Ahead, a tall levy hid the canal's waterway. To his right came the grumble of a marine engine. He ran toward the noise as Kane came racing hard along the top of the levy.

Tucker knew he couldn't hope to match the dog's speed. According to the map, the canal was narrow, no more than fifteen feet.

Doable, Tucker thought.

He shouted, "TAKE DOWN . . . DISARM!"

The shepherd dropped his head lower, put on a burst of speed, then leaped from the levy and vanished beyond the berm.

Kane flies high, thrilled by the rush of air over his fur. Here is what he lived for, as ingrained in his nature as the beat of his heart.

To hunt and take down prey.

His front paws strike the wood of the deck, but he is already moving, shifting his hind end, to bring his back legs into perfect position. He bounds off the boards and toward the cabin of the boat.

His senses swell, filling in details.

The reek of burnt oil . . .

The resin of the polished wood . . .

The trail of salt and fear that lead to that open door of the cabin . . .

He follows that scent, dragged along by both command and nature.

He bolts through the door, sees the man swing toward him, his skin bursting with terror, his breath gasping out in surprise.

An arm lifts, not in reflexive defense, but bringing up a gun.

Kane knows guns.

The blast deafens as he lunges.

10:33 A.M.

The gunshot echoed over the water as Tucker reached the top of the levy. His heart clenched in concern. Fifty yards down the waterway, a center-cabin dredge boat tilted crookedly in the canal, nosing toward the bank.

Tucker ran, fear firing his limbs. As he reached the foundering boat, he coiled his legs and vaulted high, flying. He hit the boat's afterdeck hard and slammed into the gunwale. Pain burst behind his eyes. Rolling sideways, he got to his knees and brought the Makarov up.

Through the open cabin door, he saw a man sprawled on his back, his left arm flailing, his legs kicking. His right forearm was clamped between Kane's jaws. The shepherd's muscled bulk was rag-dolling the man from side to side.

The Russian screamed in his native tongue. Tucker's grasp of the language was rudimentary, but the man's tone said it all.

Get him off me! Please!

With his gun trained on the man's chest, Tucker stepped through the cabin door. Calmly he said, "RELEASE."

Kane instantly let go of the man's arm and stepped back, his lips still curled in a half snarl.

The Russian clutched his shattered arm to his chest, his eyes wide and damp with pain. Judging by where Kane had clamped on to the man's forearm, the ulna was likely broken and possibly the radius as well.

Tucker felt no pity.

The asshole had almost shot his partner.

A few feet away lay a revolver, still smoking in the cold.

Tucker stepped forward and looked down at the man. "Do you speak English?"

"English . . . yes, I speak some English."

"You're under arrest."

"What? I don't—"

Tucker drew back his right foot and heel-kicked the man squarely in the forehead, knocking him unconscious.

"More or less," he added.

2

March 4, 12:44 P.M.
Vladivostok, Russia

"You owe me a new windshield," Bogdan Fedoseev boomed, handing Tucker a shot glass of ice-cold vodka.

He accepted it but placed the glass on the end table next to the couch. He was not fond of vodka, and, more important, he didn't trust his hands right now. The aftermath of the shoot-out at the shipyard had left Tucker pumping with adrenaline, neither an unfamiliar nor unpleasant rush for him. Even so, he wondered how much of that rush was exhilaration and how much was PTSD—a clinical acronym for what used to be called shell shock or battle fatigue, a condition all too common for many Iraq and Afghanistan veterans.

Compared to most, Tucker's case was mild, but it was a constant in his life. Though he managed it well, he could still feel it lurking there, like a monster probing for a chink in his mental armor. Tucker found the metaphor strangely reassuring. Vigilance was something he did well. Still, the Buddhist in him whispered in his ear to relax his guard.

Let go of it.

What you cling to only gets stronger.

What you think, you become.

Tucker couldn't quite nail down when and where he'd adopted this philosophy. It had snuck up on him. He'd had a few teachers—one in particular—but he suspected he'd picked up his worldview from his wanderings with Kane. Having encountered people of almost every stripe, Tucker had learned to take folks as they came, without the baggage of preconceptions. People were more alike than different. Everyone was just trying to find a way to be happy, to feel fulfilled. The manner in which they searched for that state differed wildly, but the prize remained the same.

Enough, Tucker commanded himself. Contemplation was fine, but he'd long ago decided it was a lot like tequila—best taken only in small doses.

At his feet, Kane sat at ease, but his eyes remained bright and watchful. The shepherd missed nothing: *posture, hand and eye movements, respiration rate, perspiration.* All of it painted a clear picture for his partner. Unsurprisingly, Kane had picked up on the anxiety in the air.

Tucker felt it, too.

One of the reasons he had been paired with Kane was his unusually high empathy scores. Military war dog handlers had a saying—*It runs down the lead*—describing how emotions of the pair became shared over time, binding them together. The same skill allowed Kane to read people, to pick up nuances of body language and expression that others might miss.

Like now, with the tension in the room.

"And the side mirror of the limo," Fedoseev added with a strained grin. "You destroyed both windshield and mirror. Very costly. And worst of all, you could have killed Pytor, my driver."

Tucker refused to back down, knowing it would be a sign of weakness. "At that distance and angle, the rifle I used didn't have enough foot-pounds to penetrate the limo's ballistic glass. Maybe if I was standing on the hood of the car, Pytor might have had something to worry about."

Stymied, Fedoseev frowned. "Still, very expensive things to fix on limousine, yes?"

"You can take it out of my bonus," Tucker replied.

"Bonus! What bonus?"

"The one you're going to give me for saving your life."

Standing behind Fedoseev, Yuri said, "We would have handled the—"

Fedoseev held up his hand, silencing his subordinate. Yuri's face flushed. Behind him, the pair of bodyguards at the door shifted their feet, glancing down.

Tucker knew what Yuri and his security team were thinking. *Would haves* were worthless when it comes to personal protection. The fact was, this outsider— this American and his dog—had saved their boss. Still, Yuri had intervened on Tucker's behalf with the police, smoothing over the complications that could have risen over killing the first shooter. Russian bodyguards taking down a would-be assassin was a simple matter; a former U.S. Army Ranger, not so much.

Ninety minutes after apprehending the second man, who was now in police custody, Tucker met Fedoseev and his entourage back at the Meridian Hotel, where the Russian had rented the top floor of VIP suites. The decor and furnishings were comfortable, but overly ornate. Shabby Soviet chic. Outside, snow still fell, obscuring what would have been a stunning view of Peter the Great Bay and mainland Russia.

"I do you better than bonus," Fedoseev offered. "You become part of my team. Permanent part. I am generous. Your dog will eat steak every night. He would like that, yes?"

"Ask him yourself."

Fedoseev's gaze flicked toward Kane, then he smiled and wagged his finger at Tucker. "Very funny." He tried a different angle. "You know, these two *suka* may have had a helper. If he is still around—"

Suka was one of Fedoseev's favorite slang terms. Roughly and politely, a *suka* meant *scumbag*.

Tucker interrupted. "If you're right, I'm sure Yuri will find anyone else involved in this attempted assassination."

Especially with one of the attackers already in custody.

Up here, torture was as common a tool as a knife and fork.

Fedoseev sighed. "Then your answer is?"

"I appreciate the offer," he said, "but my contract's up in two days. Past that, I've got somewhere to be."

It was a lie, but no one called him on it.

The truth was he had *nowhere* to be, and right now he liked it that way. Plus Yuri and his team were all ex-military and that background infused everything they did and said. He'd had his fill of them. Tucker had done his time in the military, and the parting had been less than amicable.

Of course, he'd loved his early days in the army and had been contemplating going career.

Until Anaconda.

He reached for the abandoned glass of vodka as the unwanted memory of the past swept over him. He hated how the cubes rattled against the crystal as he lifted the tumbler. PTSD. He considered it merely a piece of psychic shrapnel lodged near his heart.

He sipped at the liquor, letting the memory wash through him.

Not that he had any choice.

Tucker again felt the pop of his ears as the rescue helicopter lifted off, felt the rush of hot air.

He closed his eyes, remembering that day, drawn back to that firefight. He had been assisting soldiers from the Tenth Mountain Division secure a series of bunkers in Hell's Halfpipe. He had been flanked by two partners that day: Kane and Kane's littermate, Abel. If Kane had been Tucker's right arm, Abel was his left. He'd trained them both.

Then a distress call had reached his team in the mountains. A Chinook helo carrying a team of Navy

SEALs had been downed by RPG fire on a peak called Takur Ghar. Tucker and his squad were dispatched east and had begun the arduous climb to Takur Ghar when they were ambushed in a ravine. A pair of IEDs exploded, killing most of Tucker's squad and wounding the rest, including Abel, whose left front leg had been blown off at the elbow.

Within seconds, Taliban fighters emerged from concealed positions and swarmed the survivors. Tucker, along with a handful of soldiers, was able to reach a defensible position and hold out long enough for an evac helicopter to land. Once Kane and his teammates were loaded, he was about to jump off and return for Abel, but before he could do so, a crewman dragged him back aboard and held him down—where he could only watch.

As the helo lifted off and banked over the ravine, a pair of Taliban fighters chased down Abel who was limping toward the rising helo, his pained eyes fixed on Tucker, his severed leg trailing blood.

Tucker scrambled for the door, only to be pulled back yet again.

Then the Taliban fighters reached Abel. He squeezed those last memories away, but not the haunting voice forever in the back of his mind: *You could've tried harder; you could have reached him.*

If he had, he knew he would have been killed, too, but at least Abel wouldn't have been alone. Alone and wondering why Tucker had abandoned him . . .

Back in his own skin, he opened his eyes and downed the rest of the vodka in a single gulp, letting the burn erase the worst of that old pain.

"Mr. Wayne . . ." Bogdan Fedoseev leaned forward, his forehead creased with concern. "Are you ill? You've gone dead pale, my friend."

Tucker cleared his throat, shook his head. Without looking, he knew Kane was staring at him. He reached out and gave the shepherd's neck a reassuring squeeze.

"I'm fine. What were we talking—?"

Fedoseev leaned back. "You and your dog joining us."

Tucker focused his eyes on Fedoseev and on the present. "No, as I said, I'm sorry. I've got somewhere to be."

Though it was a lie, he was ready to move on, *needed* to move on.

But the question remained: What would he do?

Fedoseev sighed loudly. "Very well! But if you change your mind, you tell me. Tonight, you stay in one of the suites. I send up two steaks. One for you. One for your dog."

Tucker nodded, stood, and shook Fedoseev's hand.

For now, that was enough of a plan.

11:56 P.M.

The chirp of his satellite phone instantly woke Tucker in his room.

He scrambled for it, while checking the clock.

Almost midnight.

What now? With nothing on Fedoseev's schedule for that evening, Tucker and Kane had been given the night off. Had something happened? Yuri had already informed him earlier that the Vladikavkaz Separatist taken into custody had broken and talked, spilling everything.

So Tucker had expected a quiet night.

He checked the incoming number as he picked up the phone: a blocked number. That was seldom good.

Kane sat at the edge of the bed, watching Tucker.

He lifted the phone and pressed the talk button. "Hello?"

A series of squeaks and buzzes suggested the call was being filtered through a series of digital coders.

Finally, the caller spoke. "Captain Wayne, I'm glad I could reach you."

Tucker relaxed—but not completely. Suspicion rang through him as he recognized the voice. It was Painter Crowe, the director of Sigma Force, and the man who'd tried to recruit Tucker not so long ago after a prior mission. The full extent of Sigma's involvement in the U.S. intelligence and defense community was still a mystery to him, but one thing he did know: Sigma worked under the aegis of the ultrasecretive DARPA— the Defense Advanced Research Projects Agency.

Tucker cleared the rasp of sleep from his voice. "I assume you know what time it is here, Director?"

"I do. My apologies. It's important."

"Isn't it always? What's going on?"

"I believe your contract with Bogdan Fedoseev is almost up. In two more days, if I'm not mistaken."

Tucker should have been surprised that the caller had this information, but this was Painter Crowe, who had resources that bordered on the frightening.

"Director, I'm guessing this isn't a casual call, so why don't you get to your point?"

"I need a favor. And you've got forty-two days still left on your Russian visa."

"And something tells me you want those *days.*"

"Only a few. We've got a friend I'd like you to meet."

"I've got enough friends. Why is this one so special?"

There was a pause, one that took too long. He understood. While the call was encrypted, Tucker's room could have been bugged—probably *was* bugged, knowing the Russians. Any further details would require additional precautions.

He couldn't say such subterfuge didn't intrigue him.

He also suspected this lapse in the conversation was a test.

Tucker proved his understanding of the need for privacy by asking another question. "Where?"

"Half a mile from your hotel—a pay phone on the northeast corner of the Grey Horse Apartments."

"I'll find it. Give me twenty minutes."

He was there in eighteen, stamping his feet against the cold. Using a prepaid calling card, Tucker dialed Sigma's cover trunk line, then waited through another series of encoder tones before Crowe's voice came on the line.

The director got straight to the point. "I need you to escort a man out of the country."

The simple sentence was fraught with layers of information. The fact that Crowe didn't think their *friend* was capable of accomplishing this feat on his own already told Tucker two things.

One: The man was of high value to Sigma.

Two: Normal travel options were problematic.

In other words, someone didn't want the man leaving the country.

Tucker knew better than to ask *why* this target needed to leave Russia. Crowe was a firm believer in the need-to-know policy. But Tucker had another question that he wanted answered.

"*Why* me?"

"You're already in-country, have an established cover, and your skill set matches the job."

"And you have no other assets available."

"That, too—but it's a secondary consideration."

"Just so we're clear, Director. This is a favor. Nothing more. If you're trying to court me to join—"

"Not at all. Get our friend out of the country, and you're done. You'll make twice your usual retainer. For this mission, I'm assigning you an operations handler. Her name is Ruth Harper."

"Not you?" This surprised him, and he didn't like surprises. "Director, you know I don't play well with others, especially those I've never met face-to-face."

"Harper is good, Tucker. Really knows her stuff. Give her a chance. So will you do it?"

Tucker sighed. While he had little trust in government agencies, Crowe had so far proven himself to be a stand-up guy.

"Give me the details."

3

The door to Tucker's private berth on the train slid back, and a head bearing a blue cap peeked through.

"Papers, please," the train porter ordered, tempering his KGB-like request with a friendly smile. The sliver-thin young man could be no more than twenty, his coal-black hair peeking from under his crisp hat. He kept the buttons of his uniform well polished, clearly very proud of his job.

Tucker handed over his passport.

The porter studied it, nodded, and handed it back. The man's eyes settled nervously on Kane. The shepherd sat upright in the seat opposite Tucker, panting, tongue hanging.

"And your animal?" the porter asked.

"Service animal."

Tucker handed over Kane's packet, courtesy of Painter Crowe. The papers certified his furry companion was a working dog, adept at sensing Tucker's frequent and debilitating epileptic seizures. It was a ruse, of course, but traveling with a seventy-pound military war dog tended to raise unwanted questions.

The porter reviewed the papers and nodded. "*Da*, I see. My second cousin suffers same sickness." His gaze returned to Kane, but with more affection and sympathy now. "May I pet him?"

Tucker shrugged. "Sure. He doesn't bite."

Not unless I tell him to.

Tentatively, the porter reached out and scratched Kane under the chin. "Good doggy."

Kane regarded him impassively, tolerating the familiarity.

Tucker resisted the urge to smile.

Satisfied, the porter grinned and returned the documents to Tucker.

"I like him very much," the young man said.

"I do, too."

"If there's anything you need, you ask, *da*?"

Tucker nodded as the porter exited and slid the door closed.

He settled back, staring at the Russian scenery passing by the window, which mostly consisted of snowy trees and Soviet-bloc-era buildings as the train headed out of Vladivostok. The port city marked one end of this route of the Trans-Siberian Railway; the other was Moscow.

Not that he and Kane were traveling that far.

For reasons Crowe hadn't explained, Tucker's target wouldn't be ready for extraction for a week. So after completing his final two days with Bogdan Fedoseev, Tucker had boarded the famous Trans-Siberian Railway and settled in for the five-day journey to the city of Perm. Once there, he was to meet a contact who would take him to his target, a man named Abram Bukolov.

Tucker still had no idea *why* the man needed to leave Russia in such a clandestine manner—especially such a high-profile figure. Tucker had recognized his name as soon as Crowe had mentioned it on the phone. Tucker's previous employer, Bogdan Fedoseev, had had business dealings with this man in the past.

Abram Bukolov was the owner of Horizon Industries and arguably the country's pharmacological tycoon. A frequent face on magazine covers and television shows,

Bukolov was to prescription drugs what Steve Jobs had been to personal computing. In the years following the breakup of the Soviet Union, the pharmaceutical industry in Russia disintegrated into disarray and corruption, from the quality of the drugs themselves to the distribution networks. Thousands were thought to have died from tainted drugs or faulty doses. Through sheer force of will and inherited wealth, Abram Bukolov slowly and steadily bent the system to his benevolent will, becoming the keeper of Russia's pharmacy.

And now he wanted out, all but abandoning a multibillion-dollar empire he had spent his entire adult life building.

Why?

And what could possibly drive such a man to run so scared?

According to the encrypted dossier sent by Painter Crowe, the only clue lay in Bukolov's mysterious warning: *The Arzamas-16 generals are after me . . .*

The man refused to explain more until he was safely out of Russia.

Tucker had studied the rest of the files for this mission over and over again. Bukolov was a well-known eccentric, a personality trait that shone in every interview of him. He was clearly a driven visionary with a zealous passion to match, but had he finally snapped?

And what about these Arzamas-16 generals?

From the research notes included in the dossier, there was once a city named *Arzamas-16*. During the rule of Joseph Stalin, it was home to the Soviet Union's first nuclear weapons design center. The U.S. intelligence community simply referred to it as the *Russian Los Alamos*.

But it was only the first of the many *naukograds*, or "closed science cities," that popped up across the Soviet Union, secured by ironclad perimeters. In such places, top-secret projects under the aegis of the best Soviet scientists were conducted. Rumors abounded during the Cold War of biological weapons, mind control drugs, and stealth technology.

But Arzamas-16 no longer existed.

In its place, the region had become home to a couple of nuclear weapons test facilities—but what did anything like that have to do with Abram Bukolov?

And who could these nefarious *generals* be?

It made no sense.

He glanced over at Kane, who wagged his tail, ready for whatever was to come. Tucker settled back, deciding that was probably the best course of action from here.

Just be ready for anything.

4

March 7, 10:42 A.M.
Moscow, Russia

The large man stepped around his desk and settled into his chair with a creak of leather. He had the call up on his speakerphone. He had no fear of anyone listening. No one dared, especially not here.

"Where is the target now?" he asked. Word had reached his offices that an operative—an American mercenary with a dog—had been assigned to help Dr. Bukolov leave Russian soil.

That must not happen.

"Heading west," the caller answered in Swedish-accented Russian. "Aboard the Trans-Siberian. We know he is booked through to Perm, but whether that's his final destination, we don't know yet."

"What makes you think it would be otherwise?"

"This one clearly has some training. My instincts tell me he wouldn't book a ticket straight to his ultimate destination. He's too clever for that."

"What name is he traveling under?"

"We're working on that, too," the Swede answered, growing testy.

"And where are *you* now?"

"Driving to Khabarovsk. We tried to board the train at Vladivostok but—"

"He gave you the shake, *da*?"

"Yes."

"Let me understand this. A man and a large dog lost you and your team. Did he see you?"

"No. Of that we're certain. He is simply careful and well trained. What else have you learned about him?"

"Nothing much. I'm making inquiries, trying to track his finances, but it appears he is using a credit card that has been backstopped—sanitized. It suggests he's either more than he seems to be or has powerful help. Or both. What came of the hotel search in Vladivostok?"

"Nothing. We couldn't get close. His employer— that bastard Bogdan Fedoseev—rented out the entire penthouse. Security was too tight. But if we can reach

Khabarovsk before the train does, we'll board there. If not . . ."

The Swede's words trailed off.

Neither of them had to verbalize the problems such a failure would present.

The railway branched frequently from there, with routes heading in many different directions, including into China and Mongolia. Following their target into a foreign country—especially China—would exponentially multiply their surveillance challenges.

The speakerphone crackled again as the caller offered one hope. "If he is using sanitized credit cards, we should assume he has several passports and travel documents. If you have any colleagues in the FPS, it may be helpful to circulate his photo."

He nodded to himself, rubbing his chin. The caller was referring to Russia's Federal Border Guard Service.

"As you said," the caller continued, "a man and a large dog are hard to miss."

"I'll see what I can do. I would prefer to keep the scope of this operation limited. That's why I hired you. Sadly, I am beginning to question my judgment. Get results, or I'll be making a change. Do you understand my meaning?"

A long silence followed before a response came.

"Not to worry. I've never failed before. I'll get the information you need, and he'll be dead before he ever reaches Perm."

5

A voice over the intercom system called out first in Russian, then in English.

"Next stop, Khabarovsk."

A scrolling green LED sign on the wall of Tucker's berth repeated the multilingual message along with: DEPARTING AGAIN IN 18 MINUTES.

Tucker began gathering his things, tugging on his coat. Once done, he patted Kane. "What do you say we stretch our legs?"

They'd been cooped up in the car for most of the day, and he knew he could use a bit of fresh air. He pulled on his fur trapper's cap, attached Kane's lead, then opened the berth door.

He followed the slow trudge of fellow passengers down the corridor to the exit steps. A few eyebrows were raised at the sight of his unusual traveling companion. One matronly babushka gave him what he could best describe as the evil eye.

Taking heed of the unnecessary attention, he avoided the terminal building—a whitewashed, green-tiled Kremlin-esque structure—and guided Kane across the train tracks to a patch of scrub brush. A chest-high fence, missing more pickets than it retained, bordered the area.

As Kane sniffed and marked his territory, Tucker stretched his back and legs. Aboard the train, he had caught up on his sleep, and he had the muscle kinks to prove it.

After a few minutes, the screech of tires drew his attention past the terminal. The frantic blare of a car horn followed. He spotted a line of cars stopped at the intersection as a departing eastbound train cleared the station. As the caboose clunked over the road and the barriers rose, a black sedan swerved to the head of the line and raced into the terminal parking lot.

He checked his watch. Four minutes to departure.

Whoever was in the sedan was cutting it close.

He let Kane wander for another full minute, then walked back over the tracks to their train car. Once returned to their berth, Kane jumped into his usual seat, panting, refreshed.

A commotion out on the terminal platform drew his attention, too. A trio of men in long black leather dusters strode purposefully along the length of the train, occasionally stopping porters and showing them what looked to be a photo before moving on again. None of the men offered any credentials.

Faint alarm bells sounded in Tucker's head. But there were hundreds of people on the train, he told himself, and so far all the porters had merely shrugged or shook their heads when shown the photo.

Clearly frustrated, one of the men pulled out a cell phone and spoke into it. Thirty seconds later, he was joined by his partners, and after a brief discussion, the trio hurried back into the terminal and disappeared from view.

He watched and waited, but none of them reappeared.

He sighed in relief when the train whistle blew and the *All Aboard* was called. The train lurched forward and slowly pulled away from the station.

Only then did he settle back in his own seat.

But he was hardly settled.

7:38 P.M.

An hour later, too full of nervous energy to remain inside the berth, Tucker found himself seated in the dining car. Around him, the tables were draped with linen; the windows framed by silk curtains; the place settings china and crystal.

But his attention focused on the car's best feature.

While he had never been the type to ogle the opposite sex, the woman sitting across the aisle and one booth down was challenging his discipline.

She was tall and lithe, her figure accentuated by a form-fitting skirt and a white cashmere turtleneck sweater. She wore her blond hair long and straight, framing high cheekbones and ice-blue eyes. Picking at a salad and occasionally sipping from a glass of wine, she spent most of the meal either reading a dog-eared copy of *Anna Karenina* or staring out the window as dusk settled over the Siberian landscape. For one chance moment, she looked up, caught Tucker's eye, and smiled—genuine, pleasant, but clearly reserved.

Still, her body language was easy to read.

Thank you, but I'd prefer to be alone.

A few minutes later, the woman signaled for the check, signed her bill, then swished past Tucker's table and through the connecting door to the berth cars.

Tucker lingered over his coffee, oddly disappointed, more than he should be, then headed back to his own berth.

As he stepped into the corridor, he found the blond woman kneeling on the floor, the contents of her purse scattered at her feet, some of it rolling farther away with each jostle of the train's wheels.

Tucker walked over and dropped to a knee beside her. "Let me help."

She frowned, tucked a strand of blond hair behind her ear, and offered him a shy smile. "Thank you. Everything seems to be getting away from me lately."

Her accent was British, refined.

Tucker helped her gather the runaway items, then stood up. He nodded at her copy of *Anna Karenina*. "The butler did it, by the way."

She blinked at him, momentarily confused.

Tucker added, "In the library, with a lead pipe."

She smiled. "Well, goodness. Then there's not much point in my finishing it, is there?"

"Sorry if I ruined it for you."

"You've read it?"

"In high school," he said.

"And your verdict?"

"Certainly not beach reading. I liked it—but not enough to wade through it a second time."

"It's my *third* time. I'm a glutton for punishment, I suppose." She extended her hand. "Well, thank you again . . ."

He took her hand, finding her fingers soft, but firm. "Tucker," he said.

"I'm Felice. Thank you for your help. I hope you have a pleasant night."

It had certainly turned out *pleasant.*

She turned and started down the corridor. Ten feet away, she stopped and spoke without turning. "It doesn't seem quite fair, you know."

Tucker didn't reply, but waited until she turned to face him before asking, "What isn't?"

"You spoiling the end of a perfectly good Russian novel."

"I see your point. I take it that an apology isn't enough?"

"Not even close."

"Breakfast, then?"

Her lips pursed as Felice considered this a moment. "Is seven too early for you?"

He smiled. "See you in the morning."

With a slight wave, she turned and headed down the corridor. He watched until she vanished out of sight, enjoying every step she took.

Once alone, he opened the door to his berth and found Kane sitting on the floor staring up at him. The shepherd must have heard his voice out in the passageway. Kane tilted his head in his customary *What's going on?* fashion.

He smiled and scratched Kane between the ears. "Sorry, pal, she didn't have a friend."

6

March 8, 6:55 A.M.
Trans-Siberian Railway

The next morning, Tucker arrived five minutes early to find Felice already seated at a booth in the rear of the dining car. For the moment, they had the space to themselves. This time of the year, the sun was still not up, just a rosy promise to the east.

Tucker walked over and sat down. "You're a morning person, I see."

"Since I was a little girl, I'm afraid. It drove my parents quite mad. By the way, I ordered coffee for two, if you don't mind. I'm a much better morning person with caffeine in my system."

"That makes two of us."

The waiter arrived with a pair of steaming mugs and took their orders. Felice opted for the closest semblance to a standard big English breakfast. He nodded his approval, appreciating a woman with a good appetite. In turn, he chose an omelet with toasted black bread.

"You're the owner of that large hound, aren't you?" Felice asked. "The one that looks smarter than most people on this train."

"Owner isn't the word I would use, but yes." He offered up his service dog story, explaining about his epilepsy. "I don't know what I'd do without him."

At least that last part was true.

"Where are you two headed?" she asked.

"I'm booked to Perm, but I'm flexible. Plenty to explore out here. We might get off and sightsee if the mood strikes us. And you?"

She gave him a sly smile. "Is that an invitation?"

He gave her a shrug that was noncommittal with a hint of invitation, which only widened her smile.

She skirted over to tamer topics. "As to me, I'm headed to Moscow, off to meet some friends from my university days."

"You went to school there?"

"Goodness, no. Cambridge. Arts and humanities. *Hinc lucem et pocula sacra* and all that. *From here, light and sacred draughts.* Latin motto. Very highbrow, you see. Two of my girlfriends moved to Moscow last year. We're having a small reunion."

"You boarded in Khabarovsk?"

"Yes. And almost got run over in the parking lot for my trouble. A big black car."

"I remember hearing some honking, saw some commotion. Was that them?"

She nodded. "Three men, dressed like old-school KGB thugs. Quite gloomy looking. Very rude, marching around the platform like they owned the place, flashing their badges."

Tucker struggled to keep his brow from furrowing. "Sounds like the police. Perhaps they were looking for someone."

She took a dismissive sip of coffee. "I can only imagine."

"It's not you, is it? I'm not having breakfast with an international art thief?"

She laughed, tilting her head back and slightly to the side. "Oh, my cover has been blown. Stop the train at once."

He smiled. "According to my guide, Khabarovsk's Fedotov Gallery is a must-see for art connoisseurs. Especially for any sightseeing arts and humanities graduates from Cambridge. I almost wish I'd gotten off the train to go. Did you visit?"

She nodded, her eyes shining. "Absolutely stunning. Wish I'd had more time myself. You must go back sometime. And you, Mr. Wayne, what's your secret? What do you do when you're not traipsing around Siberia?"

"International art thief," he replied.

"Ah, I thought as much."

He patted his jacket pocket. "Excuse me," he said and pulled out his phone, glancing at the screen. "Text from my brother."

He opened the phone's camera application and surreptitiously snapped a shot of Felice's face. He studied the screen for a few more seconds, pretended to type a response, then returned the phone to his pocket.

"Sorry," he said. "My brother's getting married in a month, and he's put me in charge of his bachelor party. His wife is worried it's going to be too risqué."

Felice raised an eyebrow. "And is it?"

"Absolutely."

"Men," she said, laughing, and reached across the table and gave his forearm a squeeze.

8:35 A.M.

After finishing breakfast and lingering over coffee for another half hour, the two parted company with a promise to share another meal before Tucker disembarked at Perm.

Once free, he returned quickly to his berth, pulled out his satellite phone, and speed-dialed the new number Painter Crowe had given him. It was answered immediately.

"Tucker Wayne, I presume," a female voice answered.

"Ruth Harper."

"Correct." Harper's speech was clipped, precise, but somehow not quite curt. There was also a distinct southern accent there, too.

"What do you have for me?" Harper asked.

"No *nice to meet you* or *how are you?*"

"Nice to meet you. How are you? How's that? Warm and fuzzy enough for you?"

"Marginally," Tucker replied.

As he paced the small space, he tried to picture what she looked like. She sounded young, but with a bite at the edges that spoke of some toughness. *Maybe late thirties.* But he knew Sigma operatives had prior military experience, and Harper was likely no exception, so some of that *toughness* could be from hard lessons learned young, an early maturity gained under fire. From her seriousness, he imagined her dark-haired, wearing glasses, a battle-weary librarian.

He smiled inwardly at that image.

"So what's your take on the situation?" she asked.

"I think I've picked up a tail."

"Why do you think that, Captain Wayne?" Her tone grew grave with a trace of doubt.

"Just call me Tucker," he said and explained about the leather-jacketed men on the Khabarovsk train platform and Felice's insistence they were flashing badges.

"And they weren't?" Harper asked.

"No. They were just showing a photograph. I'm sure of it. She also claims she visited the Fedotov Gallery in Khabarovsk. It's been closed for renovations for the past month."

"And you know this detail how?"

"There's not much else to do on this train but sleep and read travel brochures."

"Anything else that makes you suspicious of her?"

"She's pretty, and she finds me fascinating."

"That certainly is odd. Are you sure she's in possession of her faculties?"

He smiled at her matter-of-fact tone. "Funny."

He decided he might—*might*—like Ruth Harper.

"Your accent," Tucker said. "Tennessee?"

She ignored his attempt to draw her out, but from the exasperated tone of her next words, he guessed he was wrong about Tennessee.

"Give me Felice's pedigree," she said, staying professional.

Tucker passed on the information he had gleaned: her name, her background at the University of Cambridge, her friends in Moscow. "And I have a picture. I assume your wizards have access to facial-recognition programs."

"Indeed we do."

"I'm sending it now."

"Okay, sit tight and I'll get back to you."

It didn't take long. Harper called back within forty minutes.

"Your instinct was sound," she said without preamble. "But you've picked up *more* than a tail. She's a freelance mercenary."

"I knew it was too good to be true," he muttered. "Let's hear it."

"Her real name is Felice Nilsson, but she's traveling under Felice Johansson. Swedish citizenship. She's thirty-three, born in Stockholm to a wealthy family. She didn't graduate from Cambridge, but from University of Gothenburg, with a master's in fine arts and music. And here's where things get interesting. Six months after graduating, she joined the Swedish Armed Forces and eventually ended up in *Särskilda Inhämtningsgruppen*."

"SIG?"

As a member of the U.S. Special Forces, Tucker had to know the competition, both allied and enemy alike. SIG was the Swedish Special Reconnaissance Group. Its operatives were trained in intelligence gathering, reconnaissance, and covert surveillance, along with being superb, hardened soldiers.

"She was one of the group's first female members," Harper added.

"What was her specialty?"

"Sniper."

Great.

"I urge you to approach her with extreme caution."

"Caution? Never would have thought of that."

Harper let out what could be taken as a soft chuckle, but it disappeared so quickly that Tucker couldn't be sure.

"Point taken," she said. "But do not underestimate her. After six years in the SIG, Nilsson resigned her commission. Eight months later, she started popping up on intel radars, first working small-time stuff as a mercenary, mostly for established groups. Then, two years ago, she struck out on her own, forming her own team—all former Swedish Special Forces. Last estimate put her roster at six to eight, including herself."

"Bored rich girl goes rogue," Tucker said.

"Maybe that's how it started, but she's got a real taste for it now. And a solid reputation. For now, the question remains, *Who hired her and why?*"

"You're in a better position to answer that than I am. But this must have something to do with your operation. Otherwise, it would be about me personally, and that doesn't seem likely."

"Agreed."

"And if that's true, if they're already on my tail, I don't have to tell you what that means."

"We've got a leak," Harper replied. "Word of your involvement must have reached those who are hunting for Dr. Bukolov."

"But who leaked that information? For the moment, let's assume it didn't come from anyone inside Sigma command. So who in Russia had my itinerary? Who knew I'd be aboard this train."

"The only person with that information was the contact you're supposed to meet in Perm."

"Who's that?"

She didn't answer immediately, and Tucker knew why. If Felice Nilsson got her hands on Tucker, the less he knew, the less he could divulge.

"Forget I asked," he said. "So the leak is either my contact or someone he told."

"Most likely," she agreed. "Either way, it has to be Abram Bukolov they're after. But the fact that Ms. Nilsson is on that train rather than out in Perm, pursuing our contact, that tells us something."

"It tells us whoever is paying her wants this to play out for some reason. This isn't all about Bukolov himself. Maybe it's something he has . . . something he knows."

"Again, I agree. And trust me when I tell you this: I don't know what that could be. When he contacted us, he was tight-lipped. He told us only enough to make sure we'd get him out." A moment of contemplative silence stretched, then she asked, "What's your plan? How do you want to play this?"

"Don't know yet. Assuming those leather jackets I saw at Khabarovsk were hers, they were in a hurry, and I think I know why. The next stop on this route is at the city of Chita, a major hub, where trains spread out in every direction. They had to tag me in Khabarovsk or risk losing me."

"Do you think her men got aboard?"

"I don't think so, but I'll have a look around. I wonder if part of their job was a distraction—a spectacle to let Felice slip aboard without fuss."

"Either way, you can bet she's in contact with them. You said there were no other stops before Chita?"

"Afraid not." Tucker checked his watch. "We'll arrive in two and a half days. I'm going to check the route map. If the train slows below thirty miles per hour, and the terrain is accommodating, we can roll off. It's the surest way to shake Felice off my trail."

"You're getting into the mountains out there, Tucker. Take care you don't tumble off a cliff."

"Glad to know you care, Harper."

"Just worried about the dog."

He smiled, warming up to this woman. His image of the battle-weary librarian was developing some softer edges, including a glint of dark amusement in her eyes.

"As to Felice Nilsson," she continued, "don't kill her unless you have to."

"No promises, Harper, but I'll keep you posted."

He disconnected and looked down at Kane, who was upright in his seat by the window. "How does a little backcountry romp sound to you, my friend?"

Kane tilted his head and wagged his tail.

So it's unanimous.

As the train continued chugging west toward Chita, Tucker spent the remainder of the day strolling the train, twice bumping into Felice. They chatted briefly. Both times she deftly probed him about his plans.

Would he be heading directly on to Perm?

What would he do when he got there?

Which hotel had he booked?

He deflected his way through her questioning with lies and vague responses. Then he spent the rest of the afternoon seeking an easy place to jump from the train.

Unlike Hollywood portrayals, one could not simply open a window or slip out between cars. While in motion, all the train's exits were locked, either directly or behind secure doors. Such security left Tucker with two choices. Either he remained aboard and attempted to shake loose of Felice at the Chita station, where she likely already had accomplices lying in wait—or he discovered a way to get through those locked exits and leap blindly from the train in the dead of night.

Not great choices.

Still, in the end, he had little trouble making the decision, leaning upon his military training and mindset. It came down to a simple adage drilled into him as an army ranger.

Act, don't react.

7

With the night darkening the berth's windows, Tucker made his final preparations. He had spent the last few hours of daylight walking through his plan, both mentally and physically, rehearsing his movements, along with timing and tracing the routines of the staff.

After one final task—a bit of breaking and entering—he called Ruth Harper.

"Did you get the photos I took of Felice's papers?"

Earlier in the day, he had snuck into her berth while she was out. He rifled carefully through her bags and compartments, discovering four passports, her credit cards, and a Swedish driver's license. He took photos of them all with his cell phone, left the room as tidy as he had entered it, and sent them to Sigma command. He wanted to know all he could about his opponent.

"Yes, we got the pictures and are running them through our databases."

"Hopefully, by the time you finish that, whatever you find will be irrelevant." Because he didn't plan to still be on the train by then. "In forty minutes, the train will have to slow down for a hairpin turn along the river outside Byankino."

"Which is *where* exactly in the vast expanse that is Siberia?"

"About three hundred miles east of Chita. A lot of small villages lie nearby and even more forest. That means lots of territory to lose ourselves in."

"I assume you don't mean that literally. The downside of such isolation is that you're going to have trouble finding transportation to Perm—at least low-visibility transport."

"I think I've got an idea about that."

"You know the saying: *No plan survives first contact with the enemy.*"

Tucker pictured Felice's face. "We've already made contact with the enemy. So it's time to get proactive."

"Your call. You're on the scene. Good luck with—"

From the door to his berth came a light knocking.

"I've got company," he said. "I'll call when I can. In the meantime, nothing to our friend in Perm, agreed?"

He didn't want his new itinerary—improvised as it was—leaked out to the wrong ears.

"Understood," Harper acknowledged.

He disconnected, walked to the door, and slid it open.

Felice leaned against the frame. "I trust it's not past your bedtime?"

The expression on her face was one of coy invitation. Not too much, but just enough.

Well practiced, he guessed.

"I was just reading Kane a bedtime story."

"I had hoped you'd join me for a late-night snack."

Tucker checked his watch. "The dining car is closed."

Felice smiled. "I have a secret cache in my berth. We could debate the literary merits of *Anna Karenina.*"

When Tucker didn't immediately reply, Felice let a little sparkle into her eye and turned up the corners of her mouth ever so slightly.

She was very good, doing her best to keep her quarry close.

"Okay," he said. "Give me ten minutes. Your berth is . . . ?"

"Next car up, second on the left."

He closed the door, then turned to Kane. "Plans have changed, pal. We're going *now*."

Kane jumped off his seat. From beneath it, Tucker pulled free the shepherd's tactical vest and secured it in place. Next he opened his wardrobe, hauled out his already-prepped rucksack, and shoved his cold-weather gear—jacket, gloves, cap—into the top compartment.

Once ready, Tucker slowly slid open his berth door and peeked out. To the right, the direction of Felice's berth, the corridor was clear. To the left, an elderly couple stood at the window, staring out at the night.

With Kane at his heels, Tucker stepped out, slid the door shut behind him, and strode past the couple with a polite nod. He pushed through the glass connector door, crossed the small alcove between the two carriages, and pushed into the next sleeper car. The corridor ahead was thankfully empty.

Halfway down, he stopped and cocked his head. Kane was looking back in the direction they'd come.

Somewhere a door had opened, then banged shut.

"Come on," Tucker said and kept walking.

He crossed through the next sleeper car and reached a glass door at the end. Beyond it, he spotted the small alcove that connected this carriage with the baggage coach.

As he touched the door handle, a voice rose behind him, from the far end of the corridor. "Tucker?"

He recognized her voice but didn't turn. He slid open the door.

"Tucker, where are you going? I thought we were—"

He stepped into the alcove with Kane and slid the glass door closed behind him. The shepherd immediately let out a low growl.

Danger.

Tucker swung around and locked eyes with a porter sharing the same cramped space, standing in the shadows off to the side. He immediately recognized the man's hard face, along with his deadly expression. It was one of Felice's team. The man had exchanged his black leather duster for a porter's outfit. Equally caught by surprise, the man lunged for his jacket pocket.

Tucker didn't hesitate, kicking out with his heel, striking the man in the solar plexus. He fell back into the bulkhead, hitting his skull with a crack and slumping to the floor, knocked out.

He reached into the man's pocket and pulled out a Walther P22 semiautomatic; the magazine was full, one round in the chamber, the safety off. He reengaged the safety and shoved the P22 into his own belt, then rummaged through the man's clothes until he found a key ring and an identification badge.

The picture it bore didn't match the slack face before him, but Tucker recognized the photo. It was the porter who had shyly petted Kane when they had first boarded. With a pang of regret, he knew the man was likely dead. Felice and company were playing hardball.

Tucker took the keys, spun, and locked the connector door just as Felice reached it.

"What are you doing?" she asked, feigning concern, a hand at her throat. "Did you hurt that poor man?"

"He'll be fine. But what about the *real* porter?"

Doubt flickered in Felice's eyes. "You're talking crazy. Just come out and we can—"

"Your English accent is slipping, Ms. Nilsson."

Felice's face changed like a passing shadow, going colder, more angular. "So what's your plan then, Mr. Wayne?" she asked. "Jump from the train and go where? Siberia is hell. You won't last a day."

"We love a challenge."

"You won't make it. We'll hunt you down. Work with me instead. The two of us together, we can—"

"Stop talking," he growled.

Felice shut her mouth, but her eyes were sharp with hatred.

Tucker stepped away from the door and unlocked the baggage car. He pointed inside and touched Kane's side. "SCENT. BLOOD. RETURN."

His partner trotted into the darkened space. After ten seconds, Kane let out an alert whine. He reappeared at Tucker's side and sat down, staring back into the baggage car.

Tucker now knew the true fate of the unfortunate porter.

"We're leaving," he said to Felice. "If you're lucky, no one will find the body before you reach Chita."

"Who's to say you didn't kill him?" Felice said. "He caught you burglarizing the baggage car, you killed him, then jumped from the train. I'm a witness."

"If you want to draw that kind of attention to yourself, be my guest."

Tucker turned, stepped over the limp body of her partner, and entered the baggage car, closing the door behind him.

Kane led him to the porter's body. The man had been shoved under a set of steel bulkhead shelves. Judging from the bruising, he had been strangled to death.

"I'm sorry," Tucker murmured.

He donned his jacket, gloves, and cap, then slung his rucksack over his shoulder. At the rear of the car, he used the porter's keys to unlock the metal door. It swung open, and a rush of wind shoved him sideways. The rattling of the train's wheels filled his ears.

Directly ahead was the caboose door.

With Kane following closely, Tucker stepped onto the open platform, shut the door behind him, then unlocked the caboose and stepped into the last car. He hurried across to the rear, through the last door— and a moment later, they were at the tail end of the Trans-Siberian Express, standing on a railed catwalk.

Beneath them, tracks flashed past. The sky was clear and black and studded with stars. To their right, a slope led to a partially frozen river; to their left, scattered snowdrifts. The locomotive was chugging up a slight grade, moving well below its average speed, but still much faster than Tucker would have liked.

He tugged the collar of his jacket up around his neck against the frigid night.

At his knee, Kane wagged his tail, excited. No surprise there. The shepherd was ready to go, come what may. Tucker knelt and cupped Kane's head in both of his hands, bringing his face down close.

"Who's a good boy?"

Kane leaned forward, until their noses touched.

"That's right. You are."

It was a routine of theirs.

Standing but keeping a grip on Kane's vest collar, Tucker navigated the catwalk steps until they were only a few feet above the racing ground. He poked his head past the caboose's side, looking forward, waiting, watching, until he saw a particularly thick snowdrift approaching.

"Ready, boy?" he said. "We're gonna jump! Steady now . . . steady . . ."

The snowdrift flashed into view. Tucker tossed his rucksack out into the darkness.

"GO, KANE! JUMP!"

Without hesitation, the shepherd leaped out into the night.

Tucker waited a beat, then followed.

8

March 8, 11:24 P.M.
Siberia, Russia

Tucker immediately realized all snowdrifts were not alike, especially in Siberia. Having gone through weeks of thawing and freezing, the drift's face had become armored by several inches of ice.

He hit the frozen surface hip-first, hoping to transition into a roll.

It was not to be.

He crashed through the top of the berm before his momentum flipped his legs up and over his head, sending him into a somersault down the drift's rear slope. He slammed onto his back and began sliding on his butt down the long, steep surface, his heels stuttering over the ice-encrusted snow. He tried jamming his elbows into the drift, to slow himself, but got no traction. To his right, alarmingly close, rose a lizard-back of boulders.

Above him, he heard a growl. He tipped his head back in time to see Kane's sleek form come galloping down the slope. The shepherd was there in seconds and clamped his teeth into Tucker's jacket collar. Once latched on, Kane sat down on his haunches and lifted his head, his strong back muscles straining to take Tucker's weight.

Ahead and a few feet to the right, a sapling jutted from the snow. On impulse, he swung his left leg out, curled it, and hooked the trunk with his ankle. The momentum whipped him around, dragging Kane along, too, before jerking them both to a sudden stop.

All was quiet.

Tucker lay perfectly still and mentally scanned his body. Nothing seemed broken. He could feel Kane's weight hanging from his collar.

"Kane? How're you doing, pal?"

The shepherd replied with a muffled growl that Tucker recognized as roughly, *Okay, but now it's time for you to do something about this.*

"Hang on, give me a second . . ."

Tucker lifted his hips, freeing his right leg from under his butt, then extended it and hooked it around the sapling trunk above the other ankle. He set his teeth, flexed his legs, and dragged himself and Kane up the slope until he could reach out and grab the sapling with his left hand. He then reached back with his other arm and snagged Kane's vest.

The shepherd unclamped his jaws, and with Tucker's help, Kane scrabbled up the slope, his nails scratching on the ice until he reached the sapling.

Finally, Tucker let his legs uncurl and swung his body around, his feet again facing downhill. He slammed his heels into the ice several times until he had formed adequate footholds, then sprawled back to catch his breath.

Kane gave his hand a lick: relief and reassurance.

Tucker sat up and got his bearings. While plunging headlong down the slope in almost complete darkness, the angle had seemed precipitous. Now he could see the grade was no more than twenty-five degrees.

Could be worse . . .

To their right, fifty feet away, a line of skeletal birches and heavy Siberian pines snaked down the slope. Far below, a dark smudge ran perpendicular to the incline.

A river. But which one? For every charted stream and lake in Siberia, a dozen more were unrecorded and unnamed. Still, rivers meant civilization. Follow one and you'll inevitably find the other.

But first he had to find his rucksack. All his supplies were inside it.

He looked around, scanning the snow, but saw nothing. It was too dark to make out any fine details. And unimpeded, his rucksack could have rolled all the way down to the river, taking with it everything he needed to survive in this harsh climate.

He had only one hope: to borrow someone's keener eyes.

Tucker turned to Kane. "SPOT RUCKSACK," he ordered.

Thankfully, *rucksack* was one of Kane's thousand-word vocabulary. When traveling, most of Tucker's worldly possessions—and survival tools—were contained in that pack.

After twenty seconds, Kane let out a low-key yelp.

Tucker twisted around and followed Kane's gaze uphill and sideways, toward the tree line. Even with Kane's guidance, it took Tucker another thirty seconds to spot it. The rucksack had become wedged into the fork of a white-barked birch tree.

He rolled onto his hands and knees, grasped Kane's vest collar with his left hand, then began sidling toward the tree line, kicking toeholds into the ice as he went.

It was slow work, eating up too much time. Halfway there, Tucker realized Kane needed no support. The shepherd's nails worked as natural pitons.

Working together, they reached the forest of Siberian pines and birches. Under the shelter of the bower, the snow was powdery and soft. Leaving Kane propped against a trunk, he climbed upward and angled toward the tree into which the rucksack was wedged.

In the distance, a branch snapped.

The sound echoed across the night's stillness—then faded.

Tucker froze. Where had the sound come from?

Above, he decided.

Slowly Tucker reached forward, grasped the nearest trunk, and laid himself flat. He scanned uphill, looking for movement. After ten seconds of silence, there came another distinctive sound: a muffled *crunch* of a footstep in the snow.

He strained as silence followed—then another *crunch*.

Somewhere above, a person was moving—not casually, but with purpose. Either a hunter or Felice. If so, she was even more dangerous than he'd anticipated. Almost fifteen minutes had passed since he and Kane had leaped from the train. Felice would have had to pinpoint their position, choose her own jumping-off point, then backtrack here at a running pace.

Possible, he realized, but such speed spoke to her skill as a hunter.

But was it her?

He turned his head. Twenty feet below, Kane lay on his belly, half buried in the softer snow. His eyes were fixed on Tucker, waiting for orders.

He signaled with his free hand: *move deeper into the trees and hunker down.*

On quiet feet, Kane moved off. Within seconds he was lost from sight.

Tucker returned his attention to their visitor. Using his elbows and knees, he burrowed himself into the powdery snowpack until only his eyes were exposed. Two minutes passed. Then five. The footsteps continued moving downhill at a stalking pace: step, pause . . . step, pause. Finally, a shadowy figure appeared from behind a tree, then stopped and crouched down.

The person's build was slim and athletic in a form-fitting dark jacket, a cut that was too modern, too tactical. Definitely not a local rural hunter. The head turned, and from beneath a dark wool cap, a wisp of blond shone in the stark starlight.

Along with something else.

A rifle barrel poked from behind a shoulder. How had Felice smuggled a sniper rifle onto the train? As he watched, she unslung her weapon and cradled it against her chest.

She was forty feet up the slope and to his right. If she kept to her line, she would pass within feet of his trapped rucksack. Not good. He was now playing cat and mouse with a SIG-trained sniper. The solution was simple if not so easily executed: kill Felice while he still had the element of surprise.

Moving with exaggerated slowness, he reached to his belt and withdrew the stolen P22. He brought it up along his body and extended it toward Felice. He aimed the front sight on her center mass, clicked off the safety, and took up the slack on the trigger.

What happened next Tucker would write off later as a soldier's intuition.

Still crouched, Felice pushed backward and disappeared behind a tree.

Crap.

He kept his gun steady, waiting for a clear shot, but from the stealthy noise of retreat, Felice was on the move, heading back up the slope, using the trunks to screen herself. After five minutes she was gone, but he could guess her plan. She intended to head deeper into the trees, then back down in a flanking maneuver. She must be gambling that he and Kane hadn't made it to the river yet, and that they didn't know she was tracking them. She would set up an ambush down below and wait.

She would be in for a *long* wait, Tucker decided.

He gave Felice another frigid five minutes' head start, then pocketed the P22, eased himself sideways out of his burrow, and began crawling toward his rucksack. He reached the tree, grabbed the bag's strap, and pulled it down to him.

He then went dead still to listen.

Silence.

He donned the rucksack, then aimed his hand toward Kane's last known position and signaled, trusting the shepherd had followed his training and kept Tucker in view.

Return, he motioned.

He waited, but it did not take long. A hushed footfall sounded above him. He craned his neck and found Kane crouched in the snow a few feet away. Tucker reached up, grabbed a handful of neck fur, and gave his partner a reassuring massage.

"FOLLOW," he whispered in his partner's ear.

Together, they began the slow climb upward, back toward the rail line.

11:50 P.M.

It took longer than he'd hoped to reach the top of the slope—only to discover that a towering, windswept drift blocked the way to the tracks, a sheer wall, three times as tall as Tucker. He would have to sidestep his way across the slope and hope to find where he had originally crashed through it so they could cross back to the railway.

Tucker took only a single step away from the tree line and out onto that treacherous, icy expanse—when he felt something shift beneath his boot. In the back of his mind he thought, *log*, but he had no time to react. The thigh-sized chunk of tree trunk, buried under a few inches of snow and held fast by the thinnest film of ice, broke free and started rolling downhill, taking Tucker and a swath of snow with it.

Avalanche.

Tucker pushed Kane aside, knowing the shepherd would try to latch on to him again. "EVADE!" he hissed.

The order countermanded Kane's instinct to protect him. The shepherd hesitated only a moment before leaping sideways and back into the shelter of the tree line.

Tucker knew he was in trouble. The sliding mass of snow was bulldozing over him, propelling him faster and faster down the slope. With the rucksack preventing him from rolling over, Tucker paddled his arms and legs, trying to mount the snow wave, to ride its tumult, but it was no use. Doing his best to survive, he drove one elbow into the ground, leaning into it. He spun on his belly until he was aimed headfirst down the slope, still on his belly.

Fifty yards away, the river loomed. The surface was black and motionless. With any luck, it was frozen over. If not, he was doomed.

Tucker's mind raced.

Where was Kane? Where was Felice?

No doubt she'd heard the miniavalanche—but was he visible within the snowy surge? He got his answer. Ahead and to his right, an orange flare spat in the night, coming from a clump of scrub bushes near the waterline.

A muzzle flash.

If nothing else, his headlong plunge had made Felice miss her first shot. The second would be closer. The third would be dead-on. Tucker reached back, freed the P22 from his pocket with a struggle, and pointed it toward the site of that flash.

He felt a sting at his neck.

Grazed by a bullet.

Ignoring the pain, he squeezed the trigger twice, wild potshots, but maybe enough to discourage the sniper.

Then he hit the river's berm and launched into the air. His heart lurched into his throat. A heartbeat later, he belly-flopped onto the ice, bounced once, then found himself rolling, flat-spinning across the river's surface. He slammed into a clump of trees jutting from the ice and came to an abrupt, agonizing stop.

Gasping for air, he rolled onto his side and fought the urge to curl into a painful ball.

He swept his arms across the ice, searching for his pistol. It had been knocked from his cold fingers as he struck the river.

Where—?

Then he spotted it. The P22 lay a few feet away in a tangle of dead branches. He reached toward it.

A chunk of ice exploded at his fingertips, shards stinging his face. The gunshot sounded like the muffled snap of a branch. She was using a noise suppressor.

"Not another inch!" Felice Nilsson called from somewhere to his right.

He craned his neck and spotted her. She was forty feet away, kneeling at the river's edge, the rifle tucked to her shoulder. At this range, she could put a bullet in his ear.

Instead, she shifted her rifle ever so slightly, from a kill shot to something that would maim and hurt. The moon, reflecting off the ice, cast the scene in stark contrast.

"Tell me where you were scheduled to meet Bukolov," she demanded.

In answer, Tucker slowly lifted his hand from the ice.

"Careful!" she barked. "I'll take it off. Don't doubt it for a moment."

"I don't," Tucker replied, raising his palm, as if pleading for her to be calm, but instead he pointed one finger at her.

"What are you—?"

Tucker rotated his hand, fingers pointing toward the ice.

"Good-bye, Felice," he said through chattering teeth.

From out of the forest behind her, Kane burst forth.

A moment ago, Tucker had noted the shepherd's furtive approach, a mere shift of shadows lit by the reflected moonlight. Kane obeyed Tucker's signal, a simple one.

Attack.

Kane races across the gap, bunching his haunches at the last moment.

He has followed the trail of the woman, catching her scent in the woods, picking it out of the spoor of deer and rabbit. He recognizes it from the train, remembers the hatred in her voice. Next came the muffled shots of the rifle and the sharper cracks of a pistol.

His other was in danger, threatened.

The last command remained etched behind his eyes.

Evade.

So he kept hidden, following the whiff of gun smoke, the musk of the hot skin, ever down toward the flow of water and creaking ice.

There, beyond the woman, he sees his partner out on the ice. He holds back a whine of concern, wanting to call out.

Then movement.

A hand raised.

A command given.

He obeys that now.

The woman turns, fear bursting from her skin. As she swings, her gun barrel dips slightly.

He sees and explodes with his hind end, springing high.

As Tucker watched, Kane slammed into Felice like a linebacker, his jaws clamping on to her arm before the pair hit the ice. Felice screamed and thrashed, but she held tight to the rifle's stock.

A sniper to the end, Tucker thought. *Lose your rifle, lose your life.*

He shoved up, ready to help his partner—only to hear a sharp *crack* erupt beneath him. A rift snaked outward from his body and headed toward Kane and Felice. Dark, icy water gushed through the fault line.

"Felice, stop struggling!" Tucker called. "Lie still!"

Panicked, deaf to his warning, she continued to struggle, her left hand still clenched around the rifle stock.

He forced himself to his knees, then his feet. The ice shifted beneath him, dipping sideways. He leaped forward, balancing on the teetering slabs as the river broke under him. He hopscotched toward Kane and Felice.

The crack reached them, then spider-webbed outward, enveloping them. With a whoosh, the ice opened up. The pair dropped headlong into the water.

With his heart thundering in his ears, Tucker stumbled forward. Fifteen feet from the hole, he threw himself into a slide, on his belly, his arms extended, trying to distinguish between the two shapes thrashing in the icy water. He saw a pale white hand slapping at the ice, spotted Kane's head surge from the water, his snout pointed at the sky.

The shepherd gasped, coughing.

Sliding parallel to the hole, Tucker grabbed Kane's vest collar and jerked hard, plucking the wet dog from the water.

From the corner of his eye, Tucker saw Felice's rifle jut out of the water; the barrel swung toward them.

Even now, she hadn't given up the fight.

She slapped at the ice with a bloody arm, while trying to bring her rifle to bear with the other hand.

Tucker rolled onto his side and kicked off with his heel, spinning on his hip. He snapped out with his other leg and struck the rifle, sending it skittering across the ice and into the snow along the opposite bank.

With a final, spasmodic flailing, Felice's arm vanished underwater, her body pulled down by the current, and she disappeared from view.

Together, Tucker and Kane crawled to the bank, but both kept watch on the shattered hole. He half expected Felice to reappear. Only after two minutes did he feel confident enough to state, "I think she's gone."

Still, he kept a vigil at the bank, probing his neck wound. The gouge was narrow but deep. Beside him, Kane did a full body shake, casting out a shower of icy water, his tail wagging off the last few drops.

Tucker checked over his partner for injuries. For his efforts, he earned a warm lick to his cold cheek, his dog's message easy to read: *Glad we're still alive.*

"I know, pal, me too," he muttered.

He shrugged off his rucksack, unzipped the side pocket, and dug out his first-aid kit. Working from feel alone, he squeezed a thick stripe of surgical glue into the wound and pinched the edges together, clenching his teeth against the sting.

Once finished, a shiver shook through him. Kane's haunches also quaked against the cold. In this weather, the effects of cold water were amplified. Hypothermia couldn't be far off.

"Let's go," he said, ready to set off, but not before completing one last duty.

Moving fifty yards downriver, he found a patch of thicker ice that easily bore his weight, allowing him to cross to the opposite bank. He walked back upstream and retrieved Felice's rifle. He examined his prize. It was the Swedish Army's standard sniper rifle: a PSG-90—variant D. After a quick inspection for damage and followed by a few quick twists and turns, he had the weapon broken down into its four component parts, none of which was longer than eighteen inches.

"Now to get warm."

He and Kane found a cluster of trees and made a temporary camp. An abandoned bird's nest and some scraps of birch bark served as perfect kindling. Within a few minutes, he had a fire blazing.

He stripped off Kane's vest and hung it over the fire to dry.

With no prompting, the shepherd stretched out beside the flames and gave a contented *hmmph*.

Settled and warm, Tucker did a quick check of his GPS unit, pinpointing their location. "Time to find out how big of a mess we're in," he mumbled.

According to the map, they were within easy walking distance of two villages: Borshchovka and Byankino. It was tempting to head for one of them, but he decided against it. Felice was clever. She surely had given her partners—or whoever hired her—a situation report after jumping from the train. If so, the two nearby villages would be the first places any search party would visit.

Of the hundreds of axioms that the army had drummed into his head, one matched this situation perfectly: *Avoid being where your enemy expects you to be.*

So he extended his search on the map. Ten miles to the northeast was the small town of Nerchinsk. There, he could regroup and decide how best to reach Perm and his contact.

He stared at the dog, at the crisp stars.

It would be easy to abandon this mission.

But blood had been spilled.

He pictured the dead porter's ashen face, remembering his smile, his joy while petting Kane. The memory, the responsibility, reminded him of another adage, burned into every ranger's mind: *Take the initiative, and get the mission done.*

He intended to do just that.

9

March 9, 5:44 P.M.
Nerchinsk, Siberia

Their day hike to Nerchinsk quickly became a slog. Around them, the landscape slowly changed from highland forest into a series of low, snow-blanketed hills, one stacked upon another, before dropping into a valley east of the town of Nerchinsk.

For the first five miles, he and Kane found themselves wading through thigh-high snow punctuated by snowdrifts twice as tall as Tucker. By early afternoon, they found themselves walking into a strong wind that found its bone-chilling way into every nook and cranny of Tucker's parka. For his part, Kane was in heaven, plowing through the powdery snow, occasionally popping to the surface, his eyes bright and tongue lolling.

Only twice did they see any signs of life. The first was a hunter, spotted in the distance, walking along a tree line. The second was a rusted fifties-era armored personnel carrier loaded down with dozens of laughing children. The rumble of the diesel engine reached them from a narrow road headed toward Nerchinsk.

Finally, eight hours after they set out and with only a few hours of daylight left, they crested a hill and the first signs of civilization came into view: a gold-domed, white-walled Russian orthodox church surrounded by a dilapidated split-rail fence that marked off a small graveyard. Many of the church's windows were boarded over, and the eaves drooped in several spots.

Tucker found a safe position behind a nearby boulder and pulled out his binoculars. A few hundred yards east of the church spread a collection of saltbox-style homes, painted in a variety of pastel blues, yellows, and reds. The town of Nerchinsk appeared quiet, with only a handful of pedestrians in view, along with a couple of boxy economy cars that puttered down the icy streets spewing clouds of exhaust.

He panned his binoculars beyond the town's outskirts, taking in the lay of the land. To the northwest, he spotted what looked to be a dilapidated airfield.

No, he realized on closer inspection.

Not air *field*, but air *base*.

Several of the base's buildings and hangars bore the red-star roundel of the Russian Air Force. Had it been abandoned? Focusing on the hangars, he was pleased to see the doors were clear of snowdrifts. *Someone* was maintaining the place, which in turn raised his hope that there might be operational aircraft.

He returned his attention to the small town, searching for either a motel or a general store. He glimpsed a soldier in an olive-drab greatcoat standing on a corner, smoking. This was no old veteran, but someone on active duty. His uniform was tidy and clean, his cap settled squarely on his head. The man finished his cigarette, tossed away the butt, then turned and headed down a side street.

"Where'd you come from?" Tucker muttered.

He kept scanning, following what he hoped was the man's path—then spotted a second anomaly. The main rotor hub of a helicopter jutted above one of the buildings at the edge of town. The chopper was big, tall enough to dwarf the building that shielded it. From the hub's mottled gray paint, it had to be military.

He didn't know what such a presence here implied, but either way, he and Kane needed to find shelter. They were both cold, tired, and with nightfall coming, the temperatures would soon plummet below zero.

He returned his attention to the ramshackle church. For the next thirty minutes, as darkness slowly enveloped them, he watched for any signs of life.

Nothing.

Still, he used the cover of snowdrifts and trees to make his way down to the churchyard. With Kane at his side, he crawled through the fence and walked around to the porch. He tried the knob. Unlocked. They slipped through and into the dim interior.

They were greeted by a wave of warmth and the tang of smoke and manure. Directly ahead, a wood-burning stove cast the interior in a flickering orange glow. A metal flue led upward from the stove toward a second floor.

Tucker kept near the door, waiting for his eyes to adjust, then called out in Russian. *"Dobriy večer?"*

No reply.

He tried again, a little louder this time, and again got no response.

Sighing, he followed the faded red carpet runner down to the domed nave. Beyond a small altar, a flaking, gold-painted wall bore religious icons and tapestries. There, he found a door, one likely leading to the church's administrative area.

He opened it with a protest of old hinges and discovered a spiral staircase. With Kane in tow, he scaled up it, ending in a small office area. Seeing the wood-slat cot in the corner, the freestanding wardrobe, and a closet-sized kitchenette, Tucker surmised it also served as a living space.

Judging by the cobwebs, no one had been up here for months. Above his head, the woodstove's pipe gushed warm air.

It would do.

He shrugged off his pack and cold-weather gear and tossed them on the cot where Kane had already settled. He spent a few minutes searching the kitchenette but found nothing save a few broken plates, a rusty tool chest under the sink, and a tarnished silver fork. In the wardrobe, he discovered an old patched greatcoat, its shoulders piled with dust.

"Looks like it's home sweet home, eh, Kane?"

The shepherd gave a tired wag of his tail.

Starving, Tucker fixed a quick meal of coffee and dehydrated camping rations, preparing enough food for both him and Kane. An upper-story window, frosted with grime, allowed him to study the village as he ate. A stranger would stand out like a sore thumb here—and raise too much suspicion—especially one who could not speak Russian with flawless fluency.

He needed a remedy, a cover.

After a bit of thought, Tucker rummaged through the tool chest and found a spool of wire. He clipped four short pieces and, using duct tape from his rucksack, sculpted the pieces into a crude equivalent of a teenager's orthodontic mouth guard. He slipped the construction between his lower lip and gum, packing it in tightly. He checked himself in the room's grungy mirror, fingering his face.

To the casual eye, it would appear Nerchinsk's latest visitor had a badly broken jaw. It would give him an easy excuse not to talk.

"Time to see a man about a plane ride," Tucker said, testing out his contraption. The sound he emitted was barely intelligible.

Perfect.

Next, he donned the dusty greatcoat from the wardrobe and tugged his *ushanka* cap back on. He pulled its brim lower over his eyebrows.

"You stay here," he ordered Kane. "Out of sight."

The shepherd, fed and warm, didn't argue.

Tucker climbed back down and slipped out the church's front door. With his shoulders hunched, he shuffled toward Nerchinsk along a road of slush and mud. He adopted what he hoped was the posture of a man who'd spent his life in the gray, frozen expanse of Siberia. The weather made that easier. The temperature had plummeted another twenty degrees. His breath billowed thickly in the air, and the icy mud squelched under his boots.

By now, the streets were empty. The yellow glow of life shone through a few dirty windows, along with the occasional flicker of neon signs, but nothing else. He made his way to the corner where the soldier had been smoking earlier. He did his best to trace the man's steps until he was a block from the helicopter.

He studied its bulk surreptitiously.

It was certainly a military aircraft: an Mi-28 Havoc attack helicopter. He knew such a craft's specs by heart. It had racks and pods enough to carry forty rockets, along with a mounted 30 mm chain gun.

But this Havoc's exterior bore no Russian roundels or emblems. Instead, it had been painted in a jagged gray/black pattern. He didn't recognize the markings. It could be the FSB—formerly known as the KGB. But what would such a unit be doing out here, in the back end of nowhere?

Tucker knew the most likely answer.

Looking for me.

Two figures stepped out from behind the chopper's tail rotor. One was dressed in a uniform, the other in civilian clothes.

Tucker retreated out of sight—but not before noting the shoulder emblems on the uniform. A red starburst against a black shield.

He had been wrong.

These men weren't *FSB*, but rather *GRU*. *Glavnoye Razvedyvatel'noye Upravleniye* served as the intelligence arm of the Russian Ministry of Defense. For covert operations, the GRU relied almost solely on Spetsnaz soldiers—the Thoroughbreds of the already-impressive Russian Special Forces stable.

If they're after me . . .

He hurried down the street, knowing his departure from this region was even more urgent—as was his overdue call to Ruth Harper.

7:55 P.M.

Tucker wandered the streets until he found a lively tavern. The neon sign above the door was in Cyrillic, but the raucous laughter and smell of beer was advertisement enough for the establishment.

This was as good a place as any to start.

He took a moment to make sure his mouth prosthetic was in place, then took a deep breath and pushed through the door.

A wall of heat, cigarette smoke, and body odor struck him like a fist to the face. A babble of country Russian—punctuated by loud guffaws and scattered curses—greeted him. Not that anyone paid attention to his arrival.

Tucker hunched his shoulders and wove his way through the mass of bodies toward what he assumed was the bar. With a bit of jostling and occasional grunting through his prosthetic, he found himself standing at a long, knotty pine counter.

Miraculously, the bartender noted his newest customer immediately and walked over. He barked something that Tucker assumed was a request for his order.

As answer, Tucker grunted vaguely.

"Eh?"

He cleared his throat and mumbled again.

The bartender leaned forward, cocking an ear.

Tucker opened his lips a little wider, exposing his mouth guard, then pantomimed a fist striking his jaw, ending it with a tired shrug.

The bartender nodded his understanding.

Tucker jerked his thumb toward a neighboring mug of beer. A moment later, a glass was pounded down in front of him, sloshing froth over the rim. He passed over a wad of rubles and pocketed the change.

Tucker felt a wave of relief. Providing no one else demanded a higher level of exchange, this might just work.

Clumsily sipping beer through his mouthpiece, he began scanning the bar for soldiers. There were a dozen or more, all army, but from the state of their clothes, none of these were active duty. In Russia, many veterans kept and wore their uniforms after leaving service, partly for necessity and partly for economic leverage. It was common practice for citizens to slip a former soldier a coin or pay for a drink or a meal. This was as much for charity as it was for insurance. Having impoverished or starving killers roaming the streets was best avoided.

Satisfied the bar was free of GRU operatives, he returned his attention to his primary interest: getting out of this place and reaching Perm. He searched for anyone who might be connected to the neighboring air base, but he spotted nothing overt. He might have to do this the hard way and—

"Your dog is beautiful," a gruff voice said at his shoulder. He spoke passable English, but heavily accented. "German shepherd?"

Tucker turned to find a short man in his sixties, with long white hair and a grizzled beard. His eyes shone a sharp ice-blue.

"Eh?" Tucker grunted.

"Oh, I see," the stranger said. "Let me guess, you are a traveling prizefighter."

Tucker's heart pounded as he glanced around. None of the other patrons seemed to be paying attention.

The man crooked his finger at Tucker and leaned closer.

"I know you are not Russian, my friend. I heard you talking to your dog at the church. You'd best follow me."

The older man turned and picked his way through the crowd, which seemed to part before him, the patrons nodding deferentially at him.

Nervous, but with no other choice, Tucker followed after him, ending up at a table in the bar's far corner, beside a stone-hearth fireplace.

With the table to themselves, the man stared at Tucker through narrow eyes. "A good disguise, actually. You have mastered the Siberian stoop—you know, the hunched shoulders, the lowered chin. The cold grinds it into you up here, bends you. So much so, if you live here long enough, it becomes one's posture."

Tucker said nothing.

"A cautious man. Good, very good. You have seen the soldiers, I assume? The Moscow boys, I mean, with the commandos and the fancy helicopter. It's the first time in years we've seen anyone like them here. And it's the *only* time an American with a giant dog has set up camp in my home. Not a coincidence, I am guessing."

Tucker said nothing.

"If I were going to turn you in, I would have already done so."

He considered this, recognized the truth of it, and decided it was time to take a chance. Covertly he removed his mouthpiece, then took a sip of beer.

"Belgian Malinois," Tucker said.

"Pardon me?"

"He's not a German. He's Belgian. And for your sake, he better be safe and sound where I left him."

"He is," the stranger said with a smile, holding out a hand. "I am Dimitry."

"I'm—"

"Do not tell me your name. The less I know, the better. I am Nerchinsk's bishop. Well, for this town and a few other villages nearby. Mine is a small flock, but I love them all the same."

The old man glanced affectionately across the crowded bar.

Tucker remembered how the others had deferred to the man, stepping out of his way. "Your English is very good."

"Satellite dish. I watch American television. And the Internet, of course. As for your Russian, well, it is—"

"Crap," Tucker finished with a smile. "But how did you know about me and my dog?"

"I was out hunting and spotted your tracks outside of town. I followed them back to my church."

"Sorry for the intrusion."

"Think nothing of it. Orthodox churches are intended as sanctuaries. The heat is always on, so to speak. And speaking of heat . . ." The man nodded to the bar's front door. "It seems you've drawn a fair share of your own heat."

Tucker shrugged. "I'm not sure if the soldiers are in town because of me, but I'm not a big fan of coincidences either."

"The last time we saw such a group in the area was before the wall came down. They were looking for a foreigner, an Englishman."

"What happened to him?"

"They found him two miles out of town. Shot him and buried him on the spot. I do not know any of the details, but he was on the run, like you and your dog."

Tucker must have paled.

Dimitry patted his arm. "Ah, but you have an advantage the Englishman lacked."

"Which is?"

"You have a friend in town."

Tucker still felt ill at ease and expressed his concern. "Do you know the phrase *look a gift horse in the mouth*?"

"As in being suspicious of good luck?"

"More or less."

"I understand your concern. So let me dispense with the formalities and settle things. Have you or do you intend to wreak havoc on Mother Russia?"

"No."

"Will you harm my flock?"

"Not unless they try to harm me."

"*Nyet*, of course not." Dimitry waved his hand dismissively. "So with that business dispensed of, I am going to assume you are simply a lost traveler, and those Moscow thugs were chasing you for stealing soap from your last hotel."

"Fair enough."

"I had my fill of the government back in the eighties, when I served as a paratrooper in Afghanistan. I killed a lot of jihadists, and the army gave me a lot of shiny ribbons. But now I am forgotten, like most of us from that war—at least the ones who truly got our knives dirty. I love my country, but not so much my government. Does that make sense to you?"

"More than you'd imagine."

"Good. Then that, my wayward friend, is why I am going to help you. I assume you and your keen-eyed partner spotted the air base?"

"We did."

"Do you know how to fly a plane?"

"No."

"Neither do I. But I have a friend who does. In fact—" Dimitry looked around the bar, half standing, before spotting what he was looking for. "There he is."

Dimitry pointed toward a pine table near the window where two men were sitting.

"Which one?"

"No, no, *underneath.*"

Tucker peered closer until he could make out a figure under the table. His legs were splayed out, and his head sharply canted to accommodate for the table-top pressing against his skull. A ribbon of dribble ran from the corner of his mouth to his coat sleeve.

"That is Fedor," Dimitry said as introduction. "Our postman. He flies in our mail."

"He's drunk."

"Massively," Dimitry agreed. "It is night, after all. In the morning, though, Fedor will be sober. Of course, that does not entirely solve your problem, does it? The Moscow thugs will be patrolling the skies during the day. Your departure must wait until tomorrow night, which means we must keep Fedor sober for, well, longer than he is accustomed." He paused with a frown. "Now I begin to see a flaw in our plan. No matter. This is a bridge we will cross later."

"Let's cross it now," Tucker said. "Fedor can't be your only pilot."

"*Nyet,* but he is the most experienced. And he is a first-rate smuggler. Nerchinsk does not live on bread alone, you see. For the right amount of money, he will get you out, right under the noses of these government men, and never tell a soul. And, as it happens, he loves dogs very much."

Tucker wasn't reassured one bit.

Dimitry downed his drink and stood up. "Come, let us collect him!"

10

Tucker woke just before dawn—a soldier's habit. With a groan from his back and a twinge of pain from his grazed neck, he pushed up from the church's attic cot and swung his bare feet to the floor.

The prior night, he and Dimitry had hauled the drunken postman across town to the church. On the way here, they had run into a trio of Spetsnaz soldiers, but none of them paid any heed, save for a few laughing gibes at the inebriated state of their companion. At the church, Dimitry offered Tucker and Kane his cot and rolled out a pair of hay-filled bedrolls for him and Fedor.

Tucker searched the attic space now, realizing he was alone.

Fedor and Dimitry were gone, along with Kane.

Quashing his panic, he went downstairs to find a naked Fedor sitting before the blazing woodstove, seated in a puddle of his own sweat. Beside him stood a plastic milk jug half filled with a clear liquid. Sober now, the man looked younger, more midthirties than forties, with dark lanky hair and a wrestler's build, most of it covered in a mat of fur, a true Russian bear.

A few feet away, Kane sat on his haunches, watching curiously. He acknowledged Tucker's arrival with a wag of his tail.

Fedor lifted the jug, tipped it to his mouth, and took a long gulp.

Bleary eyed, Fedor sloshed the container in Tucker's direction and croaked, "*Vaduh. Naturalnaya vaduh.*"

Tucker pieced together the words.

Natural water.

This must be part of Fedor's sobering ritual: extreme heat and copious amounts of water.

"Priest tells me fly," Fedor added in badly broken English. "Fly you tonight."

Tucker nodded. "*Spasiba.*"

"*Da.* Your Russian bad." He held his head between his palms. "Make my head hurt."

I don't think it's from my bad accent.

"Your dog beautiful. I love. May buy him, yes, please?"

"No, please."

Fedor shrugged and guzzled more water. "Trade fly for dog, *da?*"

"*Nyet.* Money."

Dimitry arrived, carrying in some firewood. "You see, he is already much better. Let us discuss arrangements. I will translate. It will go much faster." Dimitry spoke to his friend in rapid-fire Russian, then said to Tucker, "He will fly you tonight, but there will be surcharges."

"Go ahead."

"It does not translate well, but first you must pay him extra for missing his drinking tonight. Next, you must pay him extra because you are foreign. Finally, you must pay him extra because the Moscow men are looking for you."

"Did you tell him they were looking for me?"

"Of course not. Fedor is a drunk, not an idiot."

"Next?"

"He likes your dog—"

"Forget it. Next."

Dimitry said something to Fedor, listened, then replied to Tucker, "Where do you wish to go?"

He had already considered this. They'd likely never reach Perm in Fedor's plane. It was too far. Besides, he wasn't inclined to give away his final destination. The best hope was to reach a closer major city, one that offered plenty of options for his final leg to Perm.

"I need to reach Novosibirsk," he said.

"Very far," Dimitry translated. "It will take a lot of fuel."

Tucker waited while Fedor continued to mutter, making a big show of counting on his fingers and screwing up his face. Finally he said, in English, "Nine thousand ruble."

Tucker did the rough conversion in his head: 275 U.S. dollars. A bargain. Struggling to keep the smile off his face, he considered this for a bit, then shrugged. "Deal."

Fedor spit into his hand and held it out.

Reluctantly, Tucker shook it.

1:15 P.M.

After the fierce negotiation, Tucker and Kane spent the remainder of the morning in the church, while Dimitry and Fedor ran various errands, gathering supplies and readying the plane.

Early in the afternoon, Dimitry returned with provisions and news. "I learned there are *two* other GRU units in the region."

Tucker stood up from the woodstove. "What? Where?"

"They are positioned *west* of here, around the town of Chita. But like here, they are lazy, just smoking and lounging in hotels, *da*?"

Chita?

That was the next major stopover along the Trans-Siberian Railway. But what did that mean? He gave it some thought and came to only one conclusion. The fact that the search teams weren't actively patrolling for him, only lounging about, suggested Felice might not have had time to get out word that he had escaped the train. She must have hoped a sniper's bullet could correct her failure before her superiors learned the truth.

That was good—at least for the moment.

But as soon as the train reached Chita, and it was discovered he wasn't aboard, the search units would shift into high gear, including the unit here.

Tucker pulled out his train schedule and checked his watch. The train would reach Chita in three hours, about four hours before sunset. That meant he and Fedor couldn't wait for nightfall before departing.

"We need to take off early," he told Dimitry. "Now, if we can."

"Not possible, my friend. The fuel bowser is broken down. Fedor is working on it."

"How long?"

"I don't know, but I will go find out."

As Dimitry left, Kane walked over, sat down, and leaned against Tucker's leg, sensing the tension.

Tucker patted Kane's neck, reassuring his partner. "We've been in worse spots than this."

Not much worse, but worse.

He set his watch's countdown timer.

Three hours from now, when it was discovered he was no longer aboard the train, Nerchinsk would be swarming with Spetsnaz soldiers, all hunting for him.

2:36 P.M.

An hour later, Dimitry burst through the church's doors. The panic in his face drew both Tucker and Kane to their feet.

"They are coming!" Dimitry called out, quickly shutting the doors behind him. "The Spetsnaz."

Tucker checked his watch. It was too early. The train hadn't reached Chita yet. "Slow down. Tell me."

Dimitry crossed to them. "The soldiers are out patrolling the rest of the town. They do not seem to be in a hurry, but one is coming here nevertheless."

What did this sudden change mean? If the GRU unit had been activated, the Spetsnaz would be breaking down doors and moving Nerchinsk's inhabitants into the open. Maybe the local commander was only trying to break up the monotony.

Bored soldiers are ineffective soldiers, he thought.

Still, as Dimitry had said, it didn't matter. One of them was coming.

Tucker donned his pack and tightened the straps on Kane's vest.

"This way," Dimitry said.

He led them toward a side corner of the sanctuary and knelt before a tapestry-draped table. He scooted the table aside, lifted the rug beneath, then used the hunting knife in his belt to pry up a section of planking. It lifted free to reveal a vertical tunnel.

"What—?"

"Cossacks, Nazis, Napoleon . . . who can say? It was here long before I arrived. Get in!"

"Jump down, Kane," Tucker ordered.

Without hesitation, the shepherd dove into the opening. He landed in the dirt, then disappeared to the left.

Tucker followed, discovering the shaft was only a meter tall.

Dimitry hovered over the opening. "Follow the tunnel. It exits about two hundred meters north of here. Make your way to the east side of the air base and wait for me there. There is a shack near a crushed section of fence. Easy to find."

With that, Dimitry shut the hatch. A moment later, what little light filtered through the slats was blotted out as the rug and table were slid back into place.

A stiff pounding on the church's door echoed down to him.

Dimitry's footsteps clopped across the wooden floor, followed by the creak of hinges. "*Dobriy den!*" the bishop called out.

A sullen voice replied in kind, but Tucker didn't wait to hear what followed.

He headed off in a low crouch with Kane. After ten paces, he felt it safe enough to pull out his LED penlight and pan the cone of light down the tunnel. The dirt walls bristled with tree roots, while the roof was shored up with planks, some rotten, others new. Clearly someone had been maintaining the tunnel.

They continued on. For Kane, the going was easy as he trotted forward, scouting. Tucker had to move in a low waddle that had his thighs burning after only a few minutes. He ignored the pain and kept going. After another ten minutes, the tunnel ended at a short ladder entangled with tree roots.

A few inches above his head was a hatch. He craned his neck and pressed his ear against the wood and listened for a full minute. He heard nothing. He crouched back down beside Kane and checked his watch.

In a little over an hour, the train would reach Chita.

He had to be airborne by then.

Tucker recalled his mental map of the area. If Dimitry was correct, the hatch above his head should exit somewhere in the patch of forest that bordered the church grounds. From there, the air base lay more than a mile away, through scrub forest and open fields. Normally an easy hike, but he would have to contend with deep snowdrifts, while keeping out of sight of the newly patrolling soldiers.

He was not normally a pessimist, but he could not dismiss the pure logistics of the situation.

We'll never make it.

11

March 10, 2:48 P.M.
Nerchinsk, Russia

Tucker crouched beside Kane and carefully swung the hatch closed. The tunnel had exited beneath the shelter of a pine. Still, he swept fresh snow over the hatch to keep it hidden. Once satisfied, he wriggled his way out from beneath the boughs and into the open.

Kane followed, shaking snow from his fur.

"Ready for a little jog?" Tucker asked, acknowledging the press of time. He pointed east through the edges of a scrub forest. "SCOUT."

Kane took off, bounding through the snow, bulldozing a path.

Tucker trotted after him.

They made relatively quick progress, covering three-quarters of a mile in an hour. He could have gone faster, but he did his best to stay below snowy ridge-lines, out of direct sight of the town proper. Now was not the time to be spotted by a stray soldier.

As they reached a stand of birches, within a few hundred yards of the airbase, Tucker's watch vibrated on his wrist.

He glanced down, seeing the countdown timer had gone off.

Grimacing, he pictured the train pulling into the Chita station.

How long until someone realizes I'm not on board?

With no choice, he urged Kane onward and followed, pushing through his exhaustion, focusing on his next step through the deep snow.

After another ten minutes, they reached the edge of the air base. The perimeter fence lay fifty meters ahead, topped by barbed wire.

Suddenly, Kane stopped in his tracks, cocking his head.

Then Tucker heard it, too.

A rhythmic clanging.

He waited, then heard it again, recognizing it.

A hammer striking steel.

The sound came from ahead and to the left, not too far away. He pushed to a break in the trees, where Kane had stopped.

Beyond the fence stretched a single long runway, lined by six hangars and twice as many outbuildings, most of which seemed to be bolstered by a patchwork of sheet metal. The eastern side of the base lay a little farther to the right, out of direct view. Somewhere over there was the shack where he was supposed to rendezvous with Dimitry.

But the loud clanging continued, closer at hand, coming from the base.

Curious, Tucker pulled out his binoculars, zoomed in on the buildings, and began panning. He searched for the source of the clanging and found it at the side door of a rusty hangar.

"You've got to be kidding me," he muttered.

Standing in the doorway was Fedor. Under one arm, he clutched an aircraft propeller; in his opposite hand, an eight-pound steel mallet, which he slammed down on the propeller's leading edge.

Gong.

The sound echoed across the base to where Tucker was lying.

Gong gong gong.

He lowered the binoculars and squeezed the bridge of his nose between his index finger and thumb.

It was too late now. For better or worse, he'd hitched his wagon to this Russian bear.

He set out again, aiming right, searching ahead for the crumpled section of fence that marked the shack. At least, from here, the terrain offered decent cover. The air base had been abandoned long enough for the surrounding forest, once cut back for security purposes, to encroach upon the fence line. He kept to those trees, moving steadily, circling around to the eastern side of the base.

Tucker had just stopped to catch his breath when be heard the thumping sound of helicopter rotors. Swearing, he pushed into the shadowy bower of a Siberian pine. He whistled for Kane to join him.

As the shepherd rushed to his side, he craned his neck to the sky. The noise grew thunderous, making it difficult to discern the direction. Then the dark belly of the Havoc streaked overhead at treetop level.

The rotor wash stirred the powdery snow into a stinging whirlwind. Branches whipped overhead.

Had they been spotted?

What about their tracks through the snow?

There was something especially unnerving about being hunted from the air. His every primitive instinct was to run, but he knew that path was the quickest way to get cut in half by the Havoc's chain gun.

So he stayed hidden.

The chopper moved past, slowly circling the air base, seeming to follow the perimeter fence. He watched its slow passage, staying hidden, until he could no longer hear the rotors.

Tucker waited another ten minutes, just to be sure. He used the time to reassemble Felice's PSG-90. Once completed, he did a final check of the sniper rifle. Only then did he set out again, comforted by its weight.

In less than a hundred feet, he reached a corner of the air base. He stopped and used his binoculars to survey the eastern perimeter.

As Dimitry had promised, a section of fence had been flattened beneath a fallen tree. It lay about three hundred meters away—and there stood the shack.

The impulse was to hurry toward its relative safety, but he ignored it. Instead, he took a mental bearing and headed deeper into the trees, intending to circle wide and come at the shack from behind. He took his time, using the deepening shadows and snowdrifts as cover.

Finally, the shack came into view again. It was small, twelve feet to a side, with a mossy roof and timber walls. He saw no light and smelled no woodsmoke.

Satisfied, he bent down and pulled up Kane's camera stalk. He also made sure the radio receiver remained secure in the shepherd's left ear canal. Once done, he did a fast sound-and-video check with his phone.

With the GRU unit on the hunt, he wasn't taking any chances.

And he certainly wasn't going to enter that cabin blind.

Tucker pointed at the shack, made a circling motion with his arm, and whispered, "QUIET SCOUT."

Kane slinks from his partner's side. He does not head directly for the cabin, but out into the woods, stalking wide. His paws find softer snow or open ground, moving silently. He stays to shadow, low, moving under bowers that burn with the reek of pine pitch. Through the smell, he still picks out the bitter droppings of birds. He scents the decaying carcass of a mouse under the snow, ripe and calling out.

His ears tick in every direction, filling the world with the smallest sounds.

Snow shushes from overburdened branches, falling to the ground . . .

Fir needles rattle like bones with every gust . . .

Small creatures scrape through snow or whisper past on wings . . .

As he moves, he sights the cabin, glances back to his partner, always tracking. He glides to the far side of the shack, where the shadows are darkest, knowing this is best for a first approach, where fewer eyes will see him.

A command strikes his left ear, brash but welcoming.

"HOLD."

He steps to the nearest cover: a fallen log musky with rot and mold. He drops to his belly, legs under him, muscles tense and hard, ready to ignite when needed. He lowers his chin until it brushes snow.

His gaze remains fixed to the structure. He breathes in deeply, picking out each scent and testing it for danger: old smoke, urine of man and beast, the resin of cut logs, the taint of thick moss on shingles.

He awaits the next command, knowing his partner watches as intently as he does. It finally comes.

"MOVE IN. CLOSE SCOUT."

He rises to his legs and paces to the cabin, scenting along the ground. His ears remain high, bristling for any warning. He comes to a window and rises up, balancing on his hind legs. He stares through the murky glass, deeply and long, swiveling his head to catch every corner.

He spots no movement in the dark interior—so drops back to his paws.

He turns to stare at where his partner is hidden among the trees and keeps motionless, signaling the lack of danger.

It is understood.

"MOVE OUT. QUIET SCOUT AGAIN."

He swings away, angling around the corner. He checks each side, spies through another window, and sniffs intently at the closed door. He ends where he started.

"GOOD BOY. RETURN."

He disobeys, instead dropping again to his belly by the rotten log.

A low growl rumbles in his chest, barely heard with his own ears.

A warning.

Tucker watched the video feed jostle as Kane lowered to his belly, his nose at the snow line. He heard the growl through the radio and noted the pointed stare of the shepherd toward the deeper forest to the right of the shack.

He studied the video feed on his phone. Even with the camera, his eyesight was no match for Kane's. He squinted at the screen, trying to pick out what had seized Kane's attention. After ten long seconds, he spotted movement, fifty yards away.

A lone figure, hunched over, moved through the trees, heading toward the shack.

Tucker swore silently and dropped quietly to his chest. He shifted the sniper rifle to his shoulder, flicking off the safety.

The trespasser was also carrying a gun—an assault weapon from its shape and angles. The figure moved through thick shadows, hard to make out, camouflaged from head to toe in a woodland winter suit. He moved deftly, someone well familiar with hunting in a forest, every cautious step cementing Tucker's certainty that this was one of the Spetsnaz soldiers, not a local hunter.

Thank God for Kane's keen perception.

But why only *one*?

If there had been others, Kane would have alerted him.

It made no sense. If the Spetsnaz knew he and Kane were here, they would have come in force. This had to be a lone scout. He remembered the Havoc helo circling the perimeter of the air base. Apparently the unit commander must have sent a man or two to do the same on foot.

He raised the sniper rifle to his shoulder and peered through its scope, getting a sight picture. Once fixed, he subvocalized into the radio mike taped to his throat, passing on yet another command to his partner.

"TARGET. QUIET CLOSE."

It was an order Kane knew all too well from their time together in Afghanistan: *get as close to the enemy as possible and be ready.*

Kane began creeping toward the man.

With his partner on the move, Tucker laid his cheek against the rifle's stock and peered through the scope. The target was forty yards off, moving with practiced economy. He never paused in the open, only when behind a tree. His current line of approach would take him straight to Kane's position.

Thirty yards.

Given the angle of the man's body, Tucker knew a head shot would be tricky, so he adjusted the rifle's crosshairs and focused on a point a few inches below the man's left nipple.

The soldier stepped behind a tree and paused, ever cautious. Two seconds passed. The man emerged again from cover, ready to close in on the cabin.

It was Tucker's best chance. He squeezed the trigger ever so slightly, took a breath, let it out—and fired.

In the last millisecond, the soldier's arm shifted forward. The bullet tore through the man's elbow, shattering bone and cartilage, but veering wide from a kill shot.

The man spun counterclockwise and disappeared behind the trunk of a spruce.

"TAKEDOWN!" he called out to Kane.

He didn't wait to track his partner. Instead, he dropped the sniper rifle and charged forward, drawing his P22 pistol on the run.

Ahead and to his left, Kane leaped through the air and disappeared behind the spruce. A scream burst out, followed by a spatter of automatic fire that shred needles from the tree.

Tucker reached the spruce, grabbed a passing branch, and whipped himself around with his pistol raised. The soldier struggled on the ground, on his back. Kane straddled him, his jaws clamped on his right wrist. The assault rifle lay nearby, but the soldier had a Makarov pistol gripped in his free hand.

Time seemed to slow for Tucker. The man's gun hand turned, straining to bring the weapon to bear on Kane. Then the Makarov bucked. Kane was strobe-lit by orange muzzle flash but unharmed. In his panic and pain, the man had shot too soon.

Tucker refused to give him another chance.

Stepping sideways, he took aim and fired once. The bullet drilled a neat hole in the soldier's right temple. His body went slack.

"RELEASE," Tucker rasped out.

Kane obeyed and backed away a few steps.

Tucker placed his boot on the Makarov, which lay half buried in the snow. There was no sense in checking the man's pulse; he was dead. His mind switched to their next worry. The gunfire would have carried through the trees.

But how far? Who might have heard?

Tucker took a moment to double-check Kane for injuries. Finding none, he gave the shepherd a quick neck ruffle, then pointed in the direction the man had come.

"QUIET SCOUT."

He had to know if reinforcements were on their way.

As Kane moved off, he pocketed the Makarov, stripped off the man's camouflage suit, and stuffed it into his own pack. Though pressed for time, he spent a minute hand-shoveling snow over the corpse. The grave wouldn't stand close scrutiny, but it might buy him precious seconds.

Finally, Tucker retrieved his rifle and moved deeper into the trees, where he found a tangle of fallen logs. If necessary, it would serve as a good sniper's roost.

He checked Kane's camera, but all seemed quiet out there. Satisfied for the moment, he radioed to his partner.

"RETURN."

Thirty seconds later, Kane crouched next to him, panting.

"Good work, pal."

Kane licked Tucker's cheek.

Using the momentary lull, Tucker pulled on the camouflage suit.

"Now we wait."

4:39 P.M.

After several long minutes, the snap of branches alerted Tucker. Someone was approaching from his eight o'clock position. As he listened, the plod of footsteps grew louder, distinctly different from the soldier's cautious approach.

Not Spetsnaz.

A moment later, Dimitry appeared, lumbering through the forest.

Still, Tucker stayed hidden, waiting, suspicion ringing through him.

When Dimitry was ten feet away, seemingly alone, Tucker called out to him.

"Stop!"

Dimitry jumped, genuinely startled. He lifted both arms, showing empty hands. "Is that you, my friend?"

Tucker kept hidden. "You're making a lot of noise."

"Intentionally," Dimitry replied with a half smile. "I didn't feel like getting shot, *da*? I heard the gunfire."

"We had a visitor," Tucker admitted, relaxing somewhat. "Spetsnaz."

"Is he—?"

"Dead. Dimitry, did you turn us in?"

"*Nyet.* But you are smart to ask. I swear I have told no one about you."

"And Fedor?"

The old man shook his head. "He has his flaws, but he has never betrayed me or a customer. Besides, you must trust someone or you'll never get out of here."

Tucker both believed him and knew he was right. Even Kane wagged his tail, wanting to greet Dimitry. He finally stood up out of his blind.

Dimitry joined him, eyeing his winter suit. "New clothes, I see."

"Someone no longer needed them." Tucker pointed toward the air base. "Is Fedor ready to fly? Matters are getting a little tense out here."

"I think so. When I called him, he had just finished making some adjustments to the plane's propeller. Fine-tuning, he called it."

Tucker smiled, remembering the crude hammering. "I saw."

Together, they headed past the cabin and across the air base. Dimitry took him along a circuitous path that mostly kept them hidden, working their way toward the hangar.

"I am glad you are safe," Dimitry said. "At the church, when I left you in that tunnel—"

"What exactly is that tunnel?" Tucker interrupted, remembering the fresh boards shoring it up.

"I found it by accident one morning. I felt a strange draft coming up from the floor and started prying up boards."

"And you've been maintaining it?" he asked.

The suspicion must have been plain in his voice.

Dimitry smiled. "Myself and Fedor. I told you he was a smuggler."

Tucker raised an eyebrow toward the town's old bishop, suddenly remembering how deferential everyone in the bar had been toward Dimitry, more than could be explained by religious affection.

"Okay, perhaps Fedor has a partner," Dimitry admitted. "It is hard to maintain my flock on faith alone. But, mind you, we don't smuggle anything dangerous. Mostly medicine and food, especially during winter. Many children get sick, you understand."

Tucker could not find any fault in such an enterprise. "It's a good thing you're doing."

Dimitry spread his hands. "Out here, you do what you can for your neighbor. It is how we survive, how we make a community." He pointed ahead. "There is Fedor's hangar. I will check first. Make sure it is clear, *da?*"

With Kane at his knee, Tucker waited while Dimitry went ahead. He returned two minutes later and gestured for them to follow.

"All is good."

Dimitry led them through the main hangar doors. Lit by a lone klieg light, a single-engine prop plane filled the small space. Tucker couldn't make out the model, but like everything else at the air base, the craft seemed a hodgepodge of bits and pieces. But at least the propeller was in place.

He found Fedor kneeling beside a red toolbox on the floor.

Before they could reach him, Kane let out a low growl. The shepherd still stood by the door, staring out.

Tucker hurried to the shepherd's side, careful not to show himself. He drew Kane back by his collar. Across the base, a pair of headlights passed through the main gate, turned, and headed in their direction. It was clearly a military vehicle.

He drew his pistol and crossed to Fedor. He raised the gun and aimed it at the man's forehead. "We've got visitors. No matter what else happens, you'll be the first one to go."

Fedor's eyes got huge, and he sputtered first in Russian, then English. "I tell no one! No one!" He stood up—slowly, his palms toward Tucker. "Come, come! Follow. I show where to hide."

Tucker weighed his options as the grumble of a diesel engine grew louder. He remembered Dimitry's earlier words: *you must trust someone or you'll never get out of here.*

With no choice but to heed that wisdom, Tucker pocketed his weapon. "Show me."

Fedor hurried toward the rear of the hangar, towing everyone with him.

The big man led them to a giant orange storage tank, streaked with rust, that sat on a set of deflated rubber tires. A hose lay curled next to it. Tucker recognized an old fuel bowser used to fill the tanks of planes.

Fedor pointed to a ladder on one side. "Up! Through hatch on top."

Having already cast his dice, Tucker stepped to the ladder and crouched down. He turned to Kane and tapped his shoulder. "Up."

Backing a step, then leaping, Kane mounted Tucker's shoulder in a half-fireman carry. Together, they scaled the ladder and crawled across the bowser's roof to the hatch.

Fedor headed toward the hangar door, leaving behind a warning. "Quiet. I come back."

Hurrying, Tucker spun the hatch, tugged it open, and poked his head inside. The interior seemed dry.

At least, I won't be standing hip-deep in gasoline.

He pointed down and Kane dove through the hatch, landing quietly. Tucker followed, not as deftly, having to struggle to pull the hatch closed, too. His boots hit the bottom of the empty tank with a clang. He cringed, going still, but the rumbling arrival of the military vehicle covered the noise.

In complete darkness, Tucker drew his gun, his nose and eyes already stinging from fuel residue. But he also smelled bananas, which made no sense. He shifted to a better vantage, but his foot hit something that sounded wooden.

What the hell . . . ?

He freed his tiny penlight and flicked it on. Panning the narrow beam, he discovered the back half of the bowser's tank was stacked with crates and boxes, some marked in Cyrillic, others in various languages. He spotted one box bearing a large red cross. Medical supplies. On top of it rested a thick bunch of bananas.

Here was more of Dimitry and Fedor's smuggling operation.

It seemed he was now part of the cargo.

From outside, he heard muffled Russian voices moving around the hangar—then they approached closer. He clicked off his penlight and gripped the pistol with both hands. It sounded like an argument was under way. He recognized Fedor's tone, which sounded heated, as if in the thick of a furious negotiation. Then the conversation moved away again and became indiscernible.

After another ten minutes, an engine started, rumbling loudly, wheels squelched on wet tarmac, and the sounds quickly receded. Seconds later, feet clomped up the ladder, and the hatch opened.

Tucker pointed his pistol up.

Fedor scolded, "No shoot, please. Safe now."

Tucker called out, "Dimitry?"

"They are all gone, my friend!"

Fedor groaned. "*Da, da.* As I say, safe."

Tucker climbed up, poked his head out, and looked around. Once confident the hangar was clear, he dropped back down, collected Kane, and climbed out.

"Price higher now," Fedor announced.

Dimitry explained, "They were looking for you, but mostly they learned about our operations here. Not unusual. Every village in Siberia has such a black-market system. So people talk. The soldiers came mostly to collect what could be most kindly described as a tax."

He understood. The roving soldiers weren't above a little extortion.

"Cost me best case of vodka," Fedor said, placing a fist over his heart, deeply wounded.

"We told them that we were about to leave on a postal run," Dimitry explained. "After collecting the tax, there should be no problem getting through. Even soldiers know the mail must flow. Or their vodka here might dry up."

Tucker understood. " 'Neither snow, nor rain, nor dark of night . . .' "

Fedor looked quizzically at him. "Is that poem? You write it?"

"Never mind. How much more do I owe you?"

Fedor gave it much thought. "Two thousand rubles. You pay, *da*?"

"I'll pay."

Fedor clapped his hands together. "Happy! Time to go. Put dog in plane. Then *you* push plane out, I steer. Hurry, hurry!"

Tucker rushed to comply.

Not exactly first-class service, but he wasn't complaining.

PART II

Hunter/Killer

12

March 11, 11:15 A.M.
Novosibirsk, Siberia

"And how confident are you of Dimitry and Fedor?" Ruth Harper asked.

Tucker stood at a pay phone next to an open-air fish market. The pungent smell of sturgeon, perch, and smelt hung heavily in the cold air. He had spent the previous ten minutes bringing Harper up to speed. He was surprised how happy he was to hear that southern lilt to her voice.

If not Tennessee, then maybe—

"Do you trust those Russians?" she pressed.

"I wouldn't be making this call if either of them had ratted me out. Plus, I've been strolling the snowy streets of Novosibirsk for the past two hours. I'm clean. And it's still another twelve hundred miles to Perm. If I pick up a tail, I'll have plenty of time to shake it loose."

"Still, you're cutting the rendezvous close."

"Bukolov will keep. If they—whoever they are—had any idea where he was, they wouldn't be after me. Which reminds me, any further word about the source of that leak?"

"No luck, yet. But from the story you just told me—one involving GRU and Spetsnaz—we know the enemy has powerful connections in either the Russian government or military. I'm looking hard at the Ministry of Defense, or maybe someone at a cabinet level of the government."

"Maybe you'd better be looking at *both*."

"A scary proposition. Do you want help out there?"

Tucker considered it for a long moment. "For now, no. We've got enough players in the field. Makes it confusing enough."

Plus he liked working alone—well, not quite alone.

He gave Kane, seated at his knee, a reassuring pat.

"If I change my mind, Harper, I'll let you know."

"Do that. As it happens, I've got nobody to give you right now."

"Busy on the home front?"

"Always. World's a dangerous place. At least Sigma can offer you some logistical support. Do you have a wish list for me?"

Tucker did. After reciting the provisions he needed, he signed off. He would find all he asked for once he reached the city of Perm, secured and cached in a safe house.

But first he had to get there.

Harper had arranged clean papers and seemed confident that Russian immigration and customs did not have him on any watch list, making it safe for him to fly. Furthermore, Sigma's intelligence team had arranged another level of countermeasures, booking false tickets, hotel rooms, and car rentals. He was everywhere and nowhere.

Still, whether it was his inherent wariness of all things governmental or simply a tactical change of mind, Tucker called a local car rental agency after hanging up with Harper and booked an SUV for a one-way trip to Omskaya, some four hundred miles to the west. He had no reason to distrust Sigma, but there was no mistaking the reality of his current situation. He and Kane were out here alone, without any hope of reinforcements.

Harper had tasked him with getting Abram Bukolov safely out of Russia and to the United States. How exactly he accomplished that was his decision.

And he preferred it that way.

With Kane on a leash, he walked the mile to the rental car office and picked up the vehicle, a Range Rover of questionable age, but the engine purred and the heater worked.

Tucker took it and left Novosibirsk at midday, heading west down the highway to Omskaya. Three hours later, he pulled off the highway and drove six miles north to his *true* destination, Kuybyshev.

It never hurt to employ his own countermeasures.

Following the pictograph signs, he pulled into the local airport. Using a map and a smattering of Russian, he booked a flight to Perm.

Sixteen hours after he left Novosibirsk, his flight touched down at Perm's Bolshoye Savino Airport. He waited in cargo claim for Kane to emerge from the belly of the plane, then another hour for immigration to clear them both.

Minutes later, he and Kane were in another rental vehicle—this one a Volvo—and headed into the city proper.

From the car, he called Sigma for an update.

"Still no blips on immigration or customs," Harper informed him. "If they're still actively hunting you, they're not doing it that way."

Or they're giving me enough time to get to Bukolov before snapping shut the trap.

"Is this safe house I'm heading to manned?" he asked, intending to collect the provisions he had requested without delay.

"It won't be. It's an apartment. Call the number I gave you, let it ring three times, then again twice, then wait ten minutes. The door will be unlocked. Five minutes inside, no more."

"Are you kidding me?"

"Simplicity works, Tucker, and this is a lot simpler than meeting someone on a park bench with a flower in your lapel and your shoelace untied."

Tucker realized this made sense. In fact, one of the acronyms soldiers lived by was KISS—*Keep It Simple, Stupid.*

"Fair enough," Tucker said, but he gave voice to another troubling matter. "It's South Carolina, isn't it?"

"Pardon?"

"Your accent."

She sighed heavily, giving him his answer.

Wrong.

"Tucker, the details for your meeting tonight will also be in the safe house."

"And my contact?"

"His name and description are included in the dossier you'll find there. He's hard to miss."

"I'll call you after it's done."

"Keep out of trouble," she said.

"Are you talking about both of us, or just Kane?"

"Kane would be much harder to replace."

Tucker glanced to his partner. "Can't argue with that," he said and signed off.

Now came the hard part—grabbing Abram Bukolov without getting caught.

13

H is visit to the safe house was thankfully anticli-
mactic. He left with four new passports—two for
him and two for Bukolov—along with a roll of cash, a
pair of credit cards, a second satellite phone, and the
location of his meeting with Sigma's contact, the one
who was supposed to lead Tucker to Bukolov.

This mysterious contact was also high on his list of
suspects as the source of the intelligence leak that almost
got him killed. The man's dossier rested on the seat next
to him. He planned on studying it in great detail.

Next, Tucker took advantage of a list of local suppli-
ers left at the safe house. He traveled to a bakery whose

basement doubled as an armory. The baker asked no questions but simply waited for Tucker to make his weapon selections from a floor-to-ceiling pegboard. He then wrote down the price on a piece of paper, which he handed to Tucker with a gravelly, "No negotiate."

The next supplier, the owner of a car lot, was equally taciturn and effective. Through Harper, Tucker had preordered a black Marussia F2 SUV. Of Russian manufacture, it had a front end that only a mother could love, but it was a brute of a vehicle, often modified for use by first responders or as a mobile command center.

After paying, Tucker told the owner where to leave the vehicle—and when.

With six hours still to spare before he was supposed to meet with his contact, Tucker proceeded to the neighborhood in question: the Leninsky District on the northern side of the Kama River. Once there, he parked the Volvo and began walking. In between scouting locations and routes, he was able to relax and take in the sights.

Straddling the banks of the Kama and within the shadow of the snow-topped Ural Mountains, Perm was home to a million people. While the city had its share of Soviet-gray architecture, the older Leninsky District continued to maintain its original European charm. It was a cozy neighborhood of tree-lined streets and secluded garden courtyards, spattered with small cafés, butchers, and bakeries. To top it off, the sun shone in a cloudless blue sky, a rare sight of late.

As he strolled, no one seemed to pay much attention to him: just a man walking his dog. He wasn't alone in that regard. Much of Perm was taking advantage of the handsome day. Kane took particular interest in a pair of leashed dachshunds that passed by on the sidewalk, all three dogs doing the customary greeting of sniffing and tail wagging. Tucker didn't mind, as attached to the other end of the leash was a buxom, young beauty in a tight sweater.

The day certainly had brightened.

Eventually, as they crossed the half-mile-long bridge spanning the Kama, he abruptly found himself in a different world. On this side of the river, it was distinctly seedier and less populated. The area was mostly forest, with roads that were either dirt or deeply potholed. The few inhabitants he encountered stared at the pair as though they were alien invaders.

Luckily, where he was supposed to meet his mysterious contact was only a quarter mile from the river. He studied it from a distance, getting the lay of the land. It was a bus stop shelter across from a sullen cluster of businesses: a grocery store, a strip club, and a body shop.

Tucker finished his reconnoiter, then gladly crossed back over the bridge.

He and Kane returned to the Volvo, found a nondescript hotel in the area, checked in, and took a fast nap. Tucker knew that once he had Bukolov in hand, he might not get a chance to sleep again until he delivered the man across the border.

That is, if he ever reached the border.

In the end, he didn't sleep well at all.

8:12 P.M.

By nightfall, Tucker found himself parked in an elementary-school lot on the wrong side of the tracks—or in this case, the wrong side of the *river.* The school had boarded-up windows with a playground full of rusty, broken equipment that looked perfect for spreading tetanus.

He had picked this spot because it lay within a hundred yards of the bus stop where he was supposed to meet his contact. He shut off the engine and doused the lights and sat in the darkness for five minutes. He saw no other cars, and no one moving about. Again no one seemed to be following him. This made him feel more uneasy, not less.

It was what you *couldn't* see that usually got you killed.

He turned to Kane, motioning with a flat palm. "STAY."

He had debated the wisdom of leaving Kane behind, but if the meeting went awry, he wanted to make sure he had an escape vehicle. And considering the neighborhood, Kane's presence in the Volvo was better than any car alarm.

He often wrestled with this exact quandary. With the memory of Abel's death never far, he had to fight the temptation to keep Kane out of harm's way. But the shepherd loved Tucker, loved to work, and he hated to be separated for long.

They were a pack of two.

Even now, Kane displayed his displeasure at Tucker's order, cocking his head quizzically and furrowing his brow.

"I know," he replied. "Just mind the fort."

He took a moment to check his equipment: a Smith & Wesson .44-caliber snubnose in his belt, a hammerless Magnum revolver in his coat pocket, and a similar .38-caliber model in a calf holster. Additionally, he kept a pair of quick-loaders for each in his pockets.

This was as close to *armed to the teeth* as he could manage.

Satisfied, he got out, locked the car, and started walking.

He hopped a chest-high fence and crossed the school's playground to the north side. He followed a line of thick Russian larch trees, bare and skeletal, around a vacant lot that was dominated by mounds of garbage.

On the other side, fifty yards away, stood the bus stop. The curbside shelter was little more than a lean-to over a graffiti-scarred bench.

Across the street, under the strip club's neon sign—a silhouette of a naked lady—four thugs lounged, laughing, smoking, and chugging bottles of beer. Their heads were shaved, and they all wore jeans tucked into black, steel-toed boots.

Staying out of their sight line, Tucker checked his watch. He still had twenty minutes.

Now came the waiting.

Back at the hotel, he had read the dossier on his contact, a man named Stanimir Utkin. He was Bukolov's former student and now chief lab assistant. Tucker had memorized his face, not that it took much effort. The man stood six and a half feet tall but weighed only one hundred fifty pounds. Topped by a shock of fiery-red hair, such a scarecrow would be hard to miss in a crowd.

Right on time, a cab pulled to a stop before the bus shelter.

The door opened and out climbed Stanimir Utkin.

"Come on," Tucker mumbled. "Don't do this to me."

Not only had Utkin arrived by cab to the exact spot of their meeting—displaying a reckless lack of caution—he had come wearing what appeared to be an expensive business suit. His red hair glowed in the pool cast by the streetlamp like a beacon.

The cab pulled away and sped off.

The driver was no fool.

Like sharks smelling chum, the four thugs across the street took immediate notice of Utkin. They pointed fingers and laughed, but Tucker knew this phase wouldn't last long. Utkin was too tempting of a target, either for a mugging or a beating—or more likely, *both*.

Tucker jammed his hands into his pockets and tightened one fist around the Magnum. Taking a deep breath, he started walking fast across the open lot, keeping out of sight as he headed toward the back of the bench. He covered the distance to the bus shelter in thirty seconds, by which time Utkin had begun glancing left and right like a rat who had spotted a snake.

One of the thugs threw a bottle across the street. It shattered on the curb near Utkin's toes.

The skinny man stumbled backward, falling to his seat on the bus bench.

Oh, dear God . . .

Ten feet behind the shelter, Tucker stopped in the shadows and called out, keeping his voice low enough so only Utkin could hear him. According to the dossier, the man spoke fluent English.

"Utkin, don't turn around. I'm here to meet you."

Another beer bottle sailed across the street and shattered in the street. Harsh laughter followed.

"My name is Tucker. Listen carefully. Don't think, just turn around and walk toward me, then keep going. Do it now."

Utkin stood, stepped out from under the shelter, and headed into the abandoned lot.

One of the thugs called out, and the group started across the street, likely drawn as much out of boredom as larceny.

Utkin drew even with Tucker, who hid behind a stack of tires and trash.

He waved him on. "Keep going. I'll catch up."

Utkin obeyed, glancing frequently over his shoulder.

By now, the thugs had reached the bus stop and entered the lot.

Tucker stood up, drawing out his Magnum. He took three paces into the light, showing himself. He raised the pistol and drew a bead on the lead thug's chest.

The group came to a fast stop.

Tucker summoned one of the Russian phrases he'd been practicing. "Go away, or I will kill you."

He raised the Magnum, a mean-looking weapon. His Russian language skills might be lacking, but some communication was universal.

Still, the leader looked ready to test him, until they locked gazes. Whatever he saw in Tucker's eyes made him change his mind.

The leader waved the others off, and they wisely retreated.

Tucker turned and hurried after Utkin, who had stopped at the fence that bordered the school-yard. He was bent double, his hands on his knees, hyperventilating.

Tucker didn't slow. He couldn't trust the thugs wouldn't rally up more guys, additional firepower, and come after them. He grabbed Utkin's arm, pulled him upright, and shoved him toward a neighboring gate.

"Walk."

Coaxed and guided by Tucker, they reached the car quickly. He opened the front passenger door and herded Utkin inside. The man balked when he spotted Kane in the back. The shepherd leaned over the seat to sniff at the stranger.

Tucker placed a palm atop Utkin's head and pushed him inside. Still panicked, the man balled up in the passenger seat, twisted to the side, his eyes never leaving Kane.

Not the most auspicious introduction, but the man had left him little choice.

Tucker started the engine and drove off.

Only once back over the bridge and in more genial surroundings did Tucker relax. He found a well-lit parking lot beside a skating rink and pulled in.

"The dog won't hurt you," Tucker told Utkin.

"Does *he* know that?"

Tucker sighed and turned to face Utkin fully. "What were you thinking?"

"What?"

"The taxi, the business suit, the bad part of town . . ."

"What should I have done differently?"

"All of it," Tucker replied.

In truth, Tucker was partly to blame. From the dossier, he had known Utkin was a lab geek. He knew the meeting site was dicey. He should have changed it.

Utkin struggled to compose himself and did a surprisingly admirable job, considering the circumstances. "I believe I owe you my life. Thank you. I was very frightened."

Tucker shrugged. "Nothing wrong with being frightened. That just means you're smart, not stupid. So before we get into any more trouble, let's go get Bukolov. Where is your boss?"

Utkin checked his watch. "He should still be at the opera."

"The opera?"

Utkin glanced up, seemingly not bothered that someone seeking to escape the country, someone being hunted by Russian elite forces, should choose such a public outing.

Tucker shook his head. "You remember when I said don't be *stupid*. . ."

Over the next few minutes, he got the story out of Utkin. It seemed—faced with the possibility of never seeing the Motherland again—Abram Bukolov had decided to indulge his greatest passion: *opera*.

"They were doing one of Abram's favorites," Utkin explained. "*Faust*. It's quite—"

"I'm sure it is. Does he have a cell phone?"

"Yes, but he will have it turned off."

Tucker sighed. "Where is the opera house and when does it end?"

"In about an hour. It's being held at the Tchaikovsky's House. It's less than a mile from here."

Great . . . just great. . .

He put the Volvo in gear. "Show me."

10:04 P.M.

Ten minutes before the opera ended, Tucker found a parking spot a few blocks from the Tchaikovsky's House. As angry as he was at Bukolov for choosing to preface his defection by dressing up in a tuxedo and attending a public extravaganza, the deed was done. Still, this stunt told him something: Bukolov was either unstable, stupid, or arrogant—any of which did not bode well for the remainder of their journey.

Tucker left Kane in the car and accompanied Utkin down the street. He stopped across from the opera's brightly lit main entrance and pointed toward its massive white stone façade.

"I'll wait here," he said. "You go fetch the good doctor and walk to the car. Don't hurry and don't look at me. I'll meet you at the Volvo. Got it?"

"I understand."

"Go."

Utkin crossed the street and headed toward the main entrance.

As he waited, Tucker studied the crimson banner draped down the front of the theater. The fiery sign depicted a demonic figure in flames, appropriate for *Faust*, an opera about a scholar who makes a pact with the devil.

I hope that's not the case here.

A few minutes later, Utkin emerged with Abram Bukolov in tow. The billionaire leader of Russia's burgeoning pharmaceutical industry stood a foot shorter and forty pounds heavier than his lab assistant. He was bald, except for a monk's fringe of salt-and-pepper hair.

Following Tucker's instructions, Utkin escorted the man back to the car. Tucker gave them a slight lead, then followed. Once he was sure no one was tailing them, he joined them at the car.

"Hello!" Bukolov called, offering his hand.

Irritated, Tucker skipped the formal introductions. Instead, he used the remote to unlock the doors. "Utkin in front, Bukolov in—"

"*Doctor* Bukolov," the man corrected him.

"Whatever. *Doctor*, you're in the back."

Tucker opened the driver's door and started to climb in.

Behind him, Bukolov stopped and stared inside. "There's a dog back here."

"Really?" Tucker said, his voice steeped in sarcasm. "How did he get back there?"

"I'm not sitting next to—"

"Get in, or he'll drag you inside by your tuxedo lapels, Doctor."

Bukolov clamped his mouth shut, his face going red. It was doubtful many people had ever spoken to him like that. Still, he got in.

Two blocks later, the pharmaceutical magnate found his voice. "The opera was tremendous, Stanimir—though I doubt you would have appreciated the subtleties. Say, you, driver, what's your name? Is this your dog? He keeps staring at me."

Tucker gave Utkin a narrow-eyed glance, who got the message.

"Doctor Bukolov, why don't we talk about the opera later? We can—"

The man cut him off by tapping on Tucker's shoulder. "Driver, how long until we reach Kazan?"

Resisting the urge to break his fingers, Tucker pulled to the nearest curb and put the Volvo in park. He turned in his seat and faced Bukolov. "Kazan? What are you talking about?"

"Kazan. It's in the *oblast* of—"

"I know where it is, Doctor." The city of Kazan lay about four hundred miles to the west. "Why do you think we're going there?"

"Good God, man, didn't anyone tell you? This is unacceptable! I am not leaving the country without Anya. We must go to Kazan and collect her."

Of course we do.

"Who's Anya?" he asked.

"My daughter. I will not leave Russia without her."

11:22 P.M.

Sticking to his original plan, Tucker headed out of town, stopping only long enough to trade the Volvo for the new Marussia F2 SUV. They found the brute of a vehicle parked where he had instructed it to be left on the south end of town. It was fully gassed and carried a false license plate.

Reaching the P242, he continued west for an hour, doing his best to tune out Bukolov's rambling monologue, which ranged from the mysterious Anya, to the industrial history of the region, to Kane's *disturbingly intelligent mien.*

On the outskirts of the small town of Kungur, Tucker pulled into the hotel parking lot and decided he'd put enough distance from Perm to regroup.

He got out and called Harper and brought her up to speed.

"This is the first I've heard of this Anya," Harper said.

"You described the doctor as eccentric. You were being generous."

"He may be a bit"—she paused to consider her words—"out of touch, but there's no mistaking his brilliance. Or his desire to leave Russia. And to answer your unspoken question, we're convinced he's on the up-and-up."

"If you say so."

"Where is he now?"

"In the backseat of my SUV, having a staring contest with Kane. I had to get some air. Listen, Harper, if Anya is the brideprice to get Bukolov out of the country, that's fine, but let's make sure she's real before I head to Kazan. That's a good seven-hour drive from here."

"Agreed. Give me her full name."

"Hang on." Tucker opened his door. "Doctor, what is Anya's last name?"

"*Bukolov*, of course! She's my daughter. What kind of question—?"

Tucker straightened and spoke to Harper. "You heard?"

"I did."

The professor added, "She works at the Kazan Institute of Biochemistry and Biophysics. She's quite brilliant, you know—"

Tucker slammed the door, muffling Bukolov's ramblings.

On the phone, Harper said, "I'm on it."

Bukolov rolled down the window a few inches. "Apologies. How forgetful of me. Anya took her mother's surname—*Malinov*. Anya Malinov."

Harper heard that, too. "Got it. Name's Malinov. What's your plan, Tucker?"

"In the short term, to check into a motel. It's almost midnight here."

Tucker waited until Bukolov had rerolled up his window. He took a few additional steps away before broaching a touchier matter.

"Harper, what about Utkin?"

The lab tech continued to remain on the short list of potential leaks—but were such breaches accidental or done on purpose? Tucker trusted his gut, along with his ability to read people. He found nothing that struck a wrong nerve with the young man, beyond simple naïveté.

It seemed Harper had come to the same conclusion. "Our intelligence can find nothing untoward about Utkin. He seems as honest as they come."

"Then maybe it was a slip of the tongue. Something said to the wrong person. By Utkin . . . or maybe even by Bukolov. That guy seems a few fries short of a Happy Meal."

"I'll keep looking into it. In the meantime, I'll dig into this Anya business overnight and get back to you by morning."

With the call done, he led everyone to the hotel for the night, booking a single room with two beds. Tucker parked Kane at the door, knowing the shepherd would keep guard for the night.

He half dozed in a chair, while Bukolov puttered around the room, muttering and complaining before eventually unwinding. Around one in the morning, he sat down on the edge of the bed. Utkin was already asleep in the other.

"I'm sorry," Bukolov said. "I've forgotten your name."

"Tucker." He nodded to his partner. "That's Kane."

"I must say your dog seems well mannered enough. Thank you for coming to get me."

"You're welcome."

"Did they tell you about my discovery?" Before he could answer, Bukolov shook his head dismissively. "No, of course not. Even I didn't tell them, so how could they know?"

"Tell me about it."

Bukolov wagged a finger. "In good time. But I will say this. It is *monumental*. It will change the world of medicine—among other things. That's why they're after me."

"The Arzamas generals."

"Yes."

"Who are they?"

"Specifically? I don't know. They're too crafty for that."

Tucker stared across, sizing the other up. Was this guy suffering from a paranoid delusion? A persecution complex? Tucker fingered the healing bullet graze in his neck. That certainly was real enough.

"Then tell me about Anya," he said.

"Ah . . ." Bukolov's face softened, holding back a ghost of a smile. "She's wonderful. She's means everything to me. We've been working in tandem, the two of us—at a distance of course, and in secret."

"I thought Stanimir was your chief assistant."

"Him? Hah! He's adequate, I suppose, but he doesn't have the mind for it. Not for what I'm doing. Few people do really. That's why I must do this myself."

With that, Bukolov kicked off his shoes, sprawled back on the bed, and closed his eyes.

Tucker shook his head and settled into the chair for the night.

Bukolov whispered, his eyes still shut. "I'm not crazy, you know."

"If you say so."

"Just so you know."

Tucker crossed his arms, beginning to realize how little he actually *knew* about any of this.

March 13, 6:15 A.M.
Kungur, Russia

Despite the discomfort of the chair, Tucker slept for a solid five hours. He woke to find both of his charges still sleeping.

Taking advantage of the quiet moment, he took Kane out for a walk, let the dog stretch his legs and relieve himself. While they were still outside, Harper called.

"Anya's real," she said as introduction.

"I don't know if that's good news or bad."

If Anya were a figment of the good doctor's imagination, they could get out of Dodge immediately.

Harper continued. "We were able to confirm there's an Anya Malinov working at the Kazan Institute of Biochemistry and Biophysics, but not much else. A good portion of her file is redacted. Kazan's not as bad as the old Soviet-era *naukograds*, their closed science cities, but large swaths of the place do fall under the jurisdiction of the Ministry of Defense."

"So not only do we need to go to Kazan, but I have to extract this woman out from under the military's nose."

"Is that a problem?"

"I'll have to make it work. Not like I have a whole lot of choice. You asked me to get him out of Russia, and that's what I intend to do—him and now his daughter apparently. Which presents a problem. I've only got new passports for Bukolov. Not for Anya. And what about Utkin, for that matter? He wouldn't survive a day after we're gone. I won't leave him behind."

He flashed to Abel, panting, tongue lolling, tail wagging.

He wasn't about to abandon another teammate behind enemy lines.

Harper was silent for a few seconds. Even from halfway around the world, Tucker imagined he could hear the gears in the woman's head turning, recalibrating to accommodate the change in the situation.

"Okay. Like you, I'll make it happen. When do you plan to go for Anya?"

"Within twenty-four hours. More than that and we're pushing our luck."

"That won't work. I can't get new passports for Anya and Utkin over to you that fast. But if you gave me your route from there—"

"I don't know it yet. Considering all that's happened, it's hard to plan more than a step in advance. All I know for sure is the next step: free Anya."

"Then hold on for a minute." The line went silent, then she was back. "After you fetch Anya, can you get to Volgograd? As the crow flies, it's six hundred miles *south* of Kazan."

Tucker pulled a laminated map from his back pocket and studied it for a few seconds. "The distance is manageable."

"Good. If you can get to Volgograd, I can get you all out. No problem."

Out sounded good. So did *no problem*.

But after all that had happened, he had no faith about the outcome of either proposition.

14

By that midafternoon, Tucker stood on a sidewalk in central Kazan, staring up at a bronze monolith topped by the bust of a dour-faced man. Predictably, the plaque was written in Cyrillic.

But at least I came with my own tour guide.

"Behold the birthplace of modern organic chemistry," Abram Bukolov announced, his arms spread. "Kazan is home to the greats. Butlerov, Markovnikov, Arbuzov. The list is endless. And this fine gentleman depicted here, you surely know who he is, yes?"

"Why don't you remind us, Doctor," said Tucker.

"He is Nikolai Lobachevsky. The Russian pioneer in hyperbolic geometry. Ring any bells?"

Maybe warning bells.

Tucker was beginning to suspect Bukolov suffered from bipolar disorder. Since leaving the hotel at dawn Bukolov had cycled from barely contained excitement to sullenness. But upon reaching Kazan's outskirts a short time ago, the doctor had perked up enough to demand that they go on a walking tour of the Kazan Institute of Biochemistry and Biophysics.

Tucker had agreed for several reasons.

One: To shut Bukolov up.

Two: To scout the campus.

Three: To see if he could detect a general alert for any of them. If they were being pursued, their hunters had chosen a more discreet approach.

But most of all, he needed to find out *where* on this research campus Anya Malinov resided or worked. He hoped to sneak her out under the cover of night.

Utkin followed behind with Kane. He had a phone at his ear, trying to reach Anya. He spoke in low tones. Matters would have been easier if her father, Bukolov, knew where she lived or where her office was located.

I've never been here was his answer, almost tearful, clearly fraught with worry for his daughter.

Not trusting Bukolov to be civil, Tucker had thought it best for Utkin to make an inquiry with the institution.

Utkin finally lowered the phone and drew them all together. "We have a problem."

Of course we do.

Bukolov clutched Utkin's sleeve. "Has something happened to Anya?"

"No, she's fine, but she's not *here.*"

"What do you mean?" Tucker asked. "Where is she?"

"She's at the Kremlin."

Tucker took a calming breath before speaking. "She's in *Moscow?*"

Utkin waved his hands. "No, no. Kazan has a Kremlin also. It lies a kilometer from here, overlooking the Volga."

He pointed in the general direction of the river that bordered Kazan.

"Why is she there?" Tucker asked, sighing out his relief.

Bukolov stirred. "Of course, because of the archives!"

His voice was sharp, loud enough to draw the eye of a passing campus guard. Not wanting any undue attention, Tucker drew the group along, getting them moving back toward their hotel in town.

Bukolov continued. "She mentioned finding something." He shook his head as if trying to knock a loose gear back into place. "I forgot about it until now. Something she was going to retrieve for me. Something very important."

"What?" Tucker asked.

The doctor looked up with a twinkle in his eye. "The journal of the late, great Paulos de Klerk."

"Who is that?"

"All in good time. But De Klerk may have the last piece of the puzzle I need."

Tucker decided not to press the issue and returned his attention to Utkin. "How long until she returns to the institute?"

"Three or four days."

"We can't wait that long!" Bukolov demanded.

For once, Tucker agreed.

Utkin also nodded. "According to what I learned, security is actually tighter here on the campus than at the local Kremlin. Over where Anya lives and works at the institute, there are guards at every entrance, magnetic key card access, and closed-circuit television cameras."

Tucker blew out a discouraged breath.

Then it looks like we're breaking Anya out of the Kremlin.

3:23 P.M.

An hour later, Tucker followed a tour group onto the grounds of the Kazan Kremlin. He and a handful of others had been separated out and handed over to an

English-speaking guide, a five-foot-tall blond woman who smiled a lot but tended to bark.

"Now stay close!" she called, waving them all forward. "We are passing through the south entrance of the Kremlin. As you can guess from the massive wall we are crossing under, the structure was designed to be a fortress. Some of these structures you'll see are over six hundred years old."

Tucker searched around him. He had already done an intensive study of the Kazan Kremlin: scouring various websites, cross-referencing with Google Earth, and scanning travel blogs. A plan had begun to take shape, but he wanted to see the place firsthand.

"Here we are on Sheynkman Street," the guide expounded, "the Kremlin's main thoroughfare. Above you stands the Spasskaya Tower, known as the Savior's Tower. It is one of thirteen towers. Going clockwise, their names are . . ."

This was the third-to-last tour of the day. Tucker had Utkin working on a project back at the hotel, assisted by Bukolov. He left Kane to watch over them both.

As the group continued across the grounds, he tuned out the guide's ongoing monologue, concentrating instead on fixing a mental picture of the grounds in his head. He'd seen the *Moscow* Kremlin twice, and while that had been impressive, the Kazan version seemed somehow more majestic.

Enclosed by tall snow-white walls and turrets, the interior of the Kazan Kremlin was a mix of architectural and period styles: from the brute practicality of medieval barracks to the showy majesty of an Eastern Orthodox cathedral. Even more impressive was a massive blue-domed mosque with sky-scraping tiled towers.

Gawking all around, Tucker followed their guide for the next forty-five minutes, discovering a maze of tidy cobblestone streets, hidden courtyards, and tree-lined boulevards. He did his best to appreciate the ancient beauty, while also viewing it with the eye of a soldier. He noted guard locations, blind spots, and escape routes.

As the tour wrapped up, the group was allowed to roam relatively free in the public areas, even to take pictures for the next half hour. He sat in various places, counting the number of times he was passed by guards and visitors.

It might just work, he thought.

His phone finally rang. It was Utkin. His message was terse.

"We're ready here."

He stood and headed back to the hotel, hoping everything was in order. They had to move swiftly. One mistake and it could all come crashing down.

4:14 P.M.

Tucker studied Kane approvingly.

The shepherd stood atop the hotel bed, wearing his K9 Storm jacket, but over it, covering it completely and snugly, was a new canvas vest, midnight blue, bearing Cyrillic lettering. It spelled out KAZAN KREMLIN K9.

"Good job, Utkin," Tucker said. "You could have a new career as a seamstress."

"Actually I bought the vest at a local pet store and the letters are ironed on."

Looking closer, Tucker spotted one of the Cyrillic letters peeling off.

"I will fix that," Utkin said, stripping off the false vest.

It wasn't a great disguise, but considering Utkin had been working with Internet photos of the security personnel at the Kazan Kremlin, he had done a pretty damned good job. Besides, the disguise would only have to pass muster for a short time—and then mostly in the dark.

As Utkin finished his final touch-ups—both on the vest and on the winter parka Tucker had stripped off the dead Spetsnaz soldier—Tucker turned to Bukolov.

"Were you able to reach Anya?" he asked.

"Finally. But yes, and she will be ready as you directed."

"Good."

He noted how pale Bukolov looked and the glassy glaze to his eyes. He was plainly fearful for his daughter. It seemed hearing her voice had only stoked his anxiety.

Tucker sat down next to him on the bed, figuring the doctor could use a distraction. "Tell me more about those papers Anya was searching for. Did she find them?"

He brightened, ever the proud father. "She did!"

"And this De Klerk person, why are his journals so important?"

"If you're trying to wheedle something out of me—"

"Not at all. Just curious."

This seemed to satisfy him. "What do you know about the Boer Wars?"

"In South Africa?" Tucker frowned, taken aback by the turn of the conversation. "Just the basics."

"Then here's a primer so you'll understand the context. Essentially the British Empire wanted to keep its thumb on South Africa, and the Boer farmers disagreed, so they went to war. It was bloody and ugly and replete with atrocities on both sides, including mass executions and concentration camps. But Paulos de Klerk was not only a soldier, but a *doctor* as well. Quite a complex man. But that's not why I found him so fascinating—and certainly not why his diary is so critical to my work."

Bukolov paused and glanced around as though looking for eavesdroppers. He leaned forward and gestured for Tucker to come closer.

"Paulos de Klerk was also a *botanist.*" Bukolov winked. "Do you see?"

Tucker didn't reply.

"In his spare time, in between plying his dual trades, he studied South Africa's flora. He took copious notes and made hundreds of detailed drawings. You can find his work in research libraries, universities, and even natural history museums around the world."

"And here, too, in the archives at the Kremlin?" Tucker said.

"Yes, even before the institute in Kazan was founded, this region was considered a place of great learning. Russian czars, going back to Ivan the Terrible, who built the Kremlin here, gathered volumes of knowledge and stored them in its vaults. Vast libraries and archives, much of it poorly cataloged. It took many years to track down the various references to De Klerk, bits and pieces scattered across Russia and Europe. And the most valuable clue was found here, right under our enemies' noses. So you understand now why it's so important?"

"No, not entirely."

More like *not at all*, but he kept silent.

Bukolov leaned back, snorted, and waved him off.

That was all he would get out of the man for now.

Utkin called over to him, fitting the vest back onto Kane. "That should do it."

Tucker checked his watch.

Just enough time to catch the last tour of the day.

He quickly donned the military winter suit and tugged on a pair of black boots and a midnight-blue brigade cap. The latter items had been purchased by Utkin at a local army surplus store. He had Utkin compare the look to the photos he had taken of the guards at the Kremlin.

"It should pass," the lab tech confirmed, but he didn't sound entirely convinced.

No matter. They were out of time.

Tucker turned to his partner, who wagged his tail. "Looks like it's showtime, Comrade Kane."

15

March 13, 5:45 P.M.
Kazan, Russia

"And this concludes the day's tour," the guide told the group clustered in the cold. "Feel free to wander the grounds on your own for another fifteen minutes, then the gates will be closing promptly at six P.M."

Tucker stood with the others in a red baseball cap and knockoff Ray-Ban sunglasses, just another tourist. The disguise was in place in case he had the same blond tour guide as before. In the end, it turned out to be a man, so maybe such a level of caution was unnecessary.

At his side, Kane had initially attracted some curious glances, but as he had hoped, the service animal documents passed muster at the ticket office. It also helped that Kane could be a charmer when allowed, wriggling happily and wagging his tail. He also wore a doggie backpack with I Love Kazan printed in Cyrillic on it. The bored teenagers at the gate only gave Kane's pack a cursory exam, as they did with his own small bag.

Now free to roam, Tucker wasted little time. As casually as possible, he strode with Kane down Sheynkman Street until he reached the green-roofed barracks of the old Cadets' Quarters. He walked under its archway and into a courtyard. He ambled around and took a few pictures of a fountain and a nineteenth-century cannon display. Once done, he sat down on a nearby stone bench to wait. Beyond the arch, tourists headed back down Sheynkman toward the main exit.

No one glanced his way. No guards came into view.

Taking advantage of the moment, he led Kane across the courtyard and through a door in the southwest corner. The corridor beyond was dimly lit, lined by barrack doors. He crossed along it, noting the polished walnut floors and the boot heel impressions in the wood outside each barrack. According to the guidebook, cadets of yore stood at attention for four hours each day as their barracks underwent inspection. Tucker had thought the claim a yarn, but apparently it was true.

He came to a flight of stairs at the end of the hall and stepped over a "no access" rope. He quickly climbed to the second floor, found it empty, and searched until he located a good hiding place: an unused and derelict storage room off one of the cadets' classrooms.

He stepped inside with Kane and shut the door behind him.

Standing there, he took a breath and let it out.

Phase One . . . done.

In the darkness, he settled with Kane against one wall.

"Nap time, if you feel like it, buddy," he whispered.

Kane dropped down and rested his head on Tucker's lap.

He used the next two hours to review his plan backward, forward, and sideways. The biggest unknown was Anya. He knew little about the woman or how she would behave in a pressure situation. Nor did he know much about the escorts who guarded her here on the Kremlin premises, except for what Bukolov had learned from her.

According to him, two men—both plainclothes GRU operatives—guarded her day and night. He had a plan to deal with them, but there remained some sketchy parts to it, especially in regard to the Kremlin's K9 patrol detachment.

Over the course of the day's two tours, Tucker had counted eight dog-and-handler pairs, mostly consisting of German shepherds—which Kane could pass for. But he'd also spotted a few Russian Ovcharkas, a type of mop-coated sheepdog used by Russian military and police units.

He feared confronting any of them. He didn't kill animals, and he desperately wanted to keep it that way. Dogs did what they did out of instinct or training. Never malice. Tucker's reluctance to harm was a chink in his armor, and he knew it. Ultimately, he truly didn't know what he would do if his back were against such a wall.

In the darkness, his watch vibrated on his wrist, letting him know it was time for Phase Two.

8:30 P.M.

Tucker and Kane changed into their uniforms, a process complicated by the enclosed space and the need for quiet. Tucker already wore the police boots, their height hidden under the legs of his jeans. The rest of the clothing was split up between their two packs. He slipped into his winter military suit and tugged on the brigade cap and stuffed his old clothes into the backpack, which he stashed in the closet's rafters.

With care, he emerged back into the classroom and strode over to the windows overlooking the darkened boulevard. At this late hour, with the temperature dropping, a light icy mist had begun to fill the streets, glistening the cobblestones under the gas lamps.

Tucker stood still for another fifteen minutes, partially because he wanted to observe the routes of the night guards—but also because his arrangement with Anya required precise timing.

At nine o' clock, she would be escorted from the private research archives to the Governor's House, one of the nonpublic buildings under intense Kremlin security. Once she crossed inside there, Tucker would have no chance of reaching her.

As the time neared, Tucker attached Kane's leash and left the classroom. He went downstairs and out onto the misty boulevard. With Kane tightly heeled beside him, Tucker put a little march into his step.

At an intersection, he spotted a guard and his dog coming in his direction. Tucker called out an order in Russian to Kane, one taught to him by Utkin, though he had to practice the local accent. Kane didn't speak Russian, so Tucker reinforced the order with a hidden hand signal.

Sit.

Kane dropped to his haunches.

As the guard approached the intersection, Tucker's heart pounded.

Keep walking.

Unlike Kane, the guard refused to obey. Both man and dog suddenly stopped, staring suspiciously at the pair.

Taking a risk, Tucker raised his hand and gave the man a curt wave. The man didn't respond. *Press it,* he thought. He took two strides forward and called out brusquely in one of the phrases Utkin had taught him, which translated roughly as, "Is everything okay?"

"*Da, da,*" the guard replied and finally returned the wave. "*A u vas?*"

And you?

Tucker shrugged. "*Da.*"

The pair continued walking again, passing by Tucker and Kane.

The two quickly headed in the opposite direction, south toward the Spasskaya Tower. He had to concentrate on his steps until the acute tension worked out of his legs.

After a hundred meters, he drew even with his destination. It was called the Riding House, once a former stable, now one of the Kremlin's exhibition halls.

Thirty meters away, the guard at the Spasskaya Tower gate waved to him. He was barely discernible through the thickening mist.

Tucker lifted his arm high, acknowledging the other.

Sticking to his disguise, Tucker put on a show, shining his flashlight into the Riding House's windows and over its walls. He spotted another K9 unit crossing the square surrounding the neighboring mosque.

Tucker waved and got one in return.

"One big happy family," he muttered and kept walking.

As Anya had promised, he found the pedestrian door at the northeast corner of the building unlocked. He swung it open and scooted inside, closing the door behind him.

The interior was what he'd imagined a *riding house* would be: horse stalls lined both sides of a central hall. Only now the spaces were dominated by glass cases displaying artifacts of the cadet corps's past: saddles, riding crops, lances, cavalry swords. The room's main halogens were off for the night, but emergency lighting allowed him to see well enough.

Anya was working in the archives located in the building's cellar, the genesis of what was soon to become the Kremlin's Museum of Ancient Books and Manuscripts. How the diary of a Boer botanist had come to rest here Tucker didn't know. It was a long way from South Africa to Kazan.

He leaned down and unclasped Kane's leash.

Time to get to work.

He pointed ahead. "SCOUT AND RETURN."

He didn't want any surprises.

On quiet paws, Kane trotted off and disappeared around one of the display cases. It took him ninety seconds to clear all the former stalls. He returned, sat beside Tucker's legs, and looked up at him.

Good boy.

Together, they crossed the central room to the south wall. A door there opened to a staircase leading down. At the bottom, milky light glowed, accompanied by the distinctive hum of fluorescent lighting.

He and Kane started down.

A couple yards from the last step, an order barked out in Russian. "Who's there?"

Tucker had been expecting this and whispered to Kane, "PLAY FRIENDS."

The shepherd loved this command. He perked up his ears, sprung his tail jauntily, and trotted down the remaining steps into the corridor beyond.

Tucker followed. Ten feet down the corridor, a thick-necked man in an ill-fitting business suit frowned at the wriggling dog.

It was one of Anya's escorts.

"*Dobriy večer,*" Tucker greeted him, wishing him a good evening.

Taking advantage of the guard's divided attention, Tucker kept walking forward.

The man held up a stiff arm and rumbled something in Russian, but Tucker made out only one word—*identify*—and the tone was demanding.

Tucker gestured at Kane, playing the chagrined guard and a misbehaving dog. "Sasha . . . Sasha . . ."

When Tucker was two strides away, the man had had enough and reached into his jacket.

Tucker dropped the act and called to Kane. "PANTS."

Kane clamped his jaws on the man's pant leg and jerked backward, using every ounce of his muscled frame. The guard tipped backward, one arm windmilling, the other still reaching for his gun.

Tucker was already moving. He closed the gap and grabbed the hand going for the concealed weapon. He lashed out with his opposite fist, punching the man squarely in the center of the throat.

The guard croaked as he fell to his back, still conscious, his eyes bulging, his mouth opening and closing spasmodically as he tried to draw breath.

Tucker slipped the man's gun out of its shoulder holster—a GSh-18 pistol—and cracked its steel butt across his temple.

His eyes finally fluttered shut.

Tucker dropped to one knee and aimed the pistol down the corridor. Although the takedown had gone relatively quietly, there was no way of knowing the second escort's proximity.

When no one immediately came running, Tucker pointed ahead. "SCOUT CORNER."

Kane trotted down the corridor and stopped at the next intersection. He peeked left, then right, then glanced back with the steady stare that meant *all clear.*

Tucker joined him and searched ahead.

Unlike the floor above, the storage cellar had undergone little renovation. The walls consisted of crumbling brick, and the floor was rough-chiseled granite. The only illumination came from fluorescent shop lights bolted to the exposed ceiling joists.

On the left, stacks of boxes blocked the corridor. To the right, it was open. At the far end, a rectangle of light was cast on the opposite wall.

A door.

Tucker led the way down the hall. He flattened himself against the wall and peeked around the corner of the door.

Inside was a massive storeroom with an arched roof. It occupied the length and breadth of the main floor above. Bookcases covered all the walls. In the center, row upon row of trestle tables lined the hall, stacked with books, manuscripts, and sheaves of paper.

A raven-haired beauty in a red blouse stood at the nearest table, partially turned from the door. With her arms braced on the table, she studied an open manuscript. To her left, the second guard sat at another table, smoking and playing solitaire.

Tucker drew back, motioned for Kane to stay. Keeping to the hallway, he stepped past the open door to the opposite side. He shoved the stolen pistol into his side pocket. He signaled Kane—*distract and return*—then pointed through the open door.

Kane trotted a few yards into the massive storeroom and began barking.

A gruff voice shouted in Russian, accompanied by the sound of a chair scraping on the stone floor.

Kane trotted back through the door, and Tucker waved for him to continue down the corridor, back the way they'd come.

A moment later the guard emerged, hurrying to catch up. Tucker let him get two steps ahead, then rushed forward and swung a roundhouse punch into his kidney. Gasping, the man dropped to his knees. Tucker wrapped his right arm around the guard's throat and used his left palm to press the man's head forward. Five seconds of pressure, squeezing the carotid artery, was all it took. The man went limp in his arms. To be sure, Tucker held on for another thirty seconds before lowering him to the floor.

Kane returned to his side, wagging his tail.

Tucker patted the shepherd's side, then turned and stepped into the storeroom.

The woman was facing him now, a worried hand at her throat. Her striking blue eyes stared at him, glassy with fear, making her look even younger than her midtwenties. She took a couple of wary steps away from him, plainly skittish. But he couldn't blame her, considering the circumstances.

"You . . . you are Tucker, yes?" she asked in lightly accented English.

He held both palms toward her, trying to calm her. "I am. And you're Anya."

She nodded, sagging with relief, while also quickly composing herself. "You were almost late."

"Almost doesn't count . . . I hope."

Kane trotted forward, his tail high.

She stared down with a small, shy smile. "I must say he startled me with that sudden barking. But, my, he is a lovely animal."

"His name is Kane."

She glanced up at Tucker with those bright eyes. "As in Cain and Abel?"

His voice caught. "Just Kane now." He turned back to the door. "We should get moving."

He quickly led her back upstairs, pausing to frisk both men on the way out, taking their identification cards.

Anya followed, clutching to her chest a leather shoulder bag studded with rhinestones. It was large enough that she could've carried Kane in it. Not exactly inconspicuous. She caught him staring as they climbed up from the cellar.

"A Prada knockoff. I'm leaving my entire life behind, my career. Is one bag too much to ask?" As they stepped back into the main hall of the Riding House, she turned to him. "So what's your plan, great rescuer?"

He heard the forced humor in her voice, masking nervousness, but perhaps deeper down even a glint of steel. Now rallying, she seemed tougher than she first appeared.

"We're walking out the front gate," replied Tucker.

"Just like that?"

"As long as you can act worth a damn."

9:09 P.M.

Tucker spent a few minutes rehearsing with Anya in the main hall of the Riding House, running through what was to come. Once ready—or ready enough—he led her toward the exit door.

Before stepping back into the misty night, he reattached Kane's leash, straightened his military coat and brigade cap, then took her by the arm.

"All set?" he asked.

"This would be easier if I was *really* drunk." But she smiled and waved him on. "Let's do this."

Together, they slipped out of the Riding House and onto the boulevard. He headed immediately for the Spasskaya Tower and the main gate. He held Kane's leash in one hand, and with his other arm, he attempted to balance a struggling and stumbling Anya.

When he was thirty feet from the gated exit, the guard stepped out of his shack and called something that probably meant, "*What's going on?*"

"She was sleeping in the cadet quarters!" Tucker called out in Russian, repeating a preset phrase taught to him by Utkin for this very situation.

Anya began her performance, jabbering in Russian and generally making a fuss. Though Tucker understood none of it, he hoped the gist of her obscenity-laced tirade was what he had instructed her to say: *this guard was a thug . . . his dog stunk . . . there were no laws against sleeping in the Kremlin, let alone drinking . . . the visiting hours were much too short . . . and* that her father was the vengeful editor of the Kazan Herald.

Tucker manhandled her roughly toward the gates and yelled to the guard in another of his memorized stock phrases. "Hurry up! The police are on their way! Let's be rid of her!"

Behind them, farther down the boulevard, a voice called out to them. A glance over his shoulder revealed another K9 unit hurrying toward the commotion.

Biting back his own litany of curses, he turned and gave the approaching guard a quick wave that was meant to convey, *I've got it under control.*

Under his breath, he whispered to Kane, "Noise."

The shepherd began barking loudly, adding to the frantic confusion.

All the while, Anya never slowed her tirade.

Still, the other K9 unit closed toward them.

Improvising, Anya went red-faced and bent over double, hanging on to Tucker's arm and covering her mouth with her other hand. Her body clenched in the universal posture of someone about to toss their cookies all over the ancient cobblestones.

"Hurry up!" Tucker yelled, repeating the little Russian he knew.

Finally, turning away from the young woman about to vomit, the guard fumbled with the keys on his belt and crossed to the gate. He unlocked it and swung it open—then he waved his arm, swearing brusquely, and yelled for him to get her out of there.

Tucker hurried to obey, dragging Anya behind him.

The gate clanged closed behind them. The Kremlin K9 unit reached the exit and joined the other guard, staring after them.

Tucker waved back to the pair in a dismissive and sarcastic manner, as if to say *Thanks for leaving me to clean this mess up.*

From the ribald laughter and what sounded like Russian catcalls, his message must have translated okay.

Twenty feet from the gate, Anya started to cease her performance.

Tucker whispered to her, "Keep it up until we're out of sight."

She nodded and began shouting and tried to pull free of Tucker's grasp. He recognized the words *nyet* and *politsiya.*

No and *police.*

More laughter erupted behind him at her weak attempt at resisting arrest.

"Good job," he mumbled under his breath.

He dragged her along, angling right, until they were out of the guards' view.

Once clear, Anya stood straight and smoothed her clothes. "Should we run?"

"No. Keep walking. We don't want to draw any attention."

Still, they moved in tandem briskly and reached the forested lawn on the north side of the Church of Ascension. He pointed to the black Marussia SUV parked under a nearby tree.

They piled into the front, with Kane in the back.

Tucker started the engine, did a U-turn, and headed south. He dialed Utkin's cell phone.

"We're out. Be ready in five."

As planned, Utkin and Bukolov were waiting in the alley behind their hotel. Tucker pulled up to them, they jumped into the back with Kane, and he immediately took off.

Bukolov leaned forward to hug Anya, to kiss her cheek, tears in his eyes.

Tucker let them have their brief family reunion—then ordered everyone to keep low, out of sight. Without a glance back, he fled Kazan and headed south.

Now to get the hell out of Russia.

16

March 13, 10:42 P.M.
South of Kazan, Russia

"I can't believe you did it," Bukolov said thirty minutes later. "You really did it."

Tucker concentrated on the dark, icy road, steering the SUV south on the P240 with the heater on full blast.

"Do you think we're safe now?" Utkin asked, leaning up from the backseat, looking shell-shocked. "Everything happened so fast."

"Fast is good," said Tucker. "Smooth is better."

Truth be told, he was surprised his scheme had gone largely to plan. Still, he resisted the urge to let down his guard and relax.

The sign for a rest area flashed past his high beams. *That will do.*

Two miles south of here, they would reach a major highway junction. Before that, he wanted to do a little housekeeping. He took the ramp to the rest area, which consisted of a small bathroom and a couple of snow-mounded park benches nestled among ice-encrusted birches.

"Stretch your legs," Tucker said as he swung into a parking spot. He turned to face the others. "But first I need your cell phones, laptops, anything electronic that you're carrying."

"Why?" asked Bukolov.

Anya told him. "He thinks one of us will call someone."

"Who?" Bukolov demanded. "Who would we call?"

"It's not just that," Tucker explained. "Electronics can be tracked, even if they're not active. Hand them over."

Slowly they all complied, passing over their cell phones.

"What if one of us needs to make a call?" Anya asked.

"Then I'll arrange it," Tucker replied.

Once we're safely out of the country, and I've handed you over to Sigma.

Tucker took Kane out for a stroll and a bathroom break and let the others work some blood into their limbs after the rushed flight out of Kazan. While no one was looking, he threw all the electronic gear, including the laptops, into a creek that abutted the rest area. He kept only his own satellite phone buried in his pocket.

Ten minutes later, they were back on the road.

"What happens now?" Anya asked. "Where do we go? Are we looking for some airport?"

"We'll see," he replied cryptically, refusing to show his hand.

Tucker drove south for six hours, using the P240's relatively good condition, and put as much distance between them and Kazan as possible. Throughout the night, he headed deeper into rural farmlands, eventually crossing from one Russian *oblast* to another. At least the borders between the Russian provinces didn't have checkpoints. It would have made things much harder.

A couple of hours before dawn, Tucker reached the small town of Dimitrovgrad, a place that had never strayed far from its Soviet-era roots. He circled the major thoroughfares, looking for a hotel with the right mix of anonymity and accommodations. Discovering a suitable location, he booked adjoining rooms on the second floor, one for Anya and her father, the second for Utkin and himself. He posted Kane at the pass-door between the two rooms.

Tucker didn't want to stay in one place too long. So four hours later, he was already up and about again. He allowed the others a little more sleep and took a short stroll. He also wanted to be alone. As he drove into town last night, he had spotted an Internet café and headed over there. The place smelled of sausages and hot plastic, but at least it was empty at this hour. Five card tables bore nineties-era IBM computers, so old that the modems consisted of rubber cradles into which telephone handsets had been stuffed.

Thankfully, the proprietor, an older man who looked welded to his stool, wasn't the talkative type. Tucker deciphered the rates from a handwritten sheet on the counter and handed the fellow a hundred rubles. The man waved his arm as if to say *take your pick*.

The connection was predictably slow. He surfed several Russian newspaper websites. Using the translate feature, he found what he had been looking for—or, more accurately, what he had hoped *not* to find.

He returned to the hotel to discover both Anya and Utkin had left. Kane was sitting on the bed, watching him expectantly. A moment of frustration fired through him, but it passed quickly. He should have given Kane instructions to keep everyone in their rooms.

He shook Bukolov awake. "Where's Anya? And Utkin?"

"What?" Bukolov bolted upright in bed. "They're gone? Have they come for me?"

"Relax."

Tucker had begun to turn toward the door when it opened. Utkin and Anya stepped through. They were both carrying a cardboard tray filled with steaming Styrofoam cups.

"Where'd you go?" he snapped at them.

"To get tea," Anya replied, lifting the tray. "For everyone."

He pushed down his irritation. "Don't do it again, not without telling me."

Utkin mumbled an apology.

Anya looked embarrassed and set her tray down.

Bukolov defended his daughter, putting a protective arm around her. "Now see here, Tucker, I won't have you—"

He pointed a finger at the doctor's nose and swung it to include the others. "Once you're out of the country, you can all do as you please. Until then, you'll do as I say. Innocent blood has already been shed to get you this far, Doctor Bukolov. I won't have it wasted by stupidity. Not on anyone's part."

He stormed into the next room to cool off. Kane followed, tail low, sensing his anger.

Tucker ruffled the shepherd's fur. "It's not you. You're a good boy."

Utkin joined him, closing the door between the rooms. "I'm sorry, Tucker. I wasn't thinking."

He accepted the young man's apology, but he had another nagging question. "Were you two together the whole time?"

"Anya and I? No, not the entire time. I was up earlier than her. Went for a walk around the block. Sorry, I just needed to get out. All of this is . . . it's nerve-racking. I couldn't just sit in this quiet room while the others were sleeping."

"When did you and Anya meet up?"

He scrunched his nose in thought. "I met her in the parking lot. She had just come from the coffeehouse down the block, carrying the two trays of tea."

"Which direction was that?"

He pointed. "West."

"Did you see anyone with her? Talking to her?"

"No. You seem upset. Has something happened— something other than this, I mean?"

He sized the young man up, trying to decide if he was fabricating his side of the story or not. A liar always gave away tells, if you knew where to look. In the end, he decided his opinion of Utkin hadn't changed. He couldn't read a shred of artifice in the man's character.

Tucker explained, "I checked the Kazan news. They're reporting that Anya Malinov was kidnapped."

"Well, she was in a way."

"The reports state that she was taken from an alley outside a nightclub, by a man who killed her male companion."

Utkin sank to the bed. "Why the cover-up?"

"So they can shape events. But what strikes me as odd is that the fabricated story hit the newswires less than two hours after we left Kazan."

"That seems very fast. But does it mean something?"

"Maybe, maybe not."

"Do the reports have your description?"

"No, but by now someone is surely connecting the dots: Anya and her father and me."

"What about me?"

"They'll connect that dot, too, eventually."

Utkin paled. "That means they'll come after me once you're all gone."

"No, they won't."

"Why?"

He put a hand on the man's shoulder. "Because you're coming with us."

"What? Really?" The relief on his face gave him a puppy-dog look.

Was I ever that simple and innocent?

Tucker knew the guy needed to toughen up. "But I'm going to need you to pull your weight. Have you ever fired a gun?"

"Of course not."

"Then it's time to learn."

March 14, 9:12 A.M.

Tucker stood out on the balcony of their second-story room to get some air. He heard the pad of feet behind him and glanced over to find Anya leaning against the wall, arms crossed.

"May I speak with you?"

He shrugged.

"I'm sorry for what I did, for what my father said before . . . he was just being defensive. Protective."

"Your father is . . ." He did his best to sound diplomatic. "He's not an easy man to get along with."

"Try being his daughter."

Tucker matched her smile.

"He might not show it, but my father likes you. That's rare."

"How can you tell?"

"He doesn't ignore you. Earlier, I was just feeling boxed in. I had to get out for a while. Claustrophobic, is that the word?"

"Maybe stir-crazy?" Tucker offered.

She smiled. "This is certainly crazy. But let me ask you, why are you helping us?"

"I was asked to."

"By whom?" She immediately waved her hands. "Never mind. I should not have asked. Can you at least tell me where we are going?"

"South. With any luck, we'll make Syzran by morning. My people will meet us there."

Anya looked reassured.

"I'll drop you off at a rendezvous point in town— the Chayka Hotel. Have you thought about what you'll do once you're in the States?"

"I don't know really. I suppose that depends on what happens with my father. I have not had time to think much about it. Wherever he goes, I will go. He needs my help with his work. Where do you live?"

The question caught Tucker off guard. He had a P.O. box in Charlotte, North Carolina, but he hadn't had a permanent place to lay his head for a long time. His way of life was tough to describe to most people. He'd tried it a few times but gave up. What could he say? *I don't much like people. I travel alone with my*

*dog and do the occasional odd job. And I like it that
way.*

To shorthand the conversation now, Tucker simply
lied. "Portland, Maine."

"Is it nice there? Would I like it?"

"Do you like the ocean?"

"Yes, very much."

"Then you'd like it."

She stared wistfully across the parking lot. "I'm sure
I would."

Then you can send me a postcard and tell me about it.

He'd certainly never been there himself.

They chatted for a few more minutes, then Anya
walked back inside.

Taking advantage of the privacy, Tucker dialed
Harper. When the line clicked open, he spoke quickly.

"Tomorrow morning. Chayka Hotel in Syzran."

7:05 P.M.

With the sun fully down, the group set out again,
driving south in the darkness. Tucker took a highway
that skirted alongside the Volga River, the longest river
in Europe. Navigating from memory, he headed for
Volgograd, a city named after the river. As a precaution,
he followed a mixture of main and secondary roads.

At four in the morning, he pulled into a truck stop at the edge of the city of Balakovo. "Need a caffeine fix," he said drowsily, rubbing his eyes. "Anyone else?"

The others were half asleep. He got dismissive tired waves and irritated grunts. He headed out and returned to the SUV with a boiling cup of black coffee.

As he climbed back inside, he noted his satellite phone remained in the cup holder, where he'd left it on purpose. It appeared untouched.

Satisfied, he kept driving, covering the last hundred miles in two hours. By the time he crossed into the town of Saratov, the sun was fully up.

From the backseat, Anya roused, stretched, and looked around. "This isn't Syzran."

"No."

"I thought you said we were going to Syzran? The Chayka Hotel."

"A last-minute change of plans," he replied.

He pulled off the highway and headed to a hotel near the off-ramp.

"Won't your friends be worried?" she asked.

"Not a problem. I called them."

He turned into the parking lot and shut off the engine. Utkin stirred. Anya had to shake Bukolov awake.

Tucker climbed out. "I'll be right back with our room keys."

On his way to the lobby, his satellite phone chirped. He pulled it from his pocket and checked the screen:

No activity at the Chayka Hotel.
No activity on this phone for the past eight hours.

Satisfied, Tucker crossed through the lobby and headed toward the restroom. He relieved himself, washed his hands, finger-combed his hair, and took a breath mint from a jar near the sink. Only after five minutes did he exit the hotel and cross back to the SUV.

"No vacancies, I'm afraid," he said. "Might as well push on to Volgograd."

Utkin yawned and motioned to the new day. "I thought you told us it wasn't safe to drive during the day."

"No matter. We're pushing through."

Utkin was right. It was a risk, but with only a couple of hundred miles to go before Volgograd, it was a worthwhile gamble. And from his little test, it seemed none of his fellow travelers had taken his Chayka Hotel bait. Nor had they tried to use his phone.

So far, so good.

It seemed a safe bet to move on.

Besides, if the enemy had managed to track them, why hadn't they closed the net?

Sensing the light at the end of the tunnel, he headed out, trying to enjoy the passing scenery of this sunny morning. They were almost home free and his suspicions about Anya and the others had proven unwarranted.

Out the driver's-side window, the morning sun reflected brilliantly off the Volga River. On the other side spread rolling hills and farm tracts lying fallow under pristine blankets of snow. He rolled down the window to smell the river and fresh snow.

Everyone seemed in better spirits, talking among themselves, laughing.

"Time for a Russian history quiz," Bukolov declared merrily. "Is everyone game?"

Tucker smiled. "It's not my best subject."

"Duly noted," replied Utkin.

Anya chimed in. "Tucker, we could give you a point lead. To make it fair."

Tucker opened his mouth to reply, but the words never came out. Crossing through an intersection, he caught a glimpse of chrome, a flash of sun off a windshield, accompanied by the roar of an engine—followed by the sickening crunch of metal on metal.

Then the world rolled.

17

March 15, 8:09 A.M.
South of Saratov, Russia

With his head ringing, Tucker forced open his eyelids and searched around. It took him several seconds to register that he was hanging upside down, suspended by his seat belt, a deflated airbag waving in front of his face.

The SUV had rolled and settled onto its roof. Water poured through the vents. Improbably, the wipers were sliding across the windshield.

Groaning, he looked right and found Utkin balled up below him on the overturned ceiling, not moving. He lay face-up in about six inches of rising water.

Tucker's next worry.

Kane.

He was about to call out, to check on the others, then stopped, remembering the collision.

Someone had hit them—purposefully.

He squeezed his eyes shut and tried to think.

They'd ended up in the roadside ditch. He remembered seeing the wide drainage canal paralleling the road. The cut had looked deep—thirty feet or so—and steep sided. Though at this time of year, the bottom flowed with only a shallow creek of icy water.

He fought through gauzy thoughts to focus on two things.

First: Whoever hit them was coming.

Second: Survive.

He patted his jacket pocket. The Magnum was still there.

A splashing sounded behind him. He craned his neck and spotted a pair of furry front legs shifting through the water. He also saw Bukolov and Anya tangled and unconscious on the overturned roof. One of the woman's legs was still caught in the seat belt above.

"Kane," Tucker whispered. "Come here."

The shepherd climbed over the inert forms of Bukolov and Anya.

Fumbling, Tucker released the latch on his belt and fell as quietly as possible into the cold water. Kane joined him, bumping his nose against Tucker's cheek, giving a worried small lick.

That's my boy.

Thankfully, except for an inch-long gash above his eye, Kane seemed uninjured.

"Out," he ordered and shoved Kane toward the open driver's window. "Hide and cover."

Kane squeezed through and disappeared into the high grass covering the shadowy bank of the ditch. Tucker dove out after him. Staying low and using his elbows to propel him, Tucker dragged himself through the mud and weeds. He followed Kane's trail for ten feet up the embankment before running into the shepherd's backside.

Kane had stopped, crouched on his belly. He must have a good reason to stop. Taking a cue from the dog, he went still and listened.

Russian voices.

Two or three, farther down the canal to his left.

"Stay," Tucker whispered breathlessly to Kane.

He rolled to the right—once, twice, then a third time. He then sidled backward to the canal, putting the SUV between him and the voices. Once behind the bumper, he crouched and peeked along the vehicle's side.

Beyond the SUV, farther down the ditch, a trio of men in civilian clothes descended a shallow section of the embankment, aiming for the overturned vehicle. Each one carried a compact submachine gun—a PP-19 Bizon.

He hid away again, thinking quickly.

Something didn't make sense, jangling him with warning.

Three men, he thought. *They would be operating in pairs, which meant there had to be . . .*

Tucker risked another glance—back up toward the road.

A fourth man suddenly stepped to the highway's edge, training his Bizon down at the vehicle below.

Tucker slid back into hiding before being spotted. If the man had come a few seconds earlier, he would have caught the two exiting the SUV.

Damned lucky—but he couldn't count on such good fortune to last.

It would take skill.

He lowered to the waterline at the corner of the SUV and stuck his hands back into view, hoping the shadows there hid his signal to Kane. He placed a palm over a fist, then stuck out one finger and swung it to the right.

Stay hidden . . . move right.

He hoped Kane was watching, knowing the shepherd's sharp eyes would have no trouble discerning the movement in the darkness. It was the best he could do to communicate, especially since his partner wasn't wearing the tactical vest.

Done, Tucker shifted to the opposite corner of the bumper, farthest from the man on the road. He lowered flat to the canal, sinking to the bottom. The depth was only a foot and a half. He did his best to drape himself fully underwater. His fingers clung to weeds to help hold his belly flat. He set off with the meager current away from the SUV, heading downstream. With the morning sun still low in the sky, the steep-sided ditch lay in deep shadows, hopefully hiding his efforts. He prayed the shooter kept his focus on the SUV. Still, Tucker expected to feel rounds slam into his back at any moment.

When nothing came, he angled across the canal, to the same side as Kane and the gunman. He glided up to the bank and rolled to his back in the water. He lifted his head and blinked away the muddy residue.

Due to a slight bend in the waterway and the precipitous slope of the canal's side, the shooter on the road was out of direct view now. Closer at hand, he spotted a shifting through the grasses, coming his way, easy to miss unless looking for it.

His trick hadn't fooled Kane.

Keeping to the tallest weeds and shadows, his partner had tracked and followed him.

Like a beaching seal, Tucker slid out of the water and into the icy mud and weeds. Kane joined him. Together, they worked straight up the side of the ditch, moving as silently as possible, sticking to the thickest grasses. He heard the other three gunmen reach the SUV and start talking loudly.

He was running out of time.

He finally reached the top, peered down the road, and spotted the shooter to the left, his attention still focused on the SUV.

Tucker sank back and whispered in Kane's ear. "WAYPOINT, COVER, QUIET CLOSE, TAKE ALPHA."

He repeated the complex chain of commands.

While Kane's vocabulary was impressive, he also had an amazing ability to string together actions. In this case, Kane would need to cross the road, find cover, close the distance between himself and their target— then attack.

"Got it, buddy?" Tucker asked.

Kane bumped his nose against Tucker's. His dark eyes twinkled with his answer: *Of course I do, you stupid ass.*

"Off you go then."

Kane sweeps on silent paws across the cold pavement. On the far side, he squeezes into the deep brush, frosted brittle by the winter. He is cautious not to rattle the grasses and branches of scrub bushes. He finds the ground is a mix of ice and mud and keeps moving, slowly at first, testing the placement of each paw.

Growing confident, he moves faster.

A wind blows across the road, carrying to him the scent of his partner—as familiar as his own. It is warmth and heart and satisfaction.

He also catches a whiff of his prey ahead: the sour ripeness of unwashed flesh, the tang of gunmetal and oil, the rot of bad teeth. He fixes every slight movement with minute movements of his ears: the scuff of boot on pavement, the creak of a strap of leather, the wheeze of breath.

He moves along the edge of the road, staying hidden, weaving the darkest path.

At last, he draws even with his target. He drops low and shimmies to the road's edge, watching. The other's back is to him, but he turns every few fetid breaths to look around, even back toward where Kane hides.

Dangerous.

But the command burns behind his eyes.

He must attack.

He shifts his back legs to best advantage, firing his muscles for the charge to come. Waiting for his moment—

—then movement to the left.

His partner steps out of hiding, onto the road's shoulder. He moves wrong, tilting, stumbling. Kane knows this is false, a feigned flailing. He picks out the glint of steel held at his partner's hip, out of sight of the other.

Across the road, his target turns toward his partner and focuses fully upon him. Kane feels a surge of bone-deep approval and affection. The two are a pack, one tied to the other, working together.

With his target distracted, Kane bursts out of hiding.

Tucker stared down the barrel of the submachine gun, trying his best not to flick his gaze toward Kane, as his partner charged across the pavement.

This had been the dicey part. Much of it depended on the enemy not killing Tucker on sight. Once Kane had reached his vantage point across the road, Tucker had limped out of hiding, stumbling forward, weaving and dazed, looking like a disoriented crash victim. He held his Magnum against his thigh and kept that side turned away from the shooter.

As expected, the man had spun toward him, swinging his Bizon up.

Time slowed at that moment.

Tucker lunged forward, leading now with his Magnum.

He had to put his full faith in Kane. The pair had worked for so long together, the shepherd could read Tucker's tone and body language to infer much more than could be communicated by word or hand signal. Additionally, Kane also took in environmental cues to make astute judgments on how best to execute any orders.

All that training came to a perfect fusion now.

Kane never slowed and closed the last ten feet with a leap. Seventy pounds of war dog slammed into the man's side, and together they crashed into the dirt. Even as they landed, Kane's jaws had found their mark, closing down on his target's exposed throat with hundreds of pounds of force.

Still on the run, Tucker knee-skidded to a stop beside the man, pivoted, and fired an insurance round into the shooter's hip.

He switched the Magnum to his left hand, snatched up the Bizon with his right, and leaped over Kane. He landed on his butt in the grass and began sliding down the ditch's steep embankment.

He took in the situation below with a glance, fixing the position of the three remaining enemy combatants.

One to the left, twenty feet away . . .

One kneeling at the SUV window . . .

One standing at the bumper . . .

The grass whipped Tucker's face, and rocks slammed into his buttocks and thighs. As he plummeted, he aimed the Magnum at the man beside the bumper and opened fire, squeezing the trigger over and over again. His first shot went wide, the second caught the man in the leg, and the third in the sternum.

One down.

Tucker turned his attention next to the kneeling man, who lay directly below him. He tried to bring the Bizon to bear, but he was sliding too quickly and hit the bottom of the embankment first.

At the last moment, he kicked out with his legs and flew, body-slamming the second man against the side of the SUV. Pain burst behind his eyes—but he had the other pinned, now underwater. A blind hand rose and slapped at him, fingers clawing. Then a mud-covered face pushed out, gasping, coughing. As the man tried to gulp air, Tucker shouldered his face back underwater.

He held him down, while he swung his Bizon and pointed it toward the far side of the SUV. The third enemy appeared, still about ten feet beyond the SUV, out in the open. Tucker fired a burst of rounds. His aim was wild, but it forced the other back out of sight.

By now, the man under him had stopped struggling, drowned.

Tucker crouched up, certain the last man would come charging at him.

Nothing came for a full five count.

He heard rustling in the grass and looked up to see Kane picking his way down the embankment.

With his partner coming, Tucker sidled along the edge of the SUV and took a fast look past its bumper.

The last man was stumbling away, his back to Tucker. The Bizon hung loosely from his right hand. His feet splashed heavily in the water. Out in the open, he knew he was defeated.

"Damn it," Tucker muttered.

He couldn't let the man go, but he refused to shoot a victim in the back.

"*Stoj!*" he hollered and fired a burst into the air. *Stop!*

The man obeyed, but he didn't turn around. Instead, he dropped to his knees and threw his weapon to the side. He placed his hands on top of his head.

Kane reached him, but Tucker held him back.

"Stay, pal."

Tucker walked down the ditch to where the man was kneeling. He realized the *man* was a *boy* of about nineteen or twenty.

"Turn around," he ordered.

"I will tell no one," the boy begged in heavily accented English.

Yes, you will. Even if you don't want to, they'll make you.

Tucker was suddenly tired, spent to his core. "Turn around."

"*Nyet.*"

"Turn around."

"*NYET!*"

Tucker swallowed hard and raised the Bizon. "I'm sorry."

18

As ugly as the Marussia SUV had been, Tucker had no complaints about the vehicle. In the end, it had saved their lives.

That, and the soft mud at the bottom of the ditch.

Tucker turned his back on the overturned vehicle. The others wobbled along the shoulder of the road. After extracting them from the SUV and doing a quick triage, he managed to rouse Utkin, who helped him with Anya and Bukolov.

In all, the group had sustained bruises and a smattering of cuts and abrasions. Bukolov suffered the worst, with a dislocated shoulder and a slight concussion.

Tucker had managed to pop the old man's shoulder back into place while the doctor was still asleep. The concussion would take time and rest.

But now was *not* the time to stop moving.

Tucker led them to their new car, their attackers' dark blue Peugeot 408. Aside from a dent in the front bumper, the sedan remained unscathed. Whoever had rammed them off the road knew what they were doing. Tucker searched the car for transmitters or GPS units but found none.

As Anya helped Bukolov into the car, Utkin pulled him aside.

"What is it?" Tucker asked, wanting to get moving.

Utkin acted rather furtive. "You'd better see this."

He slipped a cell phone into Tucker's hand. It was the only phone they had found amid the attackers' possessions.

"Look at the photo I found in the digital memory."

Tucker squinted at a grainy image of himself on the screen. He was seated at a computer workstation, his hands frozen in midair over the keyboard. With a sinking feeling in his gut, he recognized the location. It was that dingy Internet café in Dimitrovgrad.

Someone had taken a picture of me.

Not knowing what to make of it, Tucker e-mailed the photo to his own phone, then deleted the original.

He scrolled to the phone's address book and found it empty; same with the recent calls. It had been sanitized. Frustrated, Tucker removed the phone's battery case and SIM card and crushed them both with his heel. He crossed the road and threw the remains down into the ditch.

He took a moment to consider the meaning of the photo. Clearly someone had been covertly following them. But how? And who? He glanced to the overturned SUV. Could there have been a hidden tracer planted on the Marussia?

He didn't know . . . couldn't know.

In fact, there were far too many unknowns.

He faced Utkin. "Have you shown the others this photo?"

"No."

"Good. Let's keep this between us for now."

A few minutes later, they were again racing south along the Volga River.

Aside from a desire to get off the main road and put some distance between themselves and the ambush site, Tucker had no immediate plan. After ten miles, he turned off the highway and onto a dirt road that led to a park overlooking the Volga. He pulled in and everyone climbed out.

Utkin and Anya helped Bukolov to a nearby picnic table.

Tucker walked to the rocky bluff above the thick-flowing river. He sat down, needing to think, to regroup. He let his legs dangle over the edge and listened to the wind whistle through the skeletal trees. Kane trotted over and plopped down beside him. Tucker rested his hand on the shepherd's side.

"How're you feeling, buddy?"

Kane thumped his tail.

"Yeah, I'm okay, too."

Mostly.

He had cleaned the gash on Kane's head, but he wondered about any psychic damage. There was no way of knowing how the shepherd felt about killing that man on the road. His partner had killed in combat before, and it seemed to have no lasting impact on him. While for Tucker, that particular onion was more layered. After Abel's death, after leaving the service, Tucker had come to appreciate certain parts of the Buddhist philosophy, but he knew he'd never match Kane's Zen mind-set, which, if put into words, would probably be something like *Whatever has happened, has happened.*

As he sat, he was torn between the instinct to run hard for Volgograd, and his desire to take it slow and cautious. Still, many things troubled him. It was why he had stopped here.

Four men, he thought. *Why only four?*

Back at the ambush site, he had checked them for identification and found nothing but driver's licenses and credit cards. But the tattoos they bore confirmed them as Spetsnaz. So why hadn't the enemy landed on them with overwhelming force? Where were the platoon of men and helicopters like back at Nerchinsk?

Somehow this current action reeked of *rogue* ops. Perhaps someone in the Russian Ministry of Defense was trying to snatch Bukolov without the knowledge of their bosses. But for now, that wasn't the most pressing question concerning Tucker.

He knew the ambush couldn't have been a chance accident.

So how did the enemy know where to find them?

He pictured the photo found on the phone.

What did that mean?

Utkin joined him, taking a seat at the bluff's edge. "Good view, yes?"

"I'd prefer to be staring at the Statue of Liberty."

That got a chuckle out of Utkin. "I would like to see that, too. I've never been to America."

"Let's hope I can get you there."

"So have you figured out a plan? Where to go from here?"

"I know we have to reach Volgograd."

"But you're worried about another ambush."

It didn't require an answer.

Changing the subject, Utkin waved an arm to encompass the river and region. "Did you know I grew up around here?"

Actually Tucker did. He'd read it from the man's dossier, but he remained silent, sensing Utkin wanted to talk, reminisce.

"It was a tiny village, along the river, about fifty miles south. My grandfather and I used to fish the Volga when I was a boy."

"It sounds like a nice childhood."

"It was, thank you. But I meant to make a point. You wish to reach Volgograd, yes?"

Tucker glanced over to him, crinkling his forehead.

"And you wish to stay off the highway," Utkin said.

"That would be good."

"Well, there is another way." Utkin pointed his arm toward the river below. "It worked for thousands of years. It can work for us now."

11:01 A.M.

Tucker had one last piece of business to address before moving on. He asked Anya to stay with Bukolov at the park. He instructed Kane to guard them. For this last chore, he needed Utkin's help.

Climbing back into the Peugeot, Tucker headed out into the tangle of the remote river roads. He followed Utkin's directions. It took less than an hour to find the abandoned farmhouse tucked away in a forest.

"This was once part of an old collective," Utkin explained. "It's at least a hundred and fifty years."

Tucker used the remote to pop the trunk.

They both stared down at the bound figure inside, his mouth secured with duct tape. He was the last of those who had ambushed them, the boy of nineteen or twenty.

"Why did you let him live?" Utkin whispered.

Tucker wasn't exactly sure. He simply couldn't execute someone in cold blood. Instead, he had clubbed the kid with the butt of his gun, bound him up, and tossed him in the trunk.

The boy stared at Tucker and Utkin with wide eyes. They pulled him out and marched him toward the farmhouse. Utkin opened the front door, which shrieked on its hinges.

The interior was what Tucker had imagined: knotty plank walls and floors, boarded-up windows, low ceilings, and layers of dust on every surface.

Tucker pushed the boy inside and sat him down on the floor. He peeled the tape from the boy's mouth.

"Can you translate?" he asked Utkin.

"Are you going to interrogate him?"

Tucker nodded.

Utkin backed up a step. "I don't want to be a part of any—"

"Not that kind of interrogation. Ask him his name."

Utkin cooperated and got an answer.

"It's Istvan."

Tucker took the boy through a series of benign personal questions designed to massage his defenses. After five minutes, the kid's posture relaxed, his rat-in-a-cage expression fading.

Tucker waved to Utkin. "Tell him I have no plans to kill him. If he cooperates, I'll call the local police and tell them where to find him."

"He's relieved, but he says you must beat him. For effect. Otherwise, his superiors will—"

"I understand. Ask him his unit."

"It's Spetsnaz, like you thought. But he and his team had been assigned to the Russian military intelligence."

"The GRU?"

"That's right."

The same as the Spetsnaz at Nerchinsk.

"Who did his unit report to at the GRU?"

"A general named Kharzin. Artur Kharzin."

"And what was their job?"

"To track down Bukolov. His group was told to intercept our car here."

"By Kharzin."

"Yes, the order came from Kharzin."

This guy must be one of Bukolov's mysterious Arzamas generals.

"And once they got hold of the doctor?" Tucker asked. "What were they to do?"

"Return him to Moscow."

"Why does General Kharzin want him?"

"He doesn't know."

Tucker pulled out his cell phone and showed the grainy image from the Internet café to their captive. "How and when did you get this?"

"By e-mail," Utkin translated. "Yesterday afternoon."

"How did they know where to intercept us?"

Utkin shook his head. "He was just given the order."

"Do you believe him?"

"Yes, I think so."

"Let's find out."

Abruptly, Tucker pulled the Magnum from his jacket pocket and pressed it against the boy's right kneecap. "Tell him I don't believe him. He needs to tell me *why* Kharzin wants Bukolov."

Utkin translated Tucker's demand.

Istvan started jabbering, white-faced and trembling.

"He says he doesn't know," Utkin blurted, almost as scared as the kid. "Something about a plant or flower. A discovery of some kind. A weapon. He swears on the life of his son."

Tucker kept the Magnum pressed against the guy's kneecap.

Utkin whispered, "Tucker, he has a son."

Tucker did his best to keep his face stony. "A lot of people have sons. He's going to have to give me a better reason than that. Tell him to think hard. Has he forgotten anything?"

"Like what!"

"Is there anyone else after us? Anyone besides the GRU?"

Utkin questioned the boy, pressing him hard. Finally, he turned and stammered, "He says there's a woman. She is helping Kharzin."

"A woman?"

"Someone with blond hair. He only saw her once. He doesn't know her name, but he believes that she was hired by Kharzin as some sort of mercenary or assassin."

Tucker pictured Felice Nilsson. She was old news. "Go on. Tell him I already know about—"

"He says after they pulled her from the river, she was taken to a hospital."

Tucker felt as though he'd been punched in the stomach.

"Has he seen her since?"

"No."

Could she truly have survived?

He remembered the strong current, the icy water. He pictured Felice swimming or being pulled along by the flow, maybe finding a break in the ice, maybe radioing for rescue. If the Spetsnaz had found Felice quickly enough, there was a slight chance she could have made it.

Tucker took the Magnum away from Istvan's knee and shoved it into his jacket pocket. The boy leaned back, gasping with relief.

Tucker was done here. As he turned away, he imagined that cunning huntress coming after him again, but he felt no fear, only certainty.

I killed you once, Felice. If I have to, I'll do it again.

19

Back in the Peugeot, Tucker continued working his way south, staying off the main road. Utkin's knowledge of the area came in very handy as he pointed to rutted tracks and cow paths that weren't on any map.

Anya broke the exhausted silence and expressed a fear she had clearly been harboring. "What did you do with the young man from the trunk?"

"Are you asking me if I killed him?" Tucker said.

"I suppose I am."

"He'll be fine."

Conditionally, he added silently. They had left Istvan duct-taped to a post at the old farmhouse.

His parting words to the kid had been clear: *This is your one free pass. Appear on the field of battle again and I'll kill you.*

"Please tell me you didn't hurt him."

"I didn't hurt him."

Tucker glanced at her in the rearview mirror. Her blue eyes stared back at him in the reflection.

She finally turned away. "I believe you."

Following Utkin's directions, Tucker drove south for another thirty miles, reaching a farming community near the Volga's banks.

"The village of Shcherbatovka," Utkin announced.

If you say so . . .

Half the buildings were either boarded up or looked abandoned. At the far end, a narrow dirt road led in a series of sharp switchbacks from the top of a bluff to a dock that hugged the river.

They all unloaded at the foot of the pier, a ramshackle structure of oil-soaked pylons and gap-toothed wooden planks.

Utkin waved to a man seated in a lawn chair at the end. Floating listlessly beside him was what looked to be a rust-streaked houseboat. Or maybe *tent* boat was the better description. A blue tarpaulin stretched over the flat main deck.

Utkin talked with the man for a few minutes then returned to the car.

"He can take us to Volgograd. It will cost five thousand rubles, not including the fuel."

The price wasn't Tucker's concern. "Can we trust him?"

"My friend, these people do not have telephones, televisions, or radios. Unless our pursuers plan to visit every fisherman personally between Saratov and Volgograd, I think we are safe. Besides, the people here do not like the government. Any government."

"Fair enough."

"In addition, I know this man well. He is a friend of my uncle. His name is Vadim. If you are in agreement, he says we can leave at nightfall."

Tucker nodded. "Let's do it."

After storing their gear in the storage shed of Vadim's boat, Tucker drove the Peugeot back toward Shcherbatovka. A mile past the village, following Utkin's crude map, he reached a deep tributary to the Volga. He drove to the edge, put the car in neutral before turning it off, and climbed out.

Kane followed him, stretching, while searching the woods to either side.

Tucker quickly tossed the keys into the creek, got behind the car, and shouldered it into the water. He waited until the Peugeot sank sullenly out of view.

He then turned to Kane.

"Feel like a walk?"

8:30 P.M.

Captain Vadim stood on the dock, a glowing stub of a cigar clenched between his back molars. The stocky, hard man, with a week of beard scruff and hardly more stubble across his scalp, stood a head shorter than any of them. Though it was already growing colder following sunset, he wore only a shirt and a pair of stained jeans.

He waved Tucker and the others toward a plank that led from the pier to his boat. He grumbled something that Tucker took as *Welcome aboard.*

Anya helped Bukolov tiptoe warily across the gangplank. Kane trotted across next, followed by Tucker and Utkin.

Vadim yanked the mooring lines, hopped aboard, and pulled the gangplank back to the boat's deck. He pointed to an outhouse-like structure that led below to the cabins and spoke rapidly.

Utkin grinned. "He says the first-class accommodations are below. Vadim has a sense of humor."

If you could call it that, Tucker thought.

"I should take my father to his cabin," Anya said. "He still needs some rest."

Bukolov did look exhausted, still compromised by his concussion. He slapped at Anya's hands as she tried to help him.

"Father, behave."

"Quit calling me that! Makes me sound like an invalid. I can manage."

Despite his grousing, he allowed himself to be helped below.

Tucker turned to find Kane standing at the blunted bowsprit, his nose high, taking in the scents.

That's a happy dog.

To the west, the sun had set behind the bluffs. The afternoon's brisk wind had died to a whisper, leaving the surface of the Volga calm. Still, underneath the surface, sluggish brown water swirled and eddied.

The Volga's currents were notoriously dangerous.

Utkin noted his attention. "Don't fall in. Vadim has no life rings. Also Vadim does not swim."

"Good to know."

With everyone aboard, Vadim hopped onto the afterdeck and took his place behind the wheel. With a rumble, the diesel engine started. Black smoke gushed from the exhaust manifolds. The captain steered the bow into the current, and they were off.

"How long to Volgograd?" Tucker asked.

Utkin glanced back to Vadim. "He says the current is faster than normal, so about ten hours or so."

Tucker joined Kane, and after twenty minutes, Anya returned topside.

She stepped over to him. Chilled, she tugged her wool jacket tighter around her body, unconsciously accentuating her curves.

"How's your father doing?" he asked.

"Finally sleeping."

Together, they stared at the dark shoreline slipping past. Stars glinted crisply in the clear skies. Something brushed Tucker's hand. He looked down to find Anya's index finger resting atop his hand.

She noticed it and pulled her hand away, curling it in her lap. "Sorry, I did not mean to—"

"No problem," he replied.

Tucker heard footsteps on the deck behind them. He turned as Utkin joined them at the rail.

"That's where I grew up," the man said, pointing downstream toward a set of lights along the west bank. "The village of Kolyshkino."

Anya turned to him, surprised. "Your family were farmers? Truly?"

"Fishermen actually."

"Hmm," she said noncommittally.

Still, Tucker heard—and he was sure Utkin did, too—the slight note of disdain in her question and response. It was an echo of Bukolov's similar blind condescension of the rich for the poor. Such sentiment had clearly come to bias Bukolov's view of Utkin as a fellow colleague. Whether Anya truly felt this way, Tucker didn't know, but parents often passed on their prejudices to their children.

Tucker considered his own upbringing. While his folks had died too young, some of his antisocial tendencies likely came from his grandfather, a man who lived alone on a ranch and was as stoic and cold as a North Dakota winter. Still, his grandfather treated his cattle with a surprisingly warm touch, managing the animals with an unusual compassion. It was a lesson that struck Tucker deeply and led to many stern conversations with his grandfather about animal husbandry and responsibility.

In the end, perhaps it was only natural to walk the path trod by those who came before us. Still . . .

After a time, Anya drifted away and headed below to join her father.

"I'm sorry about that," Tucker mumbled.

"It is not your fault," Utkin said softly.

"I'm still sorry."

9:22 P.M.

Belowdecks, Tucker lounged in what passed for the mess hall of the boat. It was simple and clean, with lacquered pine paneling, several green leatherette couches, and a small kitchenette, all brightly lit by bulkhead sconces.

Except for the captain, everyone had eventually wandered here, seeking the comfort of community. Even Bukolov joined them, looking brighter after his nap, more his old irascible self.

Tucker passed out snacks and drinks, including some jerky he'd found for Kane. The shepherd sat near the ladder, happily gnawing on a chunk.

Eventually, Tucker sat across from Bukolov and placed his palms on the dining table. "Doctor, it's high time we had another chat."

"About what? You're not going to threaten us again, are you? I won't stand for that."

"What do you know about Artur Kharzin, a general tied to Russian military intelligence?"

"I don't know anything about him. Should I?"

"He's the one hunting us. Kharzin seems to think your work involves biological weapons. So convinced, in fact, he's ordered all of us killed—except you, of course." He turned to Anya. "What do you make of all of this?"

"You'll have to ask my father." She crossed her arms. "This is his discovery."

"Then let's start with a simpler question. Who are you?"

"You know who I am."

"I know who you *claim* to be, but I also know you've been pumping me for information since we met. You're very good at it, actually, but not good enough."

Actually he wasn't as confident on this last point as he pretended to be. While Anya had asked a lot of questions, such inquiries could just as easily be born of innocent curiosity and concern for her father.

"Why are you doing this?" Anya shot back. "I thought such suspicions were settled back in Dimitrovgrad."

"And then we were ambushed. So tell me what I want to know—or I can take this discussion with your father in private. He won't like that."

She stared with raw-eyed concern and love toward Bukolov. Then with a shake of her head, she touched her father's forearm, moving her hand down to his hand. She gripped it tightly, possessively.

Bukolov finally placed his hand over hers. "It's okay. Tell him."

Anya looked up at him, her eyes glassy with tears. "I'm not his daughter."

Tucker had to force the shock not to show on his face. That wasn't the answer he had been expecting.

"My name is Anya Malinov, but I'm not Doctor Bukolov's daughter."

"But why lie about it?" Tucker asked.

Anya glanced away, looking ashamed. "I suggested this ruse to Abram. I thought, if he told you that I was his daughter, you would be more inclined to take me with you."

"You must understand," Bukolov stressed. "Anya is critical to my work. I could not risk your refusing to bring her along."

No wonder this part of the plan was kept from Harper.

"But I meant what I said before," Bukolov pressed. "Anya is critical to my work."

"And what is that *work*? I'm done with these lies. I want answers."

Bukolov finally caved. "I suppose you have earned an explanation. But this is very complicated. You may not understand."

"Try me."

"Very well. What do you know about earth's primordial history? Specifically about plant life that would have existed, say, seven hundred million years ago?"

"Absolutely nothing."

"Understandable. For many decades, a hypothesis has been circulating in scientific communities about something called LUCA—Last Universal Common Ancestor. Essentially we're talking about the earth's first multicellular plant. In other words, the *seed* or genesis for each and every plant that has ever existed on the earth. If LUCA is real—and I believe it is—it is the progenitor of every plant form on this planet, from tomatoes and orchids, to dandelions and Venus flytraps."

"You used the word hypothesis, not theory," said Tucker. "No one has ever encountered LUCA before?"

"Yes and no. I'll get to that shortly. But first consider stem cells. They are cells that hold the potential to become any other cell in the human body if coaxed just right. A blank genetic slate, so to speak. By manipulating stem cells, scientists have been able to grow an ear on a mouse's back. They've grown an entire liver in a laboratory, as if from thin air. I think you can appreciate the significance of such a line of research. Stem cell research is already a multibillion-dollar industry. And will only escalate. It is the future of medicine."

"Go on."

"To simplify it to the basics, I believe LUCA is to plant life what stem cells are to animal life. But why is that important? I'll give you an example. Say someone discovers a new form of flower in Brazil that treats prostate cancer. But the rain forests are almost gone. Or the flower is almost extinct. Or maybe the drug is prohibitively expensive to synthesize. With LUCA, those problems vanish. With LUCA, you simply carbon-copy the plant in question."

Bukolov grew more animated and grandiose. "Or, better yet, you use LUCA to replenish the rain forest itself. Or use LUCA in combination with, say, soybeans, to turn barren wastelands into arable land. Do you see the potential now?"

Tucker leaned back. "Let me make sure I understand. If you're right, LUCA can replicate *any* plant life because in the beginning, it *was* all plant life. It's as much of a genetic blank slate as stem cells."

"Yes, yes. I also believe it can *accelerate* growth. LUCA is not just a replicator species, but a *booster* as well."

Anya nodded, chiming in. "We can make flora hardier. Imagine potatoes or rice that could thrive where only cacti could before."

"All this sounds great, but didn't you say this was all an unproven hypothesis?"

"It is," Bukolov said, his eyes glinting. "But not for much longer. I'm about to change the world."

20

March 15, 9:50 P.M.
The Volga River, Russia

Tucker turned the conversation from world-changing scientific discoveries to more practical questions. Like why someone was trying to kill them?

"Back to this General Kharzin," Tucker said.

"Since we are done with the lies," Bukolov said, "I *do* know him. Not personally, just by reputation. I'm sorry. I do not trust people easily. It took me many months before I even told Anya about LUCA."

"What do you know about him? What's his reputation?"

"In a word. He's a monster. Back in the eighties, Kharzin was in charge of Arzamas-16, outside of

Kazan. After that military weapons research facility was shut down, its archives were transferred to the Institute of Biochemistry and Biophysics in Kazan."

"And then, years later they were moved into storage vaults at the Kazan Kremlin," Anya added.

"All along, Kharzin was a true believer in LUCA—though his scientists called it something different back then. But he only saw its destructive potential."

"Which is?"

"What you must understand, the primordial world was once a much harsher place. In its original habitat, such a life-form would have been highly aggressive. It would have to be to survive. If let loose today, with no defenses against it, I believe—as did Kharzin—that it would be *unstoppable*."

Tucker was beginning to see the danger.

Bukolov continued. "LUCA's primary purpose is to hijack nearby plant cells and modify them to match its own, so it can reproduce—rapidly, much like a virus. It has the potential to be the world's most deadly and relentless invasive species."

Tucker understood how this could easily become a weapon. If released upon an enemy, it could wipe out the country's entire agricultural industry, devastating the land without a single shot being fired.

"So how far along are you with this research?" he asked. "You and Kharzin?"

"In the past, we've been running parallel lines of research, trying to reverse-engineer plant life to create LUCA or a LUCA-like organism in the lab. My goal was to better the world. His was to turn LUCA into a weapon. But we both ran into *two* problems."

"Which were what?"

"First, neither of us could create a viable specimen that was stable. Second, neither of us could figure out how to control such a life-form if we succeeded."

Tucker nodded. "For Kharzin, his biological bomb needed an *off* switch."

"Without it, he wouldn't be able to control it. He couldn't safely use it as a weapon. If it is released without safeguards in place, LUCA runs the risk of spreading globally, wiping out ecosystem after ecosystem. In the end, it could pose as much risk to Russia as Kharzin's enemies."

"So what suddenly changed?" Tucker asked. "What set this manhunt in motion? Why do you need to leave Russia so suddenly?"

Clearly the old impasse between the two of them had broken.

"Because I believe I know where to *find* a sample of LUCA . . . or at least its closest descendant."

Tucker nodded. "And Kharzin learned of your discovery. He came after you."

"I could not let him get to it first. You understand that, yes?"

He did. "But where is this sample? How did you learn about it?"

"From Paulos de Klerk. The answer has been under our noses for over a century."

Tucker remembered Bukolov's story about the Boer botanist, about his journals being prized throughout the academic world.

"You see, over the years, I've managed to collect portions of his diaries and journals. Most of it in secret. Not an easy process as the man created great volumes of papers and accounts, much of it scattered and lost or buried in unprocessed archives. But slowly I was able to start collating the most pertinent sections. Like those last papers Anya smuggled out of the Kremlin."

Tucker pictured the giant Prada bag clutched to her chest.

"He kept a diary for decades, from the time he was a teenager until he died. Most of it is filled with the mundane details of life, but there was one journal— during the Second Boer War—that described a most fascinating and frightening observation. From the few drawings I could find, from his detailed research notes, I was sure he had discovered either a cluster of living

LUCA or something that acted just like the hypothetical life-form."

"Why do you think that?"

"It wasn't just me. In one page I found at a museum in Amsterdam, he described his discovery as *die oorsprong van die lewe*. In Afrikaans, that means *the origin of life*."

"So what became of this sample? Where did he find it?"

"Some cave in the Transvaal. Someplace he and his Boer unit retreated to. They were pinned down there by British forces. It was during this siege that De Klerk found the cluster of LUCA. As a botanist and medical doctor, he was understandably intrigued. I don't have the complete story about what happened in that cave. It's like reading a novel with half the pages missing. But he hints at some great misery that befell their forces."

"What happened to him?"

"Sadly, he would die in that cave, killed as the siege broke. The British troops eventually returned his belongings, including his journals and diary, to his widow. But past that we know nothing. I'm still studying the documents Anya found. Perhaps some of the blanks will be filled in."

"Is there any indication that De Klerk understood what he found?"

"No, not fully," Anya replied. "But in the papers I was collecting when you came for me in the Kremlin, he finally named his discovery: *Die Apokalips Saad.*"

"The Apocalypse Seed," Bukolov translated. "Whatever he found scared him, but he was also intrigued. Which explains his map."

"What map?"

"To the location of the cave. It's encrypted in his diary. I suspect De Klerk hoped he'd survive the siege and have a chance to return later to continue his research. Sadly that wasn't to be."

"And you have this map?"

"I do."

"Where?"

Bukolov tapped his skull. "In here. I burned the original."

Tucker gaped at the doctor.

No wonder everyone is after you.

10:18 P.M.

After the discussion, Tucker needed some fresh air to clear his head.

He and Kane stepped up on deck and waved to Vadim, who continued to man the boat's wheel. In return, he got a salute with the glowing tip of his cigar.

Settled into the bow, Tucker listened to the waves slap the hull and stared longingly at the pinpricks of lights marking homes and farmsteads, life continuing simply. He considered calling Ruth Harper. But after all that had happened, he was wary. His satellite phone was supposed to be secure, but was any communication truly safe? He decided to err on the side of caution until he got to Volgograd.

Footsteps sounded behind him. Kane stirred, then settled again.

"May I join you?" Anya asked.

Tucker gestured to the deck beside him. She sat down, then scooted away a few inches. "I'm sorry we lied to you," she said.

"Water under the boat."

"Don't you mean under the bridge?"

"Context," Tucker said, getting a nervous laugh out of the woman. "It's nice to see that."

"Me laughing? I'll have you know, I laugh all the time. You just haven't seen me at my best as of late." She hesitated. "And I'm afraid I'm about to make that worse."

He glanced over to her. "What is it?"

"Do you promise not to shoot me or throw me off the boat?"

"I can't promise that. But out with it, Anya. I've had enough surprises for one day."

"I'm SVR," she said.

Tucker blew his breath out slowly, trying to wrap his head around this.

"It stands for—"

"I know what it stands for."

Sluzhba Vneshney Razvedki. It was Russia's Foreign Intelligence Service, their equivalent of the CIA.

"Agent or officer?" he asked.

"Agent. For the last six years. But I do have a degree in biochemistry. That's real enough. It's why they sent me."

"Sent you to get close to Bukolov."

"Yes."

"And you're pretty," Tucker added. "Perfect bait for the older, widowed professor."

"It was never like that," Anya snapped. "They told me to seduce him if necessary, but I . . . I couldn't do it. Besides, it proved unnecessary. The doctor is consumed with his work. My interest and aid was enough to gain his trust."

Tucker decided he believed her. "What was the SVR after? LUCA?"

"No, not exactly. We knew Abram was working on something important. That he was close to a breakthrough. And given who he is, they wanted to know more about what he was working on."

"And now they do," Tucker replied. "When are they coming? Where's the ambush point?"

"That's just it. They're *not* coming. I've strung them along. Believe this or not, but I believe in what he is doing. When I found out what he was trying to accomplish, I changed my mind. I'm still a scientist at heart. He genuinely wants to use LUCA for *good.* Months ago, I decided I wasn't about to hand over something that important. Since then I've been feeding my superiors false information."

"Does Bukolov know?"

"No. It is a distraction he does not need. Completing his work must come first."

"What do you know about Kharzin?"

"This is the first I've heard of his involvement here, but I do know his reputation. He's ruthless, very old school, surrounds himself with like-minded ideologues. All Soviet hard-liners."

"What about your superiors? Have you been in contact with them since I got you out of the Kremlin?"

"No. You took our phones."

"What about in Dimitrovgrad . . . when you disappeared?"

"Tea," Anya replied. "I really was just getting tea. I didn't break communication silence, I swear."

"Why should I believe you? About any of this?"

"I can't offer any concrete proof. But ask yourself this: If I were still in contact with the SVR and my loyalties had not changed, why aren't they *here*?"

Tucker conceded her argument was solid.

"My real name is Anya Averin. You can have your superiors confirm what I'm saying. When we reach Volgograd, turn me over to your people. Let them debrief me. I've told you the truth!" Anya's voice took on a pleading but determined tone. "Only Abram knows where De Klerk's cave is. He never told me. Ask him. Once you get Abram out of the country and under U.S. protection, LUCA is safe from everyone—the SVR, General Kharzin—all of them."

Tucker stared across the waters at the small slumbering homesteads along the banks, free of such skullduggery. How did spies live in this world and keep their sanity?

"What are you going to do?" Anya asked.

"I'll keep your secret from Bukolov for now, but only until we reach the border."

She gave him a nod of thanks. For a second, he considered throwing her overboard anyway, but quashed the impulse.

After she left, Tucker grabbed a sleeping bag and a blanket and found a nook on the boat's forecastle.

Kane curled up on the blanket and closed his eyes. Tucker tried to do the same but failed.

He stared at the passing view, watched the moonrise above the banks. Kane had a dream, making soft noises and twitching his back legs.

Tucker tried to picture their destination.

Volgograd.

He knew the city's infamous history, when it used to be called Stalingrad. During World War II, a major battle occurred there between the German Wehrmacht and the Soviet Red Army. It lasted five months, leaving Stalingrad in rubble and two million dead or wounded.

And that's where I hope to find salvation.

No wonder he couldn't sleep.

21

March 16, 6:05 A.M.
The Volga River, Russia

With sunrise still two hours away, the river remained dark, mottled with patches of fog, but a distant glow rising ahead, at the horizon line, marked their approach toward Volgograd. As they motored along the current, the lights of the city slowly appeared, spreading across the banks of the river to either side, then spilling out into the surrounding steppes.

Tucker checked his watch, then retrieved his satellite phone and dialed Sigma. Once Harper was on the line, Tucker brought her up to speed about everything, including Anya's confession from last night.

"I'll look into her," Harper promised.

"We should be in the city proper in another hour or so. What do you have waiting for us?"

Harper hesitated a moment. "Try to keep an open mind about this."

"Whenever a sentence starts that way, I get nervous."

"What do you know about ecotourism?"

"Next to nothing."

"Well, that area of Russia has become something of a mecca for it—especially the Volga. Apparently the huge river is home to plant and animal life that's found in few other places. Consequently, a cottage business has sprung up in Volgograd—submarine ecotours."

"You're kidding. The Russians don't strike me as the ecofriendly type."

"Still, at last count, there are eleven companies that offer such tours. They make up a fleet of about forty electric minisubs. Each holds six passengers and one pilot. With a depth rating of thirty feet. Aside from conducting monthly safety checks, the government is hands-off. The subs come and go as they please."

"I like the sound of that."

Tucker could guess the rest. Sigma must have found a tour company that was strapped for cash and was willing to take a private party on an *extended* tour of the Volga.

After she passed on the details, Tucker hung up and went aft to speak with Vadim.

"Do you speak English?" Tucker asked.

"Yes. Some. If speak slow."

Tucker explained as best he could, much of it involving pantomiming. He should have woken Utkin to help with the translation.

But finally Vadim grinned and nodded. "Ah! The Volga-Don canal. Yes, I know it. I find the boat you meet. Three hours, *da?*"

"*Da.*"

"We make it. No worry. You and dog go now."

It seemed Tucker had been dismissed. He went below to find everyone awake and eating a simple breakfast of tea, black bread, and hard cheese.

Bukolov asked, "So, Tucker, what is your plan? How are you going to get me out of the country?"

"It's all been arranged." He held off mentioning the unusual means of transportation—not because of fear that the information might leak to the wrong ears, but simply to avoid a mutiny. Instead, he bucked up as much confidence as he could muster and said, "We're almost home free."

8:13 A.M.

Ninety minutes later, Vadim called down the ladder, "We are here."

Tucker led the group topside, where they found the world had been whitewashed away, swallowed by a thick, dense fog. To the east the sun was a dull disk in the overcast sky. All around, out of the mists, buoys clanged and horns blew. Flowing dark shadows marked passing boats, gliding up and down the Volga.

Vadim had them anchored near the shore, the engine in neutral.

"It is eerie, all this fog," Anya said.

"But good for us, yes?" Bukolov asked.

Tucker nodded.

Vadim resumed his post at the wheel and said something to Utkin.

"He says your friends are late."

Tucker checked his watch. "Not by much. They'll be here."

They stood in the fog, not talking, waiting.

Then an engine with an angry pitch grew louder, coming toward them. A moment later, the sharp nose of a speedboat glided out of the fog off the port bow. The speedboat drew abeam and a gaff hook appeared and latched on to their gunwale.

With a hand on his pocketed Magnum, Tucker crossed to the port side and cautiously peeked over the rail.

A bald, round-faced man with two gold front teeth smiled and handed a slip of paper up to Tucker. Nine alphanumeric characters had been scrawled on it. Tucker checked them carefully, then handed across his own slip of paper with a similar string of symbols, which the stranger studied before nodding.

It was a coded means of verifying each other, arranged by Harper.

"You are Tucker?" the man asked.

"I am. That must mean you are Misha?"

He got another gold-tinged smile, and Misha stepped back and waved his hand to the speedboat. "Thank you for choosing Wild Volga Tours."

Tucker collected the others, paid Vadim, then herded everyone onto the other boat.

Misha eyed Kane skeptically as Tucker hauled him down.

"Is he wolf?"

"He thinks so sometimes. But he's well trained."

And all the more dangerous for it, Tucker added silently.

His reassurance seemed to satisfy the boatman. "Come. Follow me."

They set off into the fog, seeming to go much faster than was wise considering the visibility. They wove in and around the river traffic. Even Tucker found himself clinging tightly to one of the boat's handgrips.

Finally, the engine changed pitch, and the boat slowed. Misha angled toward shore, and a dock appeared out of the mist. He eased them alongside the tire bumpers. Men appeared out of the fog and secured the mooring lines.

"We go now," Misha said and hopped to the pier.

Tucker led the others and followed their guide through the fog down a wide boardwalk that spanned a swampy area. At the end rose a Quonset hut with pale yellow walls and a riveted roof streaked with so much rust it looked like an abstract painting.

The group stepped inside. To their left, a pair of red-and-blue miniature submarines sat atop maintenance scaffolding. The subs were thirty feet long and seven wide with portholes lining the hull, including along the bottom. Amidships, a waist-high conning tower rose, topped by a hand-wheel-operated entry hatch. Below this, jutting from the subs' sides, were a pair of adjustable control-planes. At the bow was a clear, bulbous cone, which Tucker assumed was the pilot's seat.

Tucker turned to the others, who were staring open-mouthed at the subs, and said, "Your chariots."

No one spoke.

"Impressive, *da?*" Misha said cheerily.

"You're joking, right?" Utkin asked. "Is this how we're leaving Volgograd?"

And this, from the most pliable of the group.

Bukolov and Anya remained speechless.

"They're so very small," Utkin continued.

"But comfortable, and well stocked," Misha countered. "And reliable. It may take a while to reach your destination, but we will get you there. To date, we have had only three accidents."

Anya finally found her voice. "Accidents? What kind of accidents?"

"No injuries or fatalities. Power outages." Misha shrugged. "We got craned out of the river before the Volga mud swallowed us."

Anya turned a pleading look toward Tucker. "This is your plan? I am not—"

Surprisingly, Bukolov became the voice of reason, stepping to Anya and curling an arm around her shoulders. "Anya, I am sure it is perfectly safe."

She did not look convinced.

Leaving the others in the maintenance bay to ogle the submarines, Misha led Tucker into a side office. There, Misha's friendly grin disappeared. "What your people have asked is very difficult. Do you know how far away the Caspian Sea is?"

"Two hundred eighty-two miles," Tucker replied. "Taking into account the cruising speed of your submarines, the average recharge time for the sub's batteries, and the seasonal current of the Volga, we should reach the Caspian in eighteen to twenty-four hours."

"I see," he grumbled. "You are well informed."

"And you're being *well* paid."

Before Misha could reply, Tucker added, "I understand the risk you're taking, and I'm grateful. So, I'm prepared to offer you a bonus: ten thousand rubles if you get us there safely. On one condition."

"I am listening."

"You're our pilot. *You* personally. Take it or leave it."

He wanted more than a financial gamble by the owner of Wild Volga Tours. He wanted his skin involved in the game, too.

Misha stared hard at Tucker, then stuck out his hand. "Done. We leave in one hour."

22

March 16, 9:34 A.M.
The Volga River, Russia

Misha led the group back the way they'd come, through the swamp to the speedboat. Once aboard, the crew shoved off and headed downriver toward the tour company's embarkation point. The fog remained thick as the weak morning sun had yet to burn it away.

"What's that stink?" Utkin asked after a few minutes.

Tucker smelled it, too, a heavy sulfurous stench to the air.

"Lukoil refinery over there," Misha replied and pointed to starboard. "Much oil businesses along the river."

"This close to the Volga?" Bukolov said. "Seems like a disaster waiting to happen."

Misha shrugged. "Many jobs. No one complains."

The speedboat slowly angled back toward shore, weaving through a maze of sandbars into the mouth of an estuary. Its bow nosed into a narrow, tree-lined inlet and pushed up to a wooden pier, where the boat was tied off. At the other end of the dock, one of Misha's minisubs bobbed with the waves from their wake, rubbing against the tire bumpers.

"The *Olga*," Misha announced. "Named after my grandmother. Lovely woman, but very fat. She too bobbed in the water. But never sank."

Misha led them to the end of the dock to the *Olga*. An employee in blue coveralls climbed out of the conning tower hatch and descended the side ladder. He shook Misha's hand and exchanged a few words.

After clapping the employee on the shoulder, Misha turned to the group. "Checked, stocked, and prepared for takeoff. Who goes first?"

"Me." Anya set her jaw and stepped forward.

Tucker felt a wave of sympathy and respect for her. Frightened though she was, she'd decided to face it head-on.

Without a word, she scaled the ladder. At the top, she dropped one leg into the hatch, then the other, and disappeared into the conning tower. Utkin went next, followed by Bukolov, who muttered under his breath, "Fascinating . . . what fun."

When it came to Kane's turn, Tucker double tapped the ladder's rung. Awkwardly but quickly, the shepherd scaled the ladder, then shimmied through the hatch.

"Impressive," Misha said. "He does tricks!"

You have no idea.

Tucker followed, then Misha, who pulled the hatch closed, tugged it tight over the rubber seals, then spun the wheel until an LED beside the coaming glowed green. With the sub secure, Misha dropped down and shimmied to the cockpit.

The sub's interior was not as cramped as Tucker had expected. The bulkheads, deck, and overhead were painted a soothing cream, as were the cables and tubes that snaked along the interior. A spacious bench padded in light blue Naugahyde ran down the center of the space, long enough for each of them to lie down, if necessary.

Tucker leaned and stared out one of the portholes, noting that the sun was beginning to peek through, showing shreds of blue sky. Occasionally green water sloshed across the view as the sub rolled and bobbed. He straightened and took a deep breath, tasting the slight metallic scent to the air.

"If anyone's hungry," Misha called out from the cockpit, "there's food and drink at the back."

Tucker turned and saw that the aft bulkhead held a double-door storage cabinet.

"You'll also find aspirin, seasickness pills, and such. We'll stop every four hours for bathroom breaks. Are there any questions?"

"How deep will we be diving?" Bukolov pressed his face to one of the portholes, looking like a young boy about to go on an adventure.

"On average, eighteen feet. The Volga's main channel is at least twice that. Plenty of room for us to maneuver as needed. Plus I have a hydrophone in the cockpit. I'll hear any ships coming our way. If you'll take your seats, we will be under way."

Tucker sat on the forwardmost section of bench, and Kane settled in beneath it. The others spread out along its length, staring out portholes. With a soft whirring, the electric engines engaged, and the sub slid sideways away from the dock, wallowed a few times, then settled lower. The waters of the Volga rose to cover the portholes and flooded the sub's interior in soft green light.

As Misha deftly worked the controls, the *Olga* glided out of the estuary and into the main river channel. They were still only half submerged.

"All hands prepare to dive." Misha chuckled. "Or just sit back and enjoy."

With a muffled *whoosh* of bubbles, the sub slid beneath the surface. The light streaming through the portholes slowly dimmed from a mint green to a darker emerald. Soft halogen lights set into the underside of the benches glowed to life, casting dramatic shadows up the curved bulkheads.

After a few moments, Misha announced in his best tour-guide voice, "At cruising depth. We are under way. Prepare for a smooth ride."

Tucker found his description to be apt. They glided effortlessly, with very little sense of movement. He spotted schools of fish darting past their portholes.

Over the next hour, having slept fitfully over the past days, exhaustion settled over everyone. The others drifted away one by one, draped across the bench, each with a wool blanket and inflatable pillow.

Tucker held off the longest, but after a quiet conversation with Misha who assured him all was well, he curled up and went to sleep, too. He hung one arm over the side of the bench, resting his palm on Kane's side. The shepherd softly panted, maintaining his post beside the floor's porthole, studying every bubble and particle that swept past the glass.

1:00 P.M.

Tucker startled awake as Misha's voice came over the loudspeaker.

"Apologies for the intrusion, but we are about to make our first stop."

The others groaned and stirred.

Tucker sat up to find Kane curled on the bench with him. The shepherd stood, arched his back in a stretch, then hopped down, and trotted to the entrance of the cockpit.

"Tell your friend he cannot drive," Misha called good-naturedly.

"He just likes the view," Tucker replied.

Bukolov waddled forward and sat down beside Tucker. "I must say, you impress me."

"How so?"

"I had my doubts that you could truly help me—us— escape Russia. I see now that I was wrong to doubt you."

"We're not out yet."

"I have faith," Bukolov said with a smile. He gave Tucker's arm a grandfatherly pat, then returned to his section of bench.

Miracles never cease.

He felt his ears pop as the *Olga* angled toward the surface. The portholes reversed their earlier transformation, going from a dark green to a blinding glare as the sub broached the surface. Sunlight streamed through the glass. A moment later, forward progress slowed with a slight grinding complaint as the hull slid to a stop on sand.

Misha crawled out of the cockpit, climbed the ladder, and opened the hatch. "All ashore!"

They all abandoned ship.

Misha's expert piloting had brought the *Olga* to rest beside an old wooden dock. Their tiny cove was surrounded by tall marsh grass. Farther out, up a short slope, Tucker could see treetops.

"Where are we?" Utkin asked, blinking against the sun and looking around.

"A few miles north of Akhtubinsk. We're actually ahead of schedule. Feel free to walk around. You have thirty minutes. I'm going to partially recharge the batteries with my solar umbrella."

Tucker crossed with Kane to the shore and surveyed the immediate area around the dock. He had Kane do a fast scout to make sure they were alone. Once satisfied, he waved the others off the dock so they could stretch their legs.

"Stay close," he ordered. "If you see anyone, even in the distance, get back here."

Once they agreed, Tucker headed back to the sub. Misha had the solar umbrella already propped over the sub, recharging the batteries.

As Misha worked, he asked, "Tell me, my friend, are you all criminals? I do not judge. You pay, I don't care."

"No," replied Tucker.

"Then people are following you? Looking for you?"

"Not anymore."

I hope.

Misha nodded, then broke into a smile; his gold teeth flashed in the sun. "Very well. You are in safe hands."

Tucker actually believed him.

Anya returned early by herself and prepared to return below.

"Where are the others?" he asked.

"I . . . I did what I had to do," she said, blushing a bit. "I left the boys so they could have some privacy to do the same."

Tucker glanced down to Kane. It wasn't a bad idea. It would be another four hours before they stopped again. "How about it, Kane? Wanna go see a man about a horse?"

2:38 P.M.

As the *Olga* continued to glide down the Volga, the group dozed, stared out the portholes, or read. Occasionally Misha would quietly announce landmarks no one could see: a good spot for sturgeon fishing, or a mecca for crawfish hunting, or a village that had played a major or minor part in Russian history.

Utkin and Anya traded scientific journals and pored over them. Bukolov studied his notes, occasionally stopping to scribble some new thought or idea.

With nothing else to do himself, Tucker drifted in a half drowse—until Bukolov abruptly slid next to him and nudged him alert.

"What do you make of this?" the doctor said.

"Pardon?"

Bukolov pushed a thin journal into his hand. It was clearly old, with a scarred leather cover and sewn-in yellowed, brittle pages. "This is one of De Klerk's later journals."

"Okay, so?"

Bukolov took it back, scowled at him, and flipped the pages back and forth. He then bent the book open, spread it wide, and pointed to the inner seam. "There are pages missing from this last diary of De Klerk's. See here . . . note the cut marks near the spine."

"You're just noticing this now?" Tucker asked.

"Because the entries seemed to follow along smoothly. No missed dates, and the narrative is contiguous. Here, just before the first missing pages, he talks about one of the men in his unit complaining of mysterious stomach pains. After the missing pages, he begins talking about his Apocalypse Seed—where he found it, its properties, and so on."

Not able to read or speak Afrikaans, Tucker had to take the doctor's word for it, but the man was right. The cut marks were there.

"Why would he do this?" Tucker asked.

"I can only think of one reason," Bukolov replied. "Paulos de Klerk was trying to hide something. But what and from whom?"

7:55 P.M.

Misha announced another pit stop and guided the *Olga* toward shore. It was the third landfall of the day, near sunset. He wanted one more chance to stock up his solar batteries for the night. He pulled them up to another abandoned fishing dock. Clearly he had planned their route carefully, choosing backwater locations for their ports of call.

As the hatch was unsealed, Tucker was immediately struck by the cloying rotten-egg stench of the place, undercut by a heady mix of petroleum and burned oil.

"Ugh," Anya said, pinching her nose. "I'm staying inside. I don't have to use the bathroom that badly."

Tucker did, as did Kane. So they headed out with Utkin and Bukolov.

The cove here was surrounded by swamp, choked with densely packed grasses and reeds, interspersed with dead dwarf pines. A maze of wooden boardwalks zigzagged through the marshy area, paralleling aboveground pipes. At several intersections, car-sized steel cones protruded out of the oil-tinged water.

"Apologies for the ugly scenery," Misha called. "This is a Lukoil station—propane, I believe. Those metal funnels are burp valves. Sad. Before Lukoil bought the land, there was a fishing village here named Saray. Known for very good sturgeon. No more."

The group wandered around the dock area, which forked in several directions, all of which seemed to head inland toward the ghost town of Saray.

"Tucker, come look at this!" Utkin called somewhere to his right.

With Kane at his heels, Tucker followed the boardwalk to where the other two men were standing beside a section of submerged gas pipe. He noted the water roiling there. He plunged his hand into the marsh and slid his palm over the pipe's slimy surface until he found what he was looking for—an open control valve. He continued probing until his fingers touched a short length of chain. Dangling at the end was a padlock. Its hasp had been cut in half.

Sabotage.

"Go!" he yelled to the others. "Back to the sub!"

"What is it?" Utkin asked. "What—?"

He stiff-armed Utkin away. "Get Bukolov to the sub!"

Still kneeling, Tucker hollered to the sub, "Misha!"

"What is it?"

"A gas leak! Get under way!"

Tucker fought back the questions filling his head— like *who, how,* and *when*—and drew his gun. He searched the water and spotted a thumb-thick section of a pine branch floating nearby. He snatched it with his free hand and crammed it into the mouth of the leaking valve, like a cork in a bottle. The bubbling gas slowed to a sputter.

An ominous thumping echoed over the swamp, seeming to come from every direction at once.

Helicopter rotors.

Tucker burst to his feet and ran. Kane kept to his side.

Backlit by the setting sun, Misha was slipping through the sub's conning tower hatch. The others had already made it aboard. Misha paused when he spotted Tucker's flight.

Tucker waved his arm. "Go, go!"

Misha hollered back. "A cannery! Four miles downstream! I will wait!"

He vanished below, yanking the hatch.

Behind the *Olga,* a helicopter appeared across the river, streaking over the surface. It swooped over the sub, banked hard, then slowed to a hover above the marsh. It was a civilian chopper, not a Havoc assault bird. It seemed General Kharzin's influence and reach had limits this far from his home territory.

The helo's side door opened, and a slim figure appeared, carrying a fiery red stick in one hand. Leaning out, a long tail of blond hair whipped in the rotor wash.

Tucker's heart clenched into a tight fist.

Felice Nilsson.

Back from the dead.

From fifty yards away, he raised his pistol and fired. The bullet struck the fuselage beside Felice's head. She jerked back out of sight, but it was too late. As if moving in slow motion, the flaming flare dropped from her hand and spun downward.

Tucker swung away and took off at a sprint, Kane at his heels.

Somewhere behind he heard a *whoosh,* followed a split second later by a muffled explosion. Without looking, Tucker knew what was happening. The closely packed marsh grass had trapped the heavier-than-air propane as it leaked from the sabotaged pipe, creating a ground-hugging blanket of gas.

The flare had ignited it.

Orange-blue flames swirled through the swamp grass, chasing him. Heat seared his back. They reached an intersection and dodged left toward the river where the sub should have been. But it was already gone, sunk away.

The flames caught up with him, outpacing them, surging beneath the boardwalk. Fire spurted between the planks.

The end of the dock loomed ahead.

Tucker put his head down, covered the last few steps to the end of the boardwalk, then jumped. Kane brushed against him as they sailed through the air together—then a wall of fire erupted in front of them.

23

March 16, 8:18 P.M.
The Volga River, Russia

At the last moment, Tucker reached out and curled his arm around Kane's neck. Together, they plunged through the fire and into the river. While Kane had trained for sudden immersion, his core instinct would be to surface immediately. Cruel though it sounded, Tucker needed to prevent this.

As their plunging momentum slowed, Tucker stuck out his arm, his fingers grasping until he found a clump of roots. He clenched tight and pulled them both toward the mud. Under his other arm, Kane's body was rock hard with tension, but he did not struggle.

Tucker craned his neck backward and watched the worst of the fire blow out on the surface. The blanket of propane had quickly exhausted itself, but the swamp grass continued to burn. In his blurred vision, the flaming stalks along the marsh edges appeared like so many orange torches against the darkening sky.

One problem down, one big one to go.

Felice and the helicopter were still out there. He knew the Swede was too stubborn to assume the flames had done her work.

Tucker worked his way deeper into the swamplands bordering the river, pulling himself from one clump of roots to another. When his lungs could take no more, he let go and bobbed to the surface.

He immediately heard the thump of rotors back at the dock.

Felice continued to hunt for them, a hawk in the sky.

As he and Kane gulped air, the swamp grass crackled and smoked. Cinders hissed on the water's surface. Tucker looked at Kane. The shepherd's eyes were huge, darting left and right. Kane's animal instincts were screaming *Fire! Get away!* But his trust in Tucker and his training were holding him in place.

Tucker hugged his partner and whispered in his ear, "We're okay, we're okay . . . easy . . . hold on . . ."

The words themselves didn't matter. It was Tucker's tone and closeness that made the difference. They were together. The tension eased slightly from the shepherd's body.

Around them, the fire began dwindling as it devoured the dry tops of the marsh grass, filling the cove with smoke.

Tucker released Kane, and they half paddled, half crawled through the water, heading still deeper into the swamp, aiming for shore. Though it burned his lungs and stung his eyes, he did his best to hide their passage under the thick pall of smoke.

As they drifted into the shallows, the water was only a foot or so deep. The grasses here were greener, still smoldering. Warning bells went off in his head. Though the smoking grass provided cover, it could also serve as a beacon. Their passage risked nudging aside stalks, causing the smoky columns to shift.

From the hovering helicopter, Felice would certainly spot the irregularity.

Slowly, Tucker lowered himself to his belly and wriggled deeper into the mud. He kept Kane close.

Now, wait.

It didn't take long. With the sun setting, the helicopter crisscrossed the marshes, stirring up the smoke. It finally settled into a gliding hover over the marshy cove. He spotted the shape of the chopper through the pall.

If he could see the helicopter . . .

Not a twitch, Tucker told himself. *You're part of the swamp . . . you're mud.*

After what felt like hours, the chopper finally moved on as dusk settled. Slowly, the thump of the rotors faded away. Still Tucker didn't move. With the sun down, the temperature dropped rapidly. The cold of the water seeped into his bones. He set his jaw against it.

Wait . . .

As he'd expected, the helicopter returned a few minutes later. Ever the hunter, Felice had hoped her quarry would have taken the invitation to bolt, but Tucker knew better.

There came a sharp crack of a rifle shot. Tucker flinched. His first fear was that Felice had spotted them, but he knew immediately this wasn't the case.

Felice wouldn't have missed.

She was trying to flush them out.

Crack!

Another shot, this one closer and somewhere to their left.

Tucker eased his hand over a few inches and laid his palm on Kane's paw. The shepherd tensed, then relaxed. If Tucker remained calm, so would Kane.

Crack! Crack!

The shots were even closer still. The feeling of utter helplessness was maddening. The shots were coming at irregular intervals now, moving ever closer to their position. Tucker closed his eyes and concentrated on his breathing. His survival was now down to dumb luck: the random squeeze of a trigger, a pilot's hand on the chopper's cyclic control, the vagaries of the wind.

Crack!

This shot was to the right.

Felice had finally passed them.

Afraid to jinx their luck, Tucker held his breath until the next shot came—again to their right, even farther out.

After another agonizing five minutes, the helicopter banked away, and the thump of its rotors slowly faded.

Fearing another return, Tucker remained in the cold water for ten more minutes. By now his limbs were trembling from the cold, his teeth chattering. Night had fully fallen. Above, the sky was clear and sprinkled with stars.

Tucker sat up and rolled onto his hands and knees. He patted Kane on the rump and together they began crawling toward shore.

Once on dry land, they set off south, hugging the shoreline where there were trees for cover and veering inland when there were none, ever wary of the helicopter's return.

As he hiked, Tucker considered the implications of the ambush. How had Felice found them? The most likely suspect was Misha. He had had time to sell them out during their brief stay at the headquarters of Wild Volga Tours, as well as during the sub's voyage via radio. But for that matter, any of the others—Utkin, Anya, even Bukolov—had access during one or another of their recharging stops. Any of them could have used the sub's radio. He hated to believe it, but he also couldn't afford to ignore the possibility that one of his companions was a traitor.

Once again he was letting himself slip into a wilderness of mirrors, where everyone and no one was suspect. But he did have one last ace up his sleeve. Only he and Ruth Harper knew the endgame of their evacuation scheme. All anyone else knew was that the sub's destination was the Caspian Sea.

If Felice wanted to ambush them again, she'd have to work hard for it.

10:37 P.M.

From the edge of a copse of trees across a broad starlit meadow, Tucker spied a plank-sided building the size of an aircraft hangar along the bank of the Volga. He recalled Misha's last words.

A cannery! Four miles downstream! I will wait!

"What do you think?" Tucker whispered to Kane. "Look like a cannery to you?"

His partner simply stared up at him.

Tucker nodded. "Yeah, me too."

They took a cautious approach, circling west through the trees to bring them within a few hundred yards. He discovered a narrow canal that cut from the river toward the structure. There was little water this time of the year, and its concrete sides were crumbling. Tucker dropped down into it and used the chunks of fallen rock and other debris as stepping-stones as he followed the canal and closed the remaining distance to the cannery building.

As he drew abreast of the exterior wall, he noted a lone, rusted crane looming over the canal, its hooked cable drooping like the line from a giant's fishing pole. The air smelled faintly of rotting fish.

He found stone steps leading out of the canal and took them. Crouched near the top, he scanned the area. Aside from the croaking of frogs and the buzz of cicadas, all was quiet. From Kane's relaxed posture, the shepherd's keen senses weren't discerning anything more.

He grabbed a few pebbles off the top step and tossed one against the cannery's wall. It plinked against the wood. Still, nothing moved.

Had Misha and the others made it here? Or had they come and gone?

Tucker tossed another pebble, then a third.

From somewhere inside the building came a scuffing sound—a footstep on concrete. Kane heard it, too, his body instantly going alert. Tucker prepared to send the shepherd scouting in the dark—but then a door creaked open and a lone figure leaned out.

"Tucker?" came Misha's voice.

Tucker didn't respond.

"Tucker, is that you?" Misha repeated.

Taking a chance, he stood up and walked over. Kane followed, stalking stiffly, sensing Tucker's anxiety.

Misha sagged with relief. "Good to see you, my friend."

Despite the cordiality of the greeting, Tucker could hear the tightness in the other's voice. It was not surprising, considering the man had narrowly escaped being roasted alive in his own sub. Still, Tucker kept a wary stance, not sure how much he could trust Misha.

"You made it," the man said, eyeing him up and down.

"A little crisp along the edges but I'm okay." Tucker glanced inside and saw that the dark cannery appeared empty. "Are the others waiting at the sub?"

"Da."

"How's the *Olga?*"

"All is good. We dove before the explosion."

"They didn't shoot at you?"

"No."

"Your radio is operational?"

"Of course. Wait." He shook a finger at Tucker. "I see what you are really asking, my friend. You wonder how did they find us, *da?* You think I might have betrayed you."

Tucker shrugged. "Would you be any less suspicious?"

"Probably not." Misha's eyes stared hard into Tucker's own. "But I did not do such a thing. If I had known someone was going to firebomb my sub, I would have declined your generous offer to pilot the *Olga.* I have many other employees I don't particularly like, such as my lazy brother-in-law. But I took your money and came. And I take contracts seriously. We shook hands."

Tucker believed him. Mostly. But only time would tell.

"How can I prove this to you?" Misha asked.

"By *proving* how good of an actor you can be."

24

March 16, 11:13 P.M.
The Volga River, Russia

Misha had docked the *Olga* at the still-flooded mouth of the canal. Only the conning tower jutted above the surface, camouflaged in a nest of branches he'd cut from neighboring trees.

With Kane at his side, Tucker followed Misha into the shallows and up into the sub.

"You're alive!" Anya cried as he climbed down.

Utkin and Bukolov shook his hand vigorously, pumping his arm up and down, both smiling with an enthusiasm that seemed genuine.

"If everyone's done celebrating," Misha growled, "it's time we *talk*."

Tucker turned to him. "About what?"

"You lied to me. You told me there would be *no* danger—that *no* one was chasing you. I've had enough! I am turning around. I will return you safely to Volgograd and tell no one about this, but this voyage is over!"

Tucker took a step forward. "We had a deal."

"Not anymore."

He pulled the Magnum from his pocket and leveled it at Misha's chest.

Anya cried, "Tucker, don't."

"You're taking us the rest of the way."

"Shoot me," Misha said with a shrug. "And you'll be stranded here. Middle of nowhere. You think you can drive the *Olga*? Think you know the Volga? You will die in her mud!"

The two combatants glared at each other for a long ten seconds before Tucker lowered his gun and pocketed it. "The bastard is right."

Anya cried, "We cannot go back to Volgograd. Tucker, tell him!"

Bukolov chimed in. "This is lunacy."

"It's a setback," Tucker said, keeping his voice strained. "I'll call and arrange another means out of Volgograd." His next words were for Misha, full of menace. "If anyone is waiting for us in Volgograd, I'll put the first bullet in your head. Do we understand each other?"

"We do," replied Misha and headed for his cockpit. "Now everyone sit down so I can get under way."

As Misha eased the sub back toward the main channel, Tucker gathered the others at the rear. He kept his voice low. "Like I said, this is a setback, nothing more."

Bukolov groaned. "I will never leave this country alive. My discovery will die with me."

"Don't worry. I'll contact my friends at our next stop. Everyone try to get some sleep." He glanced back toward Misha. "I'm going to keep working on him, try to get him to change his mind."

Once the others settled to the bench, despondent and defeated, Tucker stoop-walked forward and ducked tightly next to Misha. The cockpit was cast in darkness, save the orange glow of Misha's instrument panels. Beyond the windscreen, the dark waters of the Volga swept and churned.

Tucker posted Kane two yards behind him, blocking anyone from coming forward.

"How did I do?" Misha whispered.

"An award-winning performance," replied Tucker. "Are you sure they won't notice that we're *not* heading north toward Volgograd?"

Misha pointed at the sub's windscreen, beyond which the Volga churned darkly. "How could they tell?"

True. Even Tucker was lost.

Tucker leaned forward, peering out. "How do you navigate through this sludge, especially at night?"

Misha reached above his head, pulled a sheaf of laminated paper from a cubbyhole, and handed it to Tucker. "Nautical chart of the Volga. You see the red squares along the shore? Those have been our stops so far. But usually I navigate by dead reckoning. Most of the Volga is in here." He tapped his skull. "Like a woman's body in the dark, I know her every curve and imperfection. Still, when I am a mile or so from a stop, I always broach the surface just enough for the sub's antenna to get a GPS fix."

"And how long do you think it will take us to reach Astrakhan?" Their destination lay within the Volga delta, where the river emptied into the Caspian Sea.

"We should reach the city by tomorrow afternoon, but I suspect you'd like me to stay submerged until nightfall."

"I would."

"Then that's your answer."

"And let's limit any more pit stops along the way to no longer than five minutes."

"I agree. But sometime in the morning, I'll need to dock for one more thirty-minute solar charge of the batteries in order to reach Astrakhan."

"Understood."

Tucker remained quiet for a moment, then said, "I hate to ask this, but, Misha, I need one more favor from you. Until we reach Astrakhan, no more radio communication."

Misha shrugged, clearly understanding the necessity. He reached up, unscrewed the head of the gooseneck microphone, and handed it to Tucker with a smile.

"I will now be free of my wife's nagging for a peaceful twenty-four hours."

March 17, 6:04 A.M.

The next morning, it was showtime again.

They had sailed southward for seven hours, for as long as they could manage before needing a pit stop. Misha found another quiet dark cove and put in.

Tucker ordered everyone to disembark, including Misha, who put on another display of feigned outrage.

"You disabled the radio. What do you expect me to do here by myself?"

"You could leave us. So get moving."

"Fine, fine . . ."

Everyone climbed out. While there was no dock, Misha had partially grounded the sub on a shallow sandbar. Having to wade through several inches of water in the predawn chill drew grumbled complaints as the group sought private spots amid the shrubs lining the bank.

Misha hung back with Tucker as he kept watch and whispered. "Are any of them good at astronomy?" He jerked a thumb toward the star-studded sky.

Tucker hadn't considered this. He didn't know if any of the group was adept at celestial navigation, but it probably didn't matter.

"Keep an eye on things," Tucker said to Misha and led Kane off to their own private spot. Once done, he stayed crouched in hiding and dialed Sigma's headquarters.

When Harper answered, Tucker passed on a fast request, risking only a few words. "I need a discreet airstrip near Astrakhan. I'll call back."

He hung up and stood. He made a dramatic pantomime of searching for a signal with his phone. He emphasized it by swearing softly under his breath.

Suddenly, Kane let out a low growl.

Tucker turned to find Utkin standing in the bushes ten feet away.

"Phone problem?" the man asked, zipping up his pants.

"Satellite interference."

Utkin stepped out of the shadows and walked closer. "I thought I heard you talking to someone."

"Kane. Old habit. How're you holding up?"

"Tired. Very tired. I don't think I'm suited for adventure." Utkin offered a smile, but it came out jaded. It was an expression Tucker had yet to see on the lab assistant's face.

Utkin shoved his hands in his jacket pockets and took another step toward Tucker.

Kane stood up, shifting between them.

Tucker found his fingers tightening on the butt of the Magnum.

Utkin noted the tension. "After the attack, you suspect all of us, don't you?"

"Part of the job description."

"Hmm . . ."

"If you were me, who would you suspect?"

"Any one of us," Utkin confirmed.

"Including you?"

"Including me."

"What about Bukolov and Anya? They're your friends, aren't they?"

Utkin looked at the ground and kicked a rock. "Maybe I thought so at one time. Not anymore. I was naive or maybe just wishful. How could I expect them to consider a poor fisherman's son their equal?"

Utkin turned and walked off.

Tucker stared after him.

What the hell just happened?

10:46 A.M.

The midmorning sun blazed down upon a secluded estuary where the sub had parked in the shallows, perfect for recharging the batteries.

While the solar umbrella was spread wide to catch every photon of energy, Tucker stood on the shore with his fellow passengers. "We have thirty minutes," he said. "Make the best use of it. We'll be in Volgograd soon and should be ready for anything."

The others set off amid the stands of bare willows, crowded with crows, who loudly complained at their trespass.

Tucker knelt down beside Kane and whispered, "SCOUT, HERD, ALERT."

For as long as this break lasted, the shepherd would discreetly circle the area, making sure that none of his *sheep* wandered off or drifted too close. Kane would bark a warning if there was a problem.

Satisfied, and out of direct sight, he climbed back aboard the *Olga* and started a thorough search of the group's belongings. Before reaching Astrakhan, he had to be sure that someone in the group wasn't leaking their position.

He dug through bags, shook out clothes, flipped through notebooks, everything. With experienced fingers, he probed the seams of pants, shirts, even the soles of shoes. He went so far as to pick through personal items, like thumbing through a bodice-ripper paperback of Anya's or the boxes of Utkin's playing cards—one empty, the other full of well-worn cards. He even dug through Bukolov's pouch of tobacco. As he did so, he felt a twinge of guilt, as if trespassing through the others' secret vices.

Still, for all his trespassing, he found nothing.

Next, he squeezed into the cockpit and scrutinized the instrument panel. He ran his palms over the console. Nothing anomalous jumped out at him.

He was stumped.

Only one possibility remained. Someone *had* to have used the sub's radio to transmit their position and set up that last ambush. How else could word have gotten out? He was glad he had asked Misha to disable the radio before they set off for Astrakhan. With the radio out of commission, their path from here should be unknown to their pursuers.

Tucker checked his watch, knowing he was running out of time. Ending his search, he climbed out of the conning tower and returned to the shore. Tucker whistled, raising more complaints from the nesting crows. He waved everyone back. They climbed aboard as Misha began breaking down and storing the solar array.

Tucker got Kane inside, then dropped back down next to Misha.

"Give me a minute," he said and walked a couple meters away from the sub.

Pulling out his phone, he dialed Sigma.

Harper came on the line immediately. "That was one hell of a cryptic message you left me," she said. "Had me worried."

"I'm in the wilderness, if you get my drift."

"Been there myself. I take it you don't want to go *straight* to the rendezvous as planned?"

Tucker recounted the helicopter attack. "I can't swear to this, but I suspect Felice let the sub go. Her attack was focused solely on me and Kane."

"With you gone, the rest would be easy pickings. Plus Bukolov is the prize. They don't dare risk killing him."

"Since I took out the sub's radio, it's been quiet, but I don't want to take any more chances. Better to disembark as soon as we're within sight of Astrakhan."

"Agreed. I've found an aircraft that suits our needs." She passed on the coordinates. "They're part of a charter fishing company. They fly clients south into the Volga delta on a regular basis. With a little incentive, the pilot will take you to the new rendezvous."

"Which is where?"

"An island. Just outside Russian territorial waters—or what passes for marine borders in the Caspian Sea."

"Who's meeting us?"

"They're trustworthy. I've worked with them personally in the field. You reach them, and your worries are over."

"So says the woman who described this mission as a *simple escort job*."

25

As promised, Misha reached the outskirts of Astrakhan by the afternoon. With the sub still submerged, he announced this quietly to Tucker, who squeezed into the cockpit. They studied the nautical chart together.

Checking coordinates, Tucker tapped a spot where the Volga's main channel branched into Astrakhan.

"Stop there?" Misha asked.

"*Turn* there," Tucker corrected. "Follow it for three miles, then call me again."

It took forty minutes to reach the branch.

Tucker returned to the cockpit and pointed to another spot a mile farther west.

"You are being very cagey," Misha said. "I see a small cove. Is that our destination?"

"No. Call me when you reach the next waypoint."

After another twenty minutes, Misha summoned him again.

With a smile, Tucker placed his finger on the small cove that Misha had mentioned before. "That's our destination."

"But you said—oh, I see. You are very untrusting."

"It's a recent development. Don't take it personally. How long until nightfall?"

"To be safe, two hours. I will pull us into the undergrowth along this bank. It should shield us further as we wait."

It turned out to be the longest two hours of his life. The others attempted to question him about what he was doing, but he only gave cryptic reassurances, allowing them still to believe the sub was parked underwater at some destination near Volgograd.

Finally, he ordered everyone to collect their belongings and disembark. With Tucker directing, they gathered in a clump of bushes on the shore of the cove.

Overhead, the dark sky hung with low clouds, turning the waning moon into a pale disk. Aside from the trilling of insects and the occasional croak of a frog, all was quiet.

Across the cove, a few hundred yards off, a trio of squat cabins hugged the water. A lone light burned beside the door of one. Moored to its dock floated a pair of small seaplanes.

That was their ticket out of here.

"This is not Volgograd," Utkin whispered, scrunching his face. "The air smells too clean."

Tucker ignored him and joined Misha alongside the sub. The two shook hands.

"This is where we say good-bye," Misha said. He let go of Tucker's hand but continued to hold out his open palm.

With a smile, Tucker understood. He pulled a wad of rubles from his pocket and counted out what he owed the sub's pilot—then he added an extra ten thousand on top of that. "Hazardous duty pay."

"I knew I liked you for a reason, my friend."

"You'll be able to get back to Volgograd safely?"

"Yes, I think so. And I hope you do the same—wherever you are going."

"I hope so, too."

"Because of the extra pay, I will wait here until you take off. Just in case you need me again."

"Thank you, Misha. If I don't see you again, safe sailing."

With Tucker in the lead and Kane bringing up the rear, the group headed around the curve of the cove, sticking to the trees and taller bushes.

Once near the cluster of cabins, he called a halt, knelt by Kane, and pointed forward. "SCOUT AND RETURN."

Kane skulked off and disappeared into the darkness.

Several minutes passed, then from back the way they'd come, a whispered call reached him.

"Tucker!"

It was Misha.

His heart thudding with worry, Tucker told the others to stay out of sight. He made his way back down the trail to where Misha was crouching.

"What is it?"

"This."

He passed over a black plastic object roughly the size and shape of a narrow bar of soap. A pair of insulated wires dangled from either side, ending in alligator clips.

Misha explained, "I was cleaning up after you all left, straightening and doing a systems check while I waited as promised. I found this tucked beneath my seat in the cockpit. Those clips had been spliced into the sub's antenna feed."

"It's a signal generator," Tucker muttered, his belly turning to ice. "It sends out frequency-specific pulses at regular intervals."

"Like a homing beacon."

"Yes." Tucker felt icy fingers of despair close around his heart. "That's how the enemy was tracking us."

He remembered Misha describing how he would surface the sub at regular intervals to get a GPS fix on their location, especially as they neared one of their ports of call. Each time he did it, the generator gave away their location, allowing the enemy ample time to set up an ambush once they figured out Misha's routine.

"Who put it there?" Misha asked.

Tucker glanced toward the trio hidden by the cabins.

Who indeed?

He ran everything he knew through his head—then his whole body clenched with a realization.

It couldn't be . . .

Misha read his reaction. "You know who the traitor is?"

"I think so." Tucker stuffed the signal generator into his pocket. "I suggest you shove off right now and put as much distance between you and us as possible."

"Understood. Good luck, my friend."

Tucker returned to where the group sat crouched in the darkness. By now, Kane was waiting for him. The shepherd's posture, the tilt of his ears, and the softness of his eyes told Tucker *all was clear.*

Like hell it was.

He crouched and draped an arm around Kane's neck, struggling to keep his composure.

Now what?

How much information had already been funneled to General Kharzin?

Since surfacing here, he had to assume the enemy knew where they had stopped. Surely Felice was on her way.

He didn't have the time to properly interrogate and break the traitor. That would come later. For now, by hiding his knowledge, he still had a slight upper hand.

He stared toward the seaplanes. The enemy didn't want to kill Bukolov, and with their agent sitting next to him on the plane, they'd be even less likely to try to shoot the craft down once it was airborne. In that way, both men could serve as unwitting human shields, increasing the group's chances of reaching the rendez-vous point safely. But first he had to get them all into the air.

He also intended to keep a close eye on the traitor, an eye sharper than his own. He shifted next to Kane. Shielding his hand signals, he pointed and touched the corner of his own eye.

Keep a watch on the target.

Until Tucker lifted the order, the shepherd would be on close guard—watching his target for any aggressive movements or hostile actions, judging the tone of voice, listening for the cock of a hammer or the slip of a blade from a sheath. It was a broad tool, but Tucker trusted the shepherd's instinct. If his target made the wrong move, Kane would immediately attack.

"What was that all about with Misha?" Anya whispered, drawing back his attention.

"He wanted more money. To stay silent."

"And you paid him?" Bukolov asked, aghast.

"It was easier than killing him. And besides, we're leaving now anyway."

Tucker stood up and gestured for the others to remain hidden. He crossed to the lighted cabin and knocked on the door.

It opened a few moments later. Yellow light spilled forth, framing a young woman in denim overalls. She was barely five feet tall, with black hair trimmed in a pixie haircut.

Tucker tightened his grip on the Magnum concealed in his pocket, bracing himself for any attack.

"You are Bartok?" she asked in a surprisingly bold voice for such a small body.

Bartok?

He was momentarily confused until he remembered Harper's mention of a code name.

"Yes, I'm Bartok."

"I am Elena. How many come with you on plane? Costs three thousand rubles per passenger."

She certainly didn't waste any time getting down to business.

"Four and a dog."

"Dog cost more."

"Why?"

"He crap . . . I must clean up, no?"

Tucker wasn't about to argue—not with this little firebrand. She sort of scared him. "Fine."

"Get others," she ordered him. "The plane is prepared. We are ready to leave."

With that, she stalked toward the dock area.

Tucker waved the others out of hiding and hurried to keep up with Elena. She had stopped beside one of the planes. With one leg leaning on a float, she unlatched the side door and lowered it like a ramp onto the dock's walkway.

The twin-engine seaplane, painted azure, stretched about seventy feet long, with gull wings and oval stabilizers at the tail. The fuselage was deep chested, with a bulbous cockpit.

"I don't recognize this model," he said as he joined her.

She explained proudly, her hands on her hips. "This is a Beriev Be-6. Your NATO called it *Madge*. Built the same year Stalin died."

"That's sixty years ago," Anya noted, worried.

"Fifty-nine," Elena shot back, offended. "She is old, but a very tough bird. Well maintained. Board now."

No one dared disobey.

Once everyone was aboard, Elena unhooked the lines from their cleats, hopped inside, and pulled the door closed behind her with a resounding slam. She hurried forward to the cockpit.

"Sit down!" she yelled back. "Seat belts!"

And that was the extent of their preflight safety briefing.

Bukolov and Anya were buckled into the bench along the right side of the fuselage, Utkin and Tucker on the left. Kane curled up between Tucker's feet, never letting his guard down.

The plane began drifting sideways from the dock.

Bukolov called over, "Tucker, you seem to have a proclivity for unorthodox methods of travel."

"One of my many idiosyncrasies."

"Then I assume we will be traveling to the United States aboard a zeppelin."

"Let's leave it as a surprise," he replied.

From the cockpit came a series of beeps and buzzes, accompanied by a short curse from Elena—then the sound of a fist striking something solid. Suddenly, the engines roared to life, rumbling the fuselage.

"Here we go!" Elena called.

The plane accelerated out of the cove and into the inlet. Moments later they were airborne.

7:44 P.M.

"*Bartok!*" Elena yelled once they'd reached cruising altitude. "You come up here!"

Tucker unbuckled his seat belt, scooted around Kane, and ducked into the cockpit. He knelt beside her seat. The copilot seat was empty. Through the windscreen, he saw only blackness.

"Now tell me the destination. The person on phone said *southeast*. Said you would have the destination once in air."

Tucker gave her the coordinates, which she jotted on her kneeboard.

After a few fast calculations, she said, "Fifty minutes. You know what we are looking for? A signal of some kind, *da*? The Caspian is big, especially at night."

"Once we are there, I'll let you know."

Tucker returned to the cabin. The roar of the engines had faded to a low drone. Aside from the occasional lurch as Elena hit a pocket of turbulence, the ride was smooth.

Now is as good a time as any.

Tucker stood between the two benches. "It is time we have a family meeting."

"A what?" Bukolov asked.

Tucker dove in. "Every step of the way, General Kharzin has been waiting for us. Until now I had no idea how he was doing it."

Tucker paused to look at each of them in turn.

Anya shifted under his scrutiny. "And? What are you saying, Tucker?"

He drew the signal generator from his pocket and held it up for everyone to see.

"What is that?" Bukolov asked, motioning for a closer look.

Tucker turned to Utkin. "Would you like to explain?"

The young man shrugged, shook his head.

"It's a signal generator—a homing beacon. It was attached to the *Olga*'s antenna feed. Since we left Volgograd it's been regularly sending out a signal until I disarmed it a few minutes ago. A signal that Kharzin has been listening for."

"You think one of us put it there?" Utkin asked.

"Yes."

"It could have been Misha," Anya offered. "He would know how to attach the device. It was his submarine."

"No, Misha brought this to me."

Anya's eyes grew rounder. "Tucker, you're scaring me. What do you know?"

Tucker turned to Utkin. "Is that your bag under your seat?"

"Yes."

"Pull it out."

"Okay . . . why?"

"Pull it out."

Utkin did so.

"Show me your playing cards."

"My what? I don't see why—"

"Show me."

Having noted the hardness of Tucker's tone, Kane stood up and fixed his gaze on Utkin.

"Tucker, my friend, what is going on? I do not understand, but fine, I will show you."

He unzipped his duffel and began rummaging around. After a few seconds, he froze, glanced up at Tucker, and pulled out his two boxes of playing cards. One empty, one full. Utkin held up the empty one.

Tucker read the understanding in the young man's eyes.

"But it . . . it is not mine," Utkin stammered.

Tucker grabbed the box, slid the signal generator into it, and resealed the flap. It was a perfect fit. Earlier this morning, during his search of the group's belongings, he'd found the empty box of playing cards in the young man's duffel.

Utkin continued shaking his head. "No, no, that is not mine."

Anya covered her mouth.

"Is it true?" asked Bukolov. "Tucker, is this true?"

"Ask him."

Bukolov had paled with shock. "Utkin—after all our time together, you would do this? Why? Is this tied to that past gambling problem of yours? I thought you had stopped."

Shame blushed Utkin's face to a dark crimson. "No! This is all a mistake!" He turned to Tucker, his eyes hopeless with despair. "What will you do to me?"

Before he could respond, Anya blurted out, "Tucker, do not kill him, please. He made a mistake. Perhaps someone forced him to do it. Remember, I know these people. Perhaps they blackmailed him. Isn't that right, Utkin? You had no choice. Tucker, he had no choice."

Tucker looked to Bukolov. "Doctor, how do you vote?"

Bukolov shook his head. Without looking at his lab assistant, he waved a dismissive hand. "I do not care. He is dead to me either way."

At this, Utkin broke down. He curled himself into a ball, his head touching his knees, and started sobbing.

Tucker felt sorry for Utkin, but he kept his face impassive. The lab assistant had almost cost them their lives—and he might still. Felice could already be on her way here.

That fear drew him back to the cockpit, leaving Utkin guarded by Kane.

"Can we circle?" he asked Elena. "To check our tail?"

She frowned at him. "You think we are being followed."

"Can you do it?"

Elena sighed. "Two hundred rubles extra for fuel."

"Deal."

"Okay, okay. Hold on."

She turned the wheel and the Beriev eased into a gentle bank.

After a lazy ten-minute circle above the Volga delta, Elena said, "I see no one. Easy to spot in the dark. But I will keep watching."

"Me, too." Tucker took the empty copilot's seat.

In the green glow of the instruments, he glimpsed a dark shape against the lower console between the seats. It was a machine gun, attached to the console with Velcro straps. It had a wooden stock and a stubby barrel. Just ahead of the trigger guard was a large, cylindrical magazine.

"Is that an old tommy gun?" he asked.

Elena corrected him. "That is a Shpagin machine gun. From Great Patriotic War. It was my father's. American gangsters stole the design."

"You're an interesting woman, Elena."

"*Da*, I know," she replied with a confident smile. "But don't get any ideas. I have a boyfriend. Okay, *three* boyfriends. But they don't know about each other, so it's okay."

As they neared their destination coordinates, everything still remained dark and quiet in the skies around them.

"What now, Bartok?" Elena asked.

"An island lies dead ahead at the coordinates I gave you. We're supposed to rendezvous on the eastern side, where there is a narrow beach. Once you land on the water, taxi in as close as you can, and we'll wade ashore. After that, you're done."

"Whatever you say. Best to strap in now. Touchdown in two minutes."

Tucker relayed the message to the others, then buckled in next to Elena.

"Beginning descent," she said.

The nose of the plane dipped, aiming for the dark waters below.

As they plummeted, Elena prepared for landing: flipping switches, adjusting elevator controls, tweaking the throttle. Finally, the plane straightened, racing over the water, until the pontoons kissed the surface. The Beriev shook slightly, bounced once, then settled. The seaplane's speed rapidly bled off, and the ride smoothed out.

Tucker checked his watch. They had made good time and were twenty minutes early.

"Very shallow here," Elena announced as she swung the plane's nose and headed toward the island's shore.

"Again, just get as close as you can." Tucker unbuckled and stood up. "Thanks for the ride. I—"

Over Elena's shoulder, out the side window, a dark shape appeared out of nowhere. Disoriented, Tucker's first thought was *rock*. They were passing some storm-beaten shoal sticking out of the water.

Then a strobe of navigation lights bloomed, hovering there, revealing its true nature.

Helicopter.

Tucker shouted, "Elena . . . get down!"

"What—?"

As she turned toward him, her forehead disappeared in a cloud of red mist.

26

March 17, 8:47 P.M.
The Caspian Sea

Tucker dropped to his knees, then his belly. He felt wet warmth dripping down his face and swiped his hand across it.

Blood.

He turned his head and yelled through the cockpit door. "Everyone flat on the deck!"

Kane came slinking toward him, but Tucker held up his hand, and the shepherd stopped.

"What's happening?" Anya called out, sounding terrified.

"The pilot's dead. We've got company."

He rolled and rose to his knees behind the pilot's seat. He craned his neck over Elena's slumped body and peeked out the side window.

The helicopter was gone.

Smart, Felice . . . kill the pilot and the plane's grounded.

Now she and her team could take their sweet time at capturing or killing them.

Tucker peered through the windscreen. A hundred yards ahead, the black silhouette of the island blotted out the stars. At its base, a gentle crescent of white sand beckoned.

Only then did he note that the Beriev was still moving toward their goal. He scanned the control panel, looking for—*there.* The pictogram of a spinning propeller glowed, bracketed by a plus and minus sign.

Easy enough to interpret.

Reaching around the seat, he shoved the twin throttles forward. The engines roared, and the nose lifted slightly, then settled as the Beriev's speed climbed. The plane raced for the island, skimming the water, rapidly closing the distance. He knew they would never be able to escape the more agile chopper by air.

That wasn't his plan.

He goosed the wheel, keeping them angled toward the beach.

"Brace for impact!" he shouted. "KANE, COME!"

The shepherd sprinted forward. Tucker curled his left arm around Kane's chest and turned them both so they were tucked against the bulkhead. He propped his legs against the pilot's chair and squeezed his eyes shut.

Beneath his rear end, the Beriev's fuselage shuddered as it passed the shallows. Next came a shriek, followed by a grinding of metal on sand.

The plane violently lurched left, catching a pontoon on something—a rock, a sandbar—then flipped up on its nose and cartwheeled across the beach.

Glass shattered.

From the cabin, screams and shouts.

The copilot's seat tore free and seemed to float in midair before crashing into the side window above Tucker's head.

Then the plane hit the trees, shearing off one wing. They slammed to a teetering stop, the plane stuck up on its side, the remaining wing pointed to the sky.

Tucker looked around. A pair of emergency lights in the overhead bathed the cockpit in a dull glow. Tree branches jutted through the side window. Above him, over his left shoulder, he saw a sliver of dark sky through the windscreen.

He took personal inventory of his condition and ran his hands over Kane's flanks and limbs, getting a reassuring lick in return.

Think, he commanded himself.

Felice was still out there, but her helicopter lacked pontoons, so it could not land in the water. He pictured the tree-lined beach. He didn't believe it was wide enough to accommodate the chopper's rotor span.

We have time—but not much.

They just had to survive until the plane Harper sent got here.

He called, "Everyone okay back there?"

Silence.

"Answer me!"

Bukolov called weakly, "I am . . . we are hanging in the air. Anya and myself. She hurt her hand."

"Utkin!"

"I am here, pinned under my seat."

"No one move. Let me come to you."

Tucker ordered Kane to stay put and pulled himself to the cockpit door. He swung his legs until he was sitting on the door coaming. With the plane on its side, the left bulkhead was now the floor. He found an emergency flashlight strapped to the wall. He snagged it free, turned it on, and took a moment to orient himself.

Utkin was still buckled into his seat, but it had broken loose and rolled atop him. Above him, Bukolov and Anya were strapped in place and suspended in midair.

No one seemed to be direly injured, except Anya clutched her hand to her chest, her eyes raw with pain. For now, there was nothing he could do to help her.

"Utkin, unbuckle yourself and crawl to me."

As he did so, Tucker hopped down next to him and stoop-walked aft until he was beneath Bukolov and Anya. He shined his flashlight up.

"Anya, you first. Press the buckle release with your good hand, and I'll catch you. It's not as high as it seems."

After a moment's hesitation, she hit the release and fell. Tucker caught her and lowered her to her feet.

He repeated the procedure with Bukolov.

Once down, the doctor leveled a finger at Utkin's face. "You! You almost got us killed. Again."

"Abram, I did not—"

"Quiet!" Tucker barked. "We have only a few minutes before Felice finds a way to reach us. We need to get out of here without being seen."

"How?" Anya asked, wincing. It appeared she had either sprained or broken her wrist.

"A window in the cockpit is smashed. That's our way out."

He turned and clambered back through the door that led to the cockpit. He swung his legs until he was straddling the coaming.

"Grab our packs!" he ordered. "Then Anya up first."

Moving quickly, Tucker shuttled everyone out of the cabin, past the cockpit, and through the broken window. It was a tight squeeze amid the broken branches, but it allowed them to exit directly into dense forest, keeping off the open beach.

Utkin was the last of the three to leave. He looked at Tucker. "You're wrong about me. I wish you would believe that."

"I wish I could."

As the man shimmied out, Tucker turned to Kane. "Ready to go, pal?"

Kane wagged his tail and belly-crawled after the others.

Tucker followed, but not before grabbing Elena's Shpagin machine gun. He slung it across his back, while staring down at the young woman's lifeless body.

"I'm sorry . . ."

The words sounded idiotic to him.

I'm sorry you're dead. I'm sorry I dragged you into this.

Anger stabbed into him, fiery and fierce. He used it to steady the edge of panic, to clear his head to a crystal focus.

Felice, you're dead.

He made a silent oath to make that happen.

For Elena.

Turning away, he crawled out and joined the others huddled together in the darkness of the forest. The neighboring beach looked like polished silver under the moonlight that pierced the clouds.

"What now?" Bukolov asked. "I don't see the helicopter. Perhaps they think we are dead."

"It's possible, but you're their prize, Doctor. They won't leave without knowing your true fate."

"What about your people?" Anya asked.

He checked his watch. It was still a few minutes until they were supposed to arrive.

Tucker dug through his duffel until his fingers touched the satellite phone. Even without looking, he knew the phone was shattered. The casing had split open, and the innards lay in pieces at the bottom of his pack.

"Stay here," he ordered and crawled to the edge of the sand. He scanned the sky, while straining to listen. He thought he heard the distant thump of rotors, but when he turned his head, the sound faded.

Options, Tucker thought. *What do we do?*

Felice had them pinned down.

Again, Tucker heard thumping.

The helicopter was definitely out there, moving with no lights, like before, lying in wait.

And not just for us, he suddenly realized.

No wonder she didn't immediately come after them.

He pushed back to the others. "Kharzin *knows* this is the rendezvous point, that others must be coming. Felice is out there waiting for them, intending to take them out, to catch them off guard like she did us, leaving her free to deal with us after that."

"What are we going to do?" Anya said.

"I don't know—"

Utkin suddenly bolted past Tucker, his heels kicking up sand as he broke from cover and stumbled out onto the open beach.

Tucker's first instinct was to raise the Shpagin, but he stopped himself. He still couldn't shoot an unarmed man in the back.

"Stop!" he called out to Utkin. "There's nowhere to run!"

A strobe of navigation lights burst above the treetops at the northern tip of the island. A floodlight bloomed, stabbing down to the beach. The helicopter's nose followed the beam down, picking up speed.

Utkin got caught in the light, sliding to a stop. He lifted his arm against its blinding glare and waved his other arm.

"What is that idiot doing?" Bukolov said. "Does he think they'll pick him up?"

"He'll get away," Anya cried.

Skimming the trees, the chopper reached the beach in seconds and banked over the crashed Beriev. All the while, the floodlight kept Utkin pinned down.

Suddenly fire winked from the chopper's open cabin door.

Bursts of sand kicked up, and a bullet struck Utkin's leg. He toppled forward, lay for a stunned moment, then started crawling in agony toward the trees, pushing with his good leg.

The gun flashed again from the helicopter's doorway.

A second bullet struck Utkin's other leg. He pitched flat to the sand. His arms paddled as he tried to push himself back up.

From the precision of the shooting, it had to be Felice.

He knew what she was doing, torturing Utkin to draw him out. She didn't know that the traitor had been exposed—or maybe she didn't care.

A part of Tucker knew Utkin had brought this upon himself.

But another part railed against such brutality.

He felt his ears pop, a rush of hot air, the screams of his fellow rangers filled his head. He saw a mirage of a limping dog, bloodied and in pain—

No, not again . . . never again. . .

He broke from cover, sprinted past the wreckage of the Beriev, and across the sands. He charged forward, eating up the distance until he was twenty yards away. He dropped to one knee, jerked the Shpagin to his shoulder, and took aim.

He fired a short three-round burst. The Shpagin bucked in his grip. The bullets went wide. He tucked the weapon tighter to his shoulder and fired again, squeezing and holding fast. Bullets shredded into the chopper's tail.

Smoke gushed.

The helicopter pivoted, exposing its open doorway. A lone figure stood there. Though her lower face was hidden behind a scarf, he knew it was Felice.

He opened fire again, stitching the fuselage from tail to nose.

She stumbled out of view.

Abruptly the chopper banked hard left and dove for the ocean's surface and picked up speed, heading away, trailing oily smoke.

Furious, blind with rage, he kept firing after it until it had vanished into the darkness. Critically damaged, the helicopter wouldn't be returning any time soon.

He swung over to Utkin, dropping to his knees beside him.

During the firefight, the young man had managed to roll onto his back. His left thigh was black with blood. His right poured a crimson stain into the sand, spurting from his leg, with a brightness that could only be arterial.

Tucker pressed his palm against the wound and leaned on it.

Utkin groaned heavily. One hand rose to touch the hot barrel of the machine gun. "Knew you could do it . . ."

"Quiet. Lay still."

"Someone . . . someone had to flush out that evil *suka* before she ambushed your friends . . ."

Hot blood welled through his fingers.

A sob rose in Tucker's chest, escaping in shaking gasps. "Hold on . . . just hold on . . ."

Utkin's eyes found his face. "Tucker . . . I'm sorry . . . my friend . . ."

Then he was gone.

9:02 P.M.

Tucker sat on the sand, hugging his knees. Kane lay tight against his side, sensing his grief. A small fire burned on the beach, created by igniting driftwood with some of the leaking fuel from the wreckage, a signal to those who were coming.

It seemed to have worked.

The drone of an engine echoed over the water. A moment later, a seaplane swept above the beach. Anya waved with her good arm. From the plane's side window, a flashlight blinked back at her, signaling the identity of their rescuers.

As the plane circled for a water landing, Bukolov wandered over to him. "I still don't understand why he did that."

Off to the side, Utkin's body was covered by a tarp.

"Redemption," Tucker said. "I think he purposefully drew the chopper out of hiding, so I'd have a chance to take it out before the others arrived."

"But why? Did he do it out of guilt?"

Tucker remembered his last words.

. . . *my friend* . . .

Tucker laid a hand on Kane's side. "He did it out of friendship."

PART III

Rough Country

27

March 18, 8:00 A.M.
Istanbul, Turkey

Tucker followed the embassy aide into the conference room. The space looked ordinary enough: white walls, burgundy carpet, maple table. Someone had set out glasses and pitchers of ice. He also smelled coffee, one of life's necessities at this early hour after such a long night.

Bukolov and Anya joined him as he settled into one of the leather chairs. They all squeaked heavily into place for this private meeting.

Anya's left arm was in a cast from midforearm to her knuckles. She had broken two bones in her wrist as a result of the plane crash. Her eyes were still glassy from pain relievers.

For this meeting, it would just be the three of them, seated around a speakerphone.

"Your call is being routed," said the aide, a young man in a crisp suit. He promptly left, sealing the door behind him.

Despite the unassuming decor, Tucker knew this room in the U.S. consulate was soundproofed and electronically secure. No one else would be listening in.

Tucker stared across the table at the other two.

Anya looked haunted.

Bukolov defeated.

They'd flown straight from the Caspian Sea to Turkey, arriving well after midnight. They'd been given rooms here, but it looked like none of them had slept well. Tucker had left Kane behind to give the shepherd some extra downtime.

The conference phone on the table trilled, and a voice came over the speaker. "Your party is on the line. Go ahead."

After a series of beeps, followed by a burst of static, Ruth Harper's voice came on the line.

"Tucker, are you there?"

"Yes." Again he felt the comfort of her familiar soft twang. "I have Doctor Bukolov and Anya here also."

"Very good."

In Harper's usual brusque manner, she got right down to business. "Let's start with the most pressing concern of the moment. Stanimir Utkin. How much information do you believe this mole shared with his superiors? With this General Artur Kharzin?"

Tucker had already given Harper a condensed version of the last twenty-four hours, including the betrayal and ultimate redemption by Utkin.

Bukolov answered angrily. "How much information? How about *all* of it? He had access to all my research material. I never suspected him in the slightest." He glanced over to Anya, his voice dropping further into defeat. "I never suspected anyone."

Tucker stared between them.

Anya looked down at the table. "I told Abram last night. About my involvement with Russian SVR. About my assignment. I thought he should hear it from me first."

"Anya *Averin*," Bukolov muttered. "I didn't even know your real name."

Harper spoke into the awkward silence that followed. "I made some discreet inquiries. As far as I can tell, Anya's story checks out. She *was* falsifying intelligence to her superiors."

Anya glanced to the doctor. "In order to protect you, Abram, to protect your research, so it wouldn't be abused." She reached her right hand to him. "I'm sorry. I should have told you sooner."

Bukolov turned slightly away from her. "Does she need to be here? She's of no use to me now. I have all of De Klerk's diary. I can handle the rest on my own."

"Not your decision to make, Doctor," Tucker replied.

"Not my decision? How can you say that? She betrayed me!"

Anya said, "Abram, please. I gave them nothing of your work. I protected—"

"I am done with you! Mr. Wayne, I refuse to allow her to accompany us."

Harper cleared her throat. "Let's put a pin in this, Doctor, and get back to Stanimir Utkin. For now, we must assume he gave Kharzin everything. Including the information from Paulos de Klerk's diary. Is that correct, Doctor Bukolov?"

"Unfortunately, yes."

"Then let's move on to the threat posed by that information, about the danger of LUCA falling into the hands of Kharzin?"

Bukolov took on a defensive tone. "You must understand, that if handled properly, LUCA could be an unprecedented boon to humanity. We could turn deserts into—"

"Yes, I understand that," Harper said, cutting him off. "But it's the phrase *handled properly* that worries me. Correct me if I'm wrong, but even if we're able to find a viable specimen of LUCA, we still have no way of controlling it—not you, not Kharzin's people. Is that right?"

Bukolov hesitated, frowned. "Yes," he said slowly. "No one has developed a kill switch. But I am convinced the mechanism for controlling LUCA *does* exist. So is Kharzin convinced. The general would only have to introduce a few ounces of LUCA in a handful of strategic locations, and without a kill switch in our possession, the organism would spread like wildfire, destroying all native plant life. There would be no stopping it. But the larger threat is *weaponization*."

"Explain, Doctor," said Harper.

"Take smallpox, for example. It's one of the most feared biological weapons known to man, but that threat alone is not enough. To be sure of infecting the maximum number of victims, smallpox must be weaponized—it must be deliverable over a wide area in a short period of time, so it overwhelms the population and the medical infrastructure. Kharzin will see LUCA in the same light. He's a military man. It is how they think. Weaponized LUCA, delivered strategically, could reach critical mass in hours. Yes, yes, LUCA in its raw form is dangerous, but not necessarily cata-strophic. There would be a chance we might be able to stop it. If he weaponizes it . . . it's an endgame move."

"End?" Harper asked. "As in end of the world?"

"Without a kill switch, a way of controlling what's unleashed, yes. We're talking about the fundamental destruction of the earth's ecosystem."

Harper paused, digesting the information. Tucker pictured her removing her thick set of librarian glasses and rubbing her eyes. Finally she spoke again. "How confident are you about this kill switch, Doctor?"

"I'm sure I can develop it. Even De Klerk hinted at the possibility in his diary. I just need a sample."

"From some lost cave in South Africa?" Harper added.

"Yes."

"And you think you can find this cave?"

"I believe so. Before I burned the page that explained its location, I set it to memory. But De Klerk plainly feared this organism, even bestowing it with the omi-nous title *Die Apokalips Saad.* He was so frightened that he encrypted his words, couching the route to the cave in obscure terms."

"Can you recite it now? Give us an example?"

"Here is how it starts." Bukolov formed a steeple of his fingers as he concentrated. " '*From Grietje's Well at Melkboschkuil ... bear twenty-five degrees for a distance of 289,182 krags ... there you find what is hidden beneath the Boar's Head Waterval.'"*

Harper didn't speak immediately. Tucker could almost feel the frustration coming through the speakerphone. "Does that mean anything to you?"

"Not a damned thing," Bukolov said. "I tried for a solid week after finding this page. None of the locations are on any map. Not Grietje's Well. Not Melkboschkuil. Not that Boar's Head Waterfall. And as far as I could ascertain, there is no unit of measurement called a *krag*."

Bukolov tossed his arms in the air. "It's one of the reasons I called out to you all. Surely you've got cryptographers and map experts who could decipher it. Get us on the right path to that cave."

"I will see what I can do," Harper said. "Give me a couple of hours—let me do some research—and we'll reconvene here."

The line went dead.

As they all headed out, Anya reached an arm toward Bukolov, clearly wanting to talk, to smooth matters between them. When he ignored her, Tucker read the pain in her face, the crush of her posture. She stood in the hall for a long breath, watching the man stalk off.

When she turned away, he caught a glimpse of a single tear roll across a perfect cheekbone.

It seemed betrayal wore many faces.

10:22 A.M.

Tucker used the break to walk Kane amid the courtyards of the embassy. He had been ordered not to venture beyond its gates. The multilevel compound—with its industrial white walls and rows of cell-like windows—looked more like a maximum-security prison than a consulate.

Still, the small gardens inside were handsome, blooming with purplish-pink crocuses and tangled with roses. But best of all, the warm Turkish sun helped melt the residual Russian ice from his bones and thoughts.

Even Kane had more of a dance to his step as he sniffed every corner and bush.

But soon Tucker was back inside, back at the conference table.

"I may have a couple pieces of the puzzle worked out," Harper announced as she came back on the line. "But I fear until we have boots on the ground in South Africa, the location of the cave will remain a mystery. From these obscure references, I believe De Klerk was trying to hide some meaning or significance that would only make sense to another Boer of his time."

Bukolov leaned closer. "Understandable. The Boer were notorious xenophobes, suspicious of other people and races, and especially paranoid about the British. But you said you had a couple of the clues solved. What did you learn?"

"It took consulting with a handful of Smithsonian historians, but we may have figured out De Klerk's reference to *krag* as a unit of measurement."

"What is it?" Anya asked.

"During the fighting back then, a common weapon used widely by Boer troops was a Norwegian rifle called an M1894 Krag-Jørgensen. Over time, it became simply known as a *krag*. The rifle was thirty-nine inches long. If we assume that was De Klerk's unit of measurement, the distance he described is around 178 miles."

Bukolov sat straighter, some of his normal spunk returning. "So we now know the distance from Grietje's Well to the Boar's Head Waterfall!"

"And not much else," Harper added, quickly popping that balloon. "I suspect the Boar's Head Waterfall—where this cave is hidden—is not so much a *name* as what the place *looks* like, some local landmark that you have to see to recognize."

"So obviously something that looks like the head of a boar," Tucker said.

"And that's why we'll need boots on the ground. We need someone scouring that location, likely on foot or horseback."

"To view the place from the same vantage as De Klerk did in the past," Anya said.

"Exactly." Harper shifted the topic. "But to even get there, we need to know where to *start*, where to set out from. Without that information, we're nowhere."

Bukolov nodded. "We must figure out what De Klerk meant by *Grietje's Well at Melkboschkuil.*"

"Which brings me to the *second* piece of the puzzle we've solved. The historians determined that there once was a farm called *Melkboschkuil*, owned by the Cloete family, located in the Northern Cape province of South Africa. It's historically significant because the farmstead eventually prospered and grew into the present-day city of Springbok."

"Then that's where we must go!" Bukolov slapped a palm on the table. "To Springbok . . . to find this Grietje's Well. Then it's a simple matter to measure out 178 miles at a compass bearing of twenty-five degrees, like De Klerk wrote, and look for this Boar's Head near a waterfall. That's where we'll find the cave!"

Is that all we have to do? Tucker thought sourly.

Harper also lacked the good doctor's confidence. "The only problem is I could find no reference to a place called Grietje's Well. It's likely a place known only to the locals of De Klerk's time. All we've been able to determine is that *Grietje* is Dutch for 'Wilma.'"

"So then we're looking for Wilma's Well," Tucker said.

"That's about it," Harper conceded. "Like I said. We need boots on the ground."

"And I intend to be a pair of those boots," Bukolov said. "My knowledge of De Klerk may prove the difference between success and failure out there."

Anya stirred, too, clearly wanting to go. Like the doctor, she was also well versed in De Klerk's work—and if anything, more stable.

"Understood," Harper said. "But all this presents one other problem."

Tucker didn't like the note of warning in the her tone; even her southern lilt grew heavier.

"If you draw a line from Springbok along De Klerk's bearing, it puts you squarely into the Groot Karas Mountains—in the country of Namibia."

Tucker took a deep breath and let it out audibly.

"What?" Anya asked. "What's wrong?"

"Namibia is in the middle of a bloody war," Tucker explained. "Between government forces and guerrillas."

"And those guerrillas," Harper added, "hold those mountains. They're particularly fond of kidnapping foreigners and holding them for ransom."

Bukolov puffed loudly, clearly frustrated. "There has to be a way. We cannot abandon the search now."

"We're not, but if you go, I wanted you to understand what you could be facing out there. I'll arrange some local assets to assist you in Africa, but it'll be far from safe."

Bukolov shook his head. "I must go! We must try! Before Kharzin finds some other means to discover that cave. Utkin only saw that map page briefly before I burned it, but I don't know how much he retained or shared. And maybe I inadvertently mentioned something to him. I simply don't know."

Anya spoke with more certainty. "What I do know is that General Kharzin *won't* stop. Most everyone at the SVR detests him. He's a Cold War–era warrior, a real dinosaur. He believes Russia's brightest days died with Stalin. If Utkin has been feeding him intelligence all along, then he understands LUCA's potential as a weapon. Properly introduced into an ecosystem—like a rice paddy in Japan—a single speck of LUCA would systematically destroy that ecosystem. And not just that rice paddy, but *all* of them."

"That must not happen," Bukolov pressed.

"I agree," Harper said. "I'll begin making arrangements."

11:10 A.M.

After settling some minor issues, Harper asked to speak to Tucker alone.

"Have we made a devil's deal here, Tucker? Part of me thinks we should just firebomb this cave if we find it."

"It may come down to that. But you've also made one hell of an assumption."

"Which is what?"

"That Kane and I are going to Africa."

"What? After everything we just discussed, you'd consider bailing out?"

Tucker chuckled. "No, but a girl likes to be *asked* to the dance."

Harper laughed in return. "Consider yourself asked. So what's your assessment of Anya and Bukolov. He plainly doesn't want her along."

"I say that's his problem. Anya's earned her place on this mission."

"I agree. She seems to know almost as much about LUCA as he does. And considering the stakes, it wouldn't hurt to have a different perspective on things. But the good doctor will not like it."

Tucker sighed. "The sooner Bukolov learns that his tantrums will get him nowhere, the better it will be for everyone once he reaches the United States."

"How soon can you get me a list of supplies you'll need?"

"A couple hours. I want to be under way tonight. In Springbok by noon."

"Understood."

"And I need to ask a couple of favors."

"Name them."

"First, find the family of the Beriev pilot." *Elena.* "Make sure they know where to find her body and reimburse them for the Beriev."

"And second?"

"Make sure Utkin's body is returned to his family. They're in a village called Kolyshkino on the Volga River."

"Why? The man betrayed you—almost got you all killed."

"But in the end, he saved us. And I respect that last act."

Naive or not, Tucker wanted to believe that maybe Anya was right. That Utkin had been forced against his will to betray them. But he would never know for sure. And maybe it was better that way.

"Sounds as though you liked him." Harper's voice went unusually soft, as if sensing the depth of his regret.

"I suppose I did. It's hard to explain."

Thankfully she let it go at that.

"Okay, I'll handle everything. But what about sending additional muscle your way, something beyond a few local assets?"

"I think small is better."

Besides, Tucker had all the help he needed and trusted in the form of his four-legged partner.

"You may be right," Harper agreed. "South Africa's security agencies run a tight ship. You show up big and loud, and they'll be all over you."

"I can't argue with that."

"Now, I have to ask something difficult of you," she said.

"Go ahead."

"If you get to that cave and things go sour, you make damned sure LUCA doesn't see the light of day. No matter the cost. Or casualties. Is that understood?"

Tucker inhaled deeply. "I'll get it done."

3:34 P.M.

A soft knock on his door woke him out of a slight drowse. Kane lifted his head from Tucker's chest as the two lay sprawled on the bed, napping in the day's heat.

Tucker, still in his clothes, rolled to his feet and placed his face in his hands.

Who the hell . . .

Kane hopped down, sidled to the door, and sniffed along the bottom. His tail began to wag. Someone he knew.

"Tucker, are you awake?" a voice called through the door.

Anya.

He groaned, stepped over, and unlocked the door. He wiped his eyes blearily. "What's wrong?"

Something better be *wrong.*

Anya stood in the doorway, wearing a peach-colored sundress. She smoothed it over her hips self-consciously with her good hand. "One of the consulate wives gave it to me. I'm sorry, you were sleeping, weren't you?"

She began to step away.

"No. It's all right. Come in."

"I should probably be sleeping, too. But every time I lie down . . ." She walked over to the side chair across from the bed and sat down. "I'm frightened, Tucker."

"Of going to South Africa?"

"Of course, that. But mostly about what happens *after* all this. Once we're in America."

"Anya, the government will give you a new identity, a new place to live. And with your background, you'll have no trouble finding work. You'll be fine."

"I'll be *alone*. Everything I know will be gone. Even Bukolov. You heard him. He'll barely talk to me now."

"Maybe he'll calm down and eventually understand."

She picked slightly at her cast, her voice growing pained. "He won't. I know him."

Tucker knew she was right. Bukolov was single-minded and emotionally inflexible. Now that he had De Klerk's diary in hand, Anya was no longer indispensable to his work. And in addition she had proven herself untrustworthy. For Bukolov, both of these sins were unpardonable.

Anya was right. Once in America, she would be alone. Rudderless. She would need friends.

With a sigh, he reached across and squeezed her hand.

"You'll know at least *one* person in the States," he reassured her.

Kane thumped his tail.

"Make that *two*," he added.

28

March 19, 12:02 P.M.
Cape Town, South Africa

As Tucker set foot off the plane's stairway and onto the hot tarmac of Cape Town's International Airport, a shout rose ahead. They had landed at a private terminal, shuttled here by corporate jet—a Gulfstream V—arranged by Harper.

"Mr. Wayne, sir! Over here!"

He turned to see a tall, thin black man in his midtwenties trotting toward him. He wore charcoal slacks and a starched white shirt. He gave Tucker a broad smile and stuck out his hand.

"Mr. Tucker Wayne, I presume."

He took the man's hand. "And you are?"

"Christopher Nkomo."

Kane came trotting down behind him, sliding next to Tucker, sniffing at the stranger, sizing him up.

"My goodness," the man said, "who is this fine animal?"

"That would be Kane."

"He's magnificent!"

No argument there.

Bukolov and Anya came next, shielding their eyes, as they joined him. Introductions were made all around.

"What tribe are you?" Anya asked, then blurted out, "Oh, is that impolite to ask? I'm sorry."

"Not at all, missus. I am of the Ndebele tribe."

"And your language?"

"We speak Xhosa." He waved and guided them across the tarmac toward a nest of parked Cessnas and other smaller aircraft. "But I went to university here, studying business administration and English."

"It shows," said Tucker.

"Very kind of you." He finally stopped before a single-engine plane, a Cessna Grand Caravan. It was already being serviced for flight. "With your patience, we will get all your baggage loaded quickly."

Christopher was a man of his word. It was accomplished in a matter of minutes.

"Your pilot will be with you shortly," he said, clambering up the short ladder and through the Cessna's side door. A moment later, he hopped back out, his head now adorned with a blue pilot's cap. "Welcome aboard. My name is Christopher Nkomo, and I will be your pilot today."

Tucker matched his grin. "You'll be flying us?"

"Myself and my older brother, Matthew."

A thin arm stuck out from the side window next to the copilot's seat.

"No worries," Christopher said. "I am a very good pilot and I know this land and its history like the palm of my hand. I hear you all are Boer historians, and that I am to assist you however I can."

From the tone of the man's voice, he knew they weren't historians. Harper clearly must have debriefed Christopher about the goal of their mission here.

"I am especially familiar with Springbok. My cousin has a home there. So if we are all ready, let us get aboard."

Bukolov and Anya needed no coaxing to climb out of the sun and into the dark, air-conditioned interior. Bukolov took the seat farthest from Anya. The doctor was not happy to have her along, but back in Istanbul, Tucker had left him no choice.

Tucker hung back with Christopher. "The supplies I asked for?"

"Come see."

Christopher lifted a hatch to reveal a storage space neatly packed with supplies. He pulled out a clipboard and handed it to Tucker. It listed the contents: potable water, dehydrated meals, first-aid kits, maps and compasses, knives, hatchets, a small but well-stocked toolbox.

"As for weapons and ammunition," the man said, "I was not able to provide all the exact models you requested. I took the liberty of using my own judgment."

He pulled that list out of a back pocket and passed it over.

Tucker scanned it and nodded. "Nicely done. Hopefully we won't need any of it."

"God willing," Christopher replied.

1:38 P.M.

Tucker stared at the passing landscape as the Cessna droned toward their destination. Buckled opposite Tucker, Kane matched his pose, his nose pressed to the window.

The scenery north of Cape Town was hypnotically beautiful: a dry moonscape of reddish-brown earth and savannah, broken up by saw-toothed hills. Tiny settlements dotted the countryside, surrounded by brighter patches of green scrub.

At last, Christopher swung the Cessna into a gentle bank that took them over Springbok. The town of nine thousand lay nestled in a valley surrounded by rolling granite peaks, called the *Klein Koperberge,* or Small Copper Mountains.

The plane leveled out of its banking turn and descended toward Springbok's airstrip. As they landed, the tires kissed the dirt tarmac without the slightest bounce. They rolled to the end of the runway and turned right toward the terminal, administrative offices, and maintenance hangars.

Christopher drew the Cessna to a smooth stop alongside a powder-blue Toyota SUV. A man bearing a striking resemblance to Christopher and his brother waved from the driver's seat.

Tucker called toward the cockpit, "Another brother, Christopher?"

"Yes, indeed, Mr. Wayne. That is Paul, my youngest brother. He flew up here last night to arrange things and make inquiries."

When the engines had come to a complete stop, Christopher walked back, opened the side door, and helped them out.

A palpable blast of heat struck Tucker in the face.

Anya gasped at it.

Bukolov grumbled his displeasure. "What is this fresh hell you have brought us to, Tucker?"

Christopher laughed. "Do not worry. You will get used to the heat." He stepped away, embraced his brother Paul, and motioned them into the SUV. "My brother has arranged accommodations at a guesthouse not far from here."

"Why?" Bukolov said. "How long will we be staying here?"

"At least the night. Matthew will remain here and guard your supplies. If you'll climb aboard, please."

Soon they were heading north on a highway marked R355. Barren foothills flanked both sides, their eroded reddish-orange flanks revealing black granite domes.

"This place looks like Mars," Bukolov said. "I've seen no water at all in this godforsaken land. How are we supposed to find a *well* out here?"

"Patience, Doc," Tucker said.

They finally reached the outskirts of Springbok. It could have passed for a small town in Arizona, with narrow, winding streets bordered by modest ranch homes.

Paul turned into a crescent-shaped driveway lined by thick green hedges. A hand-painted placard atop a post read KLEINPLASIE GUESTHOUSE. The SUV stopped beneath a timbered awning. A set of stone steps led up to French doors bracketed by a pair of potted palms.

After speaking to a bellman in white shorts and a crisp polo shirt, Christopher led his charges, including Kane, into the lobby.

"Oh, this is glorious," Anya said, referring more to the air-conditioning than the accommodations—though they were handsome, too.

The lobby consisted of leather armchairs, animal-hide rugs, sisal runners, and framed drawings of famous African explorers. Above them, huge rattan-bladed ceiling fans hung from exposed beams and churned the already-cool air.

Christopher checked them in, then led them to a private meeting space down the hall. They gathered around a mahogany table. Sunlight streamed through the tilt of plantation shutters. Sparkling pitchers of water, floating with sliced lemons, awaited them.

Paul eventually stepped inside and crossed to the head of the table. "Mr. Wayne," he said. "Christopher informed me of your interest in a local feature. Grietje's Well. I've been making discreet inquiries, but no such place seems to exist, I'm afraid."

"It must," Bukolov snapped, still out of sorts from the travel and heat.

"Mmm," Paul said, too gracious to argue. "However, the relationship between Springbok and water is a long and bloody one. Water was quite treasured here and fought over, as you can well imagine with the heat. So natural sources were often hidden. In fact, the town's original Afrikaans name is *Springbokfontein*."

"What does that mean?" Anya asked.

"*Springbok* is a local antelope. If you keep a sharp eye, you will see them hopping about. And *fontein* means fountain. But a fountain here simply refers to a natural spring or a watering hole."

"Or perhaps a well," Tucker added.

"Exactly so. But *man-made* wells are relatively modern features here in Springbok. Before the middle of the twentieth century, locals relied upon *fonteins*. Natural springs. That is why my brother and I believe what you are actually seeking is not a *well* but a *spring*."

"But how does this fact help us?" Tucker asked.

"Perhaps much, or perhaps not at all," Christopher replied. "But there is a man who might know that answer. Reverend Manfred Cloete."

The name struck Tucker as familiar—then he remembered a detail from the briefing back in Istanbul.

"*Cloete*," Tucker said. "That's the name of the family that once owned *Melkboschkuil* farm. The one Springbok was founded upon."

Christopher nodded. "That's correct. Manfred is indeed a descendant from that distinguished lineage, making the man not only Springbok's reverend, but the keeper of its unwritten history as well."

Paul checked his watch. "And he's waiting for us now."

2:15 P.M.

Crossing through the historic center of Springbok, Christopher turned into a paved parking lot surrounded by a low stucco wall and shaded by lush green acacia trees. Nestled within those same walls stood a sturdy stone church, with a single square steeple and a large rosette window in front. It resembled a miniature Norman castle.

"Springbok's *Klipkerk*," Christopher declared. "The Dutch Reformed Church. Now a museum."

He waved his three passengers out.

Tucker and Kane clambered from the backseat. Anya slid out the front passenger door. They had left Bukolov back at the guesthouse. The travel and the sudden heat had proved too much for the Russian's reserves. As a precaution, Paul had been left behind to watch over the doctor.

Anya waited for Tucker to join her before following Christopher toward the church. She smiled at him, slightly cradling her casted arm. She must still be in some pain, but she hadn't made a single complaint. Perhaps she feared her injury might be used as an excuse to leave her behind. Either that, or she was a real trouper.

Christopher led them along a path that took them to the rear of the church and across a broad, well-manicured lawn.

To one side, a barrel-chested man with wild white hair and a bushy beard knelt beside a bed of blooming desert flowers. He wore Bermuda shorts and nothing else. His torso was deeply tanned and covered in curly white hair.

"Manfred!" Christopher called.

The fellow looked over his shoulder, saw Christopher, and smiled. He stood up and wiped his soiled palms on a towel dangling from the waistband of his shorts. As he joined them, Christopher made the introductions.

"Ah, a pair of fellow historians," Manfred Cloete said, shaking their hands. His light blue eyes twinkled. "Welcome to *Springbokfontein*."

His accent was pure South African, a blend that sounded both British and Australian with a bit of something mysterious thrown in.

"I appreciate you seeing us, Reverend," Tucker replied.

"Manfred, please. My goodness, is that your hound?"

Kane came bounding past, doing a fast circuit of the yard.

"He is indeed. Name's Kane."

"Might tell him to be careful. Got some snakes about. Can't seem to get rid of them."

Tucker whistled, and Kane sprinted over and sat down.

"Follow me, all of you," Manfred said. "I've got some lemonade over in the shade."

He led them to a nearby picnic table, and everyone sat down.

As Manfred tinkled ice and lemonade into Anya's glass, he asked, "So, Ms. Averin—"

"Anya, please."

"Of course, always happy to accommodate a lady's request. Especially one with a wounded wing." He nodded to her cast. "What is this interest in the Boer Wars?"

She glanced to Tucker, letting him take the lead.

He cleared his throat. "It's my interest actually. A personal one. I recently discovered one of my ancestors fought during the Second Boer War. He was a doctor. I know very little else about him except that he served most of his time during the fighting at a fort somewhere around here."

"If he was a *doctor*, that would most likely put him at the Klipkoppie fort. That's where the local medical unit was stationed. It was under the command of

General Manie Roosa. Tough old bird and a bit crazy, if you ask me. The British hated fighting him. You'll find the ruins of the fort just outside of town."

Tucker frowned. On the flight down here, he had already studied the locations of various old forts, hoping for a clue. "Outside of town?" he asked. "But according to my research, the ruins of Klipkoppie are in the *center* of town."

"Pah! That dung heap beside the shopping center? That was only a forward outpost, nothing more. The ruins of the *real* Klipkoppie are two miles to the northwest. Christopher knows where."

"Then why—?"

"Easier to suck tourists into the gift shops and restaurants if it's in the center of town. Besides, the real Klipkoppie isn't much to look at, and it's hard to get to. Can't have tourists getting themselves killed." He clapped his palms against his thighs. "Right. So tell me the name of this ancestor of yours."

"De Klerk. Paulos de Klerk."

Manfred leaned back, clearly recognizing the name, staring at Tucker with new eyes. "The famous botanist?"

"You know him."

"I do. Though I can't say more than that. I actually forgot until you reminded me just now that he was a field medic. He's much better known for those flower drawings of his."

"It's actually one of his journals that drew us down here. In one of his diaries, he mentioned Grietje's Well several times. It seemed important to him."

"Water was back then. It was the difference between life and death. Especially during the wars. When the Brits laid siege to a Boer fort, one of the first things they did was try to cut off access to water. A man can go weeks without food, but only a few days without water. For that reason, the Boer started building forts atop natural springs. Because of the importance of such water sources, the troops came to name them after loved ones, usually women: wives, daughters, nieces."

Anya stirred. "And *Grietje* is Afrikaans for 'Wilma.'"

Manfred nodded. "Wilma must have been dearly loved by whoever named that spring. But like I said, the springs of most forts bore women's names. The key is to find out *which* fort it might be. Because your ancestor was a doctor, I'd still start with the ruins of Klipkoppie."

Anya stared out toward the horizon, at the dry hills. "Do you know of any wells or springs up there?"

"No, but if this spring hasn't dried up, there'll be evidence of erosion on the surface from where the waters seasonally rise and fall. Christopher will know what to look for."

Christopher appeared less convinced. "It will be hard to find. And we're still not certain Klipkoppie is the right fort. With all the old Boer strongholds around here, it could be like finding a needle in a haystack."

"Still, it gives us somewhere to start," Tucker said.

"And in the meantime," Manfred said, "I will look more deeply into the local history of your ancestor. Paulos de Klerk. Come by tomorrow afternoon and we'll talk again."

2:55 P.M.

"Should we head to the Klipkoppie fort now?" Christopher asked as they pulled out of the parking lot.

"How hard is it to reach?"

"It's not far to the base of the fort's hill, but there are no roads to the top. We must hike. Very steep, but I know the way."

Tucker checked his watch. "When does the sun set here?"

"Remember you are south of the equator. It is our late summer, the end of our rainy season. So the sun won't go down until a bit past seven o'clock."

"That gives us roughly four hours." He turned to Anya. "We can drop you back at the guesthouse on the way out of town. Let you rest. I'm not sure your orthopedist would approve of you going hiking."

"And miss this chance?" She lifted her bad arm. "It's fine. Besides, I've got my boots on. Might as well use them."

Tucker heard happy thumping on the seat next to him.

"Sounds like it's unanimous."

Christopher turned the SUV and headed away from the guesthouse. He wound through the streets to the edge of Springbok, then out into the sun-blasted countryside.

They had traveled a couple of kilometers when Christopher's phone rang.

Tucker felt a clutch of fear, wondering if they should have checked on Bukolov before setting out. But there was no way the old man could make the hike in this heat.

Christopher spoke in hushed tones on the phone, then passed the handset over his shoulder. "It's for you. It's Manfred."

Both surprised and curious, he took the phone. "Hello?"

"Ah, my good fellow, glad I was able to reach you." His words were frosted with excitement and pride. "I did some digging as soon as you left. It seems General Manie Roosa, your old ancestor's commander, had a daughter. Named Wilhelmina."

"Another version of Wilma."

"Quite right. And listen to this. In one of Roosa's field reports, he states and I quote, 'Without Wilhelmina, that British bastard MacDonald would have been successful in his siege of our fort.' I suspect he's referring to Sir Ian MacDonald, a British regimental commander back then. But I doubt Roosa's young daughter had any hand in breaking that British siege."

"He must be referring to the fort's water supply! Named after his daughter."

"And surely your ancestor would have known of this secret nickname for the well."

Tucker thanked Manfred and hung up. He relayed the information to the others.

Christopher smiled. "It seems our haystack has gotten considerably smaller."

29

March 19, 3:22 P.M.
Springbok, South Africa

Eleven miles outside of Springbok, Christopher turned onto a narrow dirt driveway that ended at a tin-roofed building. The billboard atop it read HELMAN'S GARAGE. Christopher parked in the shadow of the building, then got out and disappeared through an open bay door.

When he returned, he opened the passenger side for Anya and waved Tucker and Kane out. "Helman says we can park our vehicle here. If we are not back in three weeks, he says he will alert the police."

"Three weeks?" Anya asked, then noted Christopher's smile. "Very funny."

Christopher pulled a trio of daypacks from the SUV's trunk and passed them out. He also unzipped a rifle case and handed Tucker a heavy, double-barreled gun, along with a cartridge belt holding a dozen bullets, each one larger than his thumb.

"Nitro Express cartridges," Christopher said. "Four-seventy caliber. Are you familiar with weapons, Mr. Wayne?"

Tucker broke the rifle's breech, checked the action, and gave it a quick inspection. He pulled a pair of Nitros from the belt, popped them into the breech, and snapped the weapon closed.

"I'll manage," he said.

"Very good." Christopher's expression grew serious. "It is unlikely we will encounter anything, but there are lions in this area. I recommend that Kane stays close to us."

"He will."

"If we encounter lions, we shall try to back out of the area slowly. Lions are typically inactive during the day and mostly sleep. But if there is a charge, stay *behind* me. I will take the first shot. If I miss the shots with both barrels, or the lion fails to yield, I will drop to the ground to give you a clear field of fire. The lion will likely stop to maul me. When he does, take your shot. Do not hesitate. This is very important. Aim a few inches below the lion's chin, between the shoulders, if possible. Or if from the side, just past the armpit."

"Understood," Tucker replied.

"And finally, if you miss your shots, do not under any circumstances run."

"Why not?" asked Anya.

"Because then you will die exhausted, and that is no way to present yourself to God."

With that, Christopher prepped his own rifle and donned his pack. He also pulled out a tall walking stick with a tassel of steel bells at the top.

"Ready?" he asked.

"Hold on," Anya said. "Where is my gun?"

"I am sorry, missus. I did not think . . . I have very few female clients, you see. Plus your wrist. Please forgive me."

"It's okay, Christopher. Once one of you two drops from exhaustion, I'll have my rifle." Anya smiled sweetly. "Which way are we headed?"

"South to the trailhead, missus, then northeast into the hills."

Anya turned on her heel and headed off. "Try to keep up, boys."

She led them across a patch of scrubland to where the thin trail headed northeast. From that point, she wisely let Christopher take the lead. Almost immediately, the grade steepened, winding its way higher into the hills.

Tucker kept up the rear.

He tapped Kane's side. "CLOSE ROAM."

As was his habit, Kane trotted to either side, sometimes drifting ahead, sometimes dropping back, but he never strayed more than fifty feet in either direction. The shepherd's ears looked especially erect, his eyes exceptionally bright. Here were smells he'd never before experienced. Tucker imagined it was something of a sensory kaleidoscope for Kane.

After a kilometer or so, they passed into a narrow ravine and found themselves in shadows. A riotous profusion of desert flowers in dusty shades of pink and purple bloomed from the rock faces around them, casting out a sweet perfume, not unlike honeysuckle. The deep thrum of insects greeted them as they moved through, amplified by the tight space.

Kane stood before the wall of blooms, watching petals and leaves vibrate, his head cocked with curiosity.

"Cape honeybees," Christopher announced. "Fear not. If we do not bother them, they will not bother us."

"There must be thousands," Anya murmured.

"Many, many thousands, missus."

A quarter of a mile later, they exited the ravine and found themselves on a plain of red soil and scattered scrub brush. To their left, rolling granite hills towered hundreds of feet into the air.

Abruptly, Christopher let out a barking yelp, then another one thirty seconds later, then one more. In between yelps, he shook his walking stick, tinkling the bells attached to the handle.

"What's he doing?" Anya whispered back to Tucker.

"Letting everyone know we're here. Most wildlife doesn't want anything to do with us."

Cocking his head, Christopher stopped. He held up a closed fist and pointed to his ear: *Listen.*

After a few moments of silence came a deep huffing grunt. It echoed over the hills and faded.

Without a sound, Kane padded to the head of the column, halting several feet in front of Christopher. The shepherd angled his body to the right and sat down, his eyes fixed in the distance.

The huffing came again, then stopped.

"Male lions," Christopher said and pointed off to the left. "A few miles away. They should stay there until nightfall."

Kane continued to stare—but in the opposite direction from where Christopher had been pointing. Tucker dropped to a knee next to his partner.

"Maybe those male lions will," Tucker murmured. "But look beyond that line of scrub trees over there."

"What? I do not see . . ." Christopher's words trailed, ending with a whispered, "Oh, my."

A hundred yards away, a trio of lionesses, each well over three hundred pounds, slipped from the brush and began slowly stalking toward their group. As if by some unseen cue, the trio parted to change their angle of attack. The largest of the group took the center position.

"This is unusual," Christopher muttered. "They usually do not behave this way."

"Tell them that. They're trying to flank us."

Anya said, "What should I do?"

"Stay still," Christopher said. "Tucker, if they get around us—"

"I know."

Even as Tucker said the words, Kane stood up. The shepherd arched his back, his fur hackling up in a ridge along his spine, bushing out his tail. He dropped his head low to the ground and bared his fangs. A deep, prolonged snarl rolled from his chest. He began padding toward the lead lioness.

Christopher said, "Tucker, stop him."

"He knows what he's doing," he said, putting his faith in Kane. "Follow me. Gun ready. Anya, stay behind us."

"This is ill-advised," Christopher whispered.

Tucker rose to his feet and followed Kane, pacing carefully but steadily.

The center lioness suddenly stopped, a three-hundred-pound mountain of muscle, claw, and teeth. She crouched low, her tail slashing back and forth behind her. The other two also stopped, settling to Tucker's two and ten o'clock positions.

"What's happening?" Anya whispered.

"Kane's letting them know we're not an easy meal."

"This is remarkable," Christopher rasped. "Did you teach him this?"

"This isn't teachable," Tucker replied. "This is instinct."

The lead lionesses began huffing.

Kane let out a snapping growl and took three fast paces forward. Saliva frothed from his jaws.

Tucker murmured, "HOLD."

"Let's give our visitors a little nudge," Christopher said. "A single shot each, above their heads."

Tucker nodded. "You call it."

"Understand, if they do not bolt, they will charge."

"I'm ready."

Anya said, "I think I'm going to be sick."

"Swallow it," he warned.

Christopher turned to face the lioness to the left flank; Tucker did the same to the right. Kane stayed put, his gaze fixed to the beast in the center.

"Fire!"

Tucker lifted his rifle, propped the butt against his shoulder, and blasted over the lioness's head. She jumped, then dropped low and slunk away, back through the line of scrub bushes. Christopher's did the same as he fired.

The big lioness never budged, holding her ground as the others retreated. She stared at Kane for a few more seconds, let out another huffing grunt, then turned and walked after the other two. With a final backward glance, she disappeared from view.

Christopher wasted no time in leading them off. After putting a few hundred yards between them and the lionesses, they stopped for a water break under a rock ledge. Kane sat comfortably in the shade as though nothing unusual had happened.

No one spoke for a few minutes, then Anya said, "I've never been so terrified in my life. The look in those eyes . . . we were simply meat to them."

"Essentially, yes," Christopher said.

"I am not even sure I understand what happened."

"Lions are to be feared, but they are not stupid. Given a choice between ambushing easy prey or engaging in a fight, they will always choose the former. It is a simple matter of practicality. An injured lion is a weak lion. Tucker's dog was simply reminding them of that point. Plus it is just past the main rutting period, so plenty of young animals are around. They have abundant food. If prey had been scarce, our encounter back there would have ended badly."

4:45 P.M.

Rehydrated and with nerves calmed, the group headed out again.

After another twenty minutes, Christopher stopped and pointed into the hills. "The ruins of Klipkoppie fort are over that ridge. Now we climb a bit."

"How far?" asked Anya.

"Half a kilometer. As we go, stomp your feet occasionally so we do not surprise any snakes."

Christopher led them up a shallow gully awash with boulders, scrub brush, and the occasional tree. The trees had wide trunks that narrowed to a cluster of leafless branches that ended in single star-shaped buds.

"Looks like broccoli," Anya said.

"*Kokerboom*," Christopher called over his shoulder. "Also called Quiver trees. The San people use the hollow branches as arrows."

As the gully grew narrower, it eventually required hopping from boulder to boulder to continue the steep ascent. A few spots required Tucker to haul Kane up or assist Anya. Finally, clawing their way up the last few yards, they reached a half-crescent-shaped plateau overlooking Springbok.

They were all breathing heavily, gulping water, sweating.

"What a view," said Anya, leaning over the edge.

A sheer cliff dropped away at her toes. Behind them climbed a steep-walled granite dome. Across the plateau, the stubbed ends of timbered pillars stuck up out of the ground. More sprouted across the curve of the dome.

Squinting his eyes, Tucker could almost make out the bases of old fortifications and the foundations of long-lost buildings.

"This is the Klipkoppie," Christopher announced.

"Not much left of it," he said.

"No. Time and erosion have done their job. A hundred twenty years ago, this was a massive fort. The watchtower sat atop the dome. From here, Boer soldiers could see the entire valley below. The only access was up that narrow ravine we climbed."

"A natural choke point."

"Exactly so."

Tucker began to wander into the ruins, but a shout from Christopher halted him.

"Step carefully! This plateau is riddled with tunnels and old cellars."

"Here?" Anya asked. "This looks like solid rock."

Tucker knelt and probed the earth with his fingers. "Sandstone. Definitely workable. But it would've taken hard labor and patience to excavate here."

Christopher nodded. "Two qualities the Boers were known for. The entrances are covered by old planks—probably very fragile by now. Below us are sleeping quarters and storage areas."

Tucker called to Kane, who had wandered off to explore. "COME."

The shepherd galloped over and skidded to a stop.

Kneeling, Tucker opened his canteen and filled his cupped hand. He rubbed the water over Kane's snout and under his chin. He held his damp palm to his nose. "SEEK. EASY STEP."

Nose to the ground, Kane padded off, following the edge of the plateau.

"What's he doing?" asked Anya.

"Setting up a search parameter."

Kane began working inward, crisscrossing the dirt with his nose to the ground. Occasionally he would stop suddenly and circle left or right before resuming course.

"Tunnel openings," Tucker explained to Anya and Christopher.

"Remarkable," Christopher murmured.

Kane suddenly stopped a quarter of the way across the plateau. He circled one spot, sniffing hard, stirring up dust eddies with his breath. Finally, he lay down and shifted around to face Tucker.

"He smells moisture there."

The trio worked cautiously toward him. Christopher led the way, thumping his walking stick against the ground, testing each step.

Once they reached Kane, Tucker gave his partner a two-handed neck massage. "Atta boy."

Christopher lifted his walking stick and drove the butt of it hard into the dirt, at the spot where Kane had been so vigorously sniffing.

There came a dull *thunk*.

"Impressive beast of yours!" Christopher said.

Unfolding the small spades in their packs, the trio dug and swept away the packed dirt until a square of planking was exposed. It looked like a trapdoor into the earth. Luckily, the rough-hewn wood was rotted, desiccated by a century of heat. Jamming their spades into crannies and splits, they slowly pried the planks free and set them aside, exposing a dark shaft, about a yard across.

Lying on his belly, Tucker pointed his flashlight down the throat of the tunnel. Kane crouched next to him, panting, sniffing at the hole.

"Looks to drop about eight feet," he said, rising to his knees. "Then it branches off to the left."

"Who goes first?" Anya asked.

As if understanding her, Kane gained his feet and danced around the hole, his tail whipping fast. He looked up at Tucker, then down at the shaft.

"Take a guess," Tucker said.

"You're sending him down there?" Anya crossed her arms. "That seems cruel."

"Cruel? I think Kane was a dachshund in a former life, a breed built to flush badgers out of burrows. If there's a hole, Kane wants to crawl in and explore."

Tucker pulled the shepherd's tactical vest out of his backpack. Anticipating what was to come, Kane shook and trembled with excitement. Tucker quickly suited up his partner, synching the feed into the new sat phone Harper had supplied. He ran through a quick diagnostics check and found everything working as designed.

"Ready, Kane?"

The shepherd walked to the shaft and placed his front paws on the lip. Tucker played the beam of his flashlight across the sides and down to floor of the tunnel. He pointed.

"GO."

Without hesitation, Kane leaped into the darkness, followed by a soft *thump* as he landed at the bottom.

"SOUND OFF."

Kane barked once in reply, indicating he was okay.

Tucker punched buttons on his phone, and Kane's video feed came online. Shading the screen with his hand to reduce the sun's glare, he was able to make out the horizontal tunnel that angled away from the shaft. The camera had a night-vision feature, but Tucker tapped a button, and a small LED lamp flared atop the camera stalk, lighting Kane's way.

The sharper illumination revealed coarse walls, shored up by heavy timber. Out of the sun and wind, the wood looked solid enough, but *looks* could be deceptive. Back in Afghanistan, he'd witnessed several tunnel collapses while hunting for Taliban soldiers in their warren of caves.

Fearing the same now, he licked his lips, worried for Kane, but they both had a duty here.

Speaking into his radio mike, he said, "FORWARD. SEEK."

Hearing the command, Kane stalks forward. He leaves the glaring brightness of the day and heads into darkness, led by a pool of light cast over his shoulders.

His senses fill with dirt and mold, old wood and stone—but through it all, he fixes on a trail of dampness in the air.

It stands out against the dryness.

He needs no lights to follow it.

But he goes slowly, stepping carefully.

His ears pick out the scrunch of sand underfoot, the scrabble of chitinous legs on rock, the creak of timber.

He pushes through faint webs of dust.

He reaches another tunnel, one that crosses his path.

Which way?

A command whispers in his ear. His partner sees what he sees.

SEEK.

He steps to each direction, stretching his nose, breathing deeply, pulling the trail deep inside him, through his flared nostrils, past his tongue, to where instinct judges all.

He paces into one tunnel, then another, testing each.

Down one path, to the left, the air is heavier with moisture.

His ears hear the faintest tink of water falling to stone.

He heads toward it, his heart hammering inside him, on the hunt, knowing his target is near. The tunnel

drops deeper, then levels. Several cautious paces far-
ther and the passage opens into a cavern, tall enough to
jump and leap with joy within.

He wants to do that.

But instead he hears, HOLD.

And he does.

He stares across the sloping floor of the cave, to
a pool of glassy blackness. The sweep of his light
bathes across the surface, igniting it to a clear azure
blue.

Water.

"**Eureka,**" **Christopher** murmured.

Tucker turned to the others and passed Anya his
phone. "I'm going down there. When I reach Kane, I'll
check in, using his camera."

He turned, fished through his pack, and pulled out
his handheld GPS unit. He stuffed it into a cargo pocket
of his pants.

"I don't understand," Anya said. "Why do you have
to go down there? It doesn't look safe for someone as
big as you."

Tucker scooted to the hole and swung his legs over
the edge. "We need accurate coordinates."

"But why?" Concern shone on her face. "We know
the well is below this plateau. Isn't that close enough?"

"No. We need a compass bearing from that *exact* spot. Any miscalculation of the well's location will be compounded exponentially two hundred miles away." He pointed toward the horizon. "Make a hundred-yard mistake here, we could be off by a mile from De Klerk's coordinates. And out in the broken and inhospitable terrain of the Groot Karas Mountains, we could spend months up there and never find it."

Anya looked stunned. "I didn't think about that."

Tucker smiled. "All part of the service, ma'am." He prepared to lower himself down, then stopped. "Wait, I just realized I can't get any GPS lock underground. I'm going to have to go old school. Christopher, lend me your walking stick."

Their guide understood. "To act as a yardstick. Very clever."

"Give me thirty minutes. Unless there's a cave-in."

"If that happens," Christopher said, clapping him on the shoulder, "I'll alert the proper authorities to recover your body."

"And Kane's, too. I want him buried with me."

"Of course."

Anya frowned at them. "That's not funny."

They both turned to her. Neither of them was trying to be humorous.

That realization made her go pale.

Twisting around, Tucker lowered himself over the edge and dropped below. As his boots hit the ground, he crouched, turned on his flashlight, then ducked into the side tunnel. As he crawled on his hands and knees, he slid the walking stick end to end and counted as he went, mapping his route on a pocket notebook.

Occasionally, his back scraped the ceiling, causing miniavalanches of sand. In the confined quiet of the tunnel, the cascade echoed like hail peppering a sidewalk. He reached the intersection of tunnels and followed Kane's path to the left. Working diligently, it still took him an additional five minutes to map his way down to the cavern.

Kane heard him coming, trotted over, and licked his face.

"Good boy, good job!"

Tucker shined his flashlight around the room. Clearly the Boer troops must have spent a lot of time down here. The surrounding sandstone walls had been carved into benches and rudimentary tables, along with dozens of pigeonhole shelves. Ghosts of men materialized in his mind's eye: laughing, lounging, eating, all during one of the bloodiest and most obscure wars in history.

After jotting down the final measurements, Tucker lifted the page of his notebook toward Kane's camera and passed on a thumbs-up to the others above. He wanted a visual record of his calculations, of the coordinates of Grietje's Well, in case anything happened to him.

Satisfied, with his knowledge secure, he knelt and dipped his fingers into the water. It was cold and smelled fresh.

How long had people been using this spring?

He pictured ancient tribesmen coming here, seeking a respite from heat and thirst.

He decided to do the same. It felt like an oasis—not just from the blazing African sun, but from the pressures of his mission. The events of the past days came rushing back to him, a tumult of escapes, firefights, and death. At the moment, it all seemed surreal.

And now I am here, huddled in the bowels of a century-old Boer fort?

All because of a plant species almost as old as the earth itself.

He looked at Kane. "Can't say our lives are boring, can we?"

Confirming this, a sharp *crack* exploded, echoing down to the cave.

Tucker's first thought was *rifle fire.*

Another lion attack.

Then a deeper grumble came, a complaint of rock and sand.

He knew the truth.

Not a gunshot.

A crack of breaking timber.

A cave-in was starting.

30

March 19, 5:28 P.M.
Outside of Springbok, South Africa

Tucker shoved Kane into the tunnel as the rumbling in the earth grew louder, sounding like the approach of a locomotive.

"Escape! Outside!"

Kane obeyed the frantic, breathless command and dove out of the cave. The shepherd could move faster, so had a better chance of surviving.

No sense both of them dying.

Tucker did his best to follow. He abandoned his flashlight, freeing one hand. But he dared not discard Christopher's walking stick. He had failed to measure it before jumping down here. To do his final calculations of the spring's coordinates, he needed the stick's exact length.

Ahead, the LED lamp from Kane's camera bobbled deeper down the tunnel, outdistancing him as he scrambled on his hands and knees. Skin ripped from his knuckles as he clenched the walking stick. His knees pounded across rough rocks and hard stone.

He'd never make it.

He was right.

A grinding roar erupted ahead, accompanied a moment later by a thick rolling wash of dust and fine sand through the air.

The tunnel had collapsed.

Through the silt cloud, Kane's lamp continued to glow, jostling, but not seeming to move forward any longer. Coughing on the dust, Tucker hurried to his partner's side.

Past Kane, a wall of sand, rock, and pieces of broken timber blocked the tunnel. There was no way past. The shepherd clawed and dug at the obstruction.

Tucker pushed next to him. With his free hand against the wall, he felt the vibration of the earth. Like a chain of dominoes, more collapses were imminent. With his palm on the wall, his fingertips discovered a corner at the edge of the obstruction.

"HOLD," he ordered Kane.

As the shepherd settled back, Tucker twisted the dog's vest camera to shine the light on his hand, still pressed against the wall. He glanced over his shoulder, then back to his fingers, regaining his bearings.

He realized they had reached the *intersection* of the two tunnels.

The collapse had occurred in the passageway to the right, the one leading from the entry shaft to here. What blocked them was the flood of sand and rock that had *washed* into this intersection by the cave-in. That meant there was no way to get back out the way they'd come in. But with some luck, they might be able to dig through this loose debris to reach the tunnel on the far side. Of course, there was no guarantee that such a path would lead to freedom, but they had no other choice.

"DIG," he ordered Kane.

Shoulder to shoulder, they set to work. Kane kicked rocks and paw-fulls of sand between his hind legs. Tucker grabbed splintery shards of wood and tossed them back. They slowly but relentlessly burrowed and cleared out the debris.

With raw fingers, Tucker rolled away a large chunk of sandstone down the slope of debris. He reached into the new gap and found—nothing. He whooped and scrambled faster. He soon had enough of a path for the two of them to belly-crawl through the wash of debris and into the far tunnel.

Kane shook sand from his coat.

Crouched on his hands and knees, Tucker did the same—though his shaking was a combination of relief and residual terror.

"SCOUT AHEAD," he whispered.

Together, they set out into the unknown maze of subterranean tunnels of the old Boer fort—and it was a labyrinth. Passageways and blind chambers met them at every turn. Tucker paused frequently to run his fingertips along the roofs or to shine Kane's lamp up.

Distant booms and rumbles marked additional cave-ins.

At last, he found himself standing in a square space about the size of a one-car garage. From the carved shelves and the decayed remains of smashed wooden crates, it appeared to be an old cellar. More tunnels led out from this central larder.

He bent down and turned Kane's lamp up.

He sighed in relief.

The low ceiling was held up with wooden planks.

As he straightened, Kane growled, a sharp note of fury—then bolted for the nest of crates. He shoved his nose there, then came backpedaling, shaking his head violently. After a few seconds, he trotted back to Tucker's side, something draped from his jaws.

Kane dropped it at his feet.

It was a three-foot black snake with a triangular head that hinted at its venomous nature.

Only now, past the hammering of his heart, did he hear a low and continuous hissing. As his eyes adjusted, he saw shreds of shadow slithering over the floor, wary of the light. From the other tunnels, more snakes spilled into the chamber. The trembling of the earth was stirring them out of their nests, pushing them upward.

Tucker used the butt of the walking stick to push one away from his toes, earning a savage hiss and the baring of long fangs.

Time to get out of here.

"PROTECT," he ordered Kane.

He gripped the pole two-handed and slammed the stick upward, striking into the planks with a jangle of the rod's bells. Wood pieces showered down. He kept at it, pounding again and again through the decay and rot above his head, while Kane kept watch on the snakes.

He continued to work on the ceiling, trying to force his own cave-in, knowing he had to be near the surface. He pictured Kane's earlier cautious search of the plateau and Christopher tapping the ground as they crossed, watching for pitfalls underfoot. By now, debris had begun to fall faster: wood, sand, rock. The rain of rubble only served to further piss off the roiling snakes.

With his shoulders aching, he smashed the stick into the ceiling again, cracking a thick plank, splitting it in two.

That was the straw that broke the camel's back.

A good chunk of the roof collapsed, crashing down around Tucker's ears. A piece of wood caught him in the face, ripping a gash. Sand and dirt followed. He did his best to shelter Kane with his body.

Then a blinding brilliance.

He risked a look up to see blue sky and sunlight, as the dome of his dark world broke open. He heard surprised shouts rise outside, from Anya and Christopher.

"I'm okay!" he hollered back.

Blowing out his relief, he sank to a knee next to Kane.

"We're okay," he whispered.

Kane wagged his tail, peacocking a bit, plainly proud of the scatter of dead snakes around him. The sudden sunlight had driven the rest into hiding.

"You're enjoying all this a little too much," Tucker scolded with a smile.

6:13 P.M.

In short order, using the nylon ropes in Christopher's pack, Tucker helped evacuate Kane by hooking the rope through the dog's vest, then he followed, climbing out, hand over hand.

Once topside, Anya cleaned the gash on his cheek, slathered it with antibacterial ointment, and pasted a bandage over it.

Any further ministrations could wait until they reached the hotel.

With the sun close to setting, they hurried out of the hills. As the way was mostly downhill, they made quick progress, goaded on by the distant huffing of lions.

"Did you get what you needed?" Anya asked, marching beside him.

"Down to the inch."

This time, he had measured Christopher's walking stick.

"Good," she replied. "I'm starving, and I've had enough of a nature walk for one day."

He couldn't agree more.

Once they reached the SUV parked at Helman's Garage, Christopher headed back toward Springbok. It was a quiet, exhausted ride. Christopher called his brother Paul, confirmed all was calm at the guesthouse. Or at least mostly calm. Bukolov had rested enough to become his normal irascible self, demanding to know everything about the day's discoveries, irritated at being left out.

Tucker did not look forward to that. He wanted nothing more than a long, hot soak, followed by a dip in the guesthouse pool.

As they pulled into the parking lot, Christopher's phone rang. He balanced it to his ear as he rolled up to the hotel's steps.

Once stopped, he turned to Tucker. "It's Manfred. He asked if he could speak to you at the church. Tonight. Says he has some news that might interest you." He covered the mouthpiece. "I could put him off until tomorrow."

"I should go," Tucker said, postponing his bath and dip.

Anya rebuckled her seat belt, determined to come, too, but he leaned forward and touched her shoulder.

"I can handle this," he said. "If you handle Bukolov. Someone needs to bring him up to speed, or he'll be on the warpath."

A look of uncertainty crossed Anya's face.

Tucker said, "He'll behave. Just keep it short."

Anya nodded. "After your day, I'll take the bullet with Bukolov."

"Thanks."

As Anya disappeared through the French doors, Tucker drove back with Christopher to the church. They found the good reverend lounging where they'd last left him: at the picnic table in the yard. Only now, he was fully clothed, all in colonial white, except he remained barefoot. He smoked a pipe, waving it at them as they joined him.

"How went the expedition?" Manfred asked.

"Very well," Tucker responded.

"I believe that bandage on your face says otherwise."

"Knowledge always comes with a price."

"And apparently this one was blood."

You have no idea.

Tucker shifted forward. "Reverend, Christopher mentioned you had news."

"Ah, yes. Quite mysterious. It seems Springbok has suddenly become very popular."

"What do you mean?"

"About an hour ago, I received a call from a genealogist. She was asking about your ancestor, Paulos de Klerk."

"She?" Tucker replied, warning bells jangling inside him. "A woman?"

"Yes. With an accent . . . Scandinavian, it sounded like."

Felice.

Manfred narrowed his eyes. "Tucker, I can see from your expression, this is not welcome news. At first, I assumed the woman was part of your research team."

He shook his head. "No."

"Competition then? Someone trying to steal your thunder?"

"Something like that," he said, hating to lie to a man of the cloth. "But can you tell me if this was a local call?"

He shook his head. "The connection was made through an international operator."

So likely not local.

A small blessing there.

"What did you tell her about De Klerk?" Tucker asked.

"I told her I knew very little. He was a doctor, a botanist, and likely was stationed at Klipkoppie."

He bit back a groan, sharing a glance with Christopher.

"What about me?" Tucker asked. "Did she inquire about us?"

"Not a word. And I wouldn't have told her anything anyway. By midway into the conversation, I sensed something awry. I wanted to speak to you before I offered her any further cooperation. That's why I called you."

"Did she ask about Grietje's Well?"

"Yes, and I did mention Klipkoppie fort."

This was disastrous.

Sensing his distress, Manfred patted his hand. "But I didn't tell her *where* Klipkoppie fort was."

"Surely she'll learn—"

"She'll learn what *you* learned. That Klipkoppie fort is located in the center of Springbok. It's in all the tour books."

Tucker remembered Manfred's earlier disdain for the tourist trap. He felt a surge of satisfaction. Such a false trail could buy them even more time.

He calmed down. Mostly. Knowing Felice was on her way, he wanted to immediately return to the hotel, haul out his maps, and calculate De Klerk's coordinates to his cave based on the location of the spring.

But he also had a font of local knowledge sitting across from him, and he did not want to waste it.

"Reverend, you mentioned De Klerk was under the command of General Roosa. In your research did you encounter any mention of a siege in the Groot Karas Mountains. It was where, I believe, my ancestor died."

"No, but that doesn't mean it didn't happen. It wasn't like today's wars, with embedded journalists and cameras and such. But I can look into it."

"I'd appreciate it."

Manfred stared hard, releasing a long puff of pipe smoke. "From that hunger in your voice, I worry that you're thinking of going up into the Groot mountains."

"And if we are?"

"Well, if you discount the guerrillas, the Namibian military, the poachers, and the highway bandits, there's always the terrain, the heat, and the scarcity of water. Not to mention the indigenous wildlife that would like to eat you."

Tucker grinned. "You need to be hired by the Namibian tourist board."

"If you go," Manfred warned, eyeing him seriously, "don't look like a poacher. The Namibian military will shoot first and ask questions later. If rebels or bandits ambush you, fight for your life because if they get their hands on you, you're done. Finally, take a reliable vehicle. If you break down, you'll never reach civilization on foot."

He nodded, respecting the man's wisdom. "Thanks."

Tucker stood up and shook Manfred's hand.

As he and Christopher headed across the yard, Manfred called after them, "If your *competition* comes calling, what should I do?"

"Smile and point her to that tourist trap in the center of town."

It wasn't exactly the *trap* he wished for Felice.

That was more of a razor-sharp bear trap.

But it would do for now.

31

"Welcome to wine country," Christopher announced as the Cessna's tires touched down at the airport of Upington, a picturesque town two hundred miles northeast of Springbok. "Here is where you'll find the production fields of South Africa's finest vintages. Some quarter-million pounds of grapes are harvested each year."

Tucker had noted the rolling swaths of vineyards hugging the lush banks of the Orange River. This little oasis would also serve as their group's staging ground for the border crossing into Namibia. Not that he wouldn't mind a day of wine tasting first, but they had a tight schedule.

Last night, he had completed his calculations and had a fairly good idea of the coordinates of De Klerk's cave. Knowing Felice would not be too far behind, he had everyone up at dawn for this short hop to Upington. He intended to stay ahead of her.

Once they deplaned, Paul Nkomo chauffeured them in a black Range Rover. He drove them up out of the green river valley and off into a sweeping savannah of dense grasses, patches of dark green forest, and rocky outcroppings. After twenty minutes of driving, the Rover stopped before a steel gate. A sign beside the gate read SPITSKOP GAME PARK.

Leaning out the open window, Paul pressed the buzzer, gave his name, and the gate levered open. Paul followed the road into an acre-sized clearing and parked before a sprawling, multiwinged ranch house. A trio of barns outlined the clearing's eastern edge.

They all got out, stretching kinks.

"Not nearly as hot here," Bukolov commented cheerily, on an uptick of his mood swings.

"It is still morning," Paul warned. "It will get hot, very hot."

"Are there any lions around here?" Anya asked, staring toward the savannah.

"Yes, ma'am. Must be careful."

She looked around, found Kane, and knelt down next to the shepherd, scratching his ear appreciatively, clearly remembering his heroics yesterday and intending to stick close to him.

Christopher drew Tucker aside as the others went inside. He led Tucker to one of the barns. Inside was another Range Rover, this one painted in a camouflage of ochre, brown, and tan. Stacks of gear were strapped to the roof rack or piled in the rear cargo area.

"Your ride, Mr. Wayne."

"Impressive," Tucker said. He walked around the Rover, noting it was an older model. "How're the maintenance records?"

He recalled Manfred's warning about the dangers of getting stranded in Namibia.

"You will have no problems. Now, as for when we should depart, I—"

Tucker held up a hand. "What do you mean by *we*?"

"You, your companions, and *myself*, of course."

"Who says you're going with us, Christopher?"

The young man looked puzzled. "I thought it was understood that I was to be your guide throughout your stay in Africa."

"This is the first I've heard of it."

And he wasn't happy about it. While he would certainly welcome Christopher's expertise, the body count of late had already climbed too high. He and the others had to go, but—

"You didn't sign up for this, Christopher."

He refused to back down. "I was instructed to provide whatever assistance you required to travel into Namibia. It is my judgment that *I* am the assistance you will require most." He ticked off the reasons why on his fingers. "Do you speak any of the dialects of tribal Namibia? Do you know how to avoid the Black Mamba? How many Range Rovers have you fixed in the middle of nowhere?"

"I get your point. So let me make mine."

Tucker walked to the Rover's roof rack, pulled down a gun case, and lifted free an assault rifle. He placed it atop a blanket on the hood.

"This is an AR-15 semiautomatic rifle with a 4x20 standard slash night-vision scope. It fires eight hundred rounds per minute. Effective range four hundred to six hundred meters. Questions?"

Christopher shook his head.

"Watch carefully." Tucker efficiently field-stripped the AR, laid the pieces on the cleaning blanket, then reassembled it. "Now you do it."

Christopher took a deep breath, stepped up to the Rover, and repeated the procedure. He was slower and less certain, but he got everything right.

Next Tucker showed him how to load, charge, and manage the AR's firing selector switch. "Now you."

Christopher duplicated the process.

One last lesson.

Tucker took back the weapon, cleared it, and returned it to Christopher. "Now point it at my chest."

"What?"

"Do it."

Tentatively, Christopher did as Tucker ordered. "Why am I doing this?"

Tucker noted the slight tremble in the man's grip. "You've never done this before, have you?"

"No."

"Never shot at anyone?"

"No."

"Been shot at?"

"No."

"Never killed anyone?"

"Of course not."

"If you come along, *all* of those things will probably happen."

Christopher sighed and lowered the AR to his side. "I am beginning to see your point."

"Good. So you'll wait here for us here."

"You assume too much." He handed the AR back to Tucker. "If anyone tries to shoot at us, I will shoot back. What happens to them is God's will."

"You're a stubborn bastard," Tucker said.

"So my mother tells me. Without the *bastard* reference, of course."

11:45 A.M.

"How confident are you about your coordinates?" Harper asked.

Tucker stood in the barn next to the Range Rover. He had just finished an inventory check. Everyone else had retired out of the noonday heat for lunch, leaving him alone. He used the private moment to check in with Sigma.

"Ninety percent. It's as good as it's going to get, and it puts us ahead of the competition."

"Speaking of them, a woman matching Felice Nilsson's description and bearing a Swedish passport arrived in Cape Town this morning. Four men, also with Swedish passports, cleared customs at roughly the same time."

"Not surprising. But we've got a big head start on her. Without Utkin feeding them info, they're in the dark. And they still have to figure out the Klipkoppie mystery."

"Hope you're right. Now one last thing. You know that photo you forwarded us—the one of you in the Internet café in Dimitrovgrad?"

"Yes."

"There's something off about it."

"Define *off.*"

"Our tech people are concerned about artifacts in the image's pixel structure. It may be nothing, but we're dissecting everything you sent—including all of Bukolov's data."

"Any verdict in that department?"

"We've got a team of biologists, epidemiologists, and botanists looking at everything. There's not a whole lot of consensus, but they all agree on *one* thing."

"That it's all a hoax. We can turn around and go home."

"Afraid not," she replied. "They all agree that LUCA, if it's the real deal, could have an r-naught that's off the scale."

"And that would mean *what* in English?"

"R-naught is shorthand for *basic reproductive ratio.* The higher the number, the more infectious and harder an organism is to control. Measles has a known r-naught value between 12 and 18. If Bukolov's estimates and early experiments are valid, LUCA could clock in at 90 to 100. In practical terms, if a strain of LUCA is introduced into an acre of food crops, that entire plot of land could be contaminated in less than a day, with exponential growth after that."

Tucker took in a sobering breath.

"Find this thing," she warned, "and make sure Kharzin never gets his hands on it."

Tucker pictured the plastic-wrapped blocks of C-4 packed aboard the Rover.

"That I promise."

After they signed off, Tucker circled around to the front of the Rover and leaned over a topographical map spread across the hood. It depicted the southern Kalahari Desert and eastern Namibia. He ran a finger along the Groot Karas Mountains. He tapped a spot on the map where De Klerk's cave should be located. Once there, they had to find a feature that looked like a boar's head. But first the group had to *get* there.

"I've brought you lunch," Christopher said behind him. "You must eat."

He came with a platter piled with a spinach-and-beetroot salad and a club sandwich stuffed with steak, chicken, bacon, and a fried egg—the four essential food groups.

Kane—who had been lounging to one side of the Rover—climbed to his legs, sniffing, his nose high in the air. Tucker pinched off a chunk of chicken and fed it to him.

"What is troubling you?" Christopher asked.

Tucker stared at the map. "I'm trying to decide the best place to cross the border into Namibia. With our truckload of weapons and explosives, it's best we try to sneak across at night."

"Most correct. It is very illegal to bring such things into Namibia. Long prison sentences. And because of the smuggling operations of guerrillas and bandits, the border is patrolled heavily."

"So you understand my problem; how about a solution?"

"Hmm." Christopher elbowed him slightly to the side and pointed to the plate. "You eat. I'll show you."

He touched a town not far from the border. "Noenieput is a small agricultural collective. The South African police are lax there. Should be no problem to get through. Might have to pay . . . a tourist surcharge."

Tucker heard the trip over the last. "In other words, a bribe."

"Yes. But on the other side of the border, the Namibia police are not lax at all. Bribe or no bribe. All the paved roads are blockaded. We will have to go overland at night, like you said."

Christopher ran his finger north and tapped a spot. "This is the best place to make a run for the border."

"Why is that?"

"It's where the guerrillas most often cross. Very dangerous men."

"And that's a good thing?"

Christopher looked at him. "Of course." He pointed to the plate. "Now eat."

For some reason, he no longer had an appetite.

32

As Christopher drove, the landscape slowly changed from savannah to a mixture of rust-red sands, stark white salt flats, and scattered, isolated tall hillocks called *kopjes.* With the sun sitting on the horizon, those stony escarpments cast long shadows across the blasted plains.

Far in the distance, the crinkled dark outline of the Groot Karas Mountains cut across the sky. How were they going to reach those distant peaks? As flat as the terrain was here, a border crossing at night seemed impossible. Confirming this, small black dots buzzed slowly across the skies. They were spotter planes of the Namibian Air Force. By standing orders, they shot smugglers first and asked questions later.

Tucker tried to coax Christopher's plan out of the man, but he remained reticent. Perhaps out of a secret fear that Tucker might leave him behind once he knew the plan.

"Noenieput," Christopher announced, pointing ahead to a scatter of whitewashed homes and faded storefronts. "It has the only police station for a hundred miles. If they search our cargo, things will go bad for us."

Anya slunk lower in the front seat, clutching the door grip.

Bukolov gave off a nervous groan. The doctor shared the backseat with Tucker and Kane.

"Down," Tucker ordered the shepherd.

Kane dropped to the floorboards, and Tucker draped him with a blanket.

Ahead, a white police vehicle partially blocked the road, its nose pointed toward them. As they neared, the rack on top began flashing, plainly a signal.

But of what?

Christopher slowed and drew alongside it. He rolled down his window and stuck out his arm in a half wave, half salute. An arm emerged from the driver's side of the police vehicle, returning the gesture.

As Christopher passed, he reached out and slapped palms with the officer. Tucker caught the flash of a folded bill pass hands.

The tourist surcharge.

The Rover rolled onward.

"We made it," Anya said.

"Wait," Christopher warned, his eyes studying the side mirror. "I have to make sure I paid him enough. *Too much,* he could get suspicious and come after us. *Too little,* he might be offended and hassle us."

Thirty seconds passed.

"He's not moving. I think we're okay."

Everyone relaxed. Kane hopped back into the seat, his tail wagging as if all this was great fun.

"Three more miles," Christopher announced.

"Three miles to what?" Bukolov grumbled. "I wish you two would tell us what the hell is going on."

"Three miles, then we'll have to get off the highway and wait for nightfall," Tucker explained. Though he was no happier than the doctor at being kept in the dark about what would happen from there.

As that marker was reached, Christopher turned, bumped the Rover over the shoulder, and dipped down a steep slope of sand and rock. As it leveled out, he coasted to a stop in the lee of a boulder that shielded them from the road. They sat quietly, listening to the Rover's engine *tick tick tick* as it cooled.

Within minutes, the sun faded first into twilight, then into darkness.

"That didn't take long," Anya whispered.

"Such is the desert, miss. In an hour, it will be twenty degrees cooler. By morning, just above freezing. By midday, boiling hot again."

Tucker and Christopher grabbed binoculars, walked west a hundred yards, and scaled the side of a *kopje*. They lay flat on their bellies atop the hill and scanned the four miles of open ground between them and the border.

A deadly no-man's-land.

It seemed too far to sneak across, especially because of—

"There!" Christopher pointed to the strobe of airplane lights in the dark sky. "Namibian Air Force spotter. Each night the guerrillas do what we are doing, only in reverse. They use the cover of darkness to sneak into South Africa, where they have supporters here that provide supplies and ammunition."

Tucker watched the plane drone along the border until it finally faded into the darkness. "How many are there? How often do they pass?"

"Many. About every ten minutes."

It didn't seem possible to cross that open ground in such a short time.

"And what happens when they catch you crossing?" Tucker asked.

"The spotter planes are equipped with door-mounted Chinese miniguns. Capable of firing six thousand rounds per minute. The Namibian Air Force averages three kills a night along the long border. When we go across, you will see the wreckage of many trucks whose drivers timed their run poorly."

"Here's hoping our timing is better," Tucker said.

"Tonight, *timing* does not matter. We just need to find a rabbit." Upon that cryptic note, Christopher rolled to his feet. "We must be ready and in position."

But ready for what?

Back behind the wheel, Christopher set out with the Rover's headlights doused. Milky moonlight bathed the dunes and *kopjes.* Farther out, the Groot Karas Mountains appeared as a black smudge against the night sky.

Christopher kept the Rover to a pace no faster than a brisk walk, lest the tires create a dust wake. Christopher steered the Rover into a narrow trough between a pair of dunes, keeping mostly hidden. After a mile, they emerged beside a line of scrub-covered *kopjes.*

Crawling forward, Christopher drove alongside the row of hillocks until they ended. He then parked in the shelter of the last *kopje,* camouflaged against its rocky flank.

Only open flat ground lay ahead.

"Now we wait," Christopher said.

"For what?" Tucker asked.

"For a rabbit to run."

8:22 P.M.

Tucker held the binoculars fixed to his face. He had switched places with Anya, taking the passenger seat, so that he had a sweeping view of the open land ahead. Through the scope, he picked out the blasted wreckage of unlucky smugglers and guerrillas. Most were half buried in the roll of the windswept dunes.

Then off to the northwest, he caught a wink in the distance.

He stiffened. "Movement," he whispered.

Christopher leaned next to him, also using binoculars. "What do you see?"

"Just a glint of something—moonlight on glass, maybe."

They waited tensely. Christopher had finally revealed his plan a few minutes ago. Tucker no longer believed the young man had held off telling him as some sort of insurance plan against being abandoned. He had kept silent because his plan was pure insanity.

But they were committed now.

No turning back.

"I see it," Christopher said. "It is definitely a vehicle—a pickup truck. And he's gaining speed. Here, Tucker, this is our rabbit."

Run, little rabbit, run . . .

Through his binoculars, Tucker watched the pickup careen at breakneck speeds, heading toward South Africa. No wonder Christopher had picked an area regularly frequented by guerrillas. For his plan to work, they needed traffic.

Illegal traffic, in this case.

"If the spotters are in the area," Christopher warned, "it won't be long now."

The rebel truck continued to sprint, trying to reach the highway on the South African side. Tucker no longer needed his binoculars to track its zigzagging race through the dunes.

It had covered a mile when Christopher whispered, "There, to the south!"

Lights blinked in the sky. A Namibian spotter plane streaked like a hunting hawk across the foothills on the far side, going after the fleeing rabbit. It dove, picking up speed, drawn by the truck's dust plume. Soon the plane was flying seventy yards off the desert floor. On its current course, it would sweep past their *kopje*, where they hid.

"Time to get ready," Christopher whispered. "Buckle up and hold on."

"This is madness!" Bukolov barked.

"Be quiet, Abram!" Anya ordered.

"Any moment now . . ." Tucker mumbled.

Suddenly the plane streaked past their position and was gone.

Christopher shifted into gear and slammed the accelerator. The Rover lurched forward and began bumping over the terrain.

"Tucker, keep a close eye on that plane. If they finish off that other truck too quickly, we might still draw the spotter's attention."

"Got it." He twisted around in his seat, climbed out the open passenger window, and rested his butt on the sill. With one hand clutching the roof rack, Tucker watched the pickup truck's progress.

"Doesn't look like he's going to make it!" he called out.

"They rarely do! Hold on tight!"

The Rover picked up speed, slewing around obstacles, bouncing over rock outcroppings, and dipping into dune troughs. The cooling desert wind whipped through Tucker's hair. His heart pounded with the exhilaration.

"How far to the border now?" he shouted.

"One mile. Ninety seconds."

Tucker watched the plane suddenly bank right, running parallel now to the racing truck.

"Almost there!" Christopher called.

Fire arched from the plane's doorway and streamed toward the truck. The aircraft's minigun poured a hundred rounds per second into its target, tearing the vehicle apart in an incendiary display that lit the black desert.

The engagement quickly ended.

Smoke and flames swirled from the wreckage.

Above, the plane banked in a circle over the ruins. As it turned, their dust trail would surely be spotted.

"He's coming about," Tucker called.

He turned forward to see a waist-high stone cairn flash by the right bumper of the Rover. Any closer and it would have knocked Tucker from his perch.

"Border marker!" Christopher called. "We're across! Welcome to Namibia!"

Tucker ducked back inside and buckled up.

From the backseat, Kane crowded forward and licked his face.

"Are we safe?" Anya asked.

"We're in Namibia," Christopher replied. "So *no*."

Bukolov leaned forward, red-faced and apoplectic. "For God's sake! Are you two trying to get me killed? Actually *trying*?"

Tucker glanced back. "No, Doctor, but the day's not over yet."

33

March 20, 10:11 P.M.
Borderlands of Namibia

"Should be just over that next dune," Tucker said. He had a map on his lap and his GPS unit in hand.

"What are we looking for?" Anya asked, leaning forward between the two front seats, careful of her cast.

After their flight across the border, Christopher kept the Rover at a cautious pace, proceeding overland, using the terrain to cover as much of their movement as possible.

"There should be a paved road," Tucker replied. "One heading west into the mountains."

"Is that wise?" she asked. "Won't there be traffic?"

"Perhaps, but a vehicle with South African plates in Namibia isn't unusual. As long as we don't attract attention to ourselves, the odds are in our favor."

Christopher glanced over to her. "And on the road, we're less likely to encounter guerrillas or bandits."

"That is, until we reach the mountain trails," Tucker added. "Once we're off the paved roads and climbing into the badlands, then all bets are off."

With his headlamps still dowsed, Christopher picked his way over the last of the dunes. A blacktop road appeared ahead, cutting straight across the sands. They waited a minute, making sure no traffic was in sight, then bumped over the shoulder and out onto the smooth pavement.

Christopher flipped on his lights and headed west.

Despite its remote location, the road was well maintained and well marked but completely devoid of traffic. For the next twenty-five miles, as the road wound higher into the mountain's foothills, they saw not a single vehicle, person, or sign of civilization.

The road finally ended at a T-junction. Christopher brought the Rover to a stop. In the backseat, Bukolov was snoring loudly. Anya had also fallen asleep, curled in the fetal position against the door.

"She is lovely," Christopher said. "Is she your woman?"

"No."

"I see. But you fancy each other, yes?"

Tucker rolled his eyes. "It's complicated. Mind your business."

Still, he considered Christopher's words. Anya certainly was attractive, but he hadn't given much thought to any sort of relationship with her. She would need a friend once she reached America, and he would be that for her, but beyond that . . . only time would tell. He felt pity for her, felt protective of her, but those feelings might not be the healthiest way to start a romance. And, more important, this was the wrong place and time to think about any of it.

Especially in guerrilla-infested Namibia.

Tucker checked their GPS coordinates against the map. "We're on track," he said. "We should turn right here, go a quarter mile, then turn northwest onto a dirt trail."

"And then how far to our destination?"

"Eighteen miles."

At least he hoped so. If his bearing and range measurements were off by even a fraction of a degree, the cave could be miles from where he thought it was. Plus even if his calculations were accurate, the landmark they needed to find—the Boar's Head—could have been obliterated by time and erosion. He felt a flicker of panicky despair. Tucker tried to shove it down.

Deal with what's in front of you, Ranger, he reminded himself again.

"That's a long distance to cover," Christopher said. "And the terrain will only get rougher."

"I know." Tucker checked his watch. "It's almost midnight, and I don't want to tackle the mountains until daylight. Once we're a little higher in the foothills, we'll start looking for a place to camp and get some rest. At dawn, Kane and I will do some reconnoitering.

In the backseat, Bukolov snorted, groaned, then muttered, "My ears hurt."

"We're at three thousand feet of elevation, Professor," Christopher said. "Your ears will adjust soon. Go back to sleep."

A short time later, they were off the blacktop and bouncing slowly along a rutted dirt road. They followed the ever-narrowing tract higher into the foothills.

After an hour of this, Tucker pointed to a craggy hill with a clump of scrub forest at the top. "See if you can find a way up there."

"I'll do my best."

Christopher turned right off the trail and down an embankment. He followed a dry riverbed that wound to the hill's southern face and discovered a natural ramp that headed up. After another hundred yards, they reached a clearing surrounded by a crescent of boulders, shaded by stubby trees.

"This'll do," Tucker said, drawing Christopher to a stop.

Tucker climbed out with Kane and pointed. "SCOUT AND RETURN."

The shepherd trotted off into the darkness, exploring the edges of the clearing and what looked like several game trails. Tucker did the same, circling completely around the Rover. In the distance, he heard the huffing grunt of lions, accompanied by several roars. Other creatures screeched and howled.

He waved Anya and Bukolov out and turned to Christopher.

"Let's get the tents set up. But what do you think about a fire?"

"The flames are good at keeping curious animals at bay, but also good at attracting rebels and bandits. I vote no."

Tucker agreed. They quickly set up camp; even Bukolov pitched in before finally retiring, almost collapsing into the tent. Anya soon followed him.

"I'll take first watch," Tucker said to Christopher. "You've been driving all day. Get some sleep."

"I don't need much sleep. I'll relieve you in a couple of hours."

Tucker didn't argue.

He drifted to the Rover and leaned a hip against the bumper. Overhead, a brilliant display of crisp stars flushed the sky, accompanied with the glowing swath of the Milky Way. He listened to the cacophony of the African night: the trill of insects, the distant hoots and hollers, the rustle of wind.

It was hard to believe such beauty hid such danger.

March 21, 1:24 A.M.

As Tucker kept a drowsy guard, Kane stirred from where he'd curled beside the Rover's tire.

Tucker heard the *zip* from the tent.

He turned to see Anya push out, wrapped in a blanket. Her breath misted in the cold desert air. She slowly, shyly joined him.

"Couldn't sleep?" he whispered. "Is your wrist bothering you?"

"No. It's not that—" She ended in a shrug.

He patted the hood next to him.

She sat down, shifted closer, and tugged the blanket around Tucker's shoulders. "You looked cold."

He didn't object. He had to admit the warmth was welcome . . . as was the company.

Kane glanced at them and made a deep *harrumphing* sound, then lay back down.

"I think someone is jealous," Anya said, hiding a grin.

"He can get grumpy when he's tired."

"You know each other's moods very well."

"We've been together a long time. Since Kane was a pup. And after the years of training, we've learned each other's tics and idiosyncrasies."

He suddenly felt foolish talking about this with a beautiful woman at his hip.

But she didn't seem to mind. "It must be nice to have someone so close to you in life, someone who knows you so well."

At that moment, he realized how little he knew about the real Anya Averin—and how much he wanted to know more.

"Speaking of getting to know someone," he whispered, "I don't know anything about your past. Where did you grow up?"

There was a long pause—clearly it was hard for her to let her guard down, especially after so many years of wearing a false face.

"Many places," she finally mumbled. "My father was in the Russian Army. He was a . . . a hard man. We moved around a lot."

He heard pain there as she looked down. After a long awkward silence, she shifted away. He had clearly touched a sore point.

"I suppose I should try to sleep," she mumbled, hopping down and drawing the blanket with her. With a small wave of a hand, she headed back to the tent and ducked inside.

The night was suddenly much colder.

34

March 21, 5:16 A.M.
Groot Karas Mountains, Namibia

Christopher shook Tucker awake while it was still dark. He instantly went alert, muscles going hard, shaking off the cobwebs of fitful dreams.

"It's okay, Mr. Wayne," the man reassured him. "You asked me to wake you before the sun was up."

"Right, right . . ."

He slithered out of his sleeping bag and grabbed the AR-15 rifle resting next to it.

As he followed Christopher out of the tent, Bukolov snorted and woke from the commotion. "What's going on? What's happening?"

"Nothing, Doctor," Tucker said. "Go back to sleep."

"I could if you two would stop bumbling around like a pair of elephants." He rolled over, putting his back to them.

Across the dark tent, Anya's eyes shone toward him, then she turned away, too.

With Kane in tow, Tucker pushed out into the predawn chill. He stomped circulation back into his feet, while Kane darted over to a bush and lifted his leg.

Once the shepherd had returned, Christopher asked, "Which way will you two go and how far?"

He pointed east. "We'll scout a few miles ahead. We can move quieter than the Rover. We'll make sure nothing stands between us and the coordinates. If it looks safe, we can continue with the Rover. I should be back before noon. If I run into any trouble or you do, we've got our radios."

"Understood."

"Have the Rover packed and ready. Run if you need to. Don't fight unless you have no other choice."

"I would much prefer to come with—"

"I know you would, but someone has to guard Anya and Bukolov. That's why we're here. They're more important than me."

"I don't agree, sir. Every life is precious in the eyes of God."

Tucker knew it was foolish to argue with the young man. He just prayed that when it came to a firefight that Christopher placed *his* precious life above that of his enemy's.

With matters settled, Tucker suited up Kane, then thoroughly checked his rifle and strapped a Smith & Wesson .44-caliber snubnose to his belt. As an additional precaution, knowing he might encounter guerrilla forces, he wanted something extra in his back pocket, something with a little more bang. He fished out a block of C-4 plastic explosive from their reserves and shoved it into the cargo pocket of his pants.

That'll have to do.

Ready now, he and Kane took to a game trail that led them down the steep north face of the hill and into a short valley. He took a compass bearing, marked his map, then they set out east. The terrain of the Groot Karas Mountains was as unique and strange as the desert that bordered it. From satellite images, it appeared as though a giant hand had poured molten metal across the mountain's slopes: rock formations looped and whorled around one another forming a flowing maze, all of it broken up by plateaus, boulder-strewn ravines, and tiny crescent canyons tucked tightly against steep cliffs.

It was no wonder rebels and bandits had marked off this harsh terrain as their base of operations. Hidden here, they would be difficult to find, and harder still to root out and destroy. It seemed in both real estate and guerrilla warfare, one maxim ruled them all: location, location, location.

Tucker continued picking his way eastward, studying the detailed topographical map, judging the best course to keep parallel to the dirt road without being seen, searching for any evidence of a trap set by bandits or a bivouac of guerrilla forces. He wanted no surprises when he brought the others through here in the Range Rover.

He also relied heavily on Kane, outfitted with his tactical Storm vest.

The shepherd became an extension of his eyes and ears.

Roam. Scout. Return.

Those were Kane's standing orders as they moved through the maze of cliffs, scrub brush, and sand. Padding silently, the shepherd explored every nook and cranny. He scaled slopes, peeked over crests, ducked into blind canyons, and sniffed at cave entrances, returning every now and again to pass on an *all clear.*

After three miles, the first glimmer of the new day appeared. He pictured the sun rising above the distant

Kalahari Desert, firing the sands and stretching its light into the mountains. Tucker paused for a water break, sharing his canteen with Kane. He performed another compass check and updated his map.

Kane suddenly jerked his head up from the collapsible water bowl. Tucker froze, his eyes on the shepherd. Kane tilted his head left, then right, then took a few paces forward.

Though Tucker heard nothing, he implicitly trusted Kane's ears. Quietly, he tucked away their items and donned his pack.

"CLOSE LEAD. QUIET SCOUT."

While the shepherd's gait was naturally quiet, this order put Kane into a covert stalk mode. The shepherd took off at a fast walk, with Tucker following five paces behind. Kane slowly worked his way up a sandy ridge, moving from stone to stone so as not to trigger an avalanche of sand that could give away their position.

Tucker followed his example.

At the crest of the ridge, Kane lowered flat and stopped moving. From the intensity of the dog's gaze and the angle of his ears, Tucker knew his partner had homed in on the source of the noise.

Tucker joined him, dropping to his belly and crawling the last few feet. He peeked over the ridgeline.

Before them spread a fan-shaped valley a quarter mile long. The far side vanished into a scatter of ravines that broke through a tall, flat-topped plateau. The site had great potential to serve as a guerrilla base or a bandit hideout. It was hidden and defensible, with several escape routes nearby.

As if on cue, a pair of dark compact pickup trucks rolled into the valley from the neighboring dirt road. The two picked their way overland across the floor below. Jutting from the bed of each truck was a tripod-mounted machine gun. The hair on Tucker's neck tingled. Whether these were bandits or guerrillas, he didn't know, not that it really mattered. They were a force of armed men.

That was enough.

That, and they're right where I don't want them.

He watched the trucks continue past his position, then vanish down one of the ravines. Tucker waited a few more minutes to ensure they weren't turning back. Once satisfied, he and Kane scaled down into the valley and made their way to where the trucks had first appeared. Down a short slope, he found the remains of a still-warm campfire not far from the dirt road. Refuse littered the area, including what looked like fly-encrusted entrails, the discards of a field-dressed deer or antelope.

Tucker approached the campfire. It was small and the coals only a few inches deep. That told him the site had not been used many times. It wasn't a regular base.

Just passing through then. Maybe hunting food before returning to their main base deeper in the badlands.

"Hopefully," he muttered.

He checked his watch, recognizing it was time to head back to the others.

At his side, Kane growled, hackles rising.

Tucker dropped low next to him.

Then he heard another growl—but not from Kane.

From across the neighboring road, a fleet of dappled shadows sped over the dirt tract, a pack of dogs— from their rounded ears and spotted flanks, they were African wild dogs, *Lycaon pictus,* the second-largest canid predators in the world, topping off at eighty pounds each. As a necessity, Tucker had read up on the natural threats he might face out here. These beasts had the highest bite strength relative to body size of any carnivore. Their most common means of attack: disembowelment.

He stared at the pile of entrails, at the trickle of smoke still rising from the embers. The scent had clearly drawn them. Until now, intimidated by the larger group of men from the trucks, the pack had kept hidden, biding their time. But now, with the larger force gone, the pack was not going to tolerate a single man and a shepherd stealing from their larder.

As the pack reached the far side of the road, Tucker quickly retreated, drawing Kane with him. He shouldered the AR-15, sweeping the rifle's barrel across the pack as they burst through the scrub and into the clearing.

He didn't want to shoot—not because they were dogs, but because the gunfire would surely be heard by the departing guerrillas, likely drawing them back to the road.

He continued to retreat, hoping such a nonthreatening act would appease the dogs. Most of the pack went straight for the food, scattering a cloud of heavy flies to reach the entrails. Growls and yips rose from the feasting, amid much shouldering and complaints.

Two dogs ignored the easy pickings, clearly wanting fresh meat. They sped at Tucker and Kane. The first reached Tucker and lunged, leaping toward his groin. Expecting such an attack, he reversed his rifle and slammed the stock into the skull, catching the beast a glancing blow. The dog fell, tried to get up, stumbling and dazed. It was a male.

The female hesitated, shying from the sudden attack, juking to the side, watching them, stalking back and forth. Her lips rippled into a snarl, her hackles high. Kane paced her move for move, growling from deep inside.

Tucker knew that packs of African wild dogs were different from many other canids. An alpha female always led the pack, not a male.

Here was that leader.

Confirming this, she let out a short chirping burst from her throat, calling for support. Several of the pack lifted bloody muzzles from the feast.

Tucker knew running wasn't an option. The pack would be on them in seconds. They had to make a stand here—and make it before she got her pack fully rallied, which meant taking her out.

Still, he dared not shoot her, knowing the blast would echo far, likely to the wrong ears.

But he had another weapon.

He pointed toward the female.

"ATTACK."

Kane moves before the command leaves his partner's lips. He anticipates the instruction—and charges. Aggression already rages through him, stoked to a fiery blaze by the other. He has smelled her fury, read the territoriality in her posture, heard the threat.

She does not back down, lunging at him at the same time he leaps.

They strike hard, chest to chest, teeth gnashing at each other, catching air and fur. They roll, entangled, first him on top, then her.

She moves, fast, powerful, going for his exposed belly. She bites hard—but finds no flesh, only tough vest. He slides free from under her confusion and dismay. He lunges, snapping, shredding her ear.

She leaps back.

Now wary.

He smells her fear.

He growls deeper, from his bones. His ears lie back, his hackles trembling. He sets his front legs wider, challenging her. Saliva ropes from his curled lips, redolent with her blood.

It is enough.

She backs from his posture, from the toughness of his false hide.

One step, then another.

A new command reaches him, cutting through the crimson of his rage.

COME. FOLLOW.

He obeys, retreating but never backing down, locking eyes, still challenging the other until she falls out of view.

Tucker hurried away from the campsite, putting several hundred yards between them and the pack before slowing. He paused only long enough to run his fingers over Kane. Except for a few missing puffs of hair, he appeared unscathed.

As he'd hoped, Kane's tactical vest, reinforced with Kevlar, had not only protected the shepherd, but also clearly spooked the female with its strangeness. She was happy to let them retreat.

Backtracking along their old trail, the return journey went much faster. They arrived at the camp shortly before noon and were greeted happily by Christopher and Anya.

Bukolov offered a gruff but surprisingly genuine "Glad you are not dead."

While Anya and Bukolov prepared a cold lunch, Tucker recounted for Christopher his encounter with the guerrillas and wild dogs.

"You were lucky to survive that hungry pack, Mr. Tucker. And let us hope you are right about the soldiers, that they were simply passing through. Show me how far you mapped and we can plan the best course to avoid trouble."

Half an hour later, they were all gathered over a set of maps and charts. Christopher and Tucker had settled on the safest route to reach De Klerk's coordinates. But that was only *one* problem solved.

"Once there," Tucker said, "we need to find that landmark De Klerk mentioned, something shaped like a boar's head near a waterfall."

He turned to Bukolov and Anya. They knew De Klerk's history better than anyone. "In his diary of that siege, did De Klerk give any further clues about that waterfall. Like maybe some hint of its height?"

"No," Bukolov said.

"How about whether it was spring fed or storm runoff?"

Anya shook her head. "De Klerk described the troop's route into these mountains in only the vaguest terms."

"Then we're just going to have to get there and check every creek, stream, and trickle, looking for that waterfall."

Christopher considered this. "We are at the end of our rainy season. That highland region will likely be flowing with many small creeks and waterfalls. Which is good and bad. *Bad* because there will be many spots to explore."

Making for a long search . . .

Tucker pictured Felice closing in on them.

How much time did they have?

"How is it *good?*" Anya asked.

"The terrain here is hard and unforgiving. As a consequence, the creeks and river basins rarely change course. Year after year, they are the same. If the waterfall was flowing when your man was here, it is probably still flowing now."

"So we won't be on a wild-goose chase," Tucker said. "The waterfall is somewhere up there."

It was little consolation, but in this desolate environment, that was the best he could hope for.

Tucker rolled up the maps.

"Let's go."

35

Following Tucker's map they made slow and steady progress—the operative word being *slow.*

Christopher steered the Rover eastward along the dirt road, slipping past the guerrillas' campsite where Tucker and Kane had encountered the African wild dogs. A couple of miles after that, the trail vanished under them, so gradually that they had traveled several hundred yards before realizing they were simply in the trackless wilderness now.

Their new pattern became one of faltering stops and starts.

Every half mile or so, Tucker and Kane would have to climb out, hike to the highest vantage point, and scout the terrain ahead for signs of hidden bandits or guerrillas. They also charted the best path for the Rover, using both their eyes and the topographical maps.

As Christopher bounced up a rocky ravine, testing the extremes of the Range Rover's off-road capabilities, Tucker's GPS unit gave off a chime. He checked the screen.

"Getting close to De Klerk's coordinates. Another quarter mile or so." He glanced from the screen to the path of the ravine, calculating in his head. "It should be at the top of this next pass."

The Rover climbed the last of the approach as the ravine's walls narrowed to either side. It was a tight squeeze, but they finally reached the top of the pass and rode out onto a flat open plateau.

"Stop here," Tucker said.

They all clambered from the Rover, exhausted but excited.

"We made it," Anya said, sounding much too surprised.

Beyond that plateau, the landscape looked like a giant's shattered staircase. Flat-topped mesas and fractured crooked-top plateaus spread outward, climbing higher and higher. Brighter glints reflected the sunlight, marking countless waterfalls cascading from the heights, draped like so much silver tinsel across the landscape.

Closer at hand, confronting them, rose a thirty-foot cliff. Two wide ravines cut into its face on either side, both large enough to drive the Rover into. Between them, they framed an unusual section of cliff, shaped like a triangular nose with a blunted tip. It stuck out toward them, but its slopes were still too steep to climb.

But it was the ravines that drew Tucker's attention. The canyons were twins of each other, angling away from each other, like a giant shadowy V, only the legs of the V were slightly curved, like the upraised tusks of a—

"Boar's head," Bukolov muttered, sounding disappointed.

Tucker now appreciated the protruding cliff itself somewhat resembled a pig's flattened snout—with the twin canyons forming its tusks.

Still, Tucker understood the doctor's disenchantment. Somewhere buried in the back of his own head, he'd been picturing a magnificent granite boar's skull spewing a glittering stream of water between its tusks, spilling its bounty into a roiling pool surrounded by blooming desert flowers.

The reality was much more mundane.

Yet still just as dangerous.

Tucker urged them to grab their packs and get moving again. He pointed to the two canyons in the rock face. "While we still have daylight, we should check *both* sides. Doctor Bukolov with me. Anya with Christopher. Everyone stay on the radio. Questions?"

There were none.

With Kane at his heels, Tucker and Bukolov headed for the ravine on the right. The other pair aimed for the cleft on the left.

Tucker hiked into the gorge first, trailed by Bukolov. It was about eight or nine feet wide, filled with sand and loose rock.

"How are we going to find water in here?" Bukolov asked.

"Kane."

The shepherd pushed to his side. Dropping to a knee, Tucker tipped his canteen over his cupped palm and brought the water to Kane's nose.

"SEEK."

Kane turned away, his nose sniffing high.

You did it before, my friend. Do it again.

As if reading his mind, Kane looked up at Tucker and sprinted away, deeper down the ravine.

"He's onto something. C'mon."

The two men followed the shepherd, going slower, having to pick themselves over rubble and around boulders. They discovered Kane squatted before a section of rock wall on the left. When Tucker appeared, Kane let out a single bark. The dog jumped up, planting his front paws against the wall.

"Does that mean he's found something?" Bukolov asked.

"Let's find out."

Tucker shrugged off his pack—then pulled out and unfolded a small shovel. Crossing to the wall, he jammed in the spade's tip and gouged out a chunk of sandstone. He kept digging until he'd chipped a hole about six inches deep. It took some time and effort—but he was rewarded when he noted the change in color of the stone. Reaching in, he fingered some of the darker reddish-brown sand. The granules clung together a bit.

"It's damp back here."

"What does that mean?" Bukolov asked.

He placed his hand on the wall. "There must be a source of water somewhere behind here."

"Like a cave."

"Maybe."

Bukolov frowned. "But this wall is clearly not De Klerk's *waterfall.*"

"No. But there is a water source close by here." He patted his dog's side. "Good boy, Kane."

The shepherd resisted his praise. He sniffed at Tucker's sandy fingertips, barked three times rapidly, then jumped back on the wall.

"Shh!" Tucker said.

Kane obeyed, going silent, but he stayed with his forepaws braced on the rock face, his nose pointed up.

What are you trying to tell me?

Tucker backed away from the cliff face, shaded his eyes with a hand, and looked up.

From behind them, Christopher called, "What's happening?"

Anya was with him. "Our canyon came to a dead end. Then we heard the barking."

As they closed the distance, Christopher clearly hobbled on his left leg. "Twisted my ankle on some loose shale," he explained. "Hurts but I'm fine."

Anya stared over at Kane. "What's he found?"

"I don't—"

Then he understood.

Craning his neck, he continued down the ravine. He soon discovered what he was looking for: a jumble of boulders piled against the left side of the gorge.

"I should be able to climb that."

"Why? What the devil is going on?" Bukolov asked, dragging everyone with him.

Tucker faced them. "I'm climbing up. Something on top of the plateau has Kane all hot and bothered."

"Then I'm coming, too," Anya said.

He eyed her cast.

"I can manage. If I could climb to the top of Klipkoppie fort, I can scale this."

Christopher hung back, plainly compromised by his leg.

"Stay with Doctor Bukolov," Tucker instructed him. "We'll scout it out first."

Not knowing what was up there, Tucker wanted an extra set of eyes and ears. Bending down, he hauled Kane over his shoulders in a fireman's carry and started up the steps. It was a precarious climb in spots, but they reached the top.

Boulders littered the summit, a veritable broken maze. They had succeeded in mounting the section of cliff between the two tusk-shaped canyons. To their right, the plateau ended at the pig's snout. To the left, a pair of higher plateaus abutted against this one, like the raised shoulders of a monstrous beast.

"We're standing atop the Boar's Head," he realized aloud.

It had to be significant.

Tucker returned Kane to his feet with the instruction "SEEK."

Without hesitation, the shepherd sprinted in the direction of the taller mesas, dodging around boulders. Tucker and Anya followed, and after a few twists and turns, they found Kane sitting beside a pool of water.

On the far side, a sparkling cascade poured into it, flowing along a series of cataracts from the neighboring, higher lands.

His tail wagged happily, as if to say: *This is what I was talking about.*

"What on earth . . ." Anya whispered and stared at the dancing flow of water over rock. "Is that De Klerk's waterfall? If so, where's the cave?"

"I don't know."

Tucker took a moment to orient himself. Something was wrong with this picture. The pool next to Kane was kidney shaped, about twenty feet across. He stared at the stream flowing into it—as it likely had all season long. The pool seemed too tiny to capture all that flow.

So why hasn't this pool overflowed by now?

Then he knew the answer.

36

Tucker knelt at the pool's edge with Kane. With his head cocked to the side, he stared across the surface, watching the gentle ruffle of ripples spread outward from the cascade on the far side.

"What are you looking for?" Anya asked.

"There!" He pointed near the center of the pond, where the flow of ripples slightly churned in on themselves. "See that swirl."

"Yes, I see it, but what does it mean?"

"It means the pool is draining into something *beneath* it. That's why it's not overflowing its banks as the waterfall continues to pour into it. It drains below as quickly as it fills above."

A lilt of excitement entered Anya's voice. "You're thinking it might be draining into a cave."

"Maybe *the* cave. We're exactly at De Klerk's coordinates here."

Tucker crossed back to the edge of the cliff and called down to Christopher. "I need the climbing rope from my pack. Can you toss it up?"

"Just a minute!"

"What did you find?" Bukolov yelled to them.

"That's what I'm about to find out!" he hollered down.

Christopher pulled out the nylon climbing rope, tied a monkey's fist in one end, and hurled the end up to Tucker. He caught it on the first try and reeled the rest of the length up. Before returning to the pond, he knotted the rope around one of the poolside boulders.

Pulling on gloves, he stepped back to the waterline and flung the other end of the rope—the one with the monkey's fist still tied in it—out toward the center of the pool.

The knotted end sank—then after a few tense breaths, the remaining line between his fingers began uncoiling, snaking into the water. Slowly at first, then faster and faster. With a *twang*, the last of the line sprang taut in his fingertips, forming a straight line from the boulder to the whirlpool.

Tucker waded out a few feet, sliding his palm along the rope. When he was thigh deep, he felt a slight tidal pull of the drainage vortex. His fingers tightened on the line. He moved step by step. The tug on his legs became stronger. By the time he was waist-deep, his boots began to slide on the slippery rocks underfoot.

For safety's sake, he straddled the rope, grasped it with both hands, and began backing toward the center.

Step by cautious step.

Then his left foot plunged into nothingness. Gasping in surprise, he dropped to his right knee. Water foamed and roiled around his upper chest.

"Tucker! Careful." Anya stood on the bank, a worried hand at her throat.

Kane barked at him.

"I'm okay," he told them both.

He pulled on the rope and yanked his left foot back from the hole. He gained a firmer stance against the tide. With his right hand clutching the rope, he bent down and reached back with his left. He probed the pool's bottom until his fingers touched the rim of the hole.

"Seems wide enough," he called to Anya.

"Wide enough for what?"

"Me."

"Tucker, no. You don't know what's down there. Don't—"

He took a deep breath, sat down on his butt, slid both feet into the hole, and lowered himself downward.

The current of the vortex grabbed him hard and sucked him through the drain. His gloved fingers slid along the rope in fits and starts. Then he popped out of the flooded chute and found himself swinging in open air.

He dangled and twisted in the faucet of water pouring down from the ceiling of stone overhead. Watery light flowed down with it, but not enough to illuminate the cavernous space below him.

Spinning on the line, he lowered himself hand over hand.

Finally his boots touched solid ground. He found his footing, backed up a few steps out of the torrential stream, and let go of the rope. Bent double, gasping, he spit water, coughed, and wiped clear his eyes.

He finally straightened, expecting to see nothing but what little daylight filtered through the chute above, but as his eyes adjusted, he noted fiery slivers of sunlight shining around him—some four or five of them, coming through fissures in the roof or sloping walls.

Still, they offered scant illumination.

He plucked his flashlight out of a buttoned pocket and panned it around the roughly oval-shaped cavern. The waterfall, which marked the space's center point, flooded across the bottom of the cave, pooling in some places but mostly draining through fissures in the floor.

Turning slowly, he oriented himself with the outside landscape. *Above* his head was the boulder-strewn plateau. To his *left* would be the pig's snout, the cliff that was framed by the shadowy boar tusks. To his *right*, he spotted a pair of tunnel entrances that looked like the twin barrels of a shotgun. He imagined they led deeper into the higher plateaus that extended behind the boar's head.

Shining his light across the floor, he also saw evidence of prior habitation, washed up along the walls' edges. He spotted broken furniture that could have once been tables or beds. His beam picked out a couple of bayonets oxidized to black.

As in the cave at Klipkoppie, Tucker pictured the ghosts of soldiers coming and going here, sitting around tables lit with oil lamps, polishing those bayonets, joking and exchanging war stories.

Eyeing the shotgun tunnels, he wanted to explore further, to see where they might lead, but now was not the time to go wandering by himself.

He stared at the rope whipping within the cascade of water and sighed.

He needed the others.

Going *up* proved a hundredfold harder than the descent. Hand over hand, he hauled himself through the pounding cascade, out the hole, and back to the surface of the pool. Exhausted, he waded back to the rim and threw himself flat on the bank. He rolled to his back and let the sun warm him.

"Tucker?" Anya dropped to her knees next to him. "Are you okay?"

Kane came up on his other side, nosing him fiercely, half greeting, half scolding.

"What's down there?" Anya asked.

He only grinned at her and said, "You'll see."

5:23 P.M.

"Bless you, my boy!" Bukolov said by the bank of the pond. "And your dog!"

It took some effort to get the good doctor atop the plateau, but he proved fitter than he appeared. Even Christopher, after resting while Tucker took the plunge into the unknown, was walking more solidly on his left leg. He made it up the boulder staircase without any assistance.

Bukolov continued. "We stand at the entrance to De Klerk's cave! At the threshold of discovering the greatest boon known to mankind!"

Tucker allowed the doctor to wax purple and lay on the hyperbole.

For in fact, they *had* done it.

Christopher and Anya chuckled, standing next to the doctor.

Tucker stood off by the cliff's edge, inventorying the supplies they had shuttled up here by rope. There were still a few last items he wanted, but he could haul those by hand.

Straightening, he called to the others. "I'm going for another run to the Rover while we have daylight!"

He was acknowledged, but before he could step away, a buzzing rose from his pack. He fished out his satellite phone and answered.

"Tucker, I'm glad I could reach you." The tension in Harper's voice was obvious.

"What's wrong?"

"Where were you?"

"Down a hole. At De Klerk's coordinates. We found it. We found the—"

"*Who's* with you?"

"Everyone."

"How close?" she pressed.

"Fifty feet." Tucker withdrew farther from the others, sensing the need for privacy. He put a boulder between him and the others. "Now sixty feet. What's the matter?"

"We deconstructed that photo you sent—the one of you sitting at the computer in the Internet café in

Dimitrovgrad. It was *shopped.* It's a fake. Don't ask me to explain the technicalities, but there were pixel defects in the image—something called integration artifacts."

"Go on."

"Integration artifacts are created when you extract part of one image and overlay it onto another. You follow?"

"Like replacing a horse's ass with your boss's face. I get it. Out with it."

"The photo of you at the Internet café was created by merging *two* different images. An interior shot of the café. And a photo of you taken elsewhere. Someone shopped them together. Faked it."

"What the hell?"

"Our techs were able to separate out the original photo of you, and through extrapolation and pixel capture, they were able to rebuild some of the old details that were erased, mostly details around your hands. In the faked photo, your hands are hovering over a computer keyboard. But when the techs were done, they showed your hands were really originally holding a *steering wheel.*"

"So the picture of me that was Photoshopped was actually taken while I was driving."

"Exactly. It appears to have been taken by a cell-phone camera. It was a side profile of you, as if someone in the passenger seat shot it."

It took several pained seconds for Tucker's brain to register what Harper was telling him. He squeezed his eyes shut, her last words echoing in his mind.

. . . a side profile of you, as if someone in the passenger seat shot it . . .

"What was I wearing in the photo? I can't remember."

"Uh . . . a military winter suit."

That was the jacket he wore when he pulled Anya out of the Kazan Kremlin. After that, they fled the city. He pictured that ride.

Bukolov and Utkin had been sitting in the back.

Anya had been up front with him—in the passenger seat.

Tucker whispered, "It's Anya."

He closed his eyes, despairing. She must have covertly taken the photo with her cell phone as he drove them out of Kazan, then e-mailed it away before he ditched everyone's electronics.

He had to recalibrate his entire worldview of events—and brace a hand against the boulder to keep his legs steady.

She had lied about *just getting tea* in Dimitrovgrad. While loose, she must have made contact with Kharzin's people, told them where to arrange the Spetsnaz ambush. She must have also covertly followed Tucker, noted he had used that Internet café. Kharzin's people took advantage of that information to create the doctored photo. It was insurance, a red herring. It had been *planted* on the Spetsnaz people in case their ambush failed. In that worst-case scenario, Tucker was meant to find the photo, so he would believe the attackers had been tailing them or tracking them all along, so as to throw off suspicion from Anya.

But that was not the worst of it.

Utkin.

He suddenly found it hard to breathe. He felt sucker punched in the gut. He pictured the man bleeding to death on the beach, sacrificing himself to save them, the same people who had falsely accused and condemned him.

Still, you saved us.

And it had never been Utkin. Anya had set him up. The signal generator was *hers.* The empty pack of cards in Utkin's bag was *hers.* She knew Utkin would have a set of cards. It was easy enough to plant that evidence in his duffel.

Harper's voice blared in his ear, drawing him back to his own skin. "Tucker!"

"I'm here." He took a deep breath. "It's Anya. She's the one working with Kharzin. I should have seen it."

"There's no way you could have."

"Either way, we have to assume she's been in contact with Kharzin's people since we touched down in Africa. She was with me when I found Grietje's Well.

She knew the GPS coordinates to this spot. Which means Kharzin has them, too."

"Then that means you're likely to have company soon," Harper said. "What're you going to do?"

"We've found the cave, but not the specimens of LUCA."

"That doesn't leave you many options."

"Just one. Get Bukolov into the cave and let him go to work. While he's doing that, I'll get ready for a siege and rig the cave with C-4. If we can't hold off Felice and her team, I'll blow it all to hell."

There was a long silence on her end. "Let's hope it doesn't come to that," she finally said. "What about Anya? What are you going to do with her?"

"In the short term, I haven't decided yet."

"And the long term?"

He pictured Utkin's face. "I don't see her having a *long* term."

5:38 P.M.

Tucker knelt by his pack out of sight of the others, slicing two six-foot sections of rope.

He considered how smoothly Anya had duped him. Then again, she had done the same with her superiors at the SVR. All along she'd been a GRU mole planted there or groomed there by Kharzin. It was for *that* reason she'd been falsifying reports to the SVR—not to protect Bukolov, but to help Kharzin. Even her admission to Tucker that she was an SVR agent was clever: confess to a damning lie, throw yourself on your sword, and claim remorse. Then be a team player, struggling and suffering with everyone else. And then finally, when Utkin's treachery is revealed, come to his defense with sympathy and rationalization.

My God, Tucker thought.

He stood, stuffed the rope sections into his back pockets, and picked up his AR-15 rifle. He stalked back over to the group, all still gathered at the pond's edge.

Christopher greeted him with a wave. "I thought you were going back to the Rover to get more supplies."

Kane trotted over, his tail high, but he must have immediately sensed the black pall around his partner. The flagging tail drooped down. His entire body stiffened up, readying for action.

Anya was too skilled not to get worried. "Tucker, what's wrong?"

He lifted the rifle and pointed it at her. "Raise your arms above your head. If you so much as twitch a finger, I'll shoot you."

"What are you doing?" she replied, feigning confusion, but he noted the microexpression of fury that momentarily flashed.

"Five seconds, Anya."

"Tucker, you're scaring me."

The shock that had initially struck Christopher and Bukolov wore off. They began to voice a similar chorus of confused complaints. He ignored them.

"Three seconds."

He raised the AR to his shoulder.

Anya pushed her arms high. She looked to Bukolov and Christopher for support, fixing an expression of suffering innocence. "Tell me what is happening."

"My people deconstructed the photo of the Internet café in Dimitrovgrad. It was *you*, Anya, from the very beginning. You were the traitor. Not Utkin. He was a just a boy, and you set him up to take the fall."

The complaints from Christopher and Bukolov died away.

"Tucker, please, I don't know what—"

"Deny it one more time, Anya. One more time and I'll put a round in your foot."

She stared up and must have read his seriousness. She kept her gaze fixed on him, showing no shame, but also no satisfaction. "It was not personal. I took no joy in the bloodshed. I liked Utkin. I truly did, but it was necessary. I was given a duty, and I performed it to the best of my abilities."

Her words lacked any coldness or disdain, only a calm self-assurance.

"How long until your people get here?" he asked.

"I will not tell you."

"How are they tracking you?"

She just stared.

"Drop to your knees, then to your belly, hands flat on the rock."

She complied, moving with surprising grace.

"GUARD," he ordered Kane.

As the shepherd stalked to her side, Tucker passed his weapon to Christopher. "Keep her covered."

With her under tight watch, Tucker quickly bound her hands and ankles. He frisked her, removing anything he found, including taking her boots and socks. He examined each item, but he found no electronics or trackers.

He was fairly certain she didn't have a phone, which meant Kharzin's people had to have been tracking her. But how? He would have to search through her entire pack, strip the Rover down, too.

Tucker noted Bukolov had wandered a few paces away, his back to them.

Concerned, Tucker crossed to him. He didn't need the guy falling apart. Bukolov wasn't the most stable of personalities even on his good days.

"Doc?"

Bukolov glanced to him and away, but not before Tucker noted the tears. "He died thinking I hated him."

Utkin.

"I was such a fool," Bukolov said. "How can I forgive myself?"

"Because Utkin would want you to." He placed a hand on the doctor's shoulder. "He knew our distrust of him was based on deceit. He saved us because he wouldn't let that lie define him. We have to honor that."

Bukolov nodded, wiping his eyes. "I will try to do that."

"Forget Anya. Forget all of it. I'm going to get you inside that cave, and you're going to find that sample of LUCA. That's all that matters now."

"What about Kharzin's team?"

"Let me worry about them. Concentrate on what you came here to do. The sooner you find LUCA, the sooner we can leave—with any luck, before the enemy arrives. Are you with me, Doc?"

Bukolov straightened, took a deep breath, and nodded firmly. "I am with you."

Tucker glanced back to Anya, still on her belly, her arms tied behind her back, guarded over by Christopher and Kane.

It was time to turn her betrayal to his advantage.

37

S tanding at the edge of the pond, Tucker passed a gun
to Bukolov. It was a Smith & Wesson .38-caliber
revolver. Though it only held five rounds, it was a personal favorite: for its size, accuracy, and reliability. All
too often, surviving a firefight relied more on the *quality* of the gun than the *quantity* of the rounds. He'd
rather have five good shots than ten poor ones any day.

"Do you know how to use a gun?" Tucker asked.

Bukolov turned the revolver over in his hands.
"Finger squeezes here. Bullets come out there. I think
I can manage." He glanced down to Anya, still on her
belly and bound up. "Can I shoot her?"

"Not unless she gets free and charges you. Otherwise, we're leaving you here to *guard* her until we get back."

Christopher stood off to the side. The pair of them were going to return to the Range Rover, where Anya's pack was still stored. He intended to search both it and the SUV thoroughly. They needed to find her tracking device, and the hunt would go faster with two people.

He stared toward the sky.

They had less than an hour of daylight left.

He crossed and checked Anya's bindings and knots one final time before leaving.

"You cannot win, Captain Wayne," Anya said matter-of-factly, as if discussing the weather, in this case a coming storm. "General Kharzin will have many men with him. Elite Spetsnaz."

"I believe you."

"You may hold them off for a time, but eventually you will lose. If you surrender, it will go better for you."

"Somehow I don't see that ending with anything less than a bullet in my skull." He gave the ropes around her ankle a snug pull. "Just answer one question."

Arching her back, she glanced over her shoulder toward him.

"Knowing what you do about LUCA, *why* would you want Kharzin to have it?"

"It is not my place to question. I know my duty, and I serve."

Tucker stared at her preternatural calmness, at her steady and simple gaze. It was beginning to unnerve him a little. Here was the true Anya.

"How does Kharzin plan to use it?" he asked.

"I do not know."

Oddly enough, *this* he believed.

6:33 P.M.

"Look here," Christopher said as he knelt on the ground next to Anya's open pack. He had already dumped the contents out and had been slowly going over them, item by item.

Tucker was performing a similar search upon the Rover, knowing a wireless transmitter could have been planted in a thousand places. As he worked, he felt the growing press of time as the sun sank toward the horizon.

"What did you find?" he asked, shifting over to Christopher.

Kane came sniffing, too.

Christopher passed over what looked like a thick-barreled ballpoint pen. "Twist it open."

He did, unscrewing it and pulling the two halves apart. Inside, he discovered a cluster of fine wires, a microcircuit board, and a strip of lithium-ion batteries the size of his pinkie nail.

He smiled. *Gotcha.*

"What about the Range Rover?" Christopher asked. "Do you want me to help you look for any additional transmitters?"

"In the end, they won't matter. I just need this one in hand."

"What next then?"

"You head back to the pond. We need to hide any evidence that we're still here. That means getting you, Bukolov, and Anya down into that cave."

Tucker quickly instructed Christopher on how to get everyone lowered through the vortex.

"I should be back around dusk to join you," Tucker finished. "Call me by radio if there is any trouble."

With Christopher headed back, Tucker climbed into the driver's seat of the Range Rover. Kane clambered into the passenger seat.

He engaged the engine and slowly reversed his way back down the ravine. Once at the bottom, he headed west for ten minutes, continuing their group's original trajectory, pushing the Rover as hard as he dared, hoping Kharzin was actively monitoring his progress.

He eventually found the perfect terrain.

Three-quarters of a mile from where he'd started, Tucker stopped the vehicle at the mouth of a narrow slot-canyon, much like the one back at the coordinates. He hopped out and entered the narrow ravine. Using his flashlight, he studied the rubble-strewn floor until he discovered a deep fissure in the ground. Peering down, he saw no bottom.

Good enough.

Reaching to his pocket, he pulled out Anya's pen and dropped it down the crack.

Dig for that, General.

He hurried back to the parked Rover. If there were any more transmitters aboard, he didn't care. He wanted to draw Kharzin here. He left the keys in the ignition and set to work on the second part of his plan: a surprise welcome for the general's team.

From the cargo pocket of his pants, he pulled out the waxy block of C-4 explosives that he'd been carrying all day.

Working quickly but cautiously, he sidled under the vehicle on his back and stuffed a half block of the explosive between the muffler and the floorboard. Next, he strung a length of detonation cord to the leaf springs behind the front tire and affixed a chemical detonator.

He crawled back out and surveyed his handiwork.

If anyone tried to move or even sit inside the vehicle, the stress on the tire springs would set off the charge. With any luck, the bomb would take out one or two of Kharzin's Spetsnaz.

And while the ruse wouldn't stop Kharzin forever, it should buy Tucker and the others some valuable extra time.

He turned to Kane. "Ready for a little run?"

The tail wag was answer enough.

7:18 P.M.

Setting a hard pace, it took only ten minutes to return to the canyon and up to the pond. He found Christopher waiting for him at the pool's edge. The sun had already disappeared, but the twilight's gloaming still allowed decent light.

"Are the other two down safely in the cave?" Tucker asked, huffing heavily. "And the supplies?"

"The doctor went first with his pistol. Then Anya, all trussed up and lowered like a Christmas goose. Doctor Bukolov radioed that he has her well in hand."

"Then we should get below, too."

"Before we do that," Christopher said, "I had a thought. If I call my brothers and—"

"No. I'm not going to involve them here."

"I do not mean to bring them *here*. I love my brothers too much for that. I simply mean to ask them to wait for us at last night's campsite. I can pass on the coordinates. If we make it out of this alive, we'll still need a way *back* to civilization, especially if our Rover gets blown up."

It made sense.

Christopher talked with his brother for two minutes on the satellite phone, then disconnected. "They will be there tomorrow night."

With the matter settled, they set about getting themselves down into the cave. Christopher disappeared first through the vortex. Next, Tucker lowered Kane, cinching the line through a set of loops in his tactical vest. Tucker went last after reconfiguring the rope ties, so he could pull the rope down after him once inside.

A few moments later, soaked to the skin, Tucker stood in the cave with the others. Hauling with his shoulders, he reeled the rope down from above.

"What are you doing?" Christopher asked, watching the last of the line tumble down to the floor.

Bukolov stood up from where he sat atop their supplies next to Anya, his pistol still pointed at her head. She was flat on her belly as before.

Tucker had told no one about this last detail of his plan, or they might have balked at coming down here.

"I don't want to leave any evidence that we were ever *up* there. And I certainly don't want to leave behind any clue about how to get *down* here."

"But how are we supposed to get out of here?" Bukolov asked.

"According to De Klerk, this was an old Boer bunker." He pictured the warren of tunnels and cellars back at the Klipkoppie fort. "So I wager there's more than one way out of this cavern system."

"You're *wagering* with our lives," Bukolov warned, but he ended it with an unconcerned shrug. "But you are right, the Boer were a crafty bunch."

"And even if I'm wrong, I have a contingency plan as backup."

"Which is what?" Christopher asked.

"Let's worry about that *after* we search this place."

Tucker realized one of their team had remained unusually quiet. He stepped over to Anya and dropped to a knee.

Bukolov shuffled his legs a bit. "She had a lot to say while you were all gone. Very sly, this one. Gets in your head. She kept wheedling, pressing, promising, until finally I had to put a sock in it."

Tucker smiled. In this case, the doctor was speaking literally. He had stuffed a rolled-up sock in Anya's mouth, gagging her.

Tucker straightened back up. "That's why you're a billionaire, Doctor Bukolov. Always using your head."

Or in this particular case, his foot.

Tucker pointed to her and renewed an order with Kane. "GUARD."

The shepherd walked over to Anya and lowered his head until his snout was mere inches away, panting. Anya leaned back, her eyes flashing hatefully, finally showing cracks in that calm professional demeanor.

Bukolov chuckled. "I have grown quite fond of that dog."

7:55 P.M.

Preparing to explore, Tucker and Christopher donned headlamps. The cavern's only other illumination came from an LED lantern next to Bukolov. The doctor still sat among the supplies, guarding Anya. He had a pistol in one hand and De Klerk's diary in another, doing his best to get his bearings, to discern some clue about the whereabouts of the specimens of LUCA.

"There are many references in his damned diary," Bukolov had said a few moments ago. "To bunkrooms, officers' messes, medical wards, including a place grimly noted as the *Die Bloedige Katedraal,* or 'The Bloody Cathedral.' It seemed the Boer even brought their horses in here and wagons."

Tucker looked up at the falling chute of water.

Not through there they didn't.

"But I keep coming to one entry over and over again. It's simply noted as *Die Horro,* or 'The Horror.' It seemed important to De Klerk. But it would be easier to trace his steps through this subterranean world if I had some *map* of the place."

And that's what Tucker and Christopher intended to do, with Kane's help. Tucker figured this recon mission was a better use of the shepherd's skills than merely guarding Anya. She was already trussed up and under the baleful eye of Bukolov. Besides, where could she go?

So Christopher and Tucker headed over to the two passageways that looked like the muzzle of a double-barreled shotgun.

Tucker took the one on the right with Kane. Christopher vanished into the other. After only sixty steps, Tucker's tunnel dumped into another cavern, this one massive, with a vaulted ceiling festooned with stalactites. The floor was likewise covered in a maze of towering stalagmites. Some of the two met to form columns like in a—

"Cathedral," Tucker mumbled.

Was this the place Bukolov had mentioned?

Die Bloedige Katedraal.

As he stepped farther out, he saw the walls to either side had been carved into tiers. They definitely looked man-made, likely the handiwork of the Boers.

A scuffle of boots sounded behind him. Christopher stumbled into view thirty feet away, his light shining blindingly into Tucker's face. His tunnel had also deposited him into the Cathedral.

"Whoa, whoa!" Christopher said, sweeping his headlamp across the cavern. "How big do you think this place is?"

"Side to side, fifty yards. Maybe twice again as deep." Tucker pointed to the tiered ledges on his side. "I want to check those out. Those aren't natural. See the chisel marks and ax strikes in the sandstone?"

Tucker crossed over and hopped up onto the first ledge, then the second, finally the third, like climbing tall steps. Kane followed him up. They were now ten feet off the ground. He found more Boer handiwork on top. The highest ledge had been excavated along its length to form a crude foxhole, enough room for a soldier to duck down out of sight from the floor below.

Shining his lamp into the foxhole, he saw the bottom littered with spent shell casings. Kane jumped down to explore, sniffing at the casings, shuffling through them.

Christopher had mirrored his climb on the far side of the cavern and discovered the same. They both walked along the top tier on their respective sides, heading down along the cavern, paralleling each other.

"I'm starting to see how the Boers did it," Tucker called out. "From these foxholes, they could strafe anyone passing through the cavern below. A perfect killing floor."

"Horrible to imagine," Christopher said.

Tucker now understood the *bloody* part of the room's nickname.

"Let's keep going."

They clambered back to the floor, met in the middle, and headed farther down the belly of the monstrous cavern.

Tucker noted the telltale pockmarks gouging a nearby stalagmite, evidence of gunfire. This killing floor had seen some use.

But if so, where were the bodies from that slaughter? Had the British buried them after clearing this place out—even the Boers' remains? Was there a mass grave somewhere in these hills?

As they continued through the Cathedral, the walls began narrowing and the roof descending, until the space was only thirty feet across. Near the end of the cave, they hit a waist-high wall of burlap sandbags that stretched from wall to wall. They high-stepped over it, while Kane hurdled it. In another ten feet, with the walls ever narrowing, they ran into another line of sandbags, then after that another. Beyond the last one, the Cathedral's walls and ceiling narrowed to a four-foot-wide funnel that became a tunnel.

"Defense in depth," Tucker whispered.

"Pardon me?"

He pointed to the dark tunnel. "Your enemy comes through there. The defenders hide behind the closest row of sandbags. If the enemy breaches that wall, the defenders fall back to the next barrier."

"And the next after that . . ."

"All the way across. If the enemy makes it through that gauntlet, they still have to face the killing floor behind us. No wonder the Boer lasted so long here, where only a few could withstand many."

Tucker stepped over the last sandbag and wondered if his team would soon face similar bad odds.

"Stay here with Kane," Tucker said. "I'll be right back."

Dropping to his hands and his knees, he crawled along the shaft ahead, which almost immediately began cutting sharply left and right. As he crawled,

Tucker imagined a Boer sniper lying prone at each corner, picking off an advancing British soldier before retreating to the next corner, then repeating the process again.

After eight or ten bends Tucker reached a straight passageway. At the end of it, slivers of pale light glowed. Dowsing his headlamp, he crawled the last of the way and reached a pile of rock that blocked the path forward. He fingered the silvery light that pierced through the rubble and pulled a fist-sized rock from its edge. A few more fell with it, forming a watermelon-sized hole.

Cool night air flowed back to him.

He poked his head out and searched around outside, gaining his bearings.

He realized he had reached the other canyon—the other tusk of the boar—the one Christopher and Anya had explored earlier.

Interesting.

If nothing else, he'd found another exit.

After pulling his head back inside, he carefully returned the fallen rocks back into place, sealing the hole, making sure it remained camouflaged from the outside.

He didn't want any uninvited houseguests coming in the back door.

8:13 P.M.

Tucker returned to the sandbag barrier, where he found Christopher waiting, but he noted a missing member of their team. "Where's Kane?"

Christopher did a dance of searching around. "He was here a moment ago. That one, he is like a ghost."

True . . . and with a dog's curiosity.

He had forgotten to tell Kane to stay.

Tucker pursed his lips and let out a soft double whistle.

Kane responded with a double bark.

They followed the sound back into the Cathedral, only to discover Kane standing at the top ledge along the left wall. He stared square at Tucker—then jumped down into the foxhole and vanished out of sight. The shepherd's message was plain.

Come see what I found!

What now?

Tucker led Christopher up to the ledge. He shone his lamp's beam into the foxhole to find Kane seated before a barrel-shaped wooden door in the cavern wall.

"Seems there is more to this maze," Christopher said.

Tucker jumped down. He tested the four-foot-wide plank door. The wood was once stout, the iron joinery solid. No longer. He leaned against the other side of the foxhole and kicked out with his legs. The ancient door shattered under his heels. A passageway extended from it.

"Let's see where it leads."

He took Kane with him this time, but he had noted Christopher beginning to limp badly on the ankle he'd twisted before, so he left him to rest.

The crawl this time was mercifully short. The passageway ended at a crudely circular room, crowded with stacked boxes, but at least he could stand.

He noted *four* tunnels led out from here.

Tucker sighed.

The Boers apparently were ants in another life.

Tucker called back to Christopher. "If I'm not back in fifteen minutes, come after me."

He took a brief moment to examine the crates. Burned into their sides was the coat of arms for the Boer Orange Free State. Same as De Klerk's unit. He pulled the lid off the top crate and looked inside. He found rifle shells, canned goods, tins of kerosene, candles, hammers, nails. He examined three more crates and found similar contents.

Though he had found nothing significant, a question nagged at him: *Why hadn't the British seized this bounty when they cleared this place out?*

Without an answer, he began his search of the four tunnels, starting from the left and working his way right.

The first passage led to a mess hall: a long, narrow gallery containing trestle tables constructed from what appeared to be the remains of wagons, all of them topped with abandoned plates and pewter cups.

The second tunnel ended at a bunkroom: a gallery-style cavern, with moldy lines of bedrolls flanking the walls and dark lanterns hanging above.

Again, there was no indication that the British had been here. Nothing was ransacked; nothing looked disturbed. Tucker felt as though he were touring an abandoned theater.

Down the third passageway, he found the unit's hospital: a ward lined by thirty or so makeshift cots and stacked with crates of medical supplies.

He was about to leave, when something struck him as off.

"No blankets, no mattresses, no pillows," he murmured.

The cots had been stripped.

And why so many of them?

According to Bukolov, the Boers had arrived here with only a hundred men. This medical ward held cots for nearly a third of that number. Had that many soldiers been wounded?

With more mysteries raised than solved, Tucker moved to the fourth and final passageway. This one ended at a huge cavern, but it was barren: no crates, no equipment. Nothing. But something struck him as odd about its far wall.

Following his beam of light, Tucker crossed there and discovered a large wall of rubble. He noted blackened scorch marks to either side. Roosa must have blasted this entrance, collapsing and sealing it behind him. At least this discovery answered a question that had been nagging him: *How had Roosa gotten the horses into this cave system?* Of course, that raised in turn yet another question: *What became of the horses?*

Kane barked twice behind him.

The shepherd drew him to a tunnel opening off to the right. This one was blocked by a careful stack of boulders. Each stone wedged tightly together. Even the gaps had been stuffed with clumps of burlap.

"What the hell?" he murmured.

Using his hands and his knife, he pried at the wall of boulders until one slipped free. It crashed to the floor, almost hitting his toes. He began to lower his face to the opening, to shine his light through the gap, but yanked his head back, slapped in the face by a fierce stench.

He took a few involuntary steps backward, covering his nose and mouth with a hand. He recognized the stink immediately, flashing back to too many battle-fields, to too much death.

Flesh and fire.

He took a full minute to steel himself, then he returned to the sealed door. He now detected a whiff of kerosene through the stench, the incendiary source for whatever horrors lay beyond this blockade.

He remembered the entry read by Bukolov from De Klerk's diary.

Die Horro . . .

Holding his breath, he shoved his head through the gap and swiveled the beam of his lamp. He pointed it down first, expecting to see floor. Instead, darkness swallowed his light. He was staring into the mouth of a shaft, a black pit.

Tucker pulled back out and sat down beside Kane.

He knew what he had to do, but he railed against it.

He had no doubt *what* lay at the bottom of the pit.

But he had no answer as to *why* and *who?*

Those answers lay below—along with perhaps the secret behind De Klerk's diary. He closed his eyes, struggling to rally. He'd come too far with too much blood shed. He could not balk now.

But I want to . . . dear God, do I want to.

8:41 P.M.

"Tucker, what did you find?" Christopher asked, looking worried, perhaps noting his sickened demeanor as he returned.

"I'm not sure. But I need you to go back to the supplies, grab a coil of climbing rope, and come back here."

Christopher returned two minutes later.

"Follow me," Tucker said and led Christopher and Kane back to the large cavern and over to the doorway that closed off the pit.

"That stink . . ." Christopher said after peering through the hole. He had helped Tucker widen it by pulling out a few more rocks. "You're not going down there, are you?"

"I'm happy for you to take my place."

For once, Christopher didn't argue.

Working together, they anchored the rope around a nearby stalagmite and tossed the free end through the hole.

After ordering Kane to stay put, Tucker boosted himself through the opening and twisted around. With his gloved hands on the rope, he leaned back and braced his feet against the wall of the shaft. He took a calming breath. He tried to quiet the voice in his head that was shouting at him to go no farther.

In the end, he simply chose to ignore it.

Hand over hand, Tucker walked himself down into the pit. His headlamp danced off the rock. After ten feet he stopped, steadied himself, and looked below. The bottom of the pit was still beyond the reach of his headlamp's beam. He kept going. He stopped again at the twenty-foot mark and spotted the end of his rope coiled on a bottom of sorts, a rock ramp that tilted at a sharp angle.

Tucker lowered himself until his boots came to rest atop that ramp. He noted most of the shaft around him was scorched with an oily black soot. He kept one hand on the line—not trusting the rock's slippery surface or its steep grade. Crouching carefully, he peered over the lip of the ramp and discovered another drop-off.

Don't think, he commanded himself.

Swallowing hard, he leaned over the drop-off and shone his light down.

His beam revealed an outstretched arm, reaching up toward him, blackened to bone, fingers curled by old flames.

He shuddered, his heart pounding in his throat.

He panned the light down the forearm and biceps, where it disappeared into—

It took Tucker a few seconds for his mind to accept what he was seeing: a morass of skeletal remains and charred flesh. At the edges, he picked out scorched clothing and blankets, chunks of half-charred wood, and blackened tins of kerosene. Despite trying to avoid it, he discerned bits of individual remains.

—a torso jutting from the mire as though the man had been trying to claw his way out of quicksand.

—the disembodied hoof of a horse, its steel shoe glinting dully.

—a pair of gentleman's spectacles caught on a higher spur of rock, looking unscathed by the conflagration below, reflecting back his lamp's light.

"Good God," he murmured.

Sick to his stomach, his head full of the acrid stench of immolated flesh, he tore his eyes away and pulled himself back until he stood on trembling legs on the scorched ramp. Questions swirled.

What had happened here?

How deep was the pit?

How many were down there?

Tucker stared up, ready to escape this choked gateway to hell.

Two feet above his head, he found himself staring at the haft of a dagger. It was jutting from the rock face, so soot covered he hadn't noticed it when he first came down. He reached up, grabbed the haft, and gave it a wiggle. Dried soot flaked off and swirled in the beam of his headlamp. There was something beneath the soot, pinned by the blade into the rock.

Using his fingertips, he brushed away the soot to reveal a thick square of oilcloth. Carefully, he pried the packet off the wall and slipped it into his thigh pocket.

"Tucker!" Christopher's shout startled him. "What did you find?"

He glared up toward his friend's headlamp. "I'm coming up! Get that damned light out of my eyes."

"Oh, sorry."

He quickly and gladly hauled himself up the rock face and out of the shaft. Without saying a word, he strode several yards away from the charnel pit and finally sat down. Christopher joined him and offered a canteen.

He took a long gulp of water.

Kane slinked over, his tail low, the very tip wagging questioningly.

"I'm okay . . . I'm okay . . ."

The reassurance was as much for him as Kane.

"What was down there?" Christopher asked.

Tucker explained—though words failed to convey the true horror.

Christopher murmured, "Good Lord, why would they do that?"

"I don't know." Tucker withdrew the wrapped packet of oilcloth. "But this may hold some clue."

He turned the prize over in his hands. He found a seam in the cloth. Using the tip of his knife, he slit along it and unfolded the cloth. It was several layers thick. At the heart of the package rested a thick sheaf of papers, folded in half and perfectly preserved, showing no signs of soot or decay.

Written on the outside in what he immediately recognized as De Klerk's handwriting were two lines: one Afrikaans, the other in English, likely the same message.

Aan wie dit vind...

To whoever finds this...

He shared a glance with Christopher and unfolded the papers. What he found there was written in both languages. Tucker read aloud from the English section.

" '*However unlikely this eventuality, if this message is ever found, I feel compelled by my conscience to recount what has led to the awful events that took place here. Whether our actions will ever be recognized or understood by our loved ones is for God to decide, but I leave this life confident that He, in His infinite wisdom, will forgive us . . .' "*

The remainder of De Klerk's testament went on for several more pages. Tucker read through it all, then folded the paper and put it back in his pocket.

"So?" Christopher asked.

He stood up. "Bukolov must hear this."

38

With Kane leading the way, Tucker and Christopher made it back to the Cathedral. They had barely spoken after reading De Klerk's letter. As they turned toward the double-barrel tunnels leading out from the cavern, Kane stopped ahead of them and turned. He gazed down the length of the Cathedral, toward the distant walls of sandbags. His ears were up, his posture rigid.

What had he picked out?

"QUIET SCOUT," Tucker ordered.

Hunched low and padding softly, Kane took off across the former killing floor of the Cathedral. Tucker and Christopher followed, dodging through the forest of stalagmites. Near the end of the cavern, Kane leaped the sandbag barriers and stopped at the shaft leading out to the crooked corridor.

"HOLD," Tucker ordered softly.

Kane stopped and waited for him.

Tucker took the lead, crawling through the twisting shaft of the corridor. He reached the end, where it straightened out. The slivers of pale moonlight blazed much brighter ahead. Then he heard it—what had likely caught Kane's attention.

The faint rumble of a diesel engine.

Tucker picked his way along the last of the corridor. He dropped to his belly at the tumble of rocks. He peeked out one of the shining slivers and saw the canyon outside was lit up brightly from the headlamps of a truck parked in the canyon.

From that direction, a voice shouted in Russian.

Then a bark of laughter closer at hand.

A pair of boots stomped up to his hiding spot. A man, dressed in fatigues, dropped to a knee. Tucker froze, waiting for a shout of alarm, for gunfire.

But the soldier only tied up a loose bootlace, then regained his feet.

Tucker heard other men out there, too, moving about or talking quietly.

How many?

Then a deep baritone shouted harshly, gathering everyone back to the truck. A moment later, the timbre of the engine rose, rocks ground under turning tires, and darkness fell back over the canyon.

He listened, hearing the rumble fade slowly into the distance.

They were leaving.

These were clearly Kharzin's men. Had they come to check out where the Range Rover had stopped for a few hours? Finding nothing here, were they continuing on to where Tucker had parked the booby-trapped vehicle, drawn by the transmitter?

Tucker placed his forehead against the cool rock and let out the breath he'd been holding. Relieved, he made his way back to Christopher and Kane. The three of them hurried back to the waterfall cavern.

Nothing had changed here.

Bukolov was where they had left him. Anya had rolled to her butt and leaned against a stalagmite, her arms still bound behind her. With her chin resting on her chest, she appeared to be asleep.

"How went the search?" Bukolov asked, standing and stretching.

"We need to talk," Tucker said.

After ordering Kane to guard Anya, Tucker drew Bukolov to the mouth of one of the shotgun tunnels.

He recounted their investigation, ending with his discovery of the charnel pit.

"What?" Bukolov said. "I don't understand—"

"In that pit—staked to the wall of the shaft like a warning—I believe I found De Klerk's missing pages."

"What?" Shock rocked through the doctor.

Tucker passed the papers over. "He wrote this message in both Afrikaans and English. He must have been covering his bases, not knowing who might stumble upon that pit later: his fellow Boers or the British."

"You read it?"

Tucker nodded. "De Klerk was terse but descriptive. About three weeks after they entered these caves, several men began getting sick. Terrible stomach pains, fever, body aches. De Klerk did his best to treat them, but one by one they began dying. In the final phase of the disease, the victims developed nodules beneath the skin of their lower abdomen and throat. These eventually erupted through the skin, bursting. While the British troops laid siege to the cave, De Klerk found himself overwhelmed by patients. As hard as he tried, he couldn't find the source of the illness."

"What then?"

"On day thirty, General Roosa ordered the remainder of the cave entrances sealed shut. He had become convinced everyone was infected—or soon would be—by some kind of plague. He was afraid that if the British breached their defenses they would also become infected, and the plague would spread to the outside world."

"Not an unusual reaction," Bukolov said. "Paranoia of pandemics ran rampant during the turn of the century. Scarlet fever, influenza, typhoid. It made normally rational men do crazy things."

"I think it was more personal than that. According to De Klerk, General Roosa had lost his entire family to smallpox. Including his daughter Wilhelmina. He'd never quite gotten over it. According to De Klerk, the symptoms they saw among the men struck Roosa very close to home. It was too much like the pox that killed his family. In essence, the guy lost it."

"So everyone died here. Despite what the records show, the British never did overrun this cave?"

"That record was likely falsified by the British colonel waging this siege," Tucker said. "He came to kill Roosa and his men. And after what happened here, the end result was the same. Everyone dead. So the British colonel took credit and chalked it up as a victory."

"Craven opportunist," Bukolov muttered sourly, clearly bothered that history was so unreliable and anecdotal.

Tucker continued the story. "Shortly after Roosa and his Boers entombed themselves, the British left. The dead were dropped into the pit and burned along with their clothing, bedding, and personal belongings. Many committed suicide and were burned as well—including Roosa himself. De Klerk was the last man to go down, but before he lowered himself into the pit and put a gun to his head, he gave his diary to a passing Boer scout who discovered their hiding place. De Klerk took care not to contaminate the outsider. This was the man who returned the journals and diary to De Klerk's widow."

"And what about what he pinned to the wall of the pit?" Bukolov lifted the sheaf of papers.

"A warning for anyone who came here. On the last page of his testament, De Klerk lays out his theory of this disease. He thinks it was something the men ingested—small white bulbs that the soldiers thought were some kind of local mushroom. He even includes some beautifully detailed drawings. He wrote the name under them. *Die Apokalips Saad.*"

Bukolov's eyes shone in the dark. "LUCA."

Tucker nodded. "So it sounds like your organism infects more than just *plants.*"

"Not necessarily. You mentioned the worst of the victims' symptoms were concentrated to the throat and abdomen. The human gut is full of plant material and plantlike flora. LUCA could thrive in that environment very well, wreaking digestive havoc on the host."

"Does that mean LUCA poses a danger as a biological weapon, too?"

"Possibly. But only on a *small* scale. For humans to become infected, they would have to *eat* it or—like here—be confined in a closed space where airborne spores are concentrated."

"How sure are you about that, Doc?"

"The science is complicated, but believe me when I say this: as a biological weapon, LUCA is virtually useless on the large scale—especially when a thimbleful of anthrax could wipe out a city. But as an *ecological* threat, a weaponized version of LUCA is a thermonuclear bomb."

"Then let's make sure that never happens."

"In regards to that, I've made some progress."

10:48 P.M.

When Tucker and Bukolov rejoined the others, Anya was awake. Christopher guarded her with his AR-15 rifle, while Kane kept close watch.

Tucker ignored her and followed Bukolov to his makeshift office set up amid their stack of supplies. From the haphazard scatter of paper, notes, and journal pages, he had been busy.

"It's here," Bukolov said and grabbed De Klerk's old diary from atop one of the boxes.

With the skill of a magician cutting a deck of cards, the doctor opened to the spot where it looked like pages had been cut out. He compared it to the pages Tucker had discovered.

"Looks like a perfect match," Bukolov said.

Anya stirred, trying to see, to stand. But a deep-throated growl from Kane dropped her back to her butt.

"See. Here's a crude, early rendition of LUCA in the old diary, a hazy sketch. A first-draft effort. What we had to work from before." Bukolov fitted a sheet from Tucker's collection into place. "This page was the diary's next page. Before it was cut out. The finished masterpiece."

The page in question depicted a deftly drawn sketch of a mushroomlike stalk with ruffled edges sprouting from a bulb. Colors of each structure were called out in tiny, precise print. Other drawings showed the same plant in various stages of growth.

Bukolov pointed to the earliest of the drawings. "This is LUCA in a dormant stage. A bulblike structure. De Klerk describes it here as a butter-yellow color. His measurements indicate it's about the size of a golf ball. But don't let its simplicity fool you. This structure is pure potential. Each cell in the bulb is a blank slate, a vicious chimera, waiting to unleash its fury on the modern world. It reproduces by infection and replication, as invasive as they come, an apex predator of the flora world. But if we could tame it, unlock the keys to its unique primordial genetics, anything could be possible."

"But first we need to find it," Tucker said.

Bukolov turned to him, a confused expression on his face. "I already explained where to find it."

"When?"

"Just a moment ago, when I said, *It's here.*"

Tucker had thought the doctor was referring to De Klerk's diary. "What do you mean, it's here?"

"Or it should be." Bukolov stared around the cavern with frustration. "It is supposed to be *here.* In this cavern. At least according to De Klerk."

"Why do you think that?"

Bukolov flipped the diary to the page before with the crude drawing of LUCA. "Here he talks about finding the dormant bulbs, but he never says *where* to find them. He's a sly one. But see here in the margin of that section."

Tucker leaned over. He couldn't read the passage written in Afrikaans, but next to it was a crudely scribbled spiral.

"I always thought it was just an idle doodle," Bukolov said. "I do it all the time. Especially when I'm concentrating. My mind wanders, then so does my pen."

"But you think it's significant now."

"The drawing looks like water spilling down a bathtub drain." Bukolov pointed to the torrent of water across the room. "It wasn't a mindless squiggle. De Klerk was symbolically marking this passage about the discovery of the bulb with its location. As I said, *it's here*. Under the bathtub drain."

Bukolov closed the journal and tossed it aside. "I just have to find it. And now that I don't have to play babysitter . . ."

With a glare toward Anya, Bukolov picked up an LED lantern and set off across the cavern.

For the moment, Tucker left the doctor to his search. Knowing now that Kharzin's team was in the neighborhood, he had to prepare for the contingency that Bukolov might fail. His ruse with the booby-trapped Rover would not stop the enemy for long . . . nor did he know how many of the enemy his trick might take out.

He pictured his last glimpse of Felice Nilsson, leaning out the helicopter door, her lower face hidden by a scarf, her blond hair whipping in the wind.

It was too much to hope that she would be caught in that blast.

He had to be ready.

He crossed to the pile of boxes and packs, knelt down, and pulled over the stiff cardboard box holding the blocks of C-4.

"Christopher, can you start measuring out six-foot lengths of detonation cord? I'll need about fifteen of them."

Anya stared at them, her face unreadable.

Ignoring her, he calculated the best spots to set his charges to cause the most destruction. If Bukolov couldn't find the bulbs of LUCA, he intended to make sure no one ever did, especially General Kharzin.

He unfolded the flaps of the box of C-4 and stared inside.

With a sinking drop of his stomach, he glanced again over to Anya. Her expression had changed only very slightly, the tiniest ghost of a smile.

"How?" he asked.

The box before him was packed full of dirt, about the same weight as C-4.

Anya shrugged. "Back at the campsite this morning, after you left. All your C-4 is buried out there."

Of course, she had known of his contingency plan to blow the cave as a fail-safe and had taken steps to ensure it wouldn't happen.

But she was wrong about one fact: *all your C-4.*

He had taken a block of the explosive with him as he hunted for guerrillas and ran into the pack of dogs. Later, he used half of it to rig the Rover. He still had the other half, but it was far too little to do any real damage here.

And now they were running out of time.

If they couldn't blow the place up, that left only one path open to them: *find the source of LUCA before Kharzin's team returned.*

So there was still hope—not great, but something.

Bukolov dashed it a moment later as he returned with more bad news. "I found nothing."

11:12 P.M.

Fueled by anger and frustration, Tucker tossed the leg of an old broken chair across the cavern floor. It bounced and skittered away, splashing through a standing pool of water. Christopher and Bukolov worked elsewhere in the cavern, spread out, slowly circling the torrent of water falling through the room's center.

Tucker wasn't satisfied with Bukolov's cursory search.

He had them sifting through some of the old Boer detritus and flotsam tossed against the walls by prior flooding.

But it was eating up time and getting them nowhere.

If they had a sample of LUCA, Kane could have quickly sniffed out the dark garden hidden here, but they didn't. So he left the shepherd guarding Anya.

Christopher and Bukolov finally reached him. They'd made a complete loop of the cavern. He read the lack of success in their defeated expressions.

"Maybe I was wrong about the bathtub drain." Bukolov stared up at the water cascading through the vortex. "Maybe it was just a doodle."

Tucker suddenly stiffened next to him. "We've been so stupid . . ."

Christopher turned. "What?"

Tucker grabbed Bukolov by the shoulder. "De Klerk *was* marking the location. It *is* a drain."

The doctor looked up again toward the ceiling.

"No." Tucker pointed to the floor, to where the flood of water flowing down from above either pooled—or drained through fissures in the floor. "*That's* the drain depicted by De Klerk. The water must be going somewhere."

Bukolov's eyes went wide. "There's more cavern below us!"

Christopher stared across the cavern. "One problem. If you're right, how do we get down there?"

Tucker stared across the expanse of the room. "De Klerk has been cagey all along. He wouldn't have left the entrance open. He would have sealed or covered it somehow." Tucker circled his arm in the air. "One more time around. We need to find that opening."

It was accomplished quickly—now that they knew what to look for.

Christopher called him over. "See here!"

Tucker and Bukolov joined him beside a thigh-high boulder not far from the torrent. Excess water sluiced through a four-inch crack under it and vanished away.

"I believe the stone is covering a larger hole," Christopher said.

"I think you're right."

With both Christopher and Tucker putting their shoulders to it, they were able to dislodge and roll the boulder aside.

The hole was small, only two feet wide. All three of them leaned over the opening, shining their lights down into the depths. A cavern opened below, its floor about seven feet below them.

Tucker squinted, noting the protrusions sticking up from the floor.

For a few moments, he thought he was staring at a cluster of stalagmites, but they were too uniform, and the beam of his headlamp glinted off a hint of brass beneath a greenish patina.

"What the hell are those?" Bukolov said.

"Those are artillery shells."

39

March 21, 11:34 P.M.
Groot Karas Mountains, Namibia

Tucker lowered himself to his belly and hung his head through the opening. He panned his lamp around the space. The spread of upright shells looked like some giant's bed of nails. Turning, he faced the others.

"There're at least two dozen shells down there."

"What type of artillery are they?" Christopher asked.

"Can't be sure. Judging by the size, I'd guess twelve-pounders. British Royal Horse Artillery units used them in their cannons during the wars."

"Are they live?" said Bukolov.

"More than likely."

"Why are they here?" Christopher pressed.

Tucker considered it a moment. "I'm guessing because of the black powder inside them. The Boers were probably using the powder in the shells to reload bullets."

"The Boers had to be resourceful to survive," Bukolov commented.

So do we.

Tucker shifted around, swinging his legs toward the hole. Somewhere down below must be De Klerk's dark garden. "Doc, tell me again what to look for. Anything I should be watching for."

Bukolov shook his head. "I don't have the time to give you a crash course in botany. Nor have you read all of De Klerk's notes. I should go with you. Besides, why should you have all the fun?"

Christopher looked unconvinced. "Doctor Bukolov, perhaps you didn't hear Mr. Tucker correctly. Those shells are *live* and likely very unstable by now."

"I heard him, but how difficult can it be? I must simply avoid bumping into one of those things, correct?"

"That about covers it," Tucker said. "But it's tight down there. You'll have to crawl. It's going to be hard work."

"And I'm saving my stamina for what?" Bukolov asked. "I can do this. I have not come all this way to find LUCA only to blow myself up. God will guide my hand."

"I didn't know you believed in God."

"It's a recent development. Considering everything you've put me through."

"All right, Doc, let's do this."

"I'll need to gather a few things first. Tools, sample dishes, collection bags."

"Go get them."

As Bukolov hurried away, Tucker returned his attention to the array of shells down below. He told Christopher, "There's at least a couple of hundred pounds of black powder down there. It might just solve our explosives problem."

"Will it be enough to collapse this cavern system?"

"No, but it'll definitely take out this immediate set of caves."

Bukolov returned quickly, with everything collected into a brown leather kit with his initials on it. He eyed the hole.

"Gentlemen, I believe I could use some assistance getting down. It's not a far drop but now is not the time for a misstep."

Tucker agreed. He went first, using his arms to slowly lower himself, keeping well away from the first row of shells. Once down, he turned and helped ease Bukolov through the opening. Christopher held his arms, while Tucker guided his legs, planting the doctor's boots on firm footing.

"That should do, gentlemen." Bukolov ducked low, equipped now with his own headlamp. "Shall we proceed?"

Tucker crouched next to him. From here, there was only about four feet of clearance between the floor and the roof. The chamber extended in a gentle downward slope. The water, streaming down from above, trickled in small rivulets across the floor, carving the soft sandstone into tiny channels, like the scribblings of a mad god. The rows of shells were standing upright in the flatter and drier sections.

"We should follow the water," Bukolov said, pointing down the slope. "It's what we've been doing since we got here."

"I'll go first."

Dropping low, Tucker set the best course through the field of shells. He followed the trickles, wondering if he'd ever be dry again. The last pass through the deadly gauntlet required him to lie on his right hip and scoot through sideways. An inopportune thrust of an elbow set one tall brass round to rocking on its base. He was afraid even to touch it to stabilize it.

Both men held their breath.

But the shell steadied and went still.

Tucker helped Bukolov past this squeeze.

"I can do it," the doctor complained. "I may have gray hair, but I'm not an invalid."

Free of the artillery, they were able to slide next to each other and crawl onward. Slowly a soft light glowed out of the darkness ahead.

"Do you see that?" Bukolov asked. "Or are my eyes tired?"

Tucker shaded his headlamp with his hand. Bukolov followed his example. As the darkness ahead grew blacker, the glow brightened before their eyes.

Definitely something over there.

As Tucker set out again, the roof slowly dropped down on top of them, forcing them to their bellies. They slid alongside each other across the wet, sandy floor. Finally, the slope dumped them into a pool of water about a foot deep. It lay inside a domed chamber about the size of a compact car's cabin, with enough room to kneel up, but little more.

"Amazing," Bukolov said, craning his neck to stare around.

The arched roof glowed with a soft silvery azure, like moonlight, but there were no cracks in the roof. The light suffused from a frilly carpet of glowing moss.

"It's lichen," Bukolov said.

Okay, lichen . . .

"Some phosphorescent species. And look across the chamber!"

The pond they knelt in was shaped like a crescent moon, its horns hugging a small peninsula of sandstone jutting out into the water from the far wall. Atop the surface, a dense field of buttery-white growths sprouted about six inches tall. From bulbous bases, stalks formed thick flat-topped umbrellas, with fine filaments draping from them. They gave off a slightly sulfurous smell that hung in the still air.

"LUCA," Bukolov murmured, awed.

As they shifted closer, Tucker felt the cracks in the floor under his knees, sucking at the cloth of his pants, marking drainage angles for this pool. The smell also grew worse.

"It is okay to be breathing this?" Tucker said.

"I believe so."

Tucker wanted to believe so, too.

"They're exactly like the sketches from the diary," Bukolov said.

He had to admit the renderings by De Klerk showed a masterful hand.

The doctor splashed farther to the left. "Come see this! Look at where the field of bulbs and growths meet the wall."

Tucker leaned to look where he pointed. The bulbs and the edges of the mushrooms that touched the wall were a brownish black, as if burned by the glow of the lichen covering the wall.

"I think the lichen is producing something toxic to the LUCA." Bukolov swung toward Tucker. "Here might be the secret of the kill switch."

Tucker felt a surge that was equal parts relief and worry.

Bukolov continued. "It's what I had hoped to find here. Something had to be holding this organism in check down here. It couldn't just be the isolation of the environment."

"Then collect samples of everything and—"

Bukolov knelt back and brushed his fingertips across the roof, causing the glow to darken where he touched. "You don't understand. We are looking at a microcosm of the ancient world, a pocket of the primordial history. I have so many questions."

"And we'll try to answer them later." Tucker grabbed Bukolov by the elbow and pointed from the collection kit over the man's shoulder to the field of growth. "Get your samples while you still can."

A sharp bark echoed to them—followed by a second. Kane.

"Get to work, Doc," he ordered. "I'm going to find out what's going on."

Hurrying, he slid and crawled his way through the field of artillery shells and back to the waterfall chamber. He hauled himself out of the hole, and Christopher helped him to his feet.

"He just started barking," Christopher said.

In the pool of light cast by the single LED lamp, it appeared Anya hadn't moved. She was still tied securely. Kane stood next to her, but he was staring toward the twin shotgun tunnels.

"What is it?" Christopher asked.

"I don't know. Kane must have heard something."

Tucker remembered his earlier sighting of the Russian soldiers.

Anya called over to them. "It seems we owe you some thanks, Captain Wayne. We wouldn't have thought of this method without you. Upon your example in Russia, we decided to add another weapon to our arsenal."

She was staring at Kane.

Tucker suddenly understood her veiled implication.

Damn it, Anya, you are good.

The thought had never occurred to him. Barring technology, what was the best way to track someone?

Kane glanced back at him, clearly waiting for the order to pursue whatever he had sensed.

Tucker turned to Christopher. "Stay here and be ready to help Bukolov."

"Is there trouble?"

Isn't there always?

He pointed to Anya. "She moves . . . you shoot her."

"Understood."

Working quickly, Tucker crossed to their gear and prepared for the storm to come. He grabbed two spare magazines for his rifle, along with a red flare, stuffing them all into his thigh pockets. He then slung the AR-15 over his shoulder and picked up the Rover's plastic gas can.

Once ready, he headed for the tunnels with Kane on his heels.

It was time to test these old Boer defenses.

11:55 P.M.

Reaching the Cathedral, Tucker hurried across the stalagmite maze to the series of sandbag walls at the far end. He hurdled over the first two with Kane flying at his side—then he skidded to a stop at the third wall and dropped to his knees.

Echoing up from the crooked tunnel ahead, he heard a faint barking.

No, not barking—*baying.*

The enemy had come with hounds.

Kharzin must have sent his main body of troops, along with the dogs, straight to where he had hid the booby-trapped Range Rover. The other Russians—the ones he had spied upon earlier—were likely a smaller expeditionary force sent here to canvass the side trail as a precaution. No wonder they had seemed so lax and casual. But now that Tucker's trap had been sprung and his ruse discovered, Kharzin had returned here, bringing all his forces to bear.

But what was Tucker facing?

Only one way to find out.

He pointed to the tunnel. "QUIET SCOUT."

Kane jumped over the sandbags and dove into the shaft. Using his phone, Tucker monitored his partner's progress. Once Kane reached the straight corridor, Tucker touched his throat mike.

"HOLD. BELLY."

Kane stopped and lowered himself flat, well hidden by rubble.

Right now the corridor appeared empty with no evidence of trespass. The pile of rocks blocking the way outside looked untouched. So far, the hounds hadn't found this back door to the cavern system—at least not for the moment. But they would.

Through Kane's radio, the baying already grew louder.

Hurrying, Tucker began removing sandbags from the middle of the barricade. After creating a sufficient-sized hole, he wedged the gas can into the gap. He then replaced the sandbags, taking care to hide any trace of the can.

All the while, Tucker monitored the phone's screen, using Kane to extend his vision. Movement drew his full attention back to the screen. In the gray-green glow of Kane's night-vision camera, the slivers of light at the far end of the corridor began to break wider. More light blazed through as rocks were pulled away.

Shadows shifted out there.

They'd been discovered.

Tucker whispered to Kane, "QUIET RETURN."

The camera jiggled as the shepherd belly-crawled backward. After retreating for a spell, Kane finally turned and came running back. Moments later, he emerged and hurdled the sandbags.

Good boy.

After rechecking the placement of the gas can, Tucker pulled out a flare and jammed it between a pair of sandbags near the bottom. For now, he kept it unlit.

He turned to his partner. "STAY."

With a final rub along Kane's neck, he stepped over the sandbags, planted his rifle to his shoulder, and ducked into the shaft. He crawled until he was at the last corner of the crooked corridor. He kept hidden out of sight, peeking around the bend with his rifle extended.

He quickly dowsed his headlamp and flipped the scope to night-vision mode. With his eye to the scope, he waited.

The first Spetsnaz appeared, peeking out from the straight passageway, bathed in the moonlight flowing from the open door behind him.

Tucker laid the crosshairs between the man's eyes and squeezed the trigger. The blast stung his ears. He didn't need to see the man crumple to know he was successful.

Tucker ducked away and retreated as the bullets peppered down the shaft, likely fired blindly by the second soldier in line. He knew the enemy dared not lob or fire a grenade into such a confined space, or it risked collapsing the very tunnel they had come to find and ruin any chances of reaching the prize. As far as they knew, this was the only way inside.

Still, he never trusted the enemy to think logically.

Especially with one of their comrades dead.

So he fled on his hands and knees.

If nothing else, the ambush would give the others pause, force them to move slowly, but it wouldn't last long.

He reached the end of the tunnel, regained his feet, and hopped over the first sandbag wall. Crouching down, he ruffled Kane's neck and did a quick inspection of the gas can and flare. Satisfied, he headed back over the series of sandbag fences.

As he hopped over the last one, a booming cry echoed from the far side of the Cathedral.

It was Christopher, calling from the mouth of the shotgun tunnels across the way.

"Tucker . . . watch out!"

40

March 22, 12:18 A.M.

Groot Karas Mountains, Namibia

Kane let out a deep snarl, leaped to his feet, and took off across the Cathedral floor, heading in Christopher's direction. For the shepherd to break his last command to *stay* could only mean one thing.

An immediate and real danger.

Tucker stared down the length of the dark Cathedral.

At the other end, a star glowed, marking Christopher's headlamp.

Between here and there lay a gulf of darkness. Kane vanished into it. Tucker lifted his rifle's scope and used its night-vision capabilities to pierce the blackness. Out there, he watched a figure dashing between the stalagmites. Kane rushed at full sprint toward the shape. The jittering flight of the other was difficult to track through the forest of tall rock.

Then the shape cleared a stalagmite, her face perfectly caught by the scope for the briefest instant—then gone as she dodged away, doing her best to stay in cover, knowing he was armed.

Anya.

Free.

How?

He caught another brief glimpse, watched her lift an arm, the flash of gunmetal in her hand, a revolver, the Smith & Wesson he had given to Bukolov.

Then gone again.

New movement to the left.

Kane.

Then he vanished, too.

Next came the gunfire.

Three shots in the dark, each muzzle flash an incendiary burst through his scope—followed by a strangled yelp that tore his heart out.

He watched a small shape skid across the floor, back into the glow of his headlamp, and come to a stop.

Kane.

Anya lunged out of the darkness, vaulted over the body, and came running straight at him, firing.

Her first shot went wide. He shot back. Rock blasted behind her, his aim thrown off by the sight of Kane on the ground.

Undeterred, she fired again.

He felt a hammer blow on his hip that sent him spinning, pitching backward over the sandbags. He lost the rifle. He rolled, tried to rise to his knees, and reached for the weapon.

"Stop!" Anya shouted.

She was standing at the sandbag wall. The revolver was pointed at Tucker's head, only three feet away. He ignored her and lunged for his rifle. She pulled the trigger. He heard the click. Nothing else. He had counted out her *five* shots, the limit of that Smith & Wesson model he had given Bukolov.

Not the usual six-shooter, Anya.

He grabbed the rifle, swinging it up—but too slowly, thinking he had the upper hand. He turned in time to see the revolver flying at his face, catching him across the bridge of the nose, momentarily blinding him with a flash of pain.

She threw herself over the sandbags and bowled into him.

They went down, her on top.

Tucker saw a glint of a black blade—one of the old Boer bayonets he had spotted when he first descended into the cave. She drove it in a sideswipe for his throat. Both as defense and offense, he head-butted her, his forehead striking her nose. The plunging bayonet struck the stone *behind* his head instead of his throat.

He rolled her, straddling her. He clamped her wrist and twisted until she screamed.

The bayonet dropped.

He snatched it and held the point to her throat.

She stared up, showing no fear.

Not of death, certainly not of him.

From their long journey together, she knew he couldn't kill in cold blood—no matter how much he wanted to.

A flick of her gaze was the only warning.

A shadow hurdled the sandbags behind him. The heavy weight struck his back, catching him by surprise and slamming him down atop Anya.

The shape tumbled off his shoulders and gained his four legs, wobbly, panting, dazed. Kane's lips curled in fury, his eyes fixed to his target. Even barely moving, his partner had come to his rescue, never giving up.

Tucker stared down at Anya.

Blood bubbled up around the bayonet plunged through her throat. When Kane had struck, with the sharp point poised under her chin, their combined weight had driven the blade home.

Her mouth opened and closed, her eyes stared in disbelief and pain.

"Tucker!" Christopher shouted again, sounding like he was running toward him.

"I'm okay! Go back with Bukolov!"

Tucker climbed off Anya, watching the pool of blood spread.

She no longer breathed; her eyes stared glassily upward.

Dead.

12:36 A.M.

He knelt and called Kane over to his side. The shepherd limped over with a soft whine and pressed himself against Tucker's chest. He ran his hands along Kane's belly but felt no blood. As he worked his fingers over the vest, the dog let out a wincing yelp.

"You're okay, buddy."

As gently as he could, he pried the flattened .38-caliber round from the Kevlar and tossed it away. He followed it with a hug.

Tucker then took inventory of his own damage. Anya had clipped him with her last shot, tearing the flesh of his upper thigh. Blood soaked his pant leg, and the pain was coming on, but it was manageable for now.

A few inches to the center and the high-powered .44 round would have shattered his hip, crippling him.

Such was the changeable nature of war, where life, death, disfigurement were measured by inches and seconds. He considered his own past. How many friends had he lost to the capriciousness of fate? Take a half step to your left and you get cut in half by an AK-47. A tossed grenade bounces to the right, and you live another day, but if it bounces to the left, your legs are blown off.

He felt an icy shudder run up his spine. His eyesight swirled. In some detached part of his mind, he thought: *classic symptoms of PTSD.*

He clung to that notion.

You know this enemy.

Tucker took a half-dozen calming breaths.

You're alive. Kane's alive. Get it together and do what you came here for.

Abruptly, Kane's ears perked up, accompanied by a low growl meant only for his ears.

Rustling rose from the tunnel.

He motioned for Kane to stay.

Clicking off his headlamp, he grabbed his rifle, rose to his knees, and found a break in the sandbags to peer through. Using his night-vision scope, he spied a Spetsnaz soldier edging toward the mouth of the tunnel, cautious, likely hearing the gunplay from a moment ago.

Tucker waited until he reached the tunnel's end and shot him in the head. He followed it with a continuous barrage of fire into the tunnel to keep the others at bay. While doing this, he crossed forward, high-stepping the sandbags, knowing what he needed from the dead soldier.

He reached the corpse, clicking on his headlamp, and pulled the dead man's torso to the side.

Enemy fire blasted out of the tunnel, but he kept away from the direct line of sight. He quickly stripped off the man's portable radio. That's all he intended to grab, but he got greedy and yanked a couple of grenades off the man's tactical harness. He shoved the pilfered pair into his pocket—then he grabbed a third, pulled the pin, and threw it down the tunnel.

And ran.

He vaulted over the first wall of sandbags, stopping only long enough to yank the hidden flare's ignition loop, setting it sputtering to life. As he rolled over the second barrier, he dropped flat.

The grenade exploded, the flash bright in the darkness, the noise deafening.

Tucker gained his knees, stared back as smoke poured out, along with a sift of fine sand. The tunnel hadn't collapsed, but it would certainly discourage any more soldiers from coming through for a time.

Gathering Kane to his side, he fled across the Cathedral, his wounded leg on fire. By the time he reached the twin tunnels, his sock on that side was damp with blood. Exhausted, he reached the twin tunnels and sank to his rear with Kane.

Calling over his shoulder down the tunnel, he shouted. "Christopher!"

The young man appeared a moment later and knelt beside Tucker. "You are hurt."

"And Anya is dead. I'll take that deal. By the way, how did she get loose?"

"When Bukolov returned, I had to help him out of the hole. She came at us then. Caught us by surprise. She knocked me down and attacked Bukolov with an old bayonet she must have picked up. She tried to cut away the doctor's specimen collection kit and steal it. But he fought and the bag ripped open, scattering bulbs and sample dishes across the floor. She did succeed in grabbing Bukolov's gun. By the time I got to my rifle and fired at her, she was already running and gone."

"But how did she get loose to begin with?"

"Among her ropes, I found the ripped remains of her cast."

Tucker nodded slowly. During his fight with her, he hadn't noticed her cast was missing. While tying her up, he had bound her good wrist to her cast. He should've known better, but he never imagined her to be that tough and stoic. It had to be extremely painful to get the cast off, yet she showed not the slightest wince or bead of sweat.

With her back against the stalagmite and her hands hidden behind her, she must have slowly—using the fingers of her other hand and the rock's hard surface—broken through the plaster and worked the cast free. Afterward, she was able to tug her hands through the loose rope. From there, it was just a matter of waiting for the right moment to act.

"I'm sorry," Christopher said.

"Nothing to be sorry about. She was scary good. But I need a few things: two of the five-second chemical detonators and the first-aid kit."

As Christopher disappeared into the tunnel, Tucker put on the stolen headset and keyed the radio. "General Kharzin, come in. Are you there?"

There were a few seconds of silence, then a harsh voice answered. "This is Kharzin. I assume I am talking to Tucker Wayne?"

"That's right. I want to negotiate. We can all leave here with what we want."

"Which is what?"

"Against my advice, Bukolov wants to make a deal. A trade. Some of the LUCA samples for our lives."

"He has it then?" Kharzin asked. "He's found the source?"

"Almost," he lied. "He's in the tunnel digging as we speak. He sounds confident of success."

"Give me a few minutes to consider your offer."

That was a lie, too.

Tucker needed to teach the Russian a lesson before they could really talk.

Christopher reappeared, carrying the items Tucker had requested. "Thanks. Follow me."

He regained his feet and hobbled up the tiered steps to the right and dropped into the old Boer foxhole. He moved fifty yards along it. Christopher followed, carrying the supplies.

Once settled, Tucker pointed across the Cathedral to the small red glow, "Do you see the burning flare over there?"

"Barely, but yes."

"Put your rifle scope on the shaft entrance beyond it and tell me if you see anything."

With Christopher guarding, Tucker slit open his pant leg around the wound, then ripped open a QuikClot package from the first-aid kit and pressed it to the bullet gouge. He clenched his teeth against the burn and wrapped a pressure bandage around his thigh and knotted it in place.

He then took out the remaining half block of C-4 from his pocket. He divided what was left into two equal pieces. He returned one to his pocket, then shaped the other into a deadly pancake and carefully inserted a chemical detonator in its center. He passed the bomb over to Christopher.

"This half we'll use to blow the artillery shells."

"Hold on . . ." Christopher whispered. "I see movement. Two men, I think."

"Good. I'll take over. Take the C-4 back to the cavern and wait for me."

As he left, Tucker lifted his rifle and peered through the scope. A pair of Spetsnaz soldiers crouched at the entrance of the blasted shaft. They were in full body armor, weapons ready. Beyond them, another soldier crept out . . . and another. The last one carried an RPG launcher. An arm waved, preparing for a sweep of the cavern.

As if on cue, Kharzin's voice came over Tucker's headset. "Mr. Wayne, I have given your proposal some thought."

"And?"

"What assurances do I have that you will keep your word?"

"Hmm . . . good question." Tucker adjusted his aim on the flaming flare, then lifted the crosshairs to where he had hidden the Rover's gas can. "This is my answer."

He squeezed the trigger. As the round struck the can, gasoline jetted from the bullet's holes, ran down to the flaming flare—and ignited. With a whoosh, flames engulfed the back of the Cathedral. The soldiers began screaming. Orange backlit shadows danced on the walls. After a few seconds, the screaming stopped.

Tucker spoke into his headset. "You heard?"

"Yes, I heard."

Kharzin had to learn this lesson. It was the Russian way. From his prior employment with Bogdan Fedoseev, Tucker knew how the general would respond to the inherent weakness expressed by Tucker's offer. As expected, he would try to gain the upper hand by force, to test how weak his opponent actually was.

Now he knew.

"General, I've had twelve hours to turn this place into a death trap for you and your men. If you want to keep sending your boys in, I'll be happy to keep killing them. But I don't think you came with a limitless supply."

"You set me up."

Tucker heard a note of respect buried in the outrage.

"Do we have a deal?"

Kharzin hesitated, then sighed. "We have a deal. What are your terms?"

"Let me check Doctor Bukolov's progress. I'll get back to you in ten minutes. Cross me again, General, and things will really start to get ugly. Do you understand?"

"I do."

"One last thing. Is Felice Nilsson with you?"

"And if she is?"

"She's part of the bargain. I want her."

"Why?"

"Take a guess."

"Well, as it happens, she's not with us. She had another assignment. And speaking of personnel, I want Anya returned untouched."

Tucker heard more than mere professional concern for a colleague in the Russian's voice. This was a personal matter for the general.

He knew better than to tell the truth.

"That can be arranged," he said.

"Then we have a deal."

"Stay by your radio, General."

Tucker signed off and hopped back down, one painful step at a time.

Though the back of the Cathedral still burned, he dared not leave his rear unguarded. He pressed his forehead to Kane's. "Sorry, buddy, but I need to ask even more from you."

Kane wagged his tail.

He pointed to the flames. "HOLD. WATCH."

The shepherd dropped to his belly and stared across the cavern, ready to watch for any further intrusions.

Ever his guardian.

12:55 A.M.

As Tucker limped back into the cave, Bukolov and Christopher joined him, both clearly wanting to know what the plan was from here.

"Have you secured your samples, Doc?"

"Yes, they're packed away. What now?"

"I told Kharzin we're willing to make a deal. We'd trade half of the LUCA samples for our lives." Bukolov opened his mouth to protest, but Tucker held up a hand. "I'm stalling for time. There are only two ways out of here. One we can't climb out since I pulled that rope. And the other is crawling with Spetsnaz. So we're going to have to make a third."

"How?" Christopher asked.

"Do you remember the first spot we dug—on the ravine wall outside?"

Both men nodded.

Tucker pointed across the cavern. "It's right on the other side of that wall. I estimate it's only three or four feet thick . . . mostly soft sandstone."

Bukolov looked there in dismay. "It would take us hours to dig—"

Tucker pulled the square of C-4 from his pocket. "But only seconds to blast through."

"Would that work?" Christopher said. "Truly?"

"It's our only shot."

So they all set to work. Tucker unfolded and handed Christopher one of the shovels and instructed him to dig a hole four feet off the ground, as deep as he could make it.

As he labored, Tucker prepared the new charge and handed the C-4 patty to Bukolov. "Gently, Doctor. It's live. Just go stand by Christopher."

He then collected the first bomb he'd prepared earlier and planted it down the hole among the artillery shells.

With everything in motion, Tucker limped back over to the Cathedral and joined Kane. He put on his headset and keyed the radio. "General, are you there?"

After a few long seconds, he responded. "I am here."

"Bukolov has the samples."

"Good news."

"How many vehicles do you have?"

"Two."

"We're going to want one of them."

"I understand, considering the fate of your original vehicle." He heard the residual anger in the man's voice.

So at least his ruse with the Rover had worked.

Tucker asked, "Are both vehicles at the entrance to the cave?"

He pictured the SUV from earlier, parked in the canyon by the back door. As far as the Russian knew, that was the *only* entrance.

"Yes."

"Okay. We have wounded in here. Give me a few more minutes to get ourselves together, then I'll signal you to come in. You may bring two of your men as guards. So we're all on equal footing. I don't want any surprises. We'll make the trade in here, then you and *all* your men will get in one vehicle and drive off. Agreed?"

"Agreed. And you'll have Anya ready to travel."

"Yes. Stand by."

Tucker left Kane on guard and returned to the cavern. Bukolov was leaning against the wall, cradling the C-4 patty in his hands. "I am not enjoying this, Tucker."

"Hang in there. Christopher, how's it coming?"

Christopher stopped digging. "See for yourself. To be honest, I don't think we need that explosive. The sandstone is crumbling almost faster than I can chop at it."

Tucker examined the hole. It was already more than two feet deep.

"You're right. Over time, the moisture from this chamber must have weakened the stone, softening it. Keep going—but gently. I don't want to punch through quite yet. Doc, are you packed and ready to go?"

"I'm ready, but what am I going to do with this?" He raised the C-4 in his palms.

"It's okay to lay the C-4 patty down at your feet, just don't step on."

"I will step gingerly from here."

"Tucker, I am almost through!" Christopher called.

Tucker returned to his side and used a chisel to punch a hole through the wall. He pressed his ear to the opening and listened for half a minute. Satisfied no one was in this canyon, he widened the hole and peered out. Kharzin had all his men in the other gorge, guarding what he believed was the only entrance.

"Okay, everyone keep your voices low from here. We don't want to turn any heads in this direction." He turned to Christopher. "Go ahead and widen the hole as quietly as you can, just large enough for both of you to climb through. Then I want you to take the packs and Kane and hightail it away from here; stay hidden and keep moving east. Kane can help you. I'll catch up and find you once I'm finished here."

"What are you going to do?" Bukolov said.

"I'm going to keep Kharzin looking at me, while you all make your escape. After that, I'm going to drop your C-4 patty down with the one I already planted among those artillery shells and run like hell. When those babies blow, this whole cavern will collapse in on itself."

Christopher whispered, "I'm finished."

"Then it's time for you all to vacate the premises."

Tucker helped gather their packs and drop them through the opening and out into the chilly night. He also gathered up Bukolov's abandoned bomb and repositioned it close to the hole in the floor.

With everything ready, he used the video feed on his phone to check on Kane, staring at the screen. All looked quiet out in the Cathedral, so he touched his mike and summoned his partner back to his side.

He gave Kane a warm greeting, then passed his phone to Christopher. "No matter what happens to me, keep hiking to last night's campsite and wait for your brothers. Once you're safely back over the border, hit number one on the speed-dial and ask for Harper. Tell her what's happened and she'll take it from there."

"I will."

"And take care of Kane."

"Tucker—"

"Promise me."

"I promise. He'll be like another brother to me."

"I couldn't ask for anything better."

Christopher extended his hand, shook Tucker's, then clambered through the hole and dropped low outside.

"Now you, Doctor," Tucker said.

Without warning, Bukolov wrapped Tucker in a bear hug. "I will see you out there, yes?"

"As soon as possible."

As Bukolov climbed out, Tucker knelt beside Kane. "You've done enough here, buddy," he said, his voice cracking. "I'm going to do this last part by myself."

Kane cocked his head and stared into Tucker's eyes. A soft whine flowed to him; he plainly sensed what was to come.

Tucker stood again and whispered, "Christopher, are you there?"

"I'm here."

He lifted Kane in his arms, gave him a final long squeeze, then guided him through the hole and into Christopher's waiting hands.

"I have him, Tucker. Good luck."

"You, too."

He waited for three minutes, making sure no shouts of alarm were raised as the others fled. He took an extra moment to cover the hole with a scrap of khaki tent canvas, securing the upper corners with duct tape. He didn't want the moonlight shining through the new window, giving away the ruse when he entertained guests in a few minutes.

He then crossed back to the Cathedral and tugged back on the radio headset. He kept his headlamp off, standing in the pitch darkness.

"General Kharzin."

"Yes, I'm here."

"You can come in."

"We are on our way."

1:58 A.M.

Keeping watch, Tucker raised his rifle and peered through the night-vision scope. After two minutes, the greenish haze of lights bloomed on the far side. Moments later, three men appeared. From their body posture, he could register the horror of finding the charred remains of their comrades. The trio stepped over the sandbags, only to discover Anya's body. They knelt there even longer, clearly calling for someone to collect her. Then they started across the Cathedral floor.

When they reached the halfway point, Tucker shouted, "Stop there."

The men halted.

Into his headset, Tucker said, "General, you're—"

The pain in the other's voice cut him off. "You told me Anya was still alive!"

"Let's call it even."

"It'll never be *even*. Never. She was my daughter."

Shocked by this revelation, Tucker felt a sickening twist in his gut. He remembered Anya talking about her father. He could still hear the buried pain in her words: *My father was in the Russian Army. He was a . . . a hard man.*

Tucker now wondered how much of that pain was feigned. He could only imagine what it was like to grow up with a father like Kharzin, to be used and groomed to be little more than a finely honed tool. He remembered that it had been Anya who had first suggested to Bukolov that she pretend to be the doctor's daughter. Perhaps that ruse had its roots here. To keep things easy, Anya simply shifted the lie about one father to another.

"I'm going to kill you," Kharzin said.

"I'm sorry for your loss, General. I truly am. And you certainly can come after me, but for now, do you want revenge or your LUCA samples?"

Kharzin didn't respond for a full ten seconds. His voice was tight with grief and fury. "We will settle this personal matter later then. But I promise you it will be settled. There will be an accounting."

"I look forward to it," Tucker said. "For now, come forward. Let's be done with this."

Kharzin and his two companions started walking, proceeding slowly, suspiciously. When they were thirty feet away, Tucker saw movement across the Cathedral.

"Halt," he yelled. "What is going on back there?"

One of the men glanced over to the commotion. "They are only collecting the bodies of my men . . . and my daughter. I will not leave them behind."

"Then keep coming," he said and added a lie. "But be warned, I have other guns fixed on them if they try anything."

He took off his headset and began backing down the tunnel.

"Keep coming, General," he called out.

Tucker continued his retreat back to the waterfall cavern and didn't stop until he was a few steps from the hole.

Kharzin and his men entered the cave cautiously, searching thoroughly. The tallest man waved the other two to stand guard and continued forward alone.

This had to be General Kharzin. He was a bull of a man, stony-faced, much like his photos, but in person, he appeared younger than Tucker had expected.

Tucker raised the rifle level to the man's chest. "Nice to finally meet you, General."

Kharzin would not look at him, keeping his face averted, hard and angry. He simply thrust out his palm, even refusing to speak to the man who had killed his daughter. Perhaps not trusting himself to.

"Again, I am sorry for your loss," Tucker said.

The arm remained up, demanding. "Show me the LUCA."

Immediately, alarm bells went off in Tucker's head as the man spoke. The voice was *wrong*. He stared harder at the man's shadowy features. Though there was a resemblance to the photos he'd seen of Kharzin back in Istanbul, the man standing before him wasn't the general.

"Get on your knees!" Tucker shouted, shouldering his rifle. "Now!"

All three men knelt down.

Tucker put his headset back on. "General, this was a bad gamble."

"Did you really think I would risk handing myself over to you? And now none of this matters. Even in death, my beautiful girl did her job. She brought me what I wanted. I knew she would never fail me."

"What are you talking about?"

"You should have *searched* Anya after you killed her."

Tucker's belly turned to ice.

Kharzin said, "I'm kneeling beside my beautiful daughter right now. It appears Doctor Bukolov is missing one of his samples. Major Lipov, are you there?"

"I am here, General," the man said, speaking into his headset.

"Kill him!"

Lipov's arm shot behind his back.

Tucker shifted his rifle and fired, striking the man in the heart.

The two men on the slope yanked their guns up, but he was already moving as soon as he squeezed the trigger. The others opened fire, but he leaped sideways and slammed his heel down on the C-4 patty planted there—igniting its chemical fuse.

Five seconds . . .

With rounds ricocheting off the rock at his heels, he kicked the primed explosive down the neighboring hole and kept going.

Four . . .

Firing from the hip, he sprinted across the cavern for the canvas-covered hole.

Three . . .

He didn't slow and dove headfirst at the covering.

Two . . .

Ripping through the canvas, he sailed out the hole, landed hard on his palms, and rolled.

One . . .

He pushed himself to his knees, then his feet—and started running down the canyon.

Behind him he heard a *whomp*, followed by a second, sharper *boom*.

He kept sprinting as a string of firecrackers—the cache of artillery shells—began detonating.

Head down, legs pumping, he kept going.

Don't look back! Run!

The pressure wave hit him and sent him flying.

2:39 A.M.

Tucker landed in a heap, blinked hard, and spat out a mouthful of dirt, swearing under his breath. He had survived, gotten the others out safely—but still failed.

Kharzin had a sample of LUCA.

The rumble of engines echoed from the other canyon. The Russians were preparing to leave.

Tucker looked around. Behind him, the cliff face that he just jumped through showed little sign of damage, save for the gout of smoke and dust gushing through his exit hole. But he knew inside, that tiny microcosm of the primordial world was gone, incinerated.

But it was too little, too late.

He pictured Kharzin in one of those SUVs, clutching a buttery-white bulb.

Was there still time to catch him—and, more important, catch him by surprise?

Tucker would never make it out and around to the other canyon, and even if he did, he'd likely just be run over. Instead, he turned and headed back the way he had come, checking his pockets as he ran. He'd lost his rifle, so he would have to improvise. He sprinted, passing through the surge of smoke, and skidded to a stop beside the boulder steps that led up to the plateau. He scrambled like a monkey with his tail on fire. When he reached the top, he paused for a breath, picturing what lay below. He was now standing *atop* the cavern inside. If the blast there had weakened the structure, he might drop straight through.

Might, maybe, if . . . the hell with it.

He charged across the plateau toward the opposite canyon. As he neared the edge of the cliff, the rumble of the trucks ratcheted to twin roars. Tucker slid to a stop and looked down to see both of Kharzin's SUVs racing along the canyon floor, their headlights bouncing over the rock walls.

Tucker started running parallel to them, balanced on the cliff's edge: one eye on his footing, one eye on the SUVs. Somewhere directly ahead of him was the end of the cliff, the section shaped like a pig's snout. He ignored the voice in his head yelling for him to stop.

Instead, he ran faster and yanked out the two grenades he had stolen from the soldier he had shot. As he reached the cliff's edge, he dropped to his butt and began sliding down the steep slope of the snout. To his right, out of the corner of his eye, the first SUV raced past him. Skidding along, he pulled the pin with his teeth, but he kept the spoon pressed tightly.

Then he reached the blunted end of the snout and went airborne. The drop was only ten feet, but he was flying. He hit the ground hard and shoulder-rolled, hugging his limbs tightly, clutching the grenades to his belly. As his momentum bled away, he skidded to a stop and rose to his knees. He let the grenade's spoon pop and hurled it after the lead SUV as it swept past him.

Behind him, an engine roared. Headlights flashed over him. He spun to find the second SUV barreling straight at him. He dove right and rolled out of its way, barely making it. Flipping to his back, he pulled the pin on the second grenade and lifted his arm to throw—

Whomp.

The first grenade exploded, fouling his aim as he let loose with the second. The black chunk of armament bounced harmlessly past the second SUVs back bumper and rolled into the scrub. Escaping damage, the truck sped away, dropping down the ravine that led up here—and was gone.

Whomp.

Bushes blasted away, amid a choke of rock dust.

All that wasted fury . . .

Cursing, Tucker turned to the first SUV. Its right side was on fire, flames licking inside. From the cabin came screaming.

He ran toward the SUV, not knowing if Kharzin was in this vehicle or the one that got away. There was only way to know for sure. He ran to the far side of the burning SUV, where the flames were less intense, and yanked open the passenger door. Heat washed over him, accompanied by a few licks of fire that he dodged.

The driver lay slumped at the wheel, his back burning, his skin blackening and oozing. But his uniform marked him as a major, not a general. Same was true of the passenger. The second man had caught shrapnel in the chest and the side of his face. The man groaned and grabbed Tucker's wrist. His head turned, revealing a flayed cheek and an eye scorched black. His mouth opened, but only guttural sounds came out.

Tucker twisted his wrist, trying to free it from the man's viselike grip.

"*Nyet*," the man rasped finally. "*Nyet.*"

His other hand rose—clutching a grenade. He threw it over his shoulder into the backseat and held fast to Tucker, trapping him with a strength born of vengeance and pain.

Not hesitating, Tucker swung his fist and smashed it into the guy's face. As the man's head snapped back, he finally broke free and ran. He'd only taken a handful of steps when a sledgehammer struck him across the back.

Everything immediately went dark.

41

March 22, 7:57 A.M.
Groot Karas Mountains, Namibia

The world returned in fits and starts, fluttering pieces that lacked substance: a shadowy glimpse of a face, whispers near his ear, something cold poured through his lips.

Then something real: the lap of a warm tongue along his cheek.

I know that . . .

He forced his eyes to open, to focus, blinking several times, and found himself staring at a brown-black nose, whiskers, and the darkest amber eyes. The wet nose nudged him a few times.

He groaned.

"Sleeping Beauty awakes." That had to be Bukolov.

Tucker sensed he was somehow moving, bumping along, but his legs were immobile.

"Lie still, Mister Tucker," Christopher said as he hauled Tucker along in a makeshift travois, the sled made of branches and climbing rope.

Coming slowly alert, Tucker took in his surroundings. The sun was up, low in the sky, likely early morning from the residual chill. They were moving through forests that were too tall and thick for the upper highlands of the Groot Karas.

Nearing the foothills . . .

He finally pushed up on an elbow, causing the world to spin for a moment, then steady again. He spent another minute just breathing to clear the cobwebs from his head.

Kane sidled over, his tail wagging, a prance to his gait.

"Yeah, I'm happy to be alive, too." Tucker called to Christopher, "I think you've played oxen long enough, my friend. I can walk."

Christopher lowered the sled. "Are you sure?"

"I'll let you know when I'm back up on my legs." He reached out an arm. "Help me up."

They lifted him to his feet and held him steady as he regained his balance.

He looked around. "Where are we?"

"About a five-hour walk from the cavern," said Christopher.

Bukolov explained, "When we heard the grenades, we came as fast as we could and found you near the destroyed vehicle."

"I told you both to keep going," Tucker said. "Not to turn back, no matter what."

"I don't remember him saying that, do you, Christopher?"

"I'm sure I would have remembered that, Doctor Bukolov."

"Fine." He turned to Bukolov, his chest tightening as he relived the events of last night fully in his head. "Doc, where are your LUCA samples?"

"Right here in my satchel with the lichen—"

"Count them."

Frowning, Bukolov knelt down, opened his kit, and began sorting through it. "This isn't right. One is missing."

"What about the lichen samples?"

He counted again, nodding with relief. "All here. But what about the missing bulb?"

"Anya must have snatched it during the tumult of her escape. Kharzin has it now."

Her father . . .

"That is not good," Bukolov moaned. "With the resources at his disposal, he could wreak havoc."

"But he doesn't have the lichen. Which means he doesn't have the kill switch for controlling it."

Tucker pictured the burned bulbs and stalks that came in contact with the phosphorescent growth.

"And we do . . . or might." Bukolov looked determined. "I'll have to reach a lab where I can analyze the lichen, run challenge studies with the LUCA organism. Find out which component or chemical is toxic to our ancient invasive predator."

"Then that's what we'll do. We need that kill switch."

And soon.

10:02 A.M.

Two hours after they ditched the travois and slowly worked their way east toward their old campsite in the foothills, Kane came sprinting back from a scouting roam. He sat down in front of Tucker, stared up at him, then swung his nose toward the east.

"Something ahead," Tucker said.

Bukolov dropped back a step. "Bandits? Guerrillas?"

"Maybe. Christopher, you take the doctor into cover. Kane and I will go have a look."

Tucker followed the shepherd east down the next ravine to a string of low hills. He climbed one to gain a good vantage point and dropped to his belly.

Below and two hundred yards away, a lone SUV trundled across a salt flat, heading in their direction. He lifted his binoculars, but with the sun in his face, it took him a few moments to adjust. Finally, he was able focus through the vehicle's windshield.

He smiled when he recognized the driver.

It was the group's regular chauffeur.

Paul Nkomo.

"FETCH EVERYONE," he instructed Kane.

As the shepherd raced back to the others, Tucker stood up and waved his arms over his head. The SUV stopped, and Paul leaned out the window. A glint of sunlight on glass told him Paul was peering back at him with binoculars.

Then a thin arm returned the wave.

Christopher joined Tucker a few moments later. He frowned down at the slow approach of his younger brother. "Little Paul. He was supposed to meet us at the campsite, but as usual, he didn't listen and kept heading this way. Always the impetuous one. Always getting himself into trouble."

Tucker glanced over at his bruised, sprained, and lacerated friend. "Yeah, right," he said sarcastically, "*he's* the troublemaker of the family."

8:42 P.M.

With the assistance of their regular chauffeur, Tucker and the others reached the Spitskop Game Park shortly after nightfall, where staff awaited them with food, drink, and first aid, including veterinary care.

A man in a clean smock who told wild stories of life as an African vet cleaned Kane's wounds, listened to his heart and lungs, and palpated the area of his ribs that had taken Anya's bullet. *Nothing broken just a deep bruise* was his verdict. Only after that did Tucker allow a nurse to stitch the four-inch-long gouge in his thigh.

Hours later, Tucker found himself visiting Bukolov in a private room. The doctor had his own unique needs that went beyond food and medicine. He had borrowed a dissecting microscope and some lab equipment from a group of scientists doing research locally. Though he and the others were due to depart for the United States at midnight, Bukolov had wanted to get a jump on his investigation into a potential kill switch for LUCA.

Tucker didn't blame him. After his brief encounter with General Kharzin, he knew they dared not waste a moment. He knew Kharzin would be working just as quickly to weaponize his prize.

"How are things going?" he asked Bukolov.

The man sat hunched over the dissecting microscope. A specimen of LUCA, sliced in half, lay on the tray under the lenses. "Come see this."

Bukolov scooted back to make room for Tucker to use the eyepiece.

He found himself staring at the edge of the specimen. The outer surfaces were peeling away like the layers of an onion, the tissue pinpricked with tiny holes.

"That is a sample of dying LUCA taken from the cave," Bukolov said.

Tucker pictured that glowing primordial garden.

"I'm fairly certain what you're looking at here is a chemical burn, something given off by the lichen. *What* that chemical is I do not know, but I have a hypothesis, which I'll get to in a moment. But first let me tell you about this mysterious glowing lichen." Bukolov looked at him. "Are you familiar with lichens?"

"Considering I thought it was moss . . ."

"Oh, my dear boy, no. Lichens are much more ancient and strange. They're actually made up of *two* organisms living in a symbiotic relationship. One is a fungus. The other is something that photosynthesizes."

"Like plants."

"Yes, but in the case of lichens, it's either an algae or cyanobacteria that pairs up with the fungus." He slid over a petri dish of the glowing organism. "In this particular case, it's a *cyanobacteria*. Cyanobacteria are three to four billion years old, same as LUCA. Both inhabitants of the strange and hostile Archean eon. And likely competitors for the meager resources of that time."

"Competitors?"

Bukolov slid the lichen sample and slices of bulbs resting in another petri dish next to each other. "You see, during that Archean eon, true land plants were yet to come. These two were the earliest precursors."

He tapped the lichen. "Cyanobacteria gave rise to modern chloroplasts—the engines of photosynthesis—found in today's plants."

He shifted the sample of LUCA. "And here we have the earlier common ancestor, the stem cells of the flora world, if you will."

Tucker pictured the microcosm of that ancient world found in the cave. "And the two were in competition?"

"Most definitely. In that harsh primordial time, it was a winner-takes-all world. And I believe it was that *war* that was the evolutionary drive for the rise of today's modern plants."

"And what we saw in the cave?"

"A snapshot of that ancient battle. But as in all wars, often common ground is found, cooperation necessary for short periods of time. What we witnessed below was an uneasy détente, two enemies helping each other survive in such strict isolation. Both needed the other to live."

"Why do you think that?"

"During my studies here, I found *healthy* LUCA bulbs with dead lichen melting deep inside, being consumed. I believe *living* lichen can kill LUCA and use it as some fertilizer source. While at the same time, as the lichen die and flake from the roof and walls, it feeds the LUCA below, raining down, landing on those broad mushroomlike growths."

"You're saying they were feeding off each other."

"That. And I'm sure the constant flow of water through the chamber brought a thin and steady flow of nutrients and biomatter to them as well. I also think their relationship was more nuanced, that they helped each other out in other ways. Perhaps the lichen's bioluminescence served some beneficial advantage to the LUCA, while the sulfur-rich gas—that stink we smelled down there—given off by the germinating bulbs helped the lichen in some manner. I don't know if we'll ever understand it fully. That unique relationship was formed as much by geology as it was biology."

"And how does that help us find the kill switch?"

Bukolov held up a finger. "First, we know that the *living* lichen can kill LUCA, but not *dead* lichen. So that knowledge alone will help me narrow my search for the chemical kill switch."

He raised a second finger. "Two, we know who won that ancient battle. LUCA was vanquished, all but this small isolated garden, leaving behind only its genetic legacy in the form of modern plants. But cyanobacteria survive today, going by their more common name: blue-green algae. Because of their versatility, you can find cyanobacteria in every aquatic and terrestrial location on the planet, from the coldest tundra to the hottest volcanic vent, from freshwater ponds to sun-blasted desert rock. They are masters of disguise, merging with other organisms, like with the lichen here, but also with other plants, sponges, and bacteria. They can even be found growing in the fur of sloths."

"It almost sounds like your description of LUCA from before. An organism with limitless potential."

"Exactly!" Bukolov stared over at Tucker. "That's because cyanobacteria are the closest living organisms to LUCA today. But from my studies—on a purely genetic scale—LUCA is a thousandfold more efficient, aggressive, and tough. Released today, unchecked and untamed, LUCA would wreak untold ecological havoc across every terrain on Earth, both land and sea."

"But, Doc, it *was* defeated in the past. Like you said, it didn't survive."

"And that's the second clue to discovering the kill switch: *Why didn't LUCA survive, while cyanobacteria did?*"

Tucker had to say he was impressed with how much Doctor Bukolov had learned in such a short time. He could only imagine what he could accomplish with Sigma's laboratory resources in the States.

"I have much to ponder," Bukolov said.

Tucker's satellite phone buzzed in his pocket. "Then I'll leave you to it."

He headed out of the room and answered the call.

"How are you all doing out there?" Harper asked as the line connected. He had already debriefed her about the past day's successes and failures. "Will you be ready to go at midnight?"

"More than ready."

"I talked to the military biologists over at Fort Detrick, and they wanted to know if Doctor Bukolov had any estimate on how long it would take Kharzin to weaponize his sample of LUCA."

"That's just it. According to Bukolov, it would take very little engineering. It's a ready-made weapon. All that he really needs to figure out is the method of delivery and dispersal."

"And how long would it take General Kharzin to do that? It seems Bukolov knows this man and his resources fairly well."

"No more than a week."

"Not much time," she said dourly. "And is Bukolov any further along with the kill switch?"

"Some progress, but any real answers will have to be worked out back in the States."

"Then I have one last question. From Bukolov's assessment of the general's personality, would Kharzin unleash this bioweapon without that kill switch."

"In other words, how much of a madman is he?"

"That's about it."

"I don't have to ask Bukolov." Tucker reviewed his dealings with Kharzin from Vladivostok to now. "He'll test it. And he'll do it soon."

PART IV
Endgame

42

March 26, 7:57 A.M.
Frederick, Maryland

With a puff of pressurized air, Tucker crossed out of an airlock into the BSL-3 laboratory. He wore a containment suit and mask, much like the men and women bustling within the long, narrow space. He imagined there were more Ph.D.s in this lab than there were test tubes—of which there were a *lot*. Across the vaulted space, tables were crowded with bubbling vessels, spiral tubing, glowing Bunsen burners, and slowly filling beakers. Elsewhere, stacks of equipment monitored and churned out data, scrolling across computer screens.

Orchestrating this chaos like a mad conductor was Abram Bukolov. The Russian doctor moved from

workstation to workstation like a nervous bird, gesticu-
lating here, touching a shoulder there, whispering in an
ear, or loudly berating.

*These poor souls are going to need a vacation
after this.*

The biolab lay in the basement of a research building on the grounds of Fort Detrick, a twelve-hun-
dred-acre campus that once was home to the U.S.
biological weapons program before it was halted in
1969. But that legacy lived on, as Fort Detrick continued to be the military's biodefense headquarters,
home to multiple interdisciplinary agencies, including USAMRIID, the U.S. Army Medical Research
Institute of Infectious Diseases. They were currently
in the building that housed the Foreign Disease Weed
Science Unit, part of the Department of Agriculture.

It seemed the U.S. military was already well aware
of the national security threat posed by invasive species. Today that caution paid off, as they mobilized scientists from across the entire campus of Fort Detrick to
tackle the threat posed by a weaponized form of LUCA.

Bukolov finally noted Tucker's arrival and lifted an
arm, waving him to his side, which proved a difficult
task as the doctor headed away from him, deeper into
the lab. Tucker excused his way through the chaotic
landscape, finally reaching Bukolov beside a table

holding a five-liter glass beaker with a distillate slowly dripping into it from some condensation array. The liquid looked like burned coffee.

"This is it!" Bukolov expounded, his voice slightly muffled by his mask.

"Which is what?"

Tucker had been summoned here this morning by an urgent call from the good doctor, pulled from his temporary accommodations on base. He had been kept in the dark about what was going on at the labs here since they landed three days go in D.C. He and Bukolov had been whisked straight here under military escort.

"I was able to crack the lichen's code." He waved a half-dismissive hand toward the team around him, giving them minimal credit. "It was just a matter of determining what it was in *living* lichen that became inert or dissipated after it died. I won't bore you with the technical details, but we were able to finally distill the chemicals that created that burn, that killed LUCA cells on contact. In the end, it wasn't just *one* chemical but a mix. A precise solution of sulfuric, perchloric, and nitric—all *acids*."

Bukolov's eyes danced, as if this last part was significant. When Tucker didn't question him, the doctor gave him an exasperated look and continued. "Not only is this the kill switch, but it explains *why* the genetically superior LUCA did not survive the Archean eon, but cyanobacteria did."

"What's the answer?"

"One of the turning points of that primordial era to the next was a shifting of atmospheric conditions, an acidifying of the environment. Remember, back then, oxygen-producing plants did not exist. It was a toxic hothouse. Acid rain swept in great swaths over the earth, tides and storms burned with it."

"And that's important why?"

"Cyanobacteria were perfectly equipped to deal with this acidification of the environment. They were already masters of organic chemistry, as evidenced by their control of photosynthesis, a process of turning sunlight into chemical energy. They rode that acid tide and adapted. Unfortunately, LUCA's mastery was in the field of *genetics*. It placed all its evolutionary eggs in that one basket— and chose wrong. It could not withstand that tidal change and stumbled from its high perch in the food chain. And like sharks sensing blood in the water, cyanobacteria took advantage, incorporating that acid into their makeup and burning LUCA out of the last of its environmental niches, driving it into evolutionary history."

Bukolov pointed to the steaming dark brown mire in the beaker. "That's the acid." A single drop splashed from the distillation pipe into the soup. "That's what passed for rain long before we were even single-celled organisms floating around in mud. What we're brewing here is a form of precipitation that hasn't been seen for 3.5 billion years."

"And that will kill LUCA."

"Most definitely." Bukolov stared at him. "But even still, we must catch any such environmental fires started by LUCA *early*, preferably as soon as they're set. Once it establishes a foothold and reaches critical mass, it will explode across an environment, a raging firestorm that even this ancient rain might not put out."

"So if we're too late stopping Kharzin, even this might not be enough."

Bukolov slowly nodded, watching the slow drip of acid. "The only good news is that we ran some preliminary estimates of the threat posed by the single bulb Kharzin possesses. In the long term, he could, of course, try to grow more bulbs, but that would take much patience."

"A virtue Kharzin is sorely lacking."

"In the short term, we estimate he could macerate and extract at best a liter or two of weaponized LUCA. But it's still enough to light a fire somewhere, a fire that would quickly become a storm."

So the only question remains: Where does he strike that match?

To answer that, Tucker had only one hope.

In the shape of a deadly assassin.

And so far, she was not being cooperative.

9:12 A.M.

"Felice Nilsson could have scrubbed her credit cards," Harper told him over the phone.

Tucker spoke to her as he crossed in long strides from Bukolov's lab and headed across Fort Detrick's campus for his dormitory. "Like I said from the start, Harper. It was a long shot."

Three days ago, he had informed Sigma about his radioed conversation with Kharzin and the conspicuous absence of a certain someone to that deadly party in the mountains of Africa. Kharzin had claimed Felice was on *another* assignment, which even back then struck him as odd. She had been Kharzin's point man in the field from the start, hounding Tucker since he'd first set foot aboard the Trans-Siberian Railway. Then as Kharzin's team closed in for the kill, she was suddenly pulled off and reassigned.

Why? And to where?

Tucker had proposed that perhaps Kharzin had pointed that particular blond spear in a new direction, sending her in advance to prepare for the next stage of his plan—and likely to execute it, too.

"It was a good idea," Harper said. "To search for her whereabouts by placing a financial tracer on her. But so far we've failed to get any hits from the documents you photographed aboard the train. Not the four passports, not the five credit cards, not even the bank routing numbers you managed to find. She likely received a new set of papers."

Sighing, Tucker ran through his steps that day as he broke into her berth. He had carefully sifted through her belongings, photographed what he found, and returned everything to where he'd found them.

"Maybe I wasn't careful enough," he said. "She must have gotten wise to my trespass."

"Or she could have just gone to ground and is keeping her head low. We'll keep monitoring."

1:22 P.M.

Tucker briefly visited Bukolov after lunch and discovered the doctor was working with an engineer, devising an aerosol dispersal system for his acid solution, which to him looked like a backpack garden sprayer. But he heard phrases like *flow rate composition* and *contaminant filter thresholds,* so what did he know?

Bukolov had little time to chat, so Tucker left and decided to do something more important.

Standing on a windswept wide lawn, he hauled back his arm and whipped the red Kong ball across the field. Kane took off like a furry arrow, juking and twisting as the ball bounced. He caught up to it, snatched it in his jaws, and did a little victory prance back to Tucker's side, dropping the ball at his toes. Kane backed up, crouching his front down, his hind end high, tail wagging, ready for more.

It was good to see such simple joy—though *obsession* might be the better word, considering Kane's current deep and abiding love for that rubber Kong ball. Still, the play helped temper the black cloud stirring inside Tucker.

If only I'd been more careful . . .

Tucker exercised Kane for another few minutes, then headed back to their dorm. As he crossed the lawn, his phone rang. It was Harper again.

"Looks like you have a future career as a cat burglar after all, Captain Wayne. We got a hit on Ms. Nilsson."

"Where?"

"Montreal, Canada. Hopefully you and Kane are up for a little more cold weather."

He pictured Felice's face, remembering Utkin in the sand, bloody and crawling.

"I'll grab our long johns."

43

March 28, 10:23 A.M.
St. Ignace, Michigan

Right back where I started . . .

Tucker stood on the hotel balcony, staring out at the frozen edges of Lake Huron. Snow sifted from a low morning sky. The rest of the view could best be described as *brittle*. It was below freezing with the forecasted promise of the day climbing a whole two degrees.

He'd started this adventure in Vladivostok, a frozen city by the sea.

And here he was again: cold and facing another assassin.

Bukolov called from inside the room. "Some of us don't have the hardy constitution of a young man.

Perhaps if you close the balcony door, I won't catch pneumonia before your tardy guest arrives in the area."

He stepped back inside and pulled the slider and latched it. Kane lifted his head from where he curled on the bed.

"But for the hundredth time, Doc: you didn't have to come."

"And for the hundredth time: you may need my expertise. We have no idea how Kharzin plans to utilize his weaponized LUCA. And my solution has had no real-world field test. We may have to improvise on the fly. Now is not the time for inexperienced guesswork."

It had been two days since Sigma's cyber net had detected the credit card hit in Montreal. Unfortunately, Felice still remained a ghost, leaving only the occasional financial bread crumb behind: at a gas station outside of Ottawa, at a diner in the small town of Bracebridge. Her movements seemed headed straight for the U.S. border. Immigrations and Customs were alerted, but the northern border of the United States was an open sieve, especially in the dense woods nestled among the Great Lakes. She could easily cross undetected.

This was confirmed yesterday when they got a hit here in St. Ignace, the northernmost city in Michigan.

Ominously, she had made a single purchase from the local Ace Hardware & Sporting Goods.

A plastic backpack sprayer.

Tucker stared toward their hotel room's closet. Inside rested the battery-powered chemical dispersant rig engineered by Bukolov and filled with his acid slurry.

Since then they had had no further hits indicating her whereabouts.

Was she still in town? Had she moved on?

Waiting in the wings, ready to mobilize in an instant, were *fourteen* two-person helicopter teams, each armed with their own canisters of the kill-switch solution. Six of these teams were located in Michigan; the other eight in the surrounding states.

Whether this was enough manpower or resources for the situation, Tucker didn't know, but he left it to Harper's best judgment. Harper feared that alerting the authorities at large would invariably turn into a brute-force manhunt that Felice would easily spot. If that happened, she would bolt, scrubbing those cards. They would never get a second chance at her. They had to do this right the first time and as surgically as possible.

So for now, the job of stopping Felice and her team—*of stopping LUCA*—fell to Tucker and the other quick-alert teams.

He hoped Harper's caution was not their downfall.

7:02 P.M.

As the sun sank toward the horizon, Tucker's phone finally trilled.

"We've got something," Harper said as soon as Tucker answered. "Picked up a report on a Harbor Springs police scanner. Fifteen minutes ago, a woman matching Felice's description, accompanied by three other men, were spotted stealing a speedboat from the marina. It was heading into Lake Michigan."

Tucker leaned over a map spread out on the coffee table. "Harbor Springs . . . that's thirty miles south of us."

"You're the closest team. Get to your extraction point. A helicopter is en route to pick you up."

Tucker disconnected. "Doc, we're moving!"

Bukolov was already heading for the closet. He grabbed the backpack holding their gear, including the dispersant rig. Tucker unzipped his duffel. He slid out a noise-suppressed Heckler & Koch MP-5 SD submachine gun, donned the gun's concealed chest rig, and harnessed the weapon in place. He then pulled his jacket on over it and shoved a Browning Hi-Power 9 mm into a paddle holster in the waistband at the back of his pants.

But his real firepower leaped off the bed and followed him to the door.

With Kane at their heels, Tucker and the doctor left the room and jogged across the icy parking lot. Off in the distance, helicopter rotors chopped the sky, coming in fast. The white-and-blue Bell 429 swooped over their heads, slowed to a hover, and then touched down.

As soon as the three of them had boots and paws inside, the Bell roared and sped upward. They banked hard over Lake Huron, passing above the Mackinaw City Bridge, and headed out across Lake Michigan.

Tucker tugged on a radio headset, and the pilot's voice came over it. "Fifteen minutes to Harbor Springs, gentlemen. I have incoming for you on channel five."

Tucker punched the proper frequency. "Up on channel five," he called over the rush of the engine.

Harper came on the line. "We have the make, model, and registration number of the boat. I gave it to the pilot. The last sighting put her on a heading of two-three-nine degrees. They should be passing the city of Charlevoix right about now. It's a fast boat, Tucker. Running at about forty knots."

"What's in front of it?"

"Mostly cargo traffic from the St. Lawrence seaway. The bulk of the ships are heading for either Milwaukee or Chicago."

"Carrying what?"

"I'm working on it."

Bukolov had his headset on. "I have an idea of what's happening here, Ms. Harper. I think Felice is targeting one of those cargo ships, one that's likely carrying something organic—fertilizer, seeds, even herbicide."

"What makes you say that?"

"Because it's what I would do if I were in Kharzin's shoes. He could not have produced more than a couple of liters of weaponized agent by now. Far too little to disperse via air. Such small amounts require him to *directly* contaminate a primary source in order to ensure suitable germination and propagation—but how do you get the most bang for your buck in such a scenario? Let's say Ms. Nilsson can contaminate a cargo of agricultural products and that ship docks in Chicago or Milwaukee or another major distribution hub—"

Tucker understood. "Planting season is starting throughout the Midwest. That infected cargo could incubate in the hold and then be spread throughout the nation's heartland." He imagined the havoc that would be wreaked. "Harper, what about the Coast Guard? Can we get them mobilized, to set up some sort of blockade? We can't let that ship reach shore."

"I'll sound the alarm, but I doubt we have enough time. Doctor Bukolov, answer me this. What happens if the LUCA is introduced into a body of water?"

Tucker stared at the snow-swept lake racing under the helicopter, appreciating her concern.

"Simply speculating, much of the organism would survive. Lakes have plenty of vegetative matter to host or feed LUCA. This organism survived and thrived for millions of years during this planet's most inhospitable period. It's aggressive and highly adaptable. Nature always finds a way to go on, and LUCA is *Nature* at its most resilient."

"I was afraid you'd say that."

"What's got you worried, Harper?" Tucker asked.

"If Felice boards one of those ships and contaminates the cargo, we've got more ways to lose than win. If the ship is sunk or destroyed, LUCA still escapes."

Bukolov nodded. "Additionally, if the contamination does reach open water, it would be much harder to clean up with the kill switch."

"Then we need to stop Felice before she reaches one of those ships," Tucker said.

After signing off, he switched channels to the pilot, a young National Guard aviator named Nick Pasternak. "Give me all the speed you can, Nick."

"You got it. Hold tight."

The timbre of the engines climbed, and the Bell accelerated to its maximum speed. At 150 knots, the ice-crusted coastline rushed beneath them.

"Coming to Harbor Springs now," Nick called five minutes later. "The marina where your boat was stolen is on our nose, thirty seconds out."

"Once there, head out on the same bearing the boat took. Two-three-nine degrees. Then keep your eyes peeled. If they're still on this bearing, they've got a twenty-five-mile head start on us."

"I can close that in six minutes."

The helicopter passed over the frozen docks of the marina, turned its nose southwest, and headed out over the lake. As it raced away from the coast, Tucker watched the waters slowly change from green to blue. He strained for any sign of the stolen boat through the thickening snowfall.

Nick had better eyes. "Speedboat dead ahead! Make and model seem to be a match."

Tucker had to be certain. "Give us a close flyby."

"Will do."

The Bell swept down until it was a hundred feet off the water, speeding low over the water.

"Boat coming up in five seconds," Nick reported. "Four . . . three . . ."

Tucker pressed his face against the window. The speedboat appeared out of the storm mist. As the helicopter buzzed over it, he saw the deck was empty, no one behind the wheel.

What the hell . . .

7:33 P.M.

Bukolov stared out his window. "Nobody's aboard."

Ignoring him, Tucker radioed the pilot. "Keep on this bearing!"

The doctor turned to him. "Does that mean they already boarded one of the cargo ships?"

"Most likely."

Nick called out, "Cargo ship dead ahead!"

"I need her name," Tucker replied. "Can you get us close to—?"

"Yep, hold on. Descending."

"But don't crowd her!" Tucker warned.

If Felice was aboard that ship, he didn't want her spooked—at least not yet.

"I understand. I'll keep us a half mile out."

Tucker picked up a set of binoculars and focused on the boat.

Off in the distance, the gray bulk cut slowly through the storm, led by a tall well-lit wheelhouse, flanked by flying bridges. He imagined the pilot and crew inside there navigating the ship through the growing weather. At the stern rose a three-level superstructure, less bright. Between the two castles spread a flat deck interrupted by cranes and a line of five giant square cargo hatches. He adjusted his view down and read the name painted on the cargo ship's hull.

He radioed it to Harper. "I think we've got her. *Motor Vessel Macoma.* I need whatever you can get on her. Especially her cargo."

"Stand by." She was back in two minutes: "*Motor Vessel Macoma.* Capacity is 420 deadweight tons. It's bound for Chicago carrying fertilizer-enhanced topsoil and compost for agricultural use."

Tucker turned. "Doctor, would that fit the bill?"

"Yes . . ." Bukolov confirmed. "Such material would make the perfect incubation bed for LUCA."

Harper remained more cautious. "Tucker, are you sure this is the ship?"

"We spotted an abandoned speedboat, adrift a few miles astern of the *Macoma.* Listen, Harper, we're not going to find a neon sign guiding us. We have to roll the dice."

"I hear you. You're on scene. It's your call."

"How soon can we expect any help?" Tucker asked.

"The closest team to you is still forty minutes out. I'm working on the Coast Guard."

"Then I guess we're going in. If Felice is smart, and I know she is, she'll be rigging that ship with explosives. So the sooner we can intercede, the better."

"Then good luck to the both of you."

Tucker switched channels. "Nick, we need to get aboard that ship. Can you do it?"

"Watch me," he said, with the confidence of the very young and very foolish.

Nick descended again, a stomach-lurching drop to thirty feet. He banked until the chopper was dead astern to the *Macoma*. The dark ship filled the world ahead of them. He moved slower, closing the gap, buffeted by the storm's crosswind. The Bell's nose now lingered mere feet from the ship's rear railing.

Nick radioed his plan from here. "I'm gonna pop us higher, bring us to hover over the roof of that aft superstructure. You'll have to jump from there."

Tucker studied the towering castle rising from the ship's stern. The superstructure climbed three levels, its lights glowing through the snow.

"Go for it," he said.

"Hang on."

Nick worked the cyclic and throttle, and the Bell shot straight up. Fighting the winds, the helicopter glided forward, bobbling, struggling.

Oh, God . . .

Bukolov agreed. "Oh, God . . ."

The landing skids bumped over a top railing—then came the sound of steel grinding on steel as the skids scraped across the roof. Crosswinds skittered the craft.

Crack . . . crack . . .

From the shattering blasts, Tucker thought something had broken on the helicopter.

Nick corrected him. "Pulling out! Somebody out there with a gun, taking potshots at us."

The helicopter lifted, rising fast.

Tucker unbuckled and leaned forward, searching through the cockpit's Plexiglas bubble. A man, cloaked in storm gear, stood on the roof deck below. He slung his rifle, picked up another weapon, and rested it atop his shoulder, something larger and longer.

A grenade launcher.

Tucker yelled, "Hard left, nose down!"

Nick worked the controls, pitching the nose and leaning into a bank.

Too late.

Below, a flash of fire, a trailing blast of smoke—

—and the rocket-propelled grenade slammed into the Bell's tail rotor, sending the bird into a hellish spin.

Tucker got pitched left and landed in a heap in the cockpit's passenger seat.

Nick screamed next to him, fighting for control, "Tail strike, tail strike . . . Ah, Jesus!"

Tucker shouted and pointed to the cargo ship's main deck. "Cut the engines! Crash us! We're going down anyway. Do it!"

"Okay . . . !"

"Doctor, grab Kane!"

"I have him."

Nick worked the cyclic, bringing the nose level, then took his hand off the throttle and flipped switches. "Engines off! Hold on!"

As the roaring died around them, the Bell dropped, falling crookedly out of the sky. Suddenly a tall davit crane loomed before the windscreen. Nick jerked the cyclic sideways, and the Bell pivoted. The tail section swung and slammed against the davit tower, whipping the helicopter around as it plummeted to the deck.

With a bone-numbing thud, the helicopter hit, bounced once on its skids, then slammed its side into the aft superstructure. The still-spinning rotor blades chopped against the steel, shearing off and zipping across the deck like shrapnel, severing cables and slicing off rails.

Then all went silent, save the spooling down of the Bell's engine.

44

March 28 , 7:49 P.M.
Lake Michigan

"Who's hurt?" Tucker called out as he regained his senses after the wild plummet and crash.

"Bleeding," Nick mumbled, dazed. "My head. Not bad."

"Doc?"

"We're okay, Kane and I . . . I think."

Tucker untangled himself from his spot on the floor and crawled back to the passenger compartment. He checked on Kane, who jumped up and greeted him.

Bukolov gasped, aghast. "Dear God, man, the blood . . . your ear . . ."

Tucker carefully probed the injury. The upper part of his left ear hung down like a flap.

"Grab that first-aid kit behind—"

Nick shouted from the cockpit, "Another guy with a gun!"

"Where?"

"Left side! On the port side! Coming up the deck by the railing!"

Means I have to be on the starboard side . . .

Tucker crawled across Bukolov's legs and shoved at the side door. It was jammed. Tucker slammed into it with his shoulder a few times until the door popped open. He hurled himself out and landed hard on the roof of the cargo hold. Staying flat, he rolled away from the man climbing to the deck. As he reached the starboard edge of the raised cargo hold, he fell the yard down to the main deck.

He landed on his back, unzipped his jacket, and drew out his MP-5 submachine gun.

Bullets ricocheted across the cargo hold as the man on the far side took potshots at him from across its roof.

Tucker shouted to Kane. "CHARGE SHOOTER!"

He heard the shepherd land on the roof and begin sprinting toward the gunman. Tucker waited two beats—then popped up out of hiding. As planned, the shooter had turned toward the charging dog. Tucker fired twice, striking the guy in the chest and face.

One down . . .

"Come!" he called to Kane.

The shepherd skidded on the snow-slick surface, turned, and ran to him, jumping down beside Tucker.

Now to deal with the man who had shot their bird out of the air. The assailant with the RPG launcher had been atop the aft superstructure. But where was—?

Boots pounded to the deck from the ladder behind Tucker. He swung around. The assailant had his weapon up—but pointed at the helicopter. During the man's frantic climb down, he must have failed to witness the brief firefight, and now he missed Tucker lying in the shelter of the raised cargo only yards away in the dark.

Small miracle, but he'd take it.

He fired a three-round burst into the man's chest, sprawling him flat.

Two down . . .

That left Felice and how many others? The police report mentioned three men accompanying her on the boat, but were there more? Did she have other accomplices already on board, mixed with the crew, to expedite this takeover? Regardless, his most pressing question at the moment remained: *Where was she?*

He poked his head up and took five seconds to get the lay of the land. Their helicopter had crash-landed against the aft superstructure and on top of the rearmost cargo hold. He turned and stared down the length of open deck between him and the main bridge, studying the ship's wheelhouse and its two flying bridges.

The first order of business was to reach there, try to take control of the ship.

There was only *one* problem.

Between him and the bridge stretched two hundred yards of open deck. Aside from the other four raised cargo holds and a handful of davit cranes down the ship's midline, there was no cover.

Which meant they had *two* problems.

Somewhere aboard this ship was an expert sniper.

Tucker called toward the helicopter, "Nick . . . Doc!"

"Here!" the men called in near unison from inside the craft.

"Think you can make it over to me?"

"Do we have a choice?" Bukolov yelled back.

It seemed to be a rhetorical question. Both men immediately vacated the broken bird at the same time. Nick helped Bukolov, as the doctor was weighted down by the backpack over his shoulders. They ran low and fast together. Nick pushed Bukolov over the roof's edge to the deck, then jumped down after him.

They both collapsed next to him.

Nick had brought the first-aid kit with him and passed it over. "Looks like you could use this."

Tucker quickly fished out a winged pressure bandage. Using the pad, he pressed his ear back in place, then wound the strips around his forehead and knotted it off.

"What's this I overheard about the ship may be blowing up?" Nick asked as he worked.

"Just a possibility. The good news is that it hasn't happened yet. The bad news is that there's a highly trained sniper on board, and unless I miss my guess, she's probably looking for a decent perch to—"

A bullet zinged off the cargo hold beside Tucker's head.

They all dropped lower.

And there she is . . .

He rolled to face the others, while keeping his head down. "Nick, you stay put with the doctor."

"Wait! Do you feel that?" Bukolov asked.

Tucker suddenly did: a deep shuddering in the deck. He knew what that meant.

"The engines are picking up speed," he said. "And we're turning."

Tucker had spent the last two days studying a map of Michigan's Upper Peninsula. In his mind's eye, he overlapped the *Macoma*'s approximate position, picturing the ship slowly swinging to port. He suddenly knew *why* the ship was turning.

He yanked out his satellite phone and dialed Harper, who picked up immediately. "She's here!" he said. "On the *Macoma*. And she knows she's been exposed and knows the ship will never make Chicago now that the alarm has been raised. So she's gone to Plan B and is heading straight for land, to try to run this ship into the ground."

It also explained why her forces hadn't overwhelmed Tucker and the others by now. She and her remaining teammates must have turned their attention to the bridge and likely entrenched themselves there to keep anyone from thwarting them.

"If Felice is truly attempting to crash the ship," Harper said, "that might be good news."

"Good? How?"

"It means she hasn't had time to set up any explosives . . . or maybe she doesn't have any. Either way, I'm vectoring all teams to you now. The State Police and Coast Guard won't be far behind us. Still no one will reach you for another twenty minutes."

"We don't have that much time, Harper."

"Do what you can to delay her. Cavalry's coming."

Tucker disconnected.

"How long until we hit the coastline?" Bukolov asked after eavesdropping on the conversation. He crouched, hugging his body against the cold and snow.

"Twenty, maybe twenty-five minutes at most."

Tucker needed to get the others somewhere safer. A bit farther up the deck was a thick enclosed hinge for the cargo hold. It was only two feet high, but it offered additional shelter both from the wind and from direct view of the main bridge's wheelhouse, where Felice was surely perched.

"Follow me, but stay low," he said and got everyone into that scant bit of cover.

Nick clutched Tucker's elbow. "I was born and raised in Michigan. If this ship is heading to shore around here, that'll put them in Grand Traverse Bay, headed straight for Old Mission Point. The rocks there'll rip the hull to shreds."

"Must be why she chose that course," Bukolov said.

Tucker nodded grimly. "Doc, stay here with Kane, prep your dispersal rig, and do your best not to get shot. Felice is holed up there in the forward wheelhouse, with who knows how many others. She intends to make sure this ship stays on course for those rocks. I have to try to get to her before that happens."

Tucker also had to assume one or more of the holds was already contaminated by Felice and her team. Back at Fort

Detrick, he had trained Kane to lock on to the unusual sulfurous smell of LUCA. But before that search could commence, Tucker first had to clear the way.

He poked his head an inch above the cargo hold's lid, aimed the MP-5's scope at the wheelhouse, then dropped down again. The wheelhouse had three aft-facing windows. They all appeared untouched, which meant Felice had probably fired upon them from one of its two open flying bridges—one stuck out from the port side of the wheelhouse, the other from the starboard, the pair protruding like the eyes of a hammerhead shark.

Perhaps he could use this to his advantage.

"What's your plan?" Bukolov asked.

"Run fast and hope she misses."

"That's not a plan. Why not go belowdecks and stay out of sight?"

He shook his head. "Too easy to get lost or boxed in, and I don't know how many men she's got."

His only advantage was that Felice would be surprised by his frontal assault. How much time that surprise would buy him was the big question.

Tucker took a deep breath and spoke to the others. "Everyone stay here. When the coast is clear, I'll signal you." He ruffled Kane's neck. "That means you, too, buddy."

Kane cocked his head, seemingly ready to argue.

Tucker reinforced it with an order, pointing to Nick and Bukolov. "HOLD AND PROTECT."

He stared across the open deck.

But who's going to protect me?

8:04 P.M.

Tucker took a few deep breaths—both to steady his nerves and to remind himself that he was alive and should stay that way.

Ready as he was ever going to be, he coiled his legs beneath him, then took off like a sprinter, a difficult process with the snow and wind. But the darkness and weather offered him some cover, and he was happy to take it. All the while, he kept a constant watch on the wheelhouse for movement.

Clearing the rearmost cargo hold, he shifted a few steps to the left and ran across the deck toward the cover of the next hold. He was twenty feet from it when he spotted movement along the flying bridge on the starboard side. He threw himself in a headfirst slide and slammed against that next hold's raised side.

A bullet thudded into the lid above his head.

Not good.

He crawled to the right and reached the corner of the cargo hold and peeked around—just as another

round slammed into the steel deck beside his head. He
jerked back.

Can't stay here . . .

Once a sniper had a target pinned down, the game
was all but won.

He crawled left, trying to get as far out of view of the
starboard bridge wing as possible. When he reached
the opposite corner, he stood up and started sprinting
again, his head low.

Movement . . . the *port* bridge wing, this time.

Felice had anticipated his maneuver, running from
the starboard wing, through the wheelhouse, to the
port side, but she hadn't had time to set up yet.

Tucker lifted his MP-5 submachine gun and
snapped off a three-round burst while he ran. The bullets sparked off a ladder near a figure sprawled atop the
wing. Dressed in gray coveralls, the sniper rolled back
from Tucker's brief barrage. He caught a flash of blond
hair, the wave of a scarf hiding her face.

Definitely Felice.

Tucker kept going, firing at the wing every few steps.

Movement.

Back on the *starboard* bridge wing.

Felice had crossed through the wheelhouse again.

Tucker veered to the right, dove, and slammed into
the third hold's edge, gaining its cover for the moment.

Three holds down, two to go.

He stuck his MP-5 over the edge and fired a burst toward the starboard wing—then something slapped at his palm. The weapon skittered across the deck. He looked at his hand. Felice's bullet had gouged a dime-sized chunk from the flesh beneath his pinkie finger. He stared at it for a moment, dumbfounded, and then the blood started gushing. Waves of white-hot pain burst behind his eyes and made him nauseated.

Sonofabitch!

He gasped for breath, swallowing the pain and squeezing the wound against his chest until the throbbing subsided a bit. He looked around. The MP-5 lay a few feet away, resting close to the railing.

As if reading his thoughts, Felice put a bullet into the MP-5's stock. His weapon spun and clattered—then went over the ship's edge, tumbling into the water.

Felice shouted, muffled by her scarf. "And that, Tucker, is the end!"

45

March 28, 8:08 P.M.
Lake Michigan

Tucker tried to pin down the direction of her voice, but it echoed across the deck, seeming to come from all directions at once. He didn't know where she was. Unfortunately, the same couldn't be said for Felice. She had her sights fixed on him. Even a quick pop-up would be fatal.

He still had his Browning in its paddle holster tucked into his waistband, but the small-caliber pistol at this distance and in this weather was as useless as a peashooter.

With his heart pounding, he tried to guess Felice's approximate position. She was likely still on the starboard wing of the bridge, from where she'd shot both his hand and the MP-5. Considering him weaponless and pinned down, Felice had no reason to move. She wouldn't give up that advantage.

On the other hand, she seemed talkative and overconfident. First rule in the sniper's handbook: *You can't shout and shoot at the same time.*

Tucker yelled over to her, "Felice, the Coast Guard knows your course! They're en route as we speak!"

"Makes no difference! The ship will crash before—"

Tucker jumped up and mounted the top of the cargo hold lid. He sprinted directly toward Felice, toward the starboard wing. As he'd hoped, in replying to his taunt, she'd lifted her scarf-shrouded head from the weapon's stock—breaking that all-important *cheek weld* snipers rely upon. She tucked back down.

He dodged right—as a bullet sparked off the metal by his heels—and in two bounding steps, he vaulted himself off the lid, rolled into a ball across the main deck, and crashed into the next cargo hatch, finding cover again.

"Clever!" Felice shouted. "Go ahead . . . try it again!"

No thanks.

He had one hatch to go before he could duck under the wheelhouse bulkhead as cover. To reach there, he had no good choices and only one bad—an almost unthinkable option.

Not unthinkable—just heartbreaking.

But he couldn't let the LUCA organism escape.

Using his left hand, Tucker drew the Browning from its paddle holster. He squeezed his eyes shut, then shouted above the wind.

"KANE! CHARGE TARGET! FAST DODGE!"

The loud command strikes Kane in the heart. Up until then, he has heard the blasts, knows his partner is in danger. He has strained against the last order; it still blazes behind his eyes: HOLD. *Another's hand has even grasped the edge of his vest, reeking of fear, sensing his desire.*

But the shout finally comes. He leaps the short obstruction, ripping out of those fingers. Wind, icy and full of salt, strikes his body hard. He ducks his head against it, pushing low, getting under the wind. He sprints, finding traction with his rear pads to propel him forward.

He obeys the order, the last words.

. . . FAST DODGE.

As he flies across the deck, he jinks and jukes. He makes sudden shifts, feinting one way and going another. But he never slows.

He races toward where his ears had picked out the blasts.

Nothing will stop him.

Tucker heard Kane pounding across the deck. His heart strained toward his friend, now a living decoy, sent out by his own command to draw deadly fire. He regretted the order as soon as it left his lips—but he didn't recall it.

It was too late now. Kane was already in the line of fire. The shepherd knew his target, knew he needed to evade, but would it be enough? Were Kane's reflexes faster than Felice's?

Miss . . . miss . . . dear God, miss . . .

From the starboard bridge wing, a single shot rang out. Kane had drawn her fire, her attention . . .

Good boy.

Tucker popped up, took aim on the starboard wing, and started running that way. Felice crouched up there, rifle up to her shoulder.

He shouted to Kane. "Take cover!"

Kane instantly reacts to the new order and pivots off his left front paw. He slides on the wet, icy deck, up on his nails, spinning slightly to slam into the next raised metal square.

He stays low.

He ignores the searing pain.

But the blaze of it grows.

Felice had heard Tucker's shouted order. She pivoted toward him, bringing her rifle barrel to bear, her scope's lens glinting for a flash through the storm.

Tucker fired, three quick shots in that direction with no real hope of hitting her. The rounds pounded into the steps and railing around Felice. Not flinching, she pressed her eye to the scope.

"Charge target!" he screamed.

Kane pushes the pain deep into his bones and lunges back out of hiding. He runs straight, gaining speed with each thrust of his back legs, with each pound of his front.

He stays low against the sleet and snow, his entire focus on the steel perforated steps leading up. His target lurks above, in hiding, and dangerous.

Still he runs forward.

Then a new order is shouted, but he does not know this word. It flows through him and away, leaving no trace.

As meaningless as the wind.

So he keeps running.

———

"KILL!" **Tucker** hollered, using all his breath.

To his right, Kane passed his position and raced toward the starboard stairs, taking no evasive action as ordered. The shepherd sprinted along the deck, his head down, his focus fixed on the objective. He was pure muscle in motion, an instinctive hunter, nature's savagery given form.

"KILL!" Tucker shouted again.

It was a hollow, toothless order—the word had never been taught to Kane—but the command was not meant for the shepherd, but for Felice. It was intended to strike a chord of terror in Felice, igniting that primal fear in all of us, harkening to a time when men cowered around fires in the night, listening to the howling of wolves.

Tucker continued his sprint across the cargo hatch, firing controlled bursts in her direction. Felice shifted back, lifted her face from the stock, and glanced to her left, toward Kane.

The shepherd had closed to within twenty feet of the steps and was still picking up speed.

Felice swung her rifle around and began tracking the shepherd.

Firing upward, Tucker covered the last few feet of the cargo hatch, leaped off, and headed for the shelter of the wheelhouse bulkhead.

"KANE! BREAK TO COVER!"

Crack! Felice shot as Tucker's body crashed into the bulkhead. He bounced off it and stumbled along its length until he was in the shadows beneath the starboard bridge wing. He pointed his gun up, searching through the ventilated steel, looking for movement above.

Nothing.

He peeked behind him.

No sign of Kane.

Had his last order come in time?

No matter the dog's fate, Kane had done as asked, allowing Tucker to close the gap and get inside Felice's bubble. Her primary advantage as a sniper was gone. Now she was just another soldier with a rifle.

Which was still a dangerous proposition.

She was up there, and he was down here—and she knew it. All she had to do was wait for Tucker to come to her.

With his gun still trained on the wing above him, Tucker slid over to a neighboring hatch, one that led into the main bridge's tower. He tried the handle: *locked.* He slid farther around the bulkhead, searching for another.

As he stepped cautiously around an obstruction, leading with his Browning, a dark shape lunged toward him. He fell back a step, until he recognized his partner.

Kane ran over to Tucker, panting, heaving.

Relief poured through him—until he saw the bloody paw print in the snow blown up against the bulkhead.

Buddy . . .

He knelt down and checked Kane. He discovered the bullet graze along his shoulder. It bled thickly, matting the fur, dribbling down his leg. He would live, but he would need medical attention soon.

A growl thundered out of Kane.

Not of pain—but of *warning*.

Behind Tucker, the hatch handle squeaked, and the door banged open against the bulkhead. He spun, bringing the Browning up, but Kane was already on the move, leaping past Tucker and onto the man in three bounds. The shepherd clamped on to the hand holding the gun and shook, taking the assailant down with a loud crack of the guy's forearm.

The pistol—a Russian Makarov—clattered to the deck.

Tucker stepped to the fallen man and slammed the butt of his Browning into his temple. He went limp—only then did Kane release his arm.

"Good boy," he whispered. "Now HOLD."

Tucker moved to the hatchway and peeked past the threshold. Inside was a corridor leading deeper into the bridge's superstructure, but to his immediate right, a bolted ladder climbed up toward the wheelhouse above.

Then came a clanking sound.

A grenade bounced down the ladder, banked off the wall, and landed a foot from the hatch.

Crap . . .

He backpedaled and stumbled over the splayed arm of the downed assailant. As he hit the deck hard, he rolled to the right, to the far side of the hatch.

The grenade exploded, the blast deafening.

A plume of smoke gushed from the doorway, along with a savage burst of shrapnel. The deadly barrage peppered into the steps leading up to the bridge wing, some pieces ricocheting back and striking the wall above his body.

Both he and Kane remained amazingly unscathed.

Tucker strained to hear, perhaps expecting some final taunt from Felice—but there was only silence. She had the upper hand, and she knew it.

If that's how you want to play this . . .

8:18 P.M.

Working quickly, Tucker holstered his Browning and returned to the unconscious man. He slipped out of his own hooded parka and wrestled the man into a seated position. He then forced his coat over the man's torso, tugging the hood over his head.

The man groaned blearily but didn't regain his senses.

Straightening, Tucker hauled his limp body over a shoulder and carried the man to just inside the hatch, leaning him against the bulkhead. He took a step past him—then leaned forward, grabbed the ladder railing, and gave it a tug.

The aluminum gave a satisfying squeak.

Immediately, he got a response.

Clang . . . clang . . . clang. . .

The grenade dropped, bounced off the last step, and rolled toward him.

Twisting around, he vaulted over the seated man and dodged to the left of the hatch. The grenade exploded. More smoke blasted, and shrapnel flew, finding a target in the man at the door.

As the smoke rolled out, Tucker peeked around the hatch and kicked the macerated body deeper inside. It landed face-first on the deck, coming to a bloody rest at the foot of the ladder.

He backed out again.

Five seconds passed . . . ten seconds . . .

Felice was a hunter. He knew she would want to inspect her handiwork.

At the first scuff of boot on metal rung, he signaled to Kane and they both climbed the outside stairs to reach the open starboard wing of the bridge. Reaching the last step, he leaned forward and peered through the open hatch of the wheelhouse. It appeared empty.

He pictured Felice on the ladder, abandoning the bridge to gloat over his body.

Good.

With the Browning up and ready, Tucker quietly stepped across the threshold into the wheelhouse. He slipped to the head of the ladder, took a breath, and pointed the Browning down the rungs.

No Felice.

No one.

Just the corpse on the floor in a widening pool of blood.

Kane growled at his side.

On instinct alone, Tucker spun on his heel, jerked the Browning up, and fired—as Felice stepped through the wheelhouse's port hatch.

His sudden shot went slightly wide, catching the woman in the side, just above her hip bone. She staggered backward and landed hard on the deck.

Rushing forward, he reached the hatch in time to see her rifle rising.

"Don't," Tucker said, cradling the Browning in both hands, centered on her face. "You're done."

She lifted her head, her scarf fallen away, revealing the ruin of her handsome face. Part of her nose was gone, sewn with black suture, along with a corner of her upper lip, giving her a perpetual scowl. A thick bandage covered her left cheek.

He recalled his last sight of her, as she vanished into the icy waters. She had been found later, saved, but it seemed not before frostbite ravaged her.

She snapped her rifle up, trying to take advantage of his momentary shock—but he also remembered feisty Elena and poor Utkin. It tempered any shock and revulsion. All he saw in the ruin of her face was justice.

Holding steady, he squeezed the trigger and sent a single round through her forehead.

46

From behind Tucker, boots clanked on the outside stairs. He turned and spotted a shotgun-wielding figure charging up the ladder toward the starboard wing. Here were the boots he had heard descending the ladder earlier—not Felice.

As the man reached the top stair, his shotgun up, Kane bounded into the hatchway before him, hackles raised, growling.

The sudden materialization of the large dog knocked the man back, his shotgun barrel dropping toward Kane.

Tucker shot once, placing a bullet through his sternum. The gunman tumbled backward down the ladder.

Tucker followed him out, covering with his Browning, but the man lay on his back, snowflakes melting on his open eyes.

Tucker took a fast accounting. He'd shot three men, along with Felice, the same number as reported stealing the speedboat.

But was that all of them?

He waited a full minute more—but no other threat appeared.

Satisfied, he moved farther out onto the bridge wing and cupped his hands around his mouth. "Doc! Nick! Come forward quickly!"

As the two men joined him, running forward against the sleet and snow, Tucker peeled off the pressure bandage from his ear and called Kane to him as he knelt. He secured the bandage to the shepherd's wound and wrapped it snugly, patching his friend up as best he could for now.

Bukolov joined him in the wheelhouse as he finished. The doctor's gaze shifted across the dead bodies. "Is that all of them?"

"I think so. Time for you all to get to work. Take Kane and use his nose to sniff out which cargo holds might have been contaminated by Felice's team."

From an inner pocket of his jacket, Tucker removed a gauze sponge prescented with the sulfurous discharge from Bukolov's specimen of LUCA. He held it to the shepherd's nose.

"TRACK AND FIND."

He next turned to Nick. "Go with them," he ordered. "Keep them safe."

"Will do."

The three took off, heading belowdecks.

Remaining in the wheelhouse, Tucker crossed quickly to the computerized helm console. He hoped to find some way to turn the *Macoma*, to stop its collision course with the rocky coastline.

Off in the distance, a light glowed through the snowfall. It had to be Old Mission Point, dead on the bow.

Maybe two miles, probably a little less.

He glanced at their speed on a gauge and calculated swiftly.

Eight minutes to impact.

Tucker studied the helm. Dozen of additional gauges, switches, knobs, and readouts spread across its console—but no wheel.

Instead, he spotted a joystick with a handgrip— beside it, an LED readout marking the ship's course. He grasped the stick and eased it slightly to the right, while keeping his eyes on the course readout.

"Come on, come on . . ."

The LED digits refused to change. Frustrated, he shoved the stick all the way to the right, but to no effect. The *Macoma* continued it relentless charge for the coast.

The glow in the distance grew brighter.

What am I doing wrong—?

Backing a step to consider his options, his boot crunched on something on the floor. He glanced down to find the deck beneath the console strewn with circuit boards, each one broken in half.

Felice had sabotaged the helm.

Even in death, she continued to thwart him.

Kane suddenly appeared at the port bridge hatch, followed a half minute later by a panting Bukolov and Nick.

"We found it!" Bukolov declared. "Or rather Kane did. Remarkable nose on that fellow. They contaminated hold number five, just behind us. But it's sealed like a bank vault. Looks like someone sabotaged the locking mechanism."

Felice.

Nick stared out the window, looking ill. "That's Old Mission Point," he confirmed. "Dead ahead."

"That's awful close," Bukolov said. "If we crash before we can decontaminate that hold . . ."

LUCA would be let loose into the world.

8:27 P.M.

After explaining his inability to turn or slow the ship, Tucker wasted a full precious minute as he scanned the helm, clenching his fist all the while. There had to be *something:* an override, an emergency shut down . . .

Where's a damned plug when you need to pull one?

His eyes skipped over a gauge—then returned to it, reading it more carefully.

HOLD FIRE SUPPRESSION

Tucker suddenly stiffened and swung to Nick and Bukolov.

"Follow me!"

He slid down the ladder, followed by the two men who scrambled after him. Kane used the outside stairs to join them below. At the bottom, Tucker grabbed the shotgun from the last man he had killed.

Nick looked around. "What are we—?"

"We need to find the crew," he said.

"Why?"

"I'll explain later. Kane can help us."

Tucker searched the next few rooms on this level and found a crewman's cabin. He grabbed some dirty clothes from a hamper and placed it in front of Kane's muzzle, ruffling it to raise the scent and gain Kane's full attention.

"TRACK AND FIND," he ordered again.

The shepherd buried his nose in the garments, snuffling deeply. He finally backed a step, lifted his nose high in the air—then bounded through the door.

The three men ran after him. Kane led them on a chase deeper into the ship's bowels, but in short order, the shepherd skidded to a double set of doors, sniffing furiously along the bottom.

The door was labeled CREW DINING.

Tucker pounded on it. "Anybody there?"

Multiple voices shouted back, both frantic and relieved, overlapping one another.

He tried the knob and found it locked. "Move as far to your right as you can! And turn away from the door!"

After getting a confirmation, he waved Bukolov and Nick farther down the hall, along with Kane. He then pointed the shotgun at the door's hinges from about six inches away and turned his head.

The blast stung his ears.

He moved immediately to the second hinge and did the same. With his ears ringing, he kicked the door the rest of the way open.

Seven or eight crewmembers stood huddled together in the far corner. Felice must have rounded them up when Tucker arrived by helicopter, knowing her hopes of contaminating the cargo without anyone's knowledge were ruined.

A tall, auburn-haired woman stepped from the group. "Who are you? What's going on?"

"No time," Tucker said. "We're working with national security. Who's the engineer?"

A wiry man in a thick wool sweater and suspenders raised his hand. "I am. John Harris."

"You're familiar with the ship's fire suppression system for the cargo holds?"

Tucker pictured the label on the helm's gauge: HOLD FIRE SUPPRESSION.

Of course, a cargo ship must be equipped with a sophisticated means of controlling fires, especially those that broke out in their cavernous holds. Fire was a ship's worst enemy.

"Yes, certainly," the ship's engineer confirmed. "It's a high-pressure water mist system."

"Where is it?"

"One deck down, right below us."

"Can you isolate hold number five?"

"Yes."

"Great. This is Doctor Bukolov. Take him to the fire suppression controls—then purge the water out of the tank and refill it with what the good doctor gives you. Can you do that?"

"Yes, but—"

He turned to Bukolov. "Doc, do you have enough?"

"Yes, more than adequate, I believe."

"John, you've got your orders. Get moving."

As they set out, Tucker turned back to the other crewmembers. "Who's the captain?"

The tall woman stepped forward again and introduced herself. "Captain Maynard."

"Captain, the *Macoma* is going to run aground in about three minutes, and the helm console is locked. Where's the safest place on the ship?"

"At the stern. Chart Library. One deck below the navigation bridge."

"Go there now!" he ordered.

As the crew filed past him, the last in line, a bald man wearing a cook's apron, suddenly wobbled into him. He was holding a bloody towel up to his mouth, and there was a deep gash in his forehead. Dried blood caked his eyebrows, nose, and mouth.

Tucker asked, "What happened to you?"

The man moaned and removed the towel to reveal a split lip and a flattened nose.

More of Felice's handiwork.

"I'll get you medical help as soon as we can." He turned to Nick. "Help get this guy to safety."

Nick nodded and hooked the man around the shoulders, helping him move faster. The pair hurried after the others.

THE KILL SWITCH · 621

Tucker turned and slid down the ladder to the next deck, following Bukolov and Harris, the ship's engineer. He found the pair standing before a wall console, with a panel open next to it. Bukolov's dispersal tank rested nearby, a hose running from it through the open panel.

"The fire-suppression tanks are here," Bukolov said as Tucker joined them. "He just finished siphoning the kill switch into the right one."

Tucker checked his watch.

Two minutes.

He asked Bukolov, "Will this really work?"

"In an enclosed space like that hold? Without a doubt—that is assuming their fire suppression system works as described to me."

"It'll work," Harris said and started pressing a series of buttons, then turned a lever clockwise. A button marked with the number 5 began flashing red on the board. "It's ready."

"Punch it."

Harris stabbed it with his thumb. From the tank closet, a *whoosh* sounded, followed by a gurgling.

"It's flowing," the engineer confirmed.

"How long until it's empty?"

"It's high pressure, high volume. Forty-five seconds and the compost in that hold will be soaked thoroughly."

Tucker clapped him on the shoulder. "Good job. Now we need to reach the Chart Library and join the others."

They scrambled up the ladder, where Tucker found Kane waiting. They took off as a group down the passageway with Harris leading the way.

The deck began shivering beneath their feet.

The engineer called over his shoulder, "The keel's scraping the sandbar!"

"Keep running!"

At a sprint, Harris led them toward the stern, passing intersection after intersection. As they passed one, movement drew Tucker's attention to the right. For a fleeting second, he spotted a white-smocked figure sprint past, heading the opposite direction along a parallel corridor.

The man was wearing a backpack.

Tucker skidded to a stop, as did Kane.

A backpack . . . ?

Bukolov looked over his shoulder. "Tucker . . . ?"

"Keep going! Go, go!"

The running figure in white had been the ship's cook. He was sure of it. But why—?

Tucker went momentarily dizzy as he fixed the man's broken visage before his mind's eye: *give him thick salt-and-pepper hair, a mustache, and clean the blood off his face . . .*

General Kharzin.

No, no, no!

Tucker remembered the subterfuge back in Africa, when Kharzin had sent in a body double to take his place. This time around, he had flipped that scam on its ear: disguising himself to look like an injured member of the crew. From the fact that the crew seemed to accept Kharzin as their cook meant that the general must have assumed the role of ship's cook at some prior port, coming aboard under false pretenses in order to expedite Felice's team: to get them aboard unseen, to help them contaminate the hold, and likely to help get them back off the ship unseen.

Clever.

But once Tucker arrived and the gig was up, Felice must have beaten the man to further disguise his features. Kharzin was the mission's final layer of security. If the ship was saved, he could still slip away with a final canister of LUCA and wreak what damage he could.

Tucker couldn't let that happen.

He backtracked, turned left at the intersection, and took off after the fleeing man with Kane. When he reached the parallel corridor, he stopped short and peeked around. There was no sign of Kharzin, but somewhere forward a hatch banged against steel.

He broke from cover and kept going. The deck gave a violent shake. He lost his balance and slammed against the bulkhead.

As he righted himself, he heard faint footsteps pounding on aluminum steps.

He pointed ahead. "SEEK SOUND."

Kane sprinted down the corridor, turned right at the next intersection, and down another corridor. It ended at a set of stairs, heading toward the main deck.

Ten feet from the stairs, a hatch door banged open far above.

As he closed the distance, Tucker dropped to his knees and skidded forward with his shotgun raised. As his knees hit the bottom step, he blasted upward—just as Kharzin's rear foot disappeared from the opening.

The hatch banged shut.

Tucker bounded up the steps, watching the locking wheel begin to spin. He hit the hatch before it fully engaged. He shouldered into it, bunching his legs and straining. Finally it popped up, sending him sprawling outside onto his chest.

Kane clambered next to him.

Tucker pushed himself to his feet and looked around. To his left, General Kharzin was running forward along the deck.

Tucker shouted, "Kharzin!"

The man never looked back.

He took off after the general—then suddenly his feet flipped out from under him. He landed hard on his back. The deck bucked again, accompanied by the sound of steel scraping against sharp rocks.

Tucker and Kane went flying.

47

March 28, 8:30 P.M.
Old Mission Point

The Macoma's nine hundred thousand pounds of iron and steel plow into the cold sands of Old Mission Point, its bow bulldozing trees, rocks, and bushes ahead of it. Debris crashes over the bow railing and smashes into the forecastle. A hundred feet inland, the bow strikes a boulder off center, heaving the ship onto its starboard side, dragging the forward third of its hull across a row of jagged rocks along the shoreline before finally lurching to a heavy stop.

Tucker knew none of this.

As the world became a herculean roar of rent steel and churning rock, he recalled snatching hold of Kane's collar, of tucking the shepherd to his chest, and the pair of them tumbling over the *Macoma*'s deck. They had bounced across the cargo hatches, pinballed off the davits, and slammed into the wheelhouse's bulkhead. They finally slid across the last of the canted deck and came to rest entangled on the starboard railing.

Christ Almighty . . .

With his head hammering, he forced open his eyes and found himself staring down into a well of blackness. He blinked several times, bringing the world into focus.

A world of mud.

He stared dazedly down through the starboard rails that had caught them as the ship rolled to its side. Below him rose a giant pile of black mud, its summit less than seven feet under his nose.

He smelled the ripeness of manure and the earthiness of rot.

Compost.

Kane licked Tucker's chin. The shepherd still sprawled half on top of him. The only thing keeping them from a plunge below were the struts of the rail.

"I got you, buddy," Tucker said. "Hang on."

Under him, the hull outside hold number five—where Felice's team had introduced LUCA—looked as though a giant had taken a pair of massive tin shears to the steel. Spilling from the gash was a massive wave of slurry compost, forming a mountain under him and spreading like dark lava across the landscape of Old Mission Point.

Fifty yards away a wood sign jutted from the sludge:

LIGHTHOUSE PARK—OLD MISSION POINT

A few yards past that marched a familiar figure, mucking calf-deep through the edge of the debris, a backpack hanging off one shoulder.

Kharzin.

Tucker disentangled his left arm from the railing, reached across his body to Kane, and drew the shepherd more tightly to him.

They had to find a way *down*—not that there was a way *up*.

He saw only one possibility, a *messy* possibility.

He stared below at the steep-sloping mountain of wet compost.

"Hold on, buddy, it's going to be a bit of a drop."

Tucker shifted them to the edge of the railing and rolled off. As they fell, he clutched Kane tightly against his body. They hit hard, especially for landing in mud—then they were tumbling down the slick surface of the mire. The smell filled his every sense. Muck soon covered them in a heavy coat.

In a matter of a few moments, they rolled free of the compost mountain and out across a mix of snow and sand. Tucker stood up, weaving and unsteady. His left shoulder throbbed. Kane limped a few steps, his left rear leg tucked up against his body, but as his partner worked the kinks out of his muddy body, he brought the limb down and tentatively took a few hops.

Sprained perhaps, but not broken.

Now where was General Kharzin? He was nowhere in sight.

Kane limped forward, ready to go, but Tucker forced the shepherd down with a firm, "STAY."

You've done plenty, buddy.

Tucker drew the Browning from its holster and edged forward, sticking to the deeper shadows of the *Macoma's* canted hull. Now out of the wind and snow, he could hear the pop and metallic groan of the dying ship. It loomed above him, like a building frozen in the process of collapsing.

He noted a rope dangling from a railing ahead, marking Kharzin's exit from the ship. The end hung a good ten feet off the ground. He pictured Kharzin dropping from it.

Continuing onward, he climbed the bulldozed wave of sand and rock at the ship's bow. The tip of the ship hung like a massive shadowy hatchet in the storm overhead, waiting to fall.

Tucker reached the crest of the stony tide and peered cautiously over its lip.

Fifty yards away, a figure moved through the storm, his back to Tucker and favoring one leg. Apparently Kharzin's descent hadn't gone any easier. The man slowly limped toward a snowy tree line, marked by park benches and gravel pathways.

Tucker cautiously picked his way down the backside of the rocks and started stalking toward his target, not wanting to spook him. Whether Kharzin heard his approach or not, the man suddenly shrugged off his backpack, knelt down near a copse of leafless maples, and unzipped the bag.

A stainless steel tank shone brightly within the muddy pack. Kharzin unscrewed the nozzle hose of the sprayer and tossed it away.

Uh-oh . . .

Tucker moved swiftly forward, incautiously snapping a twig.

Kharzin turned his head.

The two of them locked eyes.

Tucker raised his pistol and charged Kharzin. The other swung around, shaking free the tank from the pack and hugging it to his chest like a shield.

Kharzin confronted him, dared him. "Go ahead! Shoot! Hit the tank or hit me . . . it doesn't matter!

Either way, the corruption inside will spill free upon your precious soil. And I'll have my revenge for my daughter, for my country!"

Tucker lowered the Browning and slowed his run to a walk.

Off in the distance came the wail of sirens.

The pair stood staring at each other, neither speaking.

Tucker considered his options. First of all, he had no idea whether Bukolov had succeeded in decontaminating the ship's hold. He smelled the ripe sludge covering his body. The monster could already be out of the bag, set loose upon the shores of Lake Michigan.

If so, the tank in Kharzin's arms was irrelevant.

Still, Tucker waited, wanting extra insurance for his next move.

Then he heard it: *thump, thump, thump*—multiple helicopters echoed over the water behind him.

Good enough.

He shot Kharzin in the right kneecap, breaking the stalemate. The man's leg buckled, and he pitched forward. As he hit the ground, the canister knocked from his arms and rolled free. Yellow liquid spilled out its open spigot, blazing a toxic trail, mapping its trajectory. As the tank came to a rest, it continued to leak weaponized LUCA.

Tucker moved forward, taking care not to step on any of the yellow lines.

Kharzin rolled onto his back, his face twisted with rage and pain.

Behind him, a helicopter swept over the bulk of the *Macoma*, then hovered for a landing at a neighboring open stretch of beach. Others buzzed higher, circling wider, stirring through the storm.

"The cavalry has arrived," he said to Kharzin.

As the skids of the first helicopter touched the rocky beach, the side door popped open, and a pair of men jumped out, both wearing anorak parkas and shouldering backpack sprayers. They should be able to quickly clean up and decontaminate the brief spill. Behind them followed another trio of men armed with assault rifles.

The group began jogging toward Tucker's position.

He returned his attention to Kharzin. "Do you see the men with the rifles?"

The general remained silent, his gaze burning with hatred.

"They're going to take you into custody, whisk you off somewhere for a long talk. But I'm not officially *with* them, you see. So before they take you away, I want you to know something."

Kharzin's eyes narrowed, showing a glint of curiosity past the pain.

"You're going to need new shoes."

He shot Kharzin in the left foot, then right—then turned away from the screaming and the blood. He'd had enough of both.

Time to go home.

He headed back to where he had left Kane.

That was home enough for him.

48

Footsteps entered the barn.

Now what?

Lying on his back, Tucker scooted his roller board out from beneath the Range Rover. He wiped the oil from his hands onto his coverall, but there was nothing to do about the splatters on his face. No doubt about it, the Rover needed a new oil pan and gasket.

As he rolled free of the bumper, he found himself staring up at the worried face of Christopher Nkomo.

"My friend," he said, "I am not comfortable accepting such a large gift."

Tucker sat up and climbed to his feet.

Kane stirred from where he had been curled on a pile of straw, patiently waiting for his partner to realize he was not an auto mechanic.

Tucker scratched at the bandage over his ear. The sutures had returned his ear to its proper place on his head and were due to come out now.

It had been ten days since the crash of the *Macoma*. It seemed Bukolov's kill switch had proved successful, the site declared LUCA free, although monitoring continued around the clock. The entire event was reported to the media as a mishap due to a fault in the ship's navigation systems during a severe winter storm. Additionally, the cordoning of the site was blamed on a hazardous spill. Under such a cover, it was easy for teams to move in with electric-powered dispersion sprayers and swamp the entire area with the kill switch as an extra precaution. It also explained the continued environmental monitoring.

The rest of the crew, along with Bukolov, were discovered safe, except for a few broken bones and lacerations. Even Nick Pasternak, the pilot, was found with only an egg-sized knot behind his ear, where Kharzin had clubbed him and made his attempted escape.

In the end, with no one reported killed, the media interest in the crash quickly faded away into lottery numbers and celebrity weddings.

Life moved on.

And so did Tucker.

Two days after the events, he and Kane landed in Cape Town. Bruised, battered, and stitched up, they both needed some rest—and Tucker knew just where he would find it.

He waved Christopher toward the shaded veranda of a colonial-era mansion. The three-story, sprawling home was located in a remote corner of the Spitskop Game Preserve, far from the tourist area of the park where he and the others had originally stayed with its bell captains and its servers dressed all in house whites. This mansion had been abandoned a decade ago, boarded up and forgotten, except by the snakes and other vermin, who had to be evicted once the restoration process began.

A crew worked busily nearly around the clock. Ladders and scaffolding hid most of the slowly returning glory of the main house. New boards stood out against old. Wide swaths of lawn—composed of indigenous buffalo grass—had already been rolled out and hemmed around the home, stretching a good half acre and heavily irrigated. Cans of paint were stacked on the porch, waiting to brighten the faded beauty of the old mansion.

Farther out, the twenty-acre parcel was dotted with barns and outbuildings, marking future renovation projects.

But one pristine sign was already up at the gravel road leading here, its letters carved into the native iron-wood and painted in brilliant shades of orange, white, and black. They spelled out the hopes and dreams for the Nkomo brothers:

LUXURY SAFARI TOURS

Tucker crossed the damp lawn and climbed the newly whitewashed porch steps. Overhead, wired outlet boxes marked the future site of porch fans. Kane trotted up alongside him, seeking shade and his water bowl.

"Truly, Mr. Tucker, sir," Christopher pressed, mounting the steps as if he were climbing the gallows. "This is too large a gift."

"I had the funds and quit calling it a *gift*. It's an investment, nothing more."

Upon completing the affair with Sigma, Tucker had noticed a sudden large uptick in his savings account held at a Cayman Island bank. The sudden largesse was not from Sigma—though that pay had been fair enough—but from Bogdan Fedoseev, the Russian industrialist whose life Tucker had saved back in Vladivostok. It seemed Fedoseev placed great stake in his own personal well-being and reflected that in the *bonus* he wired.

Tucker took that same message to heart and extended a similar generosity to the Nkomo brothers, who, like Tucker with Fedoseev, had helped keep him alive. From talking to Christopher during the long stretches of the journey to the Groot Karas Mountains, he knew of the brothers' desire to purchase the mansion and the tract of land, to turn it into their own home and business.

But they were short on funds—so he corrected that problem.

"We will pay you back when we can," Christopher promised. Tucker knew it was an oath the young man would never break. "But we must talk interest perhaps."

"You are right. We should negotiate. I say *zero* percent."

Christopher sighed, recognizing the futility of all this. "Then we will always leave the presidential suite open for you and Kane."

Tucker craned his neck up toward the cracked joists, the apple-peel curls of old paint, the broken dormer windows. He cast Christopher a jaundiced eye.

The young man smiled in the face of his doubt. "A man must hope, must he not? One day, yes?"

"When the presidential suite is ready, you call me."

"I will certainly do that. But, my friend, when will you be leaving us? We will miss you."

"Considering the state of the Rover, you may not be missing me anytime soon. Otherwise, I don't know."

And he liked it that way.

He stared again at this old beauty rising out of the neglect. It gave him hope. He also liked the idea of having a place to lay his head among friends when needed. If not a home, then at least a *way station.*

Kane finished drinking, water rolling from his jowls. His gaze turned, looking toward the horizon, a wistful look in his dark eyes.

You and me both, buddy.

That was their true home.

Together.

Tucker's phone vibrated in his pocket. He pulled it out and answered, guessing who was calling. "Harper, I hope this is a social call."

"You left in a hurry. Just wanted to check on you and Kane."

"We're doing fine."

"Glad to hear it. That means you might be up for some company."

Before Tucker could respond, a black Lincoln town car pulled into the dirt driveway, coasted forward, and came to a stop in front of the house. The engine shut off.

"I assume it's too late to object," Tucker said.

As answer, the driver's door popped open, and a woman in a dark blue skirt and white blouse exited. She was tall, with long legs, made longer as she stretched a bit on her toes, revealing the firm curve of her calves. She pushed a fall of blond hair from her eyes, sweeping it back to reveal a tanned face with high cheekbones.

Though he had never met the woman face-to-face, he knew her.

Ruth Harper.

He stood straighter, trying to balance the figure before him with the image formed in his mind from their many phone conversations.

This certainly was no *librarian*.

The only feature he got right was the pair of thick-rimmed rectangular eyeglasses perched on her nose. They gave her a studious, even sexier look.

Definitely no librarian he had ever met.

Tucker called down to her from the porch. "In some lines of work, Harper, this would be considered an ambush."

She shrugged, looking not the least bit chagrined as she climbed the steps, carrying a small box in her palms. "I called first. In the South, a lady does not show up on a gentleman's doorstep unannounced. It just isn't done."

"Why are you here?" he asked—though he could guess why, sensing the manipulation of her boss, Painter Crowe.

"First," she said, "to tell you that Bukolov sends his regards—along with his thanks."

"He said the *last* part? Doctor Bukolov?"

She laughed, a rare sound from her. "He's a new man now that he has his own lab at Fort Detrick. I even saw him smile the other day."

"A minor miracle. How's he getting along?"

"His studies are still in the rudimentary stages right now. Like with human stem cell research, it might take years if not decades to learn how to properly manipulate that unique genetic code to the benefit of mankind."

"What about to the *damage* to mankind? What's the word out of Russia?"

"Through back channels, Kharzin's superiors at the GRU have insisted they knew nothing about his actions. Whether it's true or not, we don't know. But word is that the Russian Defense Ministry is turning the GRU upside down, purging anyone associated with Kharzin."

"How about Kharzin? Is he cooperating?"

She turned and balanced the small box she had been carrying onto the porch rail. "I don't know if you heard before you left, but he lost one of his feet. He must have rolled after you shot him, contaminated the wound with some of the spilled LUCA organism. By the time anyone realized it, the only option was amputation."

"Sorry to hear that," he lied.

"As to cooperation, he knows the fate that would befall him if he ever did return to Russia, so he's grudgingly beginning to bend, revealing small details to fill in some of the blanks. Like revealing the name of a port authority agent who was paid to look the other way when and if the *Macoma* reached port in Chicago. The man's in custody now."

Good riddance.

"And it seems Kharzin's paranoia has finally proven of benefit. Prior to leaving for the States, he set up a fail-safe at his lab outside of Kazan. Without an abort code from him personally every twenty-four hours, his lab's remaining samples of LUCA would be automatically incinerated. He didn't want anyone else gaining access to them."

"So they're all gone then?"

"That's the consensus. His lab did indeed burn down. And if we're wrong, we're still the only ones who have the kill switch."

"So it's over."

"Until next time," she warned, arching an eyebrow. "And speaking of next time—"

"No."

"But you don't know—"

"No," he said more firmly, as if scolding a dog.

She sighed. "It's true, then. You and the Nkomo brothers are going into some investment together? Luxury safari adventures?"

"As always, Harper, you're disturbingly well informed."

"Then I guess the only other reason I made this long trip was to deliver *this*." She pointed to the box on the porch rail. "A small token of my appreciation."

Curiosity drew him forward. He fingered the top open, reached inside, and pulled out a coffee mug. He frowned at the strange gift—until he turned the cup and spotted the gnarled face of a bulldog on the front. The dog was wearing a red-and-white-striped cap with a prominent G on it.

He grinned as he recognized the mascot for the University of Georgia, remembering all of his past attempts at placing Harper's accent.

"Never would've taken you for a fan of the Georgia Bulldogs," he said.

She reached down and scratched Kane behind an ear. "I've always had a special place in my heart for dogs."

From the arch of her eyebrow, he suspected she wasn't only referring to the four-legged kind.

"As to the other matter," she pressed, straightening up, "you're sure?"

"Very sure."

"As in forever?"

Tucker considered this.

Kane picked up his rubber Kong ball and dropped it at Tucker's feet. The shepherd lowered his front end, hindquarters high, and glanced with great urgency toward the endless stretch of cool grass.

Tucker smiled, picked up the ball, and answered Harper's question.

"For now, I have better things to do."

Author's Note to Readers: Truth or Fiction

As with my Sigma books, I thought I'd attempt here at the end of this story to draw that fine line between fact and fiction. I like to do this, if for no other reason than to offer a few bread crumbs to those who might be interested in learning more about the science, history, or various locations tread by Tucker and Kane.

But first let's start with that illustrious duo.

Military War Dogs and Their Handlers

The first recorded use of war dogs goes back to 4000 BC, to the Egyptians who used them in battle. But the modern use of dogs in the U.S. military really started in World War I. Since then dogs have become an integral part of the U.S. military, including the dog Cairo who was involved with the takedown of Osama bin Laden.

During a USO tour of authors to Iraq and Kuwait, I got a chance to observe a few of these fighting teams in action. While in Baghdad, I also met a fellow veterinary classmate who was with the U.S. Veterinary Corp. He was able to give me great insight into the technology, the psychology, and even the aftermath of such a unique fighting team.

All the MWD (military working dog) technology found in this book is real: from the Kevlar-reinforced K9 Storm tactical vest worn by Kane to his amazing communication gear. I also tried to capture that unique and intimate psychological connection between dog and handler, described as "it runs down the lead," where over time the two learn to read each other's emotions and understand each other beyond gesture and spoken command. I also learned about how PTSD afflicts not only the soldier but also the dog, and how efforts are being undertaken to combat and treat both sufferers.

As to Kane's amazing talent, that's also based on real stories. Even Kane's vocabulary, while stellar, has been demonstrated by a dog named Chaser, a border collie who has been shown to understand over a thousand words, including grammatical structure.

Last, after three decades of working with dogs as a veterinarian, I knew I wanted to portray these stalwart war heroes as they really are—not just as soldiers with four legs, but as *real* dogs. In this book, there are scenes written from Kane's perspective. Here, I wanted readers to experience what it's like to be a war dog—to be in their *paws*—to paint an accurate portrayal of how a dog *perceives* the world, how he *functions* in combat with his unique talents and senses. I hope I did them justice.

On to the central scientific concept and threat of the novel . . .

LUCA and Cyanobacteria

LUCA (Last Universal Common Ancestor) is a scientific concept concerning the origin of life, the proverbial seed from which all life sprang. There are many different theories about how that ancient life-form might have presented itself, whether its origin is rooted in DNA or RNA, whether it needs extreme heat to survive or moderate temperatures. It remains a great unknown. In regard to the concepts of cyanobacteria as a progenitor for modern plants, all the science and details regarding this ubiquitous form of life are true, including that you can find cyanobacteria in every environmental niche on the planet, including the fur of sloths.

The Threat of Invasive Species

This is a real and ongoing threat across the globe, where foreign species invade an established ecosystem and wreak great harm: from the introduction of pythons in the Everglades, where those snakes are creating untold damage, to Asian carp in the Mississippi, which are wiping out native fish populations and sweeping toward the Great Lakes. Such threats have not escaped the notice of federal counterterrorism officials. Alarm bells are being raised that terrorists could very well use invasive species as biological weapons, where the introduction of a single virulent organism into an environment could cause great economic and physical harm, possibly irreversibly so.

Let's move on to the main history topics.

The Boer Wars

All the details of this bloody conflict are true, including the military tactics related in the prologue and the weapons used (like the "krag"). The character General

Manie Roosa was very loosely based on the real-life Boer leader Manie Maritz. And you can still find such "pocket camps" of the Boers hidden throughout South Africa, and the archaeological ruins of their forts still dot the countryside.

Arzamas-16

The Russians did indeed have closed science cities, called *naukograds*, including one named Arzamas-16, which was home to the Soviet Union's first nuclear weapons design. The U.S. intelligence community did indeed refer to it as the *Russian Los Alamos*.

Last . . .

Location, Location, Location

One of the great thrills of writing is being able to shine a light on various regions of the world. And *The Kill Switch* was no exception. Grant and I strove to make sure every detail of each location was as accurate and illuminating as possible: from life in Siberian villages to the historical magnitude of the Kazan Kremlin. Even such details like the submarine eco-tours of the Volga River are factual. I also wanted to paint an accurate picture of South Africa, its wildlife, and the regional strife of Namibia, while capturing the raw beauty of the Groot Karas Mountains. Over the course of writing this book, I grew to love these places, and I hope you enjoyed the journey, too.

Finally, let me leave you with one last *fact:* Tucker and Kane will be back—because their *true* adventure is just beginning!